PER WAHLÖÖ

A Necessary Action

Born in 1926, Per Wahlöö was a Swedish writer and jour-
nalist who, alongside his own novels, collaborated with his
partner, Maj Sjöwall, on the bestselling Martin Beck crime
series, credited as inspiration for writers as varied as Agatha
Christie, Henning Mankell, and Jonathan Franzen. In 1971
the fourth novel in the series, *The Laughing Policeman*, won
an Edgar Award from the Mystery Writers of America. Per
Wahlöö died in 1975.

JOAN TATE

Joan Tate was born in 1922 of English and Irish extraction.
She traveled widely and worked as a teacher, a rehabilitation
worker at a center for injured miners, a broadcaster, a reviewer,
and a columnist. She was a prolific writer and translator, well
known for translating many leading Swedish-language writers, including Astrid Lindgren, Ingmar Bergman, Kerstin Ek-
man, P. C. Jersild, Sven Lindqvist, and Agneta Pleijel. She
died in 2000.

A Necessary Action

A NECESSARY ACTION

A Novel

PER WAHLÖÖ

Translated from the Swedish
by Joan Tate

VINTAGE CRIME/BLACK LIZARD
Vintage Books
A Division of Random House, Inc.
New York

FIRST VINTAGE CRIME/BLACK LIZARD EDITION, JUNE 2013

Translation copyright © 1968 by Michael Joseph Ltd.

Library of Congress Cataloging-in-Publication Data for this edition has been applied for.

Vintage ISBN: 978-0-307-74474-6

www.vintagebooks.com

Printed in the United States of America
10 9 8 7 6 5 4 3 2 1

To SYLVIA

A Necessary Action

Part One

1

Willi Mohr was arrested on the seventh of October at about two o'clock, in the middle of the siesta.

He was living alone in a derelict two-storey house in Barrio Son Jofre on the southern outskirts, which was also the oldest and highest part of the town.

The man who arrested him was a middle-aged civil guard with a heavy, sleepy face and a stubby grey moustache. He was carrying his carbine on a strap over his shoulder and he had walked all the way from his post quite a way out of town. When the civil guard came to the narrow cobbled alleyway which twisted its way up to Barrio Son Jofre, he stopped and let out a deep breath. He was in no hurry.

Five minutes before he was arrested, Willi Mohr knew that someone was on his way up towards the house. He was lying on his back with his hands clasped behind his head, looking at the ceiling. He was not thinking about anything special. When he heard a quiet, gliding rustle, he turned his head and saw the cat slinking through the hole in the door. It threw a slanting narrow shadow across the rhomboid-shaped patch of sun on the floor. The animal had come straight in from the sun into the shade and its eyes widened swiftly until the pupils were quite circular and had almost eaten their way right through the pale green irises. The cat did not come into the room, but stayed just by the door, cautiously peering out into the alley. Its striped ginger tail was standing straight out, but the tip of it was moving slowly to and fro. The cat was extremely cowardly, cautious and inquisitive.

Willi Mohr lay quite still and looked out through the cat-hole. He listened, but the only things he could hear were a chicken scratching about in the dried weeds and the newborn puppies whining out in the kitchen.

He thought: I'll kill them tomorrow; all of them except one. I'll choose the one with the best markings and keep that one. I'll kill the others, but I'll wait until tomorrow.

The cat moved its head, no more than a fraction of an inch, and twitched its ear forward.

But although Willi Mohr was prepared and straining, he did not hear the steps until they were very close and then he saw a man's leg through the cat-hole, not the whole leg, but just a brown laced boot and green leggings with buckles.

The civil guard knocked on the door, quite lightly, perhaps with a pencil or the stem of his pipe, and Willi Mohr half-rose, his elbow resting on the mattress, and called: 'I'm coming.'

The cat had retreated about eighteen inches and was crouching on the floor, prepared for flight.

Willi Mohr thrust his hand between the mattress and the stone floor and pulled out his gun and notebook. He went out into the kitchen and reached in under the stone bench, feeling the damp warmth of dog. He hid the pistol and the notebook under the straw, close up against the wall, and before he could withdraw his hand, the bitch had given him a lick, large and wet and trusting.

He straightened up and wiped the dog-saliva off on to his trousers. Then he went out and opened the door.

The civil guard was standing in the sun outside, rocking back and forth on his toes and heels as he gazed thoughtfully at the house. It was certainly in very bad shape.

When the door opened, he made an attempt at a salute and then let it go over into a diffuse gesture, saying: 'Let's go, shall we?'

He had in fact got a warrant in his pocket but he was not going to take it out unnecessarily.

Willi Mohr took down his straw hat from the nail on the door-post and stepped out into the sunlight. Then he locked the door and put the key into his pocket. In the meantime, the civil guard gazed down at his trousers.

As they walked towards the alleyway, Willi Mohr looked without interest down on to the town lying spread out below

2

them. It wasn't much to look at, an irregular confusion of flat, brownish roofs at different angles and of different sizes. About three thousand people were lazing beneath those roofs, many of whom would have gladly given up their siesta for work, had there been any work. The only thing to break the monotony of the view was the church tower, but not even that managed to stand out clearly against the scorched, greyish-yellow slopes.

The mountains closed in on the town from all directions and limited the view, except in the east, where a narrow corridor between two prominent ridges opened out towards a glittering sliver of sea. It was exactly thirteen kilometres of poor, twisting, gravelled road there but it was all downhill and the driver of the mail-bus could freewheel all the way from the square in the town to the quay in the fishing settlement, which was thought to be a considerable saving.

Down there, in the village by the sea, there were perhaps still a few tourists left from some late organized holiday. Long-legged English, German and Scandinavian office girls defying the morality laws by sitting under beach umbrellas in two-piece bathing costumes, sucking at Pepsi Colas.

At night they abandonedly whimpered in someone's bed, the courier's if the worst came to the worst, and in the mornings they had suck marks on their shoulders and thighs. Thought Willi Mohr.

He hadn't been down there for a long time.

They walked along Avenida Generalissimo Franco, lying empty and desolate except for a few old crones' abandoned basket chairs and a few cats sleeping here and there in the shade along the walls of the houses. The street was not straight and not especially wide, but it was level and laid with small, flat, smooth cobblestones. It could well have been laid three hundred years before, but in fact this street was quite new, put down in honour of the Caudillo, who was to have come here once on a tour of inspection. Actually he had not come and several of the Asturian forced labourers who had been working on the project had died of starvation and consumption before the street was finished.

They had not said a word to each other since they had left the house in Barrio Son Jofre. The civil guard who had arrested Willi

3

Mohr walked on the left of him and always slightly behind him, as if to indicate his relationship with the arrested man without making too much of it.

They walked diagonally across the square. In the shadow of the village pump stood a donkey-cart, laden with the kind of weeds which for lack of anything better were used to feed the pigs. Between the high wheels slept a shrunken old man, his faded and ragged straw hat tipped over his face. The emaciated donkey was dozing, its head hanging down and its sore back covered with glossy horse-flies.

The tables and cane chairs under the permanent awning outside Café Central were vacant and the doors into the bar were only half-open to show that the place was semi-closed.

It struck Willi Mohr that he was thirsty and that the guard might possibly be so also. In addition, the Central was one of the places where he could still get credit. He pointed towards the tables and said in strained Spanish: 'What about having a glass with me?'

The civil guard shook his forefinger with a parrying gesture, but when he saw that the other man was not going to repeat his offer, he seemed to resign himself, shrugged his shoulders and went and sat down under the awning. He leant his carbine against the table and put his black shiny cap down on the marble table-top. Willi Mohr clapped his hands and only a few seconds later the abuela, a wrinkled little old woman in a shawl and long black widow's weeds, came out through the rustling jalousies. She threw a confused and questioning look from Willi Mohr to the civil guard, but she said nothing. They were given vermouth and a syphon and Willi Mohr served the drinks, first for the guard and then for himself. They raised their glasses, nodded solemnly and drank, only a gulp each.

Willi Mohr fingered his glass, thought for a moment and then asked: 'What have you brought me down for?'

The guard threw out his hands, smiled apologetically and said: 'Orders.'

He emptied his glass in one gulp and waited patiently for the other man to finish his drink.

Then they walked on, in exactly the same formation as before, out of the town, along the perfectly straight, newly-gravelled

4

road. On each side grew small, gnarled olive trees with greyish-green, satiny dusty leaves.

The guard-post lay about three-quarters of a kilometre beyond the last houses. It was quite a modest place, a long, low, stone building with three or four very small windows. A yellow and red flag hung limply at the side of the entrance and under it a civil guard was busy dipping the inner tube of his bicycle-tyre into a bowl of rusty-brown water. His bicycle was standing nearby, upside-down, with its front wheel removed.

The sudden darkness in the porch was such that anyone coming in from the outside was almost unable to distinguish the objects around him. The civil guard knocked on a door and opened it at such an angle that Willi Mohr could not see inside the room. Someone inside spoke, swiftly and concisely and with a marked lisp, indicating that the owner of the voice came from another part of the country. The guard shut the door from the outside and gave the arrested man a nudge in the back as a sign that he should proceed forward. At the farthest end of the entrance hall he unlocked another door; beyond it were three steps leading down to a long stone-paved corridor. A weak electric light bulb spread an uncertain light over a row of narrow doors reinforced with iron. The civil guard went on to the last one, opened it and pushed him over the threshold. Then the door was locked and the key turned in the lock. The cell was very small, at most five or six foot square, the walls whitewashed and the contents consisting of a wooden bunk fastened to the wall and a galvanized bucket. There were no windows, but from an aperture in the ceiling a faint light filtered through a small square of thick, opaque glass. Willi Mohr walked the three steps from the door to the wall and back again. Then he leant against the wall and thought.

A few minutes later steps were heard in the corridor, the key was turned and the door opened. The civil guard who had arrested him came into the cell with a jug of water and a worn grey blanket. He put the blanket on the bunk and the jug on the floor, beside the bucket.

He let his eyes wander from the arrested man to the bunk and said: 'You'd better sleep.'

Then he left.

Willi Mohr got the impression that the blanket and the water-jug and the advice constituted a kind of extra favour, in return for the drink in the square.

As no one had bothered to search him, at least he could smoke. And he had his belt too, so he could hang himself if he wanted to.

'If there'd been something to fasten the noose to,' he said to himself, with a slight smile.

This talking to himself was a habit he had taken to lately. Sometimes he caught himself talking to the cat and the dog too. Mostly the cat, as it seemed more intelligent and more thoughtful.

When he felt in his pockets he found he had cigarettes but no matches. He went over to the door and banged on it with his fists. Nothing happened. Probably not due to nonchalance but quite simply because no one heard him.

After a while, he resigned himself and lay down on the bunk with the thin blanket folded up under his head. It was quiet in the building. Before he fell asleep he looked at his watch. It was five minutes to three.

When Willi Mohr opened his eyes again, it was dark in the cell. He could feel the raw, damp chill coming from the stone walls and he realized that he had woken because he was cold. At this time of the year the days were hot but the nights surprisingly cold.

He lay on his back on the wooden bunk and his shoulders and the small of his back ached. With difficulty he raised his arm and had to hold his wristwatch right up to his eyes to be able to see the luminous figures. It was ten o'clock. He had already been here seven hours and evidently no one had bothered about him. It was deathly quiet and he could not even see the aperture in the ceiling.

He must have slept with his mouth open, because his tongue felt dry and stiff and his throat and mouth were sore. When he sat up on the bunk and felt round for the water-jug, he got cramp in his calves and whimpered loudly as he stretched out his toes and slowly extended his contracted muscles.

He found the water-jug and drank. Then he got up on his stiff legs and went over to hammer on the door with his clenched fists. He did not stop until it began to hurt. It was still quite quiet.

Willi Mohr shook his stiff body and sat down on the bunk. He

6

drew up his legs and crept into the corner with his back to the wall, the thin blanket round his shoulders. He thought about the fact that he did not know what he ought to be thinking.

During the hours that followed, he hammered on the door three times, but somewhat listlessly, without energy or indignation. Now and again he drank from the earthenware jug and about every tenth minute he changed his position when some part of his body began to ache. He tried to think up different tricks to stop himself constantly looking at his watch, but it didn't help. He was much too keyed to waiting and the time went unendurably slowly.

'This is going to be difficult,' he said. 'You've no prison routine.'

He must have dozed off in his corner, for suddenly he was conscious of the fact that he was awake and could not have been so a moment earlier. The cell was no longer dark, but was filled with the weak yellow light from an electric light bulb which seemed to be set behind the piece of glass in the ceiling aperture. Steps and voices could be heard and someone lifted the little flap outside and looked at him through the spy-hole. The key was turned and a small civil guard whom he had not seen before opened the door. A tall officer in a green uniform with gold braid on the sleeves and a broad band round his cap appeared in the doorway. He looked at the man on the bunk, irresolutely and a little questioningly, and then exchanged a few words with the guard. They spoke Catalonian between themselves.

Then he took a step into the room and smiled in a strained manner.

'You won't have to wait much longer now,' he said.

The officer seemed to hesitate for a moment. Then he added politely: 'I hope it hasn't been too uncomfortable for you.'

He glanced with irritation at the galvanized bucket and the dirty blanket, turned round quickly and left. The guard locked the door.

Ten minutes later the small guard returned and said: 'Come.'

At the steps at the end of the corridor, Willi Mohr said: 'What happens now?'

The man in uniform replied at once, without a moment's hesitation.

7

'You're going to be interrogated by Sergeant Tornilla.'

'Was that the man who was here?'

'No, that's the chief, Lieutenant Pujol.'

The civil guard knocked on the same door that the other guard had held ajar ten hours earlier. Then he opened it wide and stepped to one side. Willi Mohr shrugged his shoulders and walked into the room. The door was shut behind him, from the outside.

2

The room was not so small as the cell, but on the other hand it was not much larger. It contained four pieces of furniture, a small desk, a filing cabinet, a black armchair and a rickety wooden bench with room for two people. But the room still seemed full to overflowing. There was no window, but on the wall behind the desk hung a large photograph of the Caudillo in a heavy black wooden frame. Under the portrait sat a man writing in the circle of light from an electric ceiling light with a green glass shade.

When Willi Mohr came into the room, the man at once put down his pen and rose from the armchair.

He saluted meticulously, held out his hand and said with a smile: 'My name is José Tornilla. Pleased to meet you. I'm sorry to have kept you waiting.'

Willi Mohr stared at him with clear blue eyes and shook the man's hand mechanically.

So this was Sergeant Tornilla, the man with a lisping voice, the man who was to interrogate him, after letting him wait for ten hours. Middle-height, slightly plump, brown eyes, moustache, military cap with tassels, well filled to the fore, white shirt, strap diagonally across his chest, cheeks smooth from his razor, white teeth, well-manicured nails, well-brushed, faultless, straight out of the book of instructions. A nob. A blown-up gasbag.

Thought Willi Mohr.

Sergeant Tornilla walked round the desk and pulled the rickety bench a bit nearer. He smiled even more broadly and made an exaggeratedly polite gesture towards it.

'This,' he said jokingly, 'is the accused's bench.'

He articulated very clearly.

They sat down opposite each other. The man in the armchair went on smiling. He had his elbows on the desk and slowly pressed first his fingertips and then his whole hands together. As if he had happened to think of something important, he suddenly parted them, got out a cigarette packet from somewhere behind the ancient manual telephone and held it out. Bisonte, Spanish Monopoly cigarettes of American type.

Not so bad, but unjustifiably expensive. Snob cigarettes, thought Willi Mohr.

He took one and almost before he had had time to put it to his lips, the other man had stretched across the desk and lit his lighter.

Willi Mohr inhaled the smoke. It stung and hurt his throat.

Sergeant Tornilla turned his lighter upside-down and said genially:

'Austrian. Contraband—even in the police . . .'

He put it away, again pressed his fingers together and smiled. Willi Mohr noted that the man had never taken his eyes off him since he had come into the room.

Sergeant Tornilla went on smiling. It was quiet in the room for at least thirty seconds. Then he exploded into a long stream of words, speaking in a low voice, intensely, with a much more marked lisp than before.

'Verstehe kein Wort,' said Willi Mohr.

It was true. He had quite literally not understood a single word.

'I'm sorry,' said Sergeant Tornilla, 'I was forgetting you were a foreigner.'

He turned a leather-covered frame so that his visitor could see the three oval portraits, a fat woman with a fan and an elaborately embroidered shawl and two small boys in sailor suits.

'My family,' he said proudly. 'My wife and my two sons. They're eleven and nine now, both born after the war.' He paused for a moment and raised his right forefinger as if replying to a question that had never been put.

'No, not here. In Huelva. My wife and I, our families come from Huelva. These photographs weren't taken here, nor in Huelva. In Badajoz. Duty, you see. One is often moved. My sons

9

were seven on these photos. Both were photographed at their first communion, Juan and Antonio.'

He pointed at the photographs, one after the other, and repeated, as if he were learning a lesson by heart:

'Juan... Antonio... They go to school here now. When they're older perhaps we'll be moved to a bigger town—with better schools.'

He offered another Bisonte, lit it and went on talking.

Willi Mohr felt as if in some way he was unable to resist this man on the other side of the desk, neither his flow of words nor his unwavering eyes. He was tired and dirty and ill at ease, painfully conscious of the fact that he had not washed for a long time, that his trousers were stiff with turpentine and spots of paint and that his faded brown shirt was impregnated with dried sweat, that his fair hair was dirty and dishevelled and wild, and that despite his long thin body he would feel small if this man in uniform got up.

And he was hungry too.

'... this is a district where there is always plenty of time. There's a saying here which says that one is waiting for the boat. There's a lot to that, much more than you would at first think. You go down to the harbour, perhaps several miles, and you wait. In the end a boat always comes, and then it goes again and you go on waiting. If anyone asks what you are waiting for—then you are still waiting for the boat, perhaps the next boat, perhaps another boat. Some don't even go to the harbour, but they are waiting all the same, for the boat, or something else. It's difficult for a stranger at first, but gradually you learn to wait. Sometimes—and in certain situations—it has its advantages.'

Silence. Sergeant Tornilla had stopped smiling.

'That's what it's like. Here and in many other parts of our country. People here are good and simple people. They demand nothing, but they earn their living in calm and order. Perhaps they are poor, many of them, but they are happy or will be happy when all the unpleasant and worrying things they've gone through have vanished from their memories. When they've been taught to learn what is right. They're already well on the way. What they need is firm faith, an orderly rhythm of life and sufficient work so that they can live. They only want to live, like

10

most people. They have already got or are going to get what they need. All other influences, all alien influences, only do them harm. Once many of these people were led into disaster, by leaders who weren't leaders—but criminals. Not all of them were criminals, it is true, for some of them were fools. They weren't any good at taking responsibility; they were only any good at dying. It takes courage to take responsibility. It doesn't take any courage to die, but it takes courage to kill, just as it takes courage to take responsibility. By the grace of God, there were some courageous people at that time.'

Silence.

Cigarette.

Smile.

The lighter and its blue gas flame.

Willi Mohr made a discovery. He had understood what the man had said, all the time, except at the beginning. Suddenly he knew why he had understood. Sergeant Tornilla was not speaking one language, but two. Into a framework of everyday Spanish he had woven a number of German expressions. The linguistic effect was not awkward or bizarre, but fluently comprehensible.

'You speak German.'

'Yes, some. And where did I learn it? In Russia. During the war. Division Azul—The Blue Division. The Vitebsk pocket . . . encirclement . . . everything. Very instructive, in many ways.'

He smiled.

'I learnt German there. I can even carry on a conversation in German, I think. But why should I do that here, in Spain? For your sake? No, you would never learn our language, Spanish, Castellano, if everyone spoke something else to you. The people here speak very badly, a dialect, a mixed language, very impure.'

He pressed his hands together again, almost laughing now.

Willi Mohr thought: What is this, a language lesson? The direct method? Aloud he said: 'Why have you had me brought here?'

'Give me your passport.'

Willi Mohr took his passport out of his hip pocket. It was buckled with the damp. The man behind the desk leafed thoughtfully through it. Then he smiled again, apologetically.

'You live here in the town, in my district. You are the only

11

foreigner here. I want to get to know the people in my district.
You live in . . .'

'Barrio Son Jofre.'

'B-a-r-r-i-o- S-o-n J-o-f-r-e, yes, B-a-r-r-i-o S-o-n- J-o-f-r-e,
you live there. Don't kid yourself. People here can't even pro-
nounce their own names.'

He repeated the address twice, with very clear diction.

Language lesson, thought Willi Mohr obstinately.

Sergeant Tornilla went on smiling.

'Just a few minor points,' he said. 'When you live here you
have to register, for example. Although you get a renewal of your
visa to stay here from the Governor General's office every third
month, you must report here at the police station. You have
neglected to do so. You have no money. You've debts in
several places.'

Pause.

'Yes, I know. That's not necessarily a crime. But earlier, you
received money regularly from somewhere. A number of things
were different before. As far as the money is concerned, you
didn't bring it with you into the country when you came. It
wasn't registered, anyhow.'

Pause.

'No, you didn't get it from outside either. Not in a letter
either, illegally. You don't get any post, anyhow no post with
money in it. And you've not had any foreign currency. You
haven't changed any.'

Pause.

'No, nor have you changed any illegally either. You received
Spanish money. And not in letters.'

Willi Mohr felt his temples growing hot. But outwardly he was
calm, stubbornly, sullenly calm. He had fled into truculence, the
eternal defence. He said nothing.

'Well, you see, one sits here and wonders. It's one's duty, one's
eternal duty. One wonders and puts two and two together.'

He passed the packet of cigarettes across and lit his lighter.

'I hope you'll get some money soon,' he said in a friendly way.
'To be without money in a foreign country can be a handicap. If
things get too difficult, you can come here. There are perhaps
certain possibilities.'

Willi Mohr made a discovery. The man opposite him did not smoke. And yet there had been some cigarette-ends in the ash-tray from the start and someone had certainly been smoking in the room earlier. But that was foolish reasoning, due to fatigue. Naturally someone else had been in here before him.

It was silent for a very long time.

Sergeant Tornilla leafed absently through the passport.

'Where did you serve during the war?'

'I wasn't in time.'

'No, of course, you were too young.'

'Not that young.'

'No, that's right, not that young. You were eighteen when the war ended. Many of your contemporaries had already been killed then.'

'I wasn't in time.'

'Where were you when the war actually ended?'

'In Flensburg.'

'And where had you been before that?'

'In Gotenhafen.'

'For training?'

'Yes.'

'What type of training?'

'Submarine training.'

'In . . . Gotenhafen?'

'Yes.'

'It's called Gdynia, isn't it?'

'Yes.'

'You never got a commission?'

'No.'

'And then, after the war. What did you do then?'

'Went home.'

'Where to. To which place?'

'Dornburg.'

'In which part of Germany does that lie?'

'Thüringen.'

'Isn't that on the wrong side of the border?'

The question threw Willi Mohr off his balance. He did not answer it.

'How long is it since you last saw Ramon Alemany?'

13

'May I have a little water?'

'Soon. How long is it since you last saw Ramon Alemany?'

'Four months.'

'Do you know where he is now?'

'No.'

'Where did you last see him?'

'In a French port.'

'Do you remember what it was called?'

'Ajaccio.'

'Quite right, Ajaccio in Corsica. But you've seen him since?'

'No.'

'Do you know what his brother's name is?'

'Santiago.'

'When did you last speak to Santiago?'

'Don't know. In the summer perhaps.'

'Didn't you meet him three days ago?'

'Yes.'

'So you were wrong when you said you hadn't spoken to him since the summer?'

'No.'

'But you met him three days ago?'

'Yes.'

'Can you explain yourself a bit?'

'We met, but we didn't speak to each other.'

'Where did you meet him?'

'Here.'

'Here? At the guard-post?'

'At home.'

'In the house in Barrio Son Jofre?'

'Yes.'

'Repeat: I met him in the house in B-a-r-r-i-o S-o-n J-o-f-r-e.'

'I met him in the house in Barrio Son Jofre.'

'Good. Your Spanish is getting better and better. Well, had you asked Santiago Alemany to come to see you?'

'No.'

'Why did he come then?'

'Don't know.'

'Did he just come to meet you?'

'He was on his way into town with some fish.'

14

'Quite right. He was on his way to the provincial capital with fish. What did you talk about?'

'Nothing.'

'For an hour?'

'I don't remember the time.'

'What did you talk about?'

'Nothing.'

'Didn't you say a word to each other for an hour?'

'I don't remember the time.'

'Didn't you say a word to each other?'

'Perhaps a few words.'

'Did he give you money?'

Willi Mohr did not answer the question.

'Dornburg in Thüringen. Does it lie in the Russian zone?'

'Yes.'

'How long did you live there?'

'Until 1951.'

'How many years?'

'Six.'

'Why did you move?'

'I didn't like it.'

'How long did you stay in West Germany?'

'For two and a half years.'

'And then you moved away from there?'

'Yes.'

'Why?'

'I didn't like it.'

'When you had tired of West Germany, you came here?'

'Yes.'

'Do you like it here?'

Willi Mohr opened his mouth but did not reply. He realized that he could answer yes or no, but he could not bring himself to choose. As usual after a winning blow Sergeant Tornilla at once changed the subject.

'You lived in Barrio Son Jofre before, when your Danish friends were still here?'

'Norwegian.'

'Quite right. So you lived in Barrio Son Jofre, while your Norwegian friends were here?'

15

'Yes.'

'How long?'

'Three months.'

'Perhaps four?'

'It's possible.'

'Let's see, while your Norwegian friends were still here and you lived with them, didn't you also mix with the Alemany brothers then too?'

'Yes.'

'You mixed with all five, like one big family?'

'Sometimes.'

'So you've known Santiago Alemany for a long time?'

'Yes.'

'And you know Antonio Millan, too, called Antonio Rojo?'

'No.'

'Just by name?'

'No.'

'But you know Santiago Alemany?'

'Yes.'

'Do you like Santiago Alemany?'

Sergeant Tornilla had hit the target again. He changed the subject at once.

'Are your parents still alive?'

'Only my mother.'

'And she lives in . . .'

'Dornburg.'

'Quite right. She lives in Dornburg. In the Russian zone.'

'Yes.'

'Did you belong to the Communist Party when you lived in the Russian zone?'

'No.'

'Only during the last years?'

'No.'

'Was it very difficult living there?'

'No.'

'And yet you moved?'

'I didn't like it.'

'Now you paint. Paint pictures. They say you paint well.'

'Thank you.'

16

'Did you make a living as an artist in Germany?'

'No.'

'Did you paint at all when you lived there?'

'No.'

'So you began to paint when you came here?'

'Yes.'

'Do you think your Norwegians friends are alive?'

'No.'

'Is Ramon Alemany in Spain now?'

'No.'

'How do you know he's not in Spain?'

Willi did not reply. The air wavered in front of his eyes. Sergeant Tornilla asked him only two more questions.

'That shirt you're wearing, is it yours?'

'Yes.'

'Are you tired?'

'Yes.'

Sergeant Tornilla had sat still while asking his questions, quite still, his eyes steady and his fingertips pressed together. Now he stretched one hand down behind his chair and lifted up an earthenware jug of water. He rose and walked round his desk. He looked totally unmoved, just as well groomed and faultless as before. He was smiling again now, in a friendly and compassionate manner.

'You're beginning to get tired,' he said, 'but you can get much tireder than this. Do have a drink.'

Willi Mohr drank, deeply and long. Then he was given a cigarette and a light. The other man went and sat down beneath the portrait.

'You don't seem happy. But perhaps that's good for you. I read in a newspaper article, in *Vanguardia*, I think, that true art is often created under difficult, even miserable circumstances. Otherwise it's easy to be happy here. Just look at people round about you. They are poor, but many of them are happy. Look at their faces. They are simple workers and peasants—but happy, for their families, their faith, for the miracle of being alive and creating another branch of the family. It's easy to be unhappy here too, and it's easy to find trouble for yourself. If you want to. Unhappiness is easy to find for anyone who seeks it out. But this

17

is really a fine little town, when you get to know it, and the people, with a few exceptions, are good people. When the exceptions have been eliminated everything will be fine. It's a big task, eliminating the exceptions.'

Willi Mohr made yet another discovery. He had raised his eyes to stop his head sinking down and now he noticed the similarity between the man in the chair and the general on the portrait. The picture was old and the Caudillo must have been about forty when it was taken, so much the same age as Sergeant Tornilla was now. The likeness was striking. The same uniform except the badges of rank, the same kind of moustache, the same shoulder-strap, the same angle of cap. Was that why he kept his cap on indoors? Willi Mohr looked at the portrait for so long that it began to shimmer in front of his eyes, and all the time the stream of words was boring its way into his mind. Suddenly he found himself sitting and listening to the portrait, seeing the mouth move. He shook his head slightly and tried to fix his eyes on the real living face below.

'... nine years, from 1936 to '45 I was a soldier, in other words. Almost uninterruptedly throughout the war. Amongst other things, one learnt to be afraid and at the same time control one's fear. They were, whatever people say, not unhappy years, not for those who had their aims in front of them. One had to learn to eliminate the enemies, one's own and one's country's, if one didn't want to have to live with them for ever in the future. There are many ways of eliminating. I was with the Navarre army corps during the offensive at Noguera Pallaresa in April '38. Do you know about the offensive at Noguera Pallaresa? No, of course not. Smoke, my dear friend?'

Willi Mohr fumbled as he took the cigarette. The hand holding the lighter did not tremble.

'Noguera Pallaresa is a tributary of the Segre. The Segre, as you probably know, runs along the border between Aragonia and Catalonia. At the Segre, directly west of Barcelona, lies Lerida, the largest town in eastern Catalonia. Just north of Lerida, there's a town called Balaguer and even farther north, just by the Noguera Pallaresa, a town called Tremp provides Barcelona and almost the whole of northern Catalonia with drinking-water and electricity. At that time the Catalonians were

18

amongst those people who found it most difficult to think as we do. Some of them still haven't learnt. Many of our soldiers were Moroccans. The Moroccans took Lerida on the second, and it was presumed that we should continue into Catalonia. The Catalonians expected it. Everyone expected it. But General Solchaga made a diversion northwards, we took Balaguer and advanced along the Noguera Pallaresa, where the reds had hardly any troops. Four days later we stormed Tremp. The Catalonians hadn't many people there, only a few weak forces, but they panicked, almost to the last man. Many people died that day. It was up in the mountains and still winter—a good exercise for Russia. When we saw the water-reservoirs and the electricity works, we knew that a million workers would be unemployed and that one and a half million households would be without water and electricity. Barcelona is a big city. We broke its back and with that the Catalonians' backs too. And yet . . .'

He paused and looked thoughtfully at the man on the bench, as if to see whether his pupil were still reacting.

'And yet,' he said, 'Catalonia didn't capitulate until a year later. Sometimes the rot is so deep-rooted that it cannot be healed. Sometimes ignorance is so great that the teacher has to kill the pupil. For both's sake. But let's talk about something else. How long is it since you last met Ramon Alemany?'

'Four months.'

'Five months and sixteen days to be exact. You said so yourself at your interrogation. I've the record here.'

He tapped the cardboard file on his desk.

'You live in a poor part of the town,' he said, with concern. 'Barrio Son Jofre. I live in a better part, near the church, on the Avenue. A really fine house, old but well built, a garden at the back and plenty of space. Good for the children.'

Now he's going to start asking questions again, thought Willi Mohr with weary despair.

Sergeant Tornilla rose, smiled and put out his hand.

'This has been a pleasant conversation. Sometime perhaps I'll come and look at your paintings. And now, we'll meet again, I'm sure.'

Willi Mohr swayed as he rose. He was soaked in sweat and everything shimmered in front of his eyes. The other man looked

19

exactly as he had when he had risen from his chair the first time, an eternity ago.

'Just one more thing. Your passport. I'll keep it for the time being. If you want to go somewhere, perhaps you'll come here. Come when you like. They're bagatelles, I know, but . . .'

He shrugged apologetically. Smiling.

Then he walked to the door and politely held it open.

Willi Mohr stood in the porch, which seemed light in comparison with the room he had just been in.

Outside the sun was shining radiantly.

The tall officer came into the porch. He looked recently risen and newly shaven, but his forehead was already sweaty. When he saw Willi Mohr, he stopped and said uncertainly: 'I'm sorry. A mistake, wasn't it?'

He opened the door to the interrogation room and went in. Before the door closed, Willi Mohr saw Sergeant Tornilla once more.

He was sitting at his desk writing. Between the forefinger and the middle finger of his left hand was a lighted cigarette, and his face was hard and serious.

Willi Mohr walked unsteadily out into the sunlight.

3

Sergeant Tornilla was carrying on a conversation with his superior. Three remarks each.

'Well?' said Lieutenant Pujol.

'Someone had given him some water.'

'What do you think?'

'If he hasn't done it, then he will.'

'Might you be mistaken?'

'Hardly.'

20

4

Willi Mohr walked through the town, a long gangling figure in a faded shirt, paint-spotted khaki trousers and sandals. His straw hat threw a dark shadow across his sunburnt face. He was tired, but his physical energies remained. Although he was walking very slowly, his steps were light and purposeful.

On the Avenida Generalissimo Franco he met several men who were on their way to road construction work up in the mountains, heavy, unbelievably badly-paid assisted work which was carried out almost wholly without the help of machines and progressed very slowly. They were walking in silence, staring ahead with empty eyes. They were carrying straw baskets containing water-jars and bits of bread, the same baskets they would be using for their work a little later on.

Look at their faces. They are simple workers, but happy, for their faith, for the miracle of being alive . . .

He lies, thought Willi Mohr.

Then he thought about another remark—the one about his shirt.

It takes great certainty in observation to be able to identify a fifteen-year-old Hitler Jugend shirt, washed-out and faded and with all the badges removed.

It struck Willi Mohr that he had answered all the questions quite truthfully, even those which dealt with the event of three days ago. Santiago Alemany had come at about five o'clock in the afternoon and stayed for a while, but they had not spoken to each other. He had parked his fish-van outside and gone into the house and looked round, especially in the kitchen. Then he had sat down on the bottom step and played with the cat. Several times he had opened his mouth to say something, but evidently had then changed his mind. When he had gone, three dirty hundred-peseta notes had lain on the steps. All the time, Willi Mohr had sat at his easel and worked on a painting of a house and some cacti. Santiago had said good-day and good-bye and possibly a few words, but Willi Mohr had just nodded twice. He

21

had let the money lie there for two days, and then he had picked it up and paid his bill at the tienda.

5

Forty minutes after he had left the guard-post, Willi Mohr was standing in front of the house in Barrio Son Jofre. When he opened the door, the cat came up to him and brushed against his legs, and the bitch rushed out on to the floor. She whined and cringed and wagged her tail. She must have been very hungry and thirsty, just as he was.

The house in Barrio Son Jofre was built on two floors and had three rooms, apart from the kitchen. From the large room on the ground floor a stone staircase led up to the first floor. Of the two rooms above, the larger was well kept but the smaller was more or less uninhabitable. The floor was broken and part of it had fallen through into the kitchen. In the whole house there were only two pieces of furniture, a large brown wooden bedstead upstairs and a rattan chair with a woven cane seat downstairs. There was a mattress downstairs too, and a blanket, and about twenty paintings. Most of them lay on the floor, but some were fastened to the walls with drawing-pins. Beside the chair stood a metal paraffin lamp, and on a piece of sacking in one corner lay some clothes and other personal possessions. The downstairs floor was carefully swept, but upstairs, where no one had been for a long time, there was a thick layer of greyish stone-dust over everything.

Willi Mohr poured out some water into an earthenware bowl for the bitch and put some dry pieces of bread into it. Then he thrust his hand in amongst the pups and took out his pistol and the notebook. The weapon felt heavy and damp and he weighed it in his hand as he went into the room. He stood still in the middle of the floor and said to himself: 'What the hell *did* he want anyhow?'

And after a pause: 'He'll fetch me down there again and before that I must kill the other one too.'

He leafed through the notebook. The first page was dated the

22

thirtieth of July the year before, the day after Hugo had gone. He had written several pages on the first days and then the notes grew briefer and briefer, and after the fourth of September they ceased altogether. On the following pages he had jotted down figures and small sketches and then there was another note. The handwriting was firm and quite legible.

16th December, 8 a.m. Yesterday I waited all the afternoon and evening in the puerto but they did not come back. It was past two in the morning when I got home.

After this date there were a lot more notes and now the notebook was almost full.

Willi Mohr bit his lower lip and slowly shook his head.

Then he put the things back in their usual place under the mattress, took off his clothes and lay down on his back, naked, his hands clasped behind his head.

He thought: Tomorrow I'll kill the pups. I'll pick out the one with the best markings and keep it. The others I'll kill.

Just before he fell asleep he thought about the truck and the day the Scandinavians were drinking at Jacinto's bar. Fourteen months had gone by since then.

Part Two

1

The truck was a re-built 1931 model Fiat-camioneta. It had no fenders and no hood and the driver's cabin and back had been stripped and replaced with two wooden seats rather like park benches. All these alterations had been made purposefully, to make the vehicle lighter and more useful as transport for people on bad roads.

The vehicle had a history, as it had come to Spain during the Civil War with General Bergonzoli's first blackshirt division and had fallen into the hands of the worker's militia after the battle at Brihuega in March, 1937. But no one knew anything about that now, so the camioneta was not considered of any historical value.

Dan Pedersen had taken it over from an acquaintance who was a builder in Santa Margarita and although it was twenty-five years old, it functioned quite satisfactorily.

The road ran in long curves down the mountainside and down there, on the other side of the bay, the houses of the fishing settlement lay piled up along the quay. The surface of the water was calm and blue and sunlit, and out by the pier a number of people could be seen bathing. Several white yachts lay by the harbour wall and farther in, along the quay itself, were half a dozen dirty yellow trawlers with their nets draped like mourning veils round their masts. Despite the distance, one could see groups of lightly-clad tourists standing on the quay, looking at the fishing-boats.

It was the beginning of August and very hot. The truck rolled swiftly down, its engine switched off, and all that could be heard was the squeal of the mechanical brakes and the noise of stones striking the underneath of the vehicle. The road was narrow and rough, but then it also led to the most distant and isolated houses in the community.

There were three people in the truck. Dan Pedersen, who was driving, and beside him Siglinde, his wife. On the bench behind sat Willi Mohr, his straw hat pulled down over his forehead as protection against the clouds of dust. Now and again he had to use both arms and legs against the bodywork to prevent himself from being thrown off on the sharp corners.

He was looking at the girl's slim, sunburnt neck and when the breeze raised her short blond hair, he saw a string of small drops of sweat along the roots of her hair. He also saw that the hairs were darker at the roots and realized that she had bleached her hair and wondered why.

'Don't drive so damned fast,'said Siglinde. 'The dust's choking me.'

Dan did not reply. He thought: The Scandinavians have got their money and now they're drinking at Jacinto's. They've forgotten that they owe me two thousand pesetas and that I've not paid the rent for two months and have hardly enough money for food. But they've also forgotten that this is a pretty small place and that one finds things out almost at once. And now they've damn well got to pay up. Hope I can get hold of Santiago and Ramon, for there's going to be a row, and the German here's not much use. He's only good for sitting goggling at Siglinde when she's sunbathing, and why not, as that's what I'd do too, if I didn't already know what she looks like all over.

Dan Pedersen did in fact use the term Scandinavians, but with a certain contempt, forgetting that he himself belonged to that same group.

At this time of the year there were perhaps a couple of hundred foreigners in the puerto and about a dozen of them were residents, people of various nationalities, mostly painters or writers, or at least pretending to be, and most of them were Swedes or Finns. Among them was a small group which never had any money. They were the Scandinavians. They were very fond of their liquor.

Siglinde thought: There's going to be trouble, I know it, as I know Dan, and I hope we meet Santiago or Ramon on the way, because this German's not much use, although he seems kind,

26

and he can't paint either, poor thing, and it's hell Dan let him come and live with us, so that now I can't sunbathe naked.'

She was a young woman of fairly ordinary nordic type, healthy and strong and moderately beautiful. She was wearing pants and bra, dusty thonged sandals and a pale blue dress with shoulder-straps. She was blond and grey-eyed and much more sunburnt than genuine blondes usually get.

The man in the back seat stared coolly at her bare shoulders and held a silent monologue with himself.

What on earth have I got to do with these people? I'm as indifferent to them as they are to me. But what could I do when Hugo went and I was left with nowhere to live and not a word of the language? Stay at a boarding-house? Then my money would not have been enough and I was to stay here a year and paint. I said I would and I'm going to. Even if it is meaningless, really. Anyhow, I can't understand what people like Hugo see in this country and this sort of place. It's warm, but that's about all. Now these people are expecting me to help them in some private row, and I suppose I ought to, as I've lived with them for a week. I don't know what it's all about but what does that matter.

They had come down on to the smooth shore road which ran in a curve round the inner part of the bay, connecting the village with the little group of houses lying near the lighthouse and the pier. Dan started the engine, which rattled alarmingly. He drove quickly and carelessly round the bay.

Two nights earlier a couple of fishing-boats had happened to get a shoal of turtles in their nets, and halfway to the village the damaged nets were stretched out on a rack which was about a hundred yards long. The nets took up one half of the road and about every ten yards men and women were sitting mending the holes.

At the third net-mender, Dan Pedersen braked the camioneta and stopped.

'Hullo,' he said.

When the shadow of the vehicle fell over him, Santiago Alemany raised his head, and with two fingers pushed his straw hat off his forehead. He was sitting with his legs stretched out in the sun-scorched gravel and had stretched the net out by hooking his big toe in one of the holes.

27

'What's up?' he said.

'The Scandinavians have got their money and are drinking at Jacinto's.'

'I heard. Even when you sit here, you get to know everything.'

'Are you coming with us?'

Santiago Alemany carefully worked the net loose and rose. His movements had a studied leisureliness, giving him a kind of grandeur, although he was bare-footed and rather dirty from the work, and although his faded clothes were of a very indefinite colour.

He was twenty-seven, roughly the same age as the people in the truck, and had calm light-brown eyes, a broad forehead and not especially dark hair.

He is well built, thought Siglinde, who often thought about such things.

'A calamity,' he said, gesturing towards the net. 'This ought to be finished today. Or tomorrow.'

He laughed, took out a crumpled packet of Ideales and handed them round. Everyone took one except Willi Mohr, who had not yet got used to the pungent local tobacco. And the fact that he did not understand what they were talking about also put him into a state of apathetic passivity.

Santiago climbed up on the truck and sat down beside Willi Mohr.

'Let's take little brother with us,' he said. 'He's useful ... in this sort of situation.'

When the truck started up, the nearest net-mender turned his head and called behind him, without ceasing to work:

'Now Santiago's gone off with the foreigners again—as usual.'

Ramon Alemany was sitting right at the end of the row, bent forward, fumbling with the stitches. The family likeness was there, but he was in many ways very different from his brother. When he saw the truck, he at once untangled himself from the nets, flung them down and jumped up, small, muscular and with lively eyes. Under his carelessly knotted shirt could be seen his hairy, sweaty chest and large, dark brown nipples.

He clambered up on to the back bench and eagerly shook everyone by the hand.

28

The brothers spoke to each other in Catalonian. Both laughed. Dan Pedersen drove on.

Singlinde turned and smiled at the three people behind her.

Willi Mohr did not understand a thing. He felt utterly indifferent to them all.

2

The clump of houses in the harbour lay basking in the sun, today just as on every summer day. From the broad level quay, narrow dark alleys ran upwards between leaning white house-walls. Some of the cafés on the harbour side had tried to live up to the demands of the present by setting up coloured umbrellas over the tables. One of the bar-owners was wearing a white jacket. On the quay a large number of foreigners were either sitting at café tables or strolling aimlessly about, looking at the boats and the catch of turtles which had been tethered with floats to rings. Red-burnt tourists in shorts and colourful shirts were wandering about in the alleys among half-naked children and thin black pigs. A couple of civil guards were standing in the shade of the fish-shed. They were absently watching the crowd on the quay. A small priest in a wide, flat hat was tripping along the row of houses. His long black skirts flapped round his legs and he kept his eyes on the ground, as if to avoid seeing such horrors.

Tourism had broken through in the puerto. The desperate need for foreign currency had persuaded the authorities to ease the restrictions on entry into the country. Here, as in hundreds of other places along the coast, the outer forms were in the process of loosening up. Strangers no longer received printed notes to say that it was forbidden to show yourself out of doors with a naked torso, or appear in shorts, two-piece bathing costumes or dresses with shoulder-straps, or to kiss in the street or to insult the Caudillo and his almighty realm. Foreigners must be treated well, as they brought money to the state. Money which was to be used for the poor and the ignorant. Soon the civil guard would be equipped with automatic weapons in place of their out-of-date old carbines.

A number of private individuals also made money out of the foreigners. These were the people who had their own businesses and had already been in a good position before. The ordinary people were just as poor as ever, though they had possibly become more conscious of their situation.

And that was where the risk lay.

The police had been reinforced, but at the same time their role had become more one of observation. Like the priesthood, the civil guard now worked preferably in silence and they mostly waited until the winter.

The patrols from La Policia Secreta very rarely showed themselves during the summer months and then only very late at night.

A number of people, especially irresponsible young men, who were much too young to have experienced the great battle for righteousness, seemed inclined to sacrifice their humility, faith, truth and purity for other forms of life and ideals.

Their names were carefully registered by the supervisors of both worldly and heavenly powers, a natural procedure, which on the whole they survived. Far worse was to land in the quagmire between the life they had been brought up in and the diffuse visions of something else, told to them by sun-shocked Scandinavians and half-naked German office girls.

In September the tourists went away and the hunt for Communists could begin again.

As could the battle for souls.

The ordinary personnel in the civil guard was often changed, according to an involved circulation system decided at regional headquarters in the town up in the mountains.

It was thirteen kilometres up there. From the quay one could see the town like a blurred shadow against the greyish-yellow of the mountain.

In the town in the mountains there were people who knew what was happening in the village by the sea without ever having to go there.

They cut off the village by the sea as if it were an enemy bridgehead during the war. They closed an iron ring round it, but very few strangers ever noticed that detail.

From the puerto only one road led into the mountains.

30

3

Dan Pedersen swung round into one of the side-streets and pressed the accelerator down as far as it would go to clear the slope. He energetically blew the horn and children, pigs and cats fled out of the way. Some strolling tourists pressed themselves against the wall and stared in surprise with round blue eyes. Then the camioneta stopped outside Jacinto's bar.

It lay at the highest point in the village, only a block away from the church, and from the outside there was not much to see. There were no tables on the street, only a couple of basket chairs for the abuele and abuela, and the pale-blue, peeling letters on the notice above the doorway were only just decipherable against the whitewashed wall. In front of the entrance hung a primitive jalousie made of string and squashed bottle-tops.

Before, the bar had been a place for villagers, but now it was being annexed more and more by the small colony of resident foreigners.

Siglinde stayed in the truck with her legs crossed and one elbow resting on her knee, her chin supported on her hand. She did not want to go in with them, not because she was afraid, but simply because she did not feel like it. The noise from within indicated that the Swedes and Finns had already been at it for some time.

They were singing.

When the jalousies fell back again behind Willi Mohr, who was last in, most of the singing stopped.

Siglinde tried to make out from the sounds what was going on. Then she shrugged her shoulders and resignedly shook her head.

Inside in the bar, a fight broke out almost at once.

The person who owed Dan Pedersen most money was a Swedish painter. He was tall, dark and handsome, but also very frightened of being beaten up. He considered himself a successful seducer and his secret terror was that someone would do violence to his greatest advantage, his face. He was also stupid and tried to cover his physical cowardice with arrogance.

31

The Swede was sitting at a table near the door, together with a small bearded man, who also maintained he was a painter and who was definitely a Finn. Another Finnish painter, famous in his own country, was standing by the bar itself, drunk and conciliatory. He was bare-footed and wearing a blue and white track suit. Four other Scandinavians were there, amongst them two girls. Behind the bar stood Jacinto. He was looking satisfied and was just having a drink with the famous Finn. The abuela, who was small and chubby and wrapped in a dirty shawl, brought another bottle of champagne to the table by the door.

The champagne infuriated Dan Pedersen. True it was of the cheapest kind, which cost only twelve pesetas a bottle, but it still gave the scene an air of inappropriate and unearned luxury. He said something uncontrolled and when the Swede smiled superciliously, Dan grabbed hold of his shoulder. The little Finn rose to his feet and hit him hard with his fist on the back of his neck and Dan fell across the Swede's outstretched leg. As he fell, he saw Jacinto slink out the back way and heard the abuela call for help. Then his head hit the iron leg of the table and he temporarily retired from the game.

When the Swede saw the devastating effect of tripping Dan up, he rose and walked towards the door. Willi Mohr was standing in the way and thought he ought to hit him. But then he saw that the Swede was frightened and so he hesitated. Ramon, who had been ill-placed from the start, pushed Willi Mohr aside and knocked the Swede down with two swift blows in the stomach. Then he kicked him hard in the side. At the same time, Santiago had succeeded in coming up behind the Finn and flinging his arms round him. Ramon came nearer, crouching with his fists clenched, but although the Finn had his arms locked to his sides he succeeded in kicking his opponent in the chest. Ramon staggered back a few steps. Two of the other Scandinavians hung amateurishly on to Santiago from behind and he was forced to let the Finn go.

Suddenly it was quite quiet, and Willi Mohr saw that what two seconds earlier had really been some kind of unreal game, had now suddenly grown serious.

Ramon and the Finn were moving round opposite one another in a small circle, crouching with their raised arms bent like

32

mechanical grabs. The skin on their faces was stretched tightly over their features.

They could well kill each other, quite without cause, thought Willi Mohr in astonishment.

The jalousies rattled and two civil guards in green uniforms came in from the street. One of them hit Ramon Alemany over the head from behind with the barrel of his carbine. Ramon fell and rolled round on the stone floor with both arms round his head. Then he lay still on his side, curled up, his arms and legs jerking like a dying animal.

The other civil guard had raised his carbine over the Finn, but stopped when he saw that he was a foreigner. He lowered his weapon and contented himself with poking the barrel into the Finn's chest. The Finn looked contemptuously at the carbine, then straightened up and relaxed.

'I'll say one thing. The North is always the North,' said the conciliatory gentleman at the bar, raising his glass, as if he were saluting some sportive success.

Calm was once again restored to Jacinto's bar.

Dan Pedersen got up. He was bleeding from a scratch on his cheek.

The tall Swede was still sitting, groaning and holding his stomach.

Ramon lay stretched out unconscious. His brother had knelt beside him and was carefully lifting his head off the stone floor.

The fight was over. It had lasted at the most two or three minutes.

Dan Pedersen had not got his money.

4

Two hours later Dan Pedersen, Willi Mohr and Santiago Alemany were standing leaning against a whitewashed wall inside the civil guard's cuartel, just behind the church. They were smoking cigarettes and looking unconcernedly at the corporal, who for the moment was the puerto's most senior police official. There was also a wooden counter in the room, and a basket chair, in which

33

the guard on duty usually sat and slept with his collar unbuttoned and his carbine across his knees. For the moment, Siglinde Pedersen was sitting in it, her skirt modestly pulled down and her brown legs crossed. She had taken off her sandals and was impatiently swinging one foot up and down.

The cabo was quite a young man in an elegant uniform and black leather boots. His forehead was beaded with sweat and he was walking irritably up and down in front of the men leaning against the wall. Now and again he glanced timidly down at Siglinde's sunburnt feet.

'This will have to be the last time now,' he said. 'We're friendly people, but we don't tolerate anything. We've tolerated a great deal from you already, drunkenness, blasphemy, indecency . . .'

'Indecency?' said Dan Pedersen, stiffening.

'Yes, we call it that,' said the cabo hastily. 'I know that they are said to look at things differently in your country. But that is as maybe, and this is something quite different. Provocation without precedent, almost assault . . .'

'It wasn't really our fault,' said Dan Pedersen.

'Don't try that on,' said the cabo, shaking his forefinger. 'Don't try telling us we've got it wrong. We know our job. I've heard what Jacinto and the abuela and even those drunks had to say. There's nothing to argue about. You started it. And don't try saying that this isn't a proper investigation. I knew you'd say that, but this time it won't work. I've had six men on this.'

'In my country,' said Dan Pedersen, 'one policeman or at the most one and a half is enough for a place this size. And you've got fifteen.'

'Seventeen,' said the cabo. 'And there's no such thing as half a policeman. But this isn't a nice little chat. You must leave now, and at once.'

'And my wife?'

'She too,' said the cabo, without looking at Siglinde.

'Do look at her,' said Dan Pedersen. 'She's alive and won't bite. Do look. You aren't allowed to do that very often, you poor bastard.'

The cabo stopped abruptly in front of him.

'Be very careful now,' he said slowly. 'Be very careful, if you

34

don't want to spend the rest of your time in this country in a very small room. I'm able to . . .'

'All right, when must we move?'

'At once.'

'Where to?'

'Wherever you like. Out of the district.'

'Up into the town, for example?'

The cabo shrugged his shoulders.

'But then we can come here every day if we want to?'

The cabo shrugged his shoulders again.

'Idiotic,' said Dan Pedersen.

'Within twenty-four hours,' said the cabo. 'Preferably before. Otherwise I'll have to make a case of it and put it before the courts. And I'd rather not do that, for your sake, and for my own.'

At least he is honest, thought Dan Pedersen. Aloud he said: 'And the German?'

'He can stay.'

'Where can he live then?'

'That's nothing to do with me.'

The cabo looked indifferently at Willi Mohr. Then he turned to look at Santiago Alemany, who was leaning with his back against the wall and looking up at the ceiling.

'What have you got to say, then?' he said provocatively.

'It wasn't our fault and all I did was to try and separate them.'

'You never do anything,' said the cabo, looking bitterly at Santiago. 'You never do anything, but you're always there. You don't even work properly like your father and brother. They go out with the boats nearly every night—but you're content to sit in bars with foreigners and drive into town with the fish at the most twice a week.'

Santiago Alemany opened his mouth and moistened his lips with his tongue.

'That can be quite hard work sometimes,' he said.

He had meant to say something quite different.

'What did you do with your brother, by the way?'

Santiago moistened his lips again.

'I took him home,' he said. 'He needed rest.'

From her place in the basket chair Siglinde saw that his eyes

35

had turned hard and cold. Perhaps no one else had noticed it.

'Your brother'll get prison; a week, perhaps fourteen days. Well, he'll manage.'

'Sure,' said Santiago Alemany.

'And remember what I've said,' said the cabo, turning to Dan Pedersen again. 'At the latest tomorrow, preferably tonight. And now, good-bye.'

When they went out to the truck, the cabo stayed behind the jalousies and looked at Siglinde. Her blue dress was tight across her hips and behind as she walked, and the grey dust swirled round her naked feet.

'Cretins,' said the cabo to himself and went back into the room. He took out the local telephone from under the counter and impatiently jiggled the cradle.

This corporal had no future ahead of him in the police. He had been sent to the puerto because he was considered to be a modern type, who handled foreigners well. He suffered from an inferiority complex on behalf of his country and studied foreign methods. His superiors at regional headquarters were following his actions with rising distrust.

Outside Dan Pedersen said to Willi Mohr: 'We've got to move now. It was our fault you got involved in all this. You can come with us if you like. I know of a house up there, which we can rent cheaply. It's at the southern end of the town and there's no electric light, but it'll do.'

'Have you any money? I'm flat broke,' he said to Santiago.

Santiago took a roll of worn dirty notes out of his pocket.

'How much do you need?'

'Only fifty.'

Santiago separated out a hundred-peseta note.

Dan Pedersen smiled as he put it in his pocket.

'And what do you think?' he said to Siglinde.

'You're crazy, but it doesn't matter. It'll probably be all right up there.'

'You're a good kid. Do you know what I thought when I saw you in there? You're an insulting truth in this goddam country.'

He paused and looked her up and down. Then he said: 'I want to sleep with you later.'

'We'll see,' said Siglinde, and she smiled.

She looked optimistically towards the distant spot in the mountains, expecting something of the future.

Dan Pedersen had spoken German to Willi, Spanish to Santiago and Norwegian to his wife. He was on form, despite relative setbacks, and he thumped the others on the back. They began to climb up into the camioneta.

For the first time for a long time, Willi Mohr felt something stir inside him. He felt a slight burrowing curiosity about what was to happen next.

'I've got some money,' he said.

'Good,' said Siglinde, 'then we can live off you until things straighten out.'

They dropped Santiago off at the nets, halfway round the bay.

'We'll move tonight, when it's a bit cooler,' said Dan Pedersen. 'Will you come with the fish-van?'

'Of course,' said Santiago Alemany, raising his hand in farewell.

When the truck had driven away, he sat down on the ground, threaded the net over his big toe and went on where he had left off.

He said nothing to those sitting nearest him and neither did anyone say anything to him.

5

It was three in the afternoon when a civil guard by the name of Pablo Canaves knocked Ramon Alemany unconscious with his carbine in Jacinto's bar.

Ramon Alemany came round fifteen minutes later. He laughed and talked but walked very unsteadily, and he seemed almost incapable of recognizing people round him. His brother helped him home and put him to bed. Then he washed the blood from his injuries and bathed the bump on the back of his head with cold water. By then Ramon had already fallen asleep.

He slept heavily for four hours. When his father came and woke him up, Ramon Alemany got up with a headache. He also found it difficult to see, and over and over again had to shake his head to get the lines to meet and fall into the usual everyday pattern. It hurt very much when he shook his head. He tried eating a piece of bread dipped in olive oil, but at once felt very sick and vomited.

Immediately afterwards he carried two containers of paraffin down to the fishing-boat. They were full and together weighed more than a hundred-and-sixty pounds. He did not once put them down on the way, and when he climbed over the railing, red and black spots danced before his eyes. He could see only very indistinctly and spoke slurringly and disconnectedly. His father thought he had been drinking and hit him several times across the back of his neck with a piece of rope, but not especially hard.

At the same time, Pablo Canaves had gone off duty. He was married, lived in the puerto and was sitting at home in his bare kitchen in his stockinged feet, his uniform jacket unbuttoned. He talked to his wife as he ate a plateful of boiled rice and two salted sardines.

'I knocked a man unconscious today,' he said.

'Who?'

'Ramon Alemany.'

'Oh—him!'

6

The town was quite small and yet was the largest and the most important in the district. It lay high up and was wholly surrounded by mountains, except in the east, where a narrow crooked valley opened out to the sea. The mountains were quite steep but very eroded, and the yellow-grey stony slopes were thinly covered with pines and low, thorny bushes. To the east, towards the sea, there were terraced fields of olive and almond trees and there was quite a number of farms there too, most of them derelict and abandoned. From the town ran two roads, one down to the puerto, the other southwards, parallel with the coast and in the direction of the provincial capital seventy kilometres

38

away. The main road was asphalted and climbed in long bends up towards a pass in the mountain range. For ten years, work had been in progress to continue it northwards to open up negotiable communications with several isolated villages. But the work was carried out in such difficult circumstances that it was making no noticeable progress.

It was not necessary for anyone travelling directly from the provincial capital to the puerto to take the road round through the town in the mountains, for there was also a through road which ran into the main road twelve kilometres south of the town. This road was old and very bad, but it saved time and had a view over the sea. A lot of people made use of it. Three thousand people lived in the town up in the mountains, of which about five hundred were fully employable men. Most were peasants or farmworkers, but as the land could not support them, many worked on road construction projects, assisted employment. This work was on a quota and could only just employ those who applied for assistance. The daily pay had a ceiling of very low sums.

A little way out of the town, on the western slope, there was a military camp for two hundred men of the marine infantry. The soldiers were peasant boys who handled their carbines clumsily and awkwardly. They could often be heard exercising and shooting up in the mountains, but they were only to be seen in the town on Saturday and Sunday evenings.

There were also ten bars, a civil guard-post of thirty-five men, twelve priests and a doctor. Most cases of sickness were nursed by a few nuns who wandered in and out of the houses like angels of death, with hypodermic syringes hidden under evil-smelling robes.

This was the town up in the mountains. It was a quiet place and to the outsider it gave an impression of quiet contemplation and sublime calm.

7

Dan Pedersen had rented a house in Barrio Son Jofre, just by the southern entrance to the town, and he moved there with Siglinde and Willi Mohr. Their possessions were somewhat varied, souvenirs, a dog, a cat, household articles, typewriters, clothes, books, raffia baskets, sketching blocks and even the odd piece of furniture, for Dan and his wife had lived in the country for nearly two years and had managed to accumulate quite a few oddments. Willi Mohr on the whole owned no more than he could carry, his rucksack, his box of oils and a roll of canvases.

The whole lot was loaded on to the camioneta and Santiago Alemany's fish-van and then they set off on the thirteen-kilometre climb up to the town. Dan Pedersen drove and Siglinde and Willi Mohr sat in the back trying to keep some sort of order in the carelessly stowed load. Santiago Alemany followed behind them in his fish-van, which was a Ford of the smallest kind and very old. Everyone was on good form and they sang, loudly and vociferously, to drown the sound of the engines.

Halfway up, they had to stop and fill up with water before the radiator boiled dry on the Ford, and a moment later they passed two civil guards who, seeing they were foreigners, at once waved them on. Just this side of the entrance to the town they passed yet another road patrol, two men in green uniforms, who were standing leaning on their bicycles by the ditch.

A fortified poor-house, thought Dan Pedersen, and at once forgot what he had thought.

The house in Barrio Son Jofre had stood empty for a long time, but the owner had had it swept out, water brought in, and in the dark it did not look at all bad.

'There's one habitable room up there and one down here,' said Dan Pedersen to his wife. 'Which one do you want?'

'The one up there, with the window,' said Siglinde.

Dan asked: 'What do you think of it, the whole place, I mean?'

Despite everything, he was still feeling a little uncertain.

'It'll be fine,' said Siglinde.

40

As long as it doesn't go on too long, she thought.

Outside, Santiago had lit a paraffin lamp and was unloading together with Willi Mohr.

'Unload the camioneta first,' said Dan Pedersen, 'and let the things stay out there, and we'll go up and fetch the other things at once.'

The owner of the house, who ran the Café Central up in the square, was an old friend of Dan's. He had promised to lend him a bed and a mattress for the time being. The bed was too big for the fish-van.

Ten minutes later their luggage lay in a heap in front of the door.

'The strongest can come and help,' said Dan Pedersen. 'The bed's as large as a cathedral.'

Willi Mohr climbed up on to the truck. He was used to heavy manual work.

'Fine,' said Dan. 'You two can carry the things in in the meantime.'

He was satisfied with the division of labour, as he had known Santiago for a long time and trusted him.

Dan Pedersen at once wound the starting-handle of the truck and drove off. Siglinde was standing outside the house. It was dark and silent and they could hear the sound of the engine until the truck stopped right up in the square.

Santiago began carrying things into the house. In the room on the ground floor, the paraffin lamp spread a weak flickering light, and the ginger cat sniffed suspiciously round the walls.

It took almost half an hour for Santiago to move everything into the house. He did it leisurely and carefully, placing each thing where Siglinde thought it ought to go.

The last thing he carried in was Dan's typewriter. He took it up to the room above and put it carefully down on to the floor.

Then he straightened up and lit a cigarette. Siglinde had opened the shutters and was standing looking out. The paraffin lamp below threw stray reflections of light up the stairs, and through the open window came a warm breeze from the sun-warmed mountains.

When Santiago had finished his cigarette, he was just about to drop the butt on to the floor, when he changed his mind and took

41

two steps forward and flicked it out of the window. It fell on to the cobblestones in a shower of sparks.

He was now standing just behind Siglinde. She was barefooted and was still wearing the blue dress with shoulderstraps. She was standing quite still.

They said nothing. Santiago opened his mouth and moistened his lips with his tongue.

It was quiet outside.

He took a step nearer and put his hands on her bare, downy shoulders.

Siglinde did not move. He was standing close up to her. All he had on was a clean shirt and pair of cotton trousers and she felt him very close, sensed his breath and perhaps the swift beats of his heart. And yet she let his hands remain, just for a moment, just to feel what it felt like.

With a swift consistent movement, he pulled her dress and bra straps down from her shoulders, pressed his lips to her neck, below her ear, and put both hands round her naked breasts.

Not at all brutally, but uncertainly and groping, almost as if he were afraid of touching her.

Her breasts were soft, firm and round, and he held them in his hands, the nipples stiff and rough against the sensitive skin of his palms.

He changed his grip and weighed her breasts in his hands, the tips of his forefingers resting gently on her nipples. He bit carefully in the soft angle between neck and shoulder.

Through the thin material of her dress she felt his sex, hard and upright, against a point just below the small of her back.

Siglinde had felt what it was like.

She freed herself, turned round and hit him across the face, quite hard, with the back of her hand.

He took a step back into the darkness.

She quickly pulled up her dress and bra straps, but he had time to see her naked breasts with their large dark nipples, which seemed black against her sunburnt skin.

'Don't ever try to do that again,' she said scornfully.

She was not really indignant. But she had found herself in similar situations so many times in her life that she knew exactly which tone of voice was the most effective.

42

She walked past Santiago Alemany, over towards the stairs. She didn't look at him and anyhow would not have been able to distinguish his features in the poor light.

Siglinde was pottering about down below and quite a long time went by before Santiago came down. His face was controlled and closed and he constantly seemed to fix his eye on a spot behind her somewhere.

She looked at him and almost imperceptibly shrugged her shoulders.

She had tested herself a little just before, a little too much, too. Not for her own sake, true, for in spite of the actual physical contact, she had not really felt a thing. She liked sleeping with men, but only one at a time and preferably the same one for as long a consecutive period of time as possible. In addition she was thoroughly satisfied and generally considered herself to be happy.

She would really like to have said 'Don't sulk, now,' but she was too wise for that and said instead: 'Give me a cigarette, there's a good boy.'

A flicker of surprise shone in Santiago's eyes and the mask cracked for one brief moment.

Siglinde thought: You poor wretch you. It's hell that you can't find anyone who wants to. Good God, there should be a rescue corps of sensible women set up, women who could be sent here as instructors and sweep out all this hypocrisy and stupidity and complexes, before those fat masturbating priests and nuns have time to destroy this generation too.

When she looked at Santiago his face had changed yet again. His look was calm and reflective, and he moistened his lips with his tongue as he systematically sorted out the things on the floor.

A moment later they heard the truck start up and come nearer.

Dan Pedersen and Willi Mohr had been forced to take the bed to pieces to get it on the vehicle. Now they had to carry the sections upstairs and put it together again. When they had done it, Siglinde went up to look and burst out laughing. It was a huge wooden bedstead of stained oak with carved ornamentation along the sides. It would have held four people with comfort and it was a miracle that in a country so short of wood it had not been broken up years ago. Presumably no one had had the energy to set about the task. Siglinde tried it out and pronounced it creaking, dignified and pretentious.

Then they all went up to the Café Central and drank a bottle of white wine. The place was large and poor and almost empty. Near the door sat a few civil guards playing cards and at the far end was a rickety ping-pong table.

Dan Pedersen and Santiago played for a while. Dan was the better player and won in three straight sets, each time with a secure margin. When they changed ends for the last game, he said: 'How's things with Ramon?'

'Not too good. Concussion, I think. But he got up and went out with the boat.'

'With concussion? He shouldn't have done that.'

'He's very strong.'

'Yes, but there are limits.'

Half an hour later, they parted at the cross-roads, Santiago shaking hands with them, one after another.

'You'll be stopped by the patrols,' said Dan.

'They've stopped me so many times I think they're sick of it now,' said Santiago.

He drove all the way without once being stopped.

The others stood outside the house in Barrio Son Jofre. The cobblestones felt warm and friendly under their feet, and the star-studded sky arched over them between the mountains.

'Apropos that corporal,' said Siglinde. 'Why doesn't Santiago work like the others?'

'It's not just a matter of hauling up a whole lot of fish,' said Dan Pedersen. 'The problem is to sell it and get a decent price. If there were enough people like Santiago, then this country wouldn't look as it does.'

'You two are good friends, aren't you?' said Willi Mohr.

'We've known each other a long time. Yes, we're friends. Friendship is something special here, something to do with sacred principles, something important and meaningful. You'll understand after a while.'

'Genuine friendship isn't something you pick up in the street,' he added. 'It's as rare as love.'

He pushed open the creaking door and they stepped into their new home.

44

While Willi Mohr was undressing, he heard Dan and Siglinde moving about and talking upstairs. After a while the bed creaked and the wavering light on the stairs went out.

Willi Mohr thought about Barbara Heinemann.

'Good-night, Willy, sleep well,' called Dan and Siglinde from above.

'Good-night, sleep well,' said Willi Mohr.

He smiled in the darkness and tried to think: Perhaps after all . . .

Tomorrow he would paint.

8

Dan Pedersen was outwardly a man without inhibitions, whether physical or spiritual. He found it easy to make friends, easy to work, easy to love. He was outward-looking and open to impulses and impressions, had a mobile intellect and a quick temper, often falling victim to occasional weaknesses and depressions. Like his wife, he was the product of a comfortable life and a tolerant upbringing. He had gone to Spain because it was cheap there and he would be able to finish a very bad serial he was writing under an assumed name and for which he had already been paid an advance. Later he took another advance and was now waiting until it was absolutely necessary for him to do some writing. As a professional writer he was what is usually called nimble-fingered. He could write so that what he wrote seemed good without it any way being so. In general he knew how things should be done but was seldom able to do them himself. He liked Spain very much, but he had liked Norway very much too, even during the war. He liked drinking too, but drank to excess only rarely. He often felt uncertain, but that was not often noticeable.

Siglinde was like him in many ways, and in some ways she was his superior. She was more farsighted and practical, but she was also more conscious of the threats in life. All her life she had borne a latent fear for a variety of things, fears which often varied in reason and character and which she tried to suppress because she thought them foolish. She possessed an immediate attractiveness, which appeared shallow and which made people think of sexuality. She was really a wholly normal girl with a normal physique, though here, in this phantom world of suppressed emotions, she played a peculiar rôle, and she herself noticed it, but did not bother about it because it seemed absurd to her. In the puerto they had often had trouble with peeping toms. In fact she was a shy person and could not, for instance, say certain things without sweating all over.

Willi Mohr was a bad painter, although he was technically skilful. He lacked spark and an artistic sense of purpose, and he energetically tried to replace what he lacked with industry and obstinacy, without for one moment believing or even wishing that this would be successful. Generally speaking, he was incapable of involving himself in anything, he believed, not even in his own problems, which he found quite meaningless. He was caught in a closed circuit and he himself considered that he could not with certainty remember any occasion on which he had been really happy or really miserable. He was locked in an attitude of physical and intellectual perfection, and if he had really been in a position to hope, he would have hoped for a miracle.

These three people lived together in the house in Barrio Son Jofre for four months and six days, from the ninth of August to the fifteenth of December.

While they were living there, a number of things happened. The summer ebbed away into a last spell of explosive heat, with burning hot days and steaming, sweaty nights. Then came a brief autumn with continuous warm rain, when the underground streams from the mountains roared along under the surface of the ground. Dried-up wells were filled and plant life, which never resigns itself, came to life again and waited for the sun, which would soon come back and burn it all up again. After the rain came the winter, the most exciting time of the year, and also the most pleasant. The winter could be said to begin in November. Beautiful, glass-clear sunny days were followed by astonishing storms and apocalyptical thunderstorms. One never knew what it would be like from one day to the next.

The people in the house in Barrio Son Jofre came to learn each other's patterns of behaviour and adapted themselves

46

accordingly. They soon acquired a tenable daily routine which was self-evident and required no discussion. Dan Pedersen finally set to work to earn his advance. He sat on the second step of the staircase and wrote. The typewriter was on a chair in front of him and the light from the open door fell on to his paper. He liked it there, despite the fact that the cat insisted on lying on his heap of typescript and despite the fact that he had to move every time Siglinde wanted to go upstairs. As she walked past, he used to run his hand down her naked leg.

Willi Mohr had borrowed some tools and had knocked up an easel. Then he sat by the door, six feet from the staircase, and painted. It took him about a week to paint a picture and then he took the drawing-pins out of the piece of hardboard, pinned the canvas on to the wall and never looked at it again.

Sometimes Dan looked at his pictures and said critically: 'You must try and get free, Willi. That's technically skilful but there's nothing in it. No feeling either, but most of all no content.'

He tapped the heap of typescript with his pipe.

'This is at least utterly false and repulsive,' he said, 'and I also know why I'm doing it.'

He sighed and wrote another sentence.

Willi Mohr smiled sardonically and went on dabbing with his brush.

Now and again Siglinde took out her sketching-block and sat down on the outside steps to draw the cat. She did it quickly and elegantly, with bold simplifications. When Dan told her it was good, she refused to believe him, although he was right. She was talented, but could never see any point in drawing a cat.

'Things that are quite meaningless can't possibly be any good,' she said.

Otherwise she did the housekeeping and that involved the burden of the daily chores. She had to cook all the food on an open fire, and this she did very well. Presumably it was due to her that the house in Barrio Son Jofre bloomed in the middle of its grotesque decay.

The previous tenants, a group of Asturian labourers, who had been taken from their homes and put to assisted work on the roads, had not been so well placed. Inscriptions on the walls bore witness to their despair and hatred.

47

Siglinde did all the shopping.
Willi Mohr fetched the water.
Dan Pedersen collected the wood.

No one had consciously created this organization. It had just come about.

Dan Pedersen's royalties did not come and would be some time coming too. Willi Mohr paid. He was relatively well off and kept his money in his wallet at the bottom of his rucksack. Above the wallet lay a 9 mm Walther pistol, an army model, carefully wrapped in a cloth.

As they had no form of lighting except candles and the old paraffin lamp, their working day coincided with the daylight. At dusk they went up to the bar in the square and drank something. Sometimes they played ping-pong, but Dan always won. Willi Mohr usually got beaten by Siglinde too, and this annoyed him a little.

Once, just before falling asleep, he realized that this was a healthy sign.

The people in the house in Barrio Son Jofre had a daily routine, but they did not allow themselves to be enslaved by it. Once or twice a week they started up the old truck and went down to the puerto. When it was warm they bathed from the cliffs or from the breakwater by the pier and they swam in the green salty water. Occasionally they stayed long into the night and knocked about Jacinto's bar or some other place. On these occasions they were always together with Santiago or Ramon, usually both.

One of the Alemany brothers often used to come up to the town. Then they brought fish with them, which Siglinde cooked on the open fire and which they ate together.

Willi Mohr went out fishing three times with the others. Santiago and Ramon had a motor-boat which was used at night for calamary fishing. It was large and well-made and eminently suitable for pleasure trips.

On these three occasions they went quite far out, to a small archipelago of rocky islands, and they fished with hooks close under the cliff walls. The archipelago was bare and uninhabited, but full of hidden bays.

They bathed there too and once Ramon Alemany looked at

Dan Pedersen and laughed and said: 'You've a very beautiful wife.'

Siglinde was standing two steps away, dripping wet in her blue bathing-costume. She looked healthy and strong and happy.

Dan Pedersen slapped her jokingly on the backside and said: 'Siglinde? Oh, her bottom's far too big.'

Santiago was sitting in the boat watching them. He did not laugh.

Willi Mohr noticed the little scene and tucked it away in his mind.

He caught several small fish that day and one that was large and flat and blue, but it did not amuse him much.

He thought: I won't go with them next time.

9

At the end of October, a prominent fascist official came to the puerto. He was a member of parliament and a military man and had been persuaded there by his wife, who liked visiting idyllic and untouched parts of the country. They stayed for three days with a very rich director of a bank in the provincial capital, who had long ago built himself a large summer residence and equipped it with a staff of servants, near the lighthouse, but had practically never stayed there. With them the couple had their twenty-year-old daughter and her fiancé, a senior official in the Portuguese Embassy. They drove from the provincial capital in a large cream-coloured American car, towing a trailer on which was a little mahogany racing-boat equipped with a brand new outboard motor of a kind that cannot be bought on the open market.

The daughter was studying economics at Madrid University and belonged to the small group of emancipated Spanish women. She went about in white slacks, a red jumper, and French cork-soled shoes, which made her look a trifle long-legged.

She and her Portuguese fiancé had the servants put the racing-boat into the sea, start the motor and then they set off round the pier. It was windy beyond the mountains, but in the bay the water was green and calm. When they had got about two

49

hundred yards behind the lighthouse, they slowed down and moved closer to each other on the seat. She unbuttoned her bra and pulled down the zip of her slacks, and then they busied themselves with an occupation which would have filled the member of parliament with wonder and doubts, had he been equipped with a pair of binoculars.

Three minutes later they lost the engine, which had been badly fixed on and had shaken loose with the vibration. It hissed as it fell into the water and immediately sank to the bottom and stayed there, forty feet below, jammed between two large stones. A couple of small squids fled in terror, each in a different direction.

The girl at once lost interest, took away the young man's hand and pulled up her zip. Although it was less than half an hour before the civil guard's barque towed the racing boat into the pier, the engine appeared to be a wholly indispensable toy. The barque went out again.

The young corporal with the shiny boots looked thoughtfully at the engine through a glass-bottomed box. He got one of his men to let down a drag-rope, but soon saw that it was not worth it. Then he sounded the depth and shook his head. When the barque returned, the member of parliament's daughter was standing on the jetty, looking at him coldly and challengingly.

The cabo knew exactly how long it would take to get hold of a diver or a frogman from the provincial capital, and his smile was not entirely convincing. Thirty seconds later he happened to think of Ramon.

It was in the middle of the siesta and the Alemany brothers were lying asleep in the room behind the kitchen when the cabo came in. He shook Ramon awake and said: 'General Moscardo's daughter has lost an outboard engine out at the approaches. Can you get it up?'

'Of course,' said Ramon, blinking drowsily. 'I'll dive with stones.'

Santiago had woken and sat up.

'How far down is it lying?'

'Twenty, twenty-five feet, and they must have it up at once.'

'Not for nothing, I hope,' said Santiago.

'No,' said the cabo, 'the General is sure to pay.'

50

'And that trouble in the bar?' said Santiago.

'That can be forgotten,' said the cabo, looking at the ceiling, 'as long as the engine is really got up.'

'Sure?'

'Yes, sure.'

Santiago went over to the door and called: 'Francisca, come here.'

His sister came in. She was a shy virgin of twenty-four, who had already grown too fat and had lost most of her freshness. Every time Santiago saw her, he was filled with loathing. He was convinced that they would never marry her off.

'I want you to hear what the cabo has to say,' he said. 'He says that Ramon won't be prosecuted for that row in the bar, as it appears he is innocent if he dives down to get a motor-boat engine. Didn't you say that?'

'Yes, perhaps that's what I said,' said the cabo sourly.

Then he turned irritably to Ramon.

'Hurry now. It's urgent.'

Ramon remained lying on his bed and looked at his brother.

'Shall I?' he asked.

'Yes, come on, let's go.'

'You needn't come,' the cabo said to Santiago.

'Try stopping me.'

Both the girl from Madrid and the young Portuguese came with them in the barque. They thought it was all beginning to be exciting now and when all was said and done perhaps it had not been such a silly thing to have gone and lost the engine.

'Look how small and squat and muscular he is, and all hairy,' said the member of parliament's daughter, when Ramon pulled off his clothes.

Santiago heard her but did not react. He was busy studying the sea bed through the glass-bottomed box.

'Twenty-four feet!' he snorted. 'Let's skip this, Ramon.'

'Forty feet, they plumbed,' said the girl from Madrid.

Santiago looked contemptuously at the cabo.

'Take us back,' he said.

'I can try,' said Ramon, peering down into the water.

'Think about Jacinto's bar,' said the cabo, drumming with his gloved fingers on the railing.

51

'It'll probably work,' said Ramon.

Santiago peered down again.

'D'you think so?' he said.

'Yes, I think it'll work.'

Santiago leant close to his brother and whispered into his ear:

'Try, but don't take any risks. If you feel it's not going to work, then drop the stone at once and come up. Do you hear what I say, at once . . .'

Ramon nodded. He lifted the large stone up from the bottom of the boat, took it in his arms and climbed over the railing.

'This is fascinating,' whispered the girl from Madrid.

Aloud she said: 'I really do hope he gets it up. It's my engine and it was awfully expensive.'

'It's my brother,' said Santiago, looking bitterly at her.

'Let me look,' she said hastily, getting down on her knees on the bottom of the boat. 'Give me that thing.'

Santiago gave her the glass-bottomed box. It was calm and in the clear water he could still see Ramon without the help of the box. The white figure grew slowly smaller and smaller. Time seemed to come to a halt and the seconds grew long and clear.

'I think he's got it, no, I don't know,' said the girl excitedly.

Santiago thought: Damned idiot, he'd go on down to a hundred feet with that stone if it was that deep. And if the engine is stuck, he'll stay there until he drowns.

He was drenched with sweat.

'It won't work,' said the Portuguese.

'Yes, yes! He's coming now. Terrific,' said the girl.

Santiago saw his brother through the water. The blurred white figure grew larger, slowly. Unendurably slowly.

He won't make it, thought Santiago. If anything happens to him, I'll chuck this whole mob into the sea.

'Drop it, drop it, for God's sake,' he whispered. 'Drop their stupid little toy and who cares what happens to it.'

'Come on, come on, good boy, oh, come on!' said the girl from Madrid.

Ramon's black head shot out of the water and at the same moment Santiago grabbed his arm.

The civil guard caught hold of the engine and the cabo made

his contribution by wetting his uniform jacket right up to the shoulder.

'Good, oh, goodie,' said the girl, clapping her hands.

Ramon was waving his arms about desperately and his breath was coming in great rasps. The Portuguese helped drag him over the railing and lie him down on the bottom of the boat. Santiago knelt down beside his brother and stayed there until they had come round the lighthouse.

'Fascinating,' said the girl quietly to her fiancé. 'Did you see, like an animal, with only one aim in mind . . .'

When they arrived back, Ramon was able to stand up again. He was still very pale in the face, breathing heavily and raspingly, and Santiago had to help him up the jetty.

The fun was over. The glow in the girl's eyes had gone.

'Have you got any loose change on you?' she said to her fiancé.

The man dug into his pocket and drew out a fistful of coins and small notes. He held them out, almost shamefacedly, and Santiago took them hesitantly.

'Well, goodbye then,' said the General's daughter.

She stopped for a moment in front of Ramon, looked him up and down and smiled at him in a way that could mean many things.

'Come on, let's go,' said Santiago.

He put his arm round his brother and they walked towards the fish-van.

'How are you feeling?'

'My head's aching again. How much did we get?'

'Don't know. Couple of hundred, perhaps.'

'Not bad. That's more than we usually earn from your mysterious affairs.'

'Huh . . . and we don't do that just for money, anyhow.'

'No, of course not. Did you see what a girl she was? You, she'd make a good tail, wouldn't she? Think of tearing off those trousers of hers and . . . She was even better than the Norwegian woman!'

'How you talk, little brother,' said Santiago, looking round seriously.

Then he bent down and began winding the starting-handle of the old Ford.

10

At the beginning of December the weather changed. The temperature rose swiftly and the wind dropped. It was just as hot as in the height of summer and the few resident foreigners in the puerto began bathing again. The fishing boats, which had been in harbour a couple of weeks because of the bad weather, went out to sea and made good catches. In the town up in the mountains, the heat lay heavily and immobile between the stone walls. It was hard to work in the daytime and the hot nights did not lend themselves to sleep.

The good weather lasted for two weeks.

Part Three

1

When the sun went down, the heat became more and more apparent, as if it had been materialized into something dry and black and dusty and it closed in even more round the houses and people.

The inhabitants of the house in Barrio Son Jofre had eaten and were sitting out on the steps. They were smoking and looking out into the darkness in silence.

They had not done any work, but had spent nearly the whole day in the puerto, lying stretched out in the shade of a cliff about two strides from the water. When they had gone back, they had felt rested and refreshed, with a dawning desire to work, but now this had already gone and they knew it would be a long time before the night would bring them any relief.

Siglinde shifted restlessly and crushed her cigarette out between her fingers.

'I can't stand this silent dark heat tonight too,' she said. 'Let's go down to the puerto again, where at least there's a slight breeze. It seems to be easier to breathe when you're nearer the water, somehow.'

'It'll be better in an hour or two,' said Dan Pedersen.

'It's just those hours I don't want. If you're not coming, I'm going down by myself.'

'You daren't.'

'Why not?'

She sounded genuinely surprised.

'You can hardly start the truck.'

'You've no idea what I can and can't do.'

They all three went, as usual with Dan and Siglinde in the front and Willi Mohr on the bench behind.

55

Halfway to the puerto, Dan Pedersen ran over a sheep and killed it. The whole flock was standing quite still on the road beyond a sharp bend and as the camioneta had its engine switched off, the meeting was equally surprising for both parties. Dan braked sharply but it was no use. The nearest animal was knocked over by the bumper and fell partly under the front wheel. Only a few days before, the mail bus had killed fifteen sheep at once in exactly the same way. The shepherd was a weak-minded old man who had sold most of his bells and had not got the sense to keep the flock moving along the edges of the road. So it was not a very serious accident, but the sheep, a ewe, was undoubtedly dead and lay on its back with pitifully splayed legs. The shepherd came up to the truck and jabbered excitedly as he gesticulated with his gnarled stick. The sheep-dog crept up to bite Dan Pedersen's leg. Dan swore and kicked out at it.

'Yes, yes, we'll pay you tomorrow,' he said irritably. 'We'll go up to the owner and pay him. But we'll damn well have the meat in that case.'

The shepherd jabbered on in his almost incomprehensible dialect.

Two civil guards came up out of the darkness and shone their torches. When the shepherd caught sight of them, he stopped abruptly and seemed to sink into his rags. He stood there with his head down, as if waiting to be beaten. His whole body was shaking, but perhaps that was just old age.

'We must apologize,' said one of the civil guards. 'Sheep should not be on the road and they're supposed to have proper bells on them.'

The other one went up to the shepherd, lifted his head by putting his finger under his chin, and barked a few sentences in gutteral Catalonian. Then he boxed the old man's ears and the old man began to weep.

Dan Pedersen and Willi Mohr climbed up into the camioneta again.

The civil guards saluted.

The truck rolled on.

Five minutes later the bay opened out before them and they saw the scattered lights of the puerto. Out at sea they could see the petrol lamps of the calamary boats like a pearl necklace of etched white points of light against the dark water.

Dan Pedersen let the camioneta free-wheel until it stopped by itself in the middle of the quay.

They sat down outside one of the bars facing the harbour and ordered vermouth and iced-water. It was a trifle cooler here, and it smelt of the sea.

They had only been sitting there five minutes when Santiago and Ramon came sauntering along the quay. They shook hands, pulled out two cane chairs and sat down at the table.

Dan Pedersen went into the bar and fetched a chess set, placed the board between himself and Santiago and began to set out the pieces.

Willi Mohr sipped carefully at his vermouth as he watched the others.

Ramon looked listless and depressed, although he hurried to smile when he felt himself observed. Several times he held his forehead and the back of his head as if he were trying to loosen an invisible noose. Now and again he looked covetously at Siglinde's naked feet and long bare legs.

Siglinde kept shifting her body as if she were uncomfortable and she kept changing the position of her legs. Sometimes her eyes flickered from one person to another. In between she looked at Dan, her eyes running down the length of his body and often resting on his face or hands. She seemed nervous. Perhaps it's the heat, thought Willi Mohr, who had no great experience of women.

The chess game was rather uneven at first. Dan Pedersen made some inspired moves in the middle of the game and took several pieces. A moment later he grew careless and lost a piece. Then he concentrated and played coldly and systematically to make the most of his lead.

Willi Mohr gradually went over to watching only his opponent.

Santiago saw that he was losing and his situation worsened slowly and inexorably, but he did not give up. The look in his eyes deepened and grew more and more ill-humoured. He made no more mistakes, but it was already too late. For each move he was driven nearer and nearer to the impotence which is one of the logical conclusions of this nerve-racking game.

Not until Dan Pedersen took his queen with his freed pawn, did Santiago give up.

Willi Mohr had the impression that he would have done almost anything to hinder his defeat.

'Did you win?' said Ramon.

Santiago shook his head and his brother's face clouded. When he noticed that Willi Mohr was looking at him, he laughed again.

'You played well today,' said Dan Pedersen magnanimously. 'I slackened off for a while, I know, but you played well all the same. But you concentrated too late.'

They shook hands and Santiago smiled, not very convincingly.

Dan Pedersen put the chessmen away, got up and took the set into the bar.

Siglinde irritably changed the position of her legs again and let her eyes follow him.

It was quiet in the puerto and everyone was waiting for the small cool breeze from the sea. Only a few people were still sitting outside the cafés facing the harbour. It would soon be one o'clock and the bar-owners with no more customers had begun to close up.

'I know what we ought to do now,' said Dan Pedersen. 'We ought to go and bathe once more and then go to bed.'

'Out by the lighthouse in that case,' said Santiago.

'Aren't there a lot of civil guards out there?'

'Only one or two. They patrol the mole and the shoreline. It's usually quite easy to see where they are.'

'We haven't any bathing-costumes,' said Siglinde.

She didn't say it in protest. She was simply being informative about the fact.

'That doesn't matter, does it?' said Dan Pedersen. 'We all know each other, and anyhow it's dark.'

Siglinde shrugged her shoulders. It really did not matter.

58

2

Siglinde came out of the water last. She was swimming in a wide circle with long lazy strokes and the luminescence of the sea floated in fine phosphorescent streaks along her body.

She and Dan and Willi Mohr were bathing farthest out by the lighthouse, where the breakwater ended in a circular pierhead made of concrete and large, crudely cut blocks of stone. Santiago and Ramon, who had swimming trunks, were a few yards farther in. To appear without a bathing-costume was a punishable pleasure and the risk of being caught not worth taking.

The night was thick and black and inpenetrable, but every sixteenth second the light from the lighthouse swung round over their heads. Each time it brought with it a pale uncertain light, weak and nebulous, but still sufficiently strong that one could make out objects round about.

They had left their clothes on the parapet.

Dan Pedersen had climbed up on to the parapet and all that could be seen was the glowing tip of his cigarette.

Willi Mohr was standing right up by the edge of the pier, looking at the distant lights of the puerto.

They enjoyed the pleasant coolness as the air slowly dried their skins.

There was no sign of Siglinde, except the thin pale green tracks in the darkness showing that she had swum towards the shore.

Soon afterwards the water could be heard pouring off her body.

'Help her up, will you,' said Dan Pedersen. 'The stones are hellish sharp down there.'

When Willi Mohr heard Siglinde trying to find a foothold on the rocks, he took a step down the stone stairway and put out a hand in the dark.

She found it at once, and her hand was cold and wet and firm. He pulled her slowly until she had her balance and he felt very clearly the well-trained elasticity in her body as she thrust off with her foot and swung herself up on to the flat stones.

Willi Mohr could not see her, but he knew she was standing just beside him on the stairway.

59

At that moment the light from the lighthouse cut through the darkness above and for one or two seconds he saw her in the light of its trailing reflection.

She was standing with her feet apart, her toes turned slightly inwards, her arms hanging loosely, and she was holding her head to one side to shake the water from her ears and to get the short blond wisps of hair away from her forehead. Her shoulders and breasts and forearms were covered with circular drops of water, which looked so firm and definitively shaped that one ought to be able to pick them off one by one without breaking them and collect them in one's hand like small glass pearls. Her nipples were large and stiff and the skin in the finely-drawn circles round them was wrinkled and contracted. Lower down the water ran down her hips and in two clear channels from the soft hollow above her navel, down over her curved stomach and was then caught up in the curly patch of hair growing up from her loins. The hair was black and thick and glittered with thousands of small drops of water.

She was standing so close that Willi Mohr saw all this very clearly, but he had no time to notice her face.

He tried to avoid being influenced by the functional beauty in her body. For the first time since they had met, it occurred to him that she was beautiful.

And this was a completely objective observation. He thought.

Then the light had gone and he heard someone draw in his breath just behind him.

Dan Pedersen was still sitting on the concrete wall, his cigarette glowing in the darkness.

Willi Mohr heard Siglinde moving, listlessly and roughly. Then she walked swiftly past him and over towards the parapet.

When the lighthouse beam swung round the next time, she had already put on her dress and was smoothing it down over her wet body. She had evidently not bothered to put on her underclothes.

Willi Mohr thought he saw someone standing a few yards away.

'The patrol is coming this way now,' said Santiago, from out of the darkness.

His voice was calm and ordinary.

60

'Yes,' said Siglinde. 'Get dressed you lot, please.'

'God, how you do nag,' said Dan.

He jumped down and began to pull on his trousers.

'I could stay here for hours,' he said to Willi Mohr, who was standing nearest to him. 'Good idea, this bathe.'

'Very,' said Willi Mohr.

They had driven as far as they could and the camioneta was standing on the tarmacadam slope just beside the irregular pile of rough blocks of stone which constituted the foundations of the breakwater. As they climbed over the stones, two civil guards came up from behind the truck and shone their torches on them. They saluted Siglinde and nodded to Dan Pedersen and Willi Mohr. Then they took Santiago and Ramon to one side, made them raise their hands above their heads and searched them, idiotically thoroughly and lengthily.

Finally they switched off their torches and disappeared into the darkness.

'What were they looking for?' said Dan Pedersen.

Santiago grimaced and shrugged his shoulders.

'Don't know,' he said.

'I'd never put up with that,' said Dan.

3

Dan Pedersen drove quite slowly on the way back from the puerto. Perhaps he was thinking about the sheep and the weak-minded old man. The engine roared and rattled and now and again in the beams of the headlights they saw the eyes of cats prowling along the edges of the road. The night was still warm but the breeze in the open truck was pleasant. Willi Mohr was sitting, as usual, behind Siglinde.

He noticed that she was still finding it difficult to sit still. On four or five occasions she put her arm along Dan's shoulders and then at once took it away again. Once she leant her head against his shoulder.

Willi Mohr could not help thinking that he had seen her naked only a short time ago.

4

They came to the house in Barrio Son Jofre and Willi took the large key out of the crack in the wall and began to fiddle with the lock.

Siglinde suddenly made herself small, crept up against Dan Pedersen and put her arm round his waist, which was bare below the edge of his carelessly knotted shirt.

When they had taken two steps up the stairs, she stood on her toes and whispered something in his ear.

'Darling old thing, what *is* the matter with you?' he said.

As if he had just become aware of her presence.

She stood on tiptoe again, bit him lightly on the ear and whispered: 'I want you. I've wanted you all day. I'm all peculiar.'

He put his arm round her shoulders and felt her skin turning warm and damp. Although he could not see it, he knew she was blushing.

'Isn't it awful,' she said.

They walked slowly up the rest of the stairs. Then he turned her towards him and put his arms round her. They kissed and through her thin frock, he felt her body, soft and warm and alive. Then he let her go and went into the room.

Siglinde let the raffia basket containing her sandals and underclothes and cigarettes drop to the floor and remained where she was, with her back to the wall, as if she were something someone had put down and would soon come and fetch.

Dan Pedersen lit a candle and stuck it on one of the bedposts. Then he closed the shutters, took the blankets off the bed and laid them out on the floor. Now and again he looked at Siglinde, who was still standing by the wall, watching him. She smiled, an uncertain stiff smile.

He put one hand against the wall to support himself as he took off his rope-sandals. Then he unknotted his shirt, hung it over a bedpost and took off his trousers, unhurriedly. Finally he took off his watch and put it down on the stool by the bed.

Siglinde was still standing by the wall over by the stairs and although he was at the other end of the room, she could see him very clearly in the soft vibrating light. He was rather thin but very sunburnt and the white triangle from his swimming trunks was sharply outlined like an alien area on his body. She liked looking at him, especially his waist and stomach and his sex. And his legs, which were long and sinewy and covered with almost white hairs.

When he came towards her across the floor, she bit the tip of her tongue and stared at his body.

She did not move.

Dan Pedersen stroked her lightly across the cheek with the back of his fingers. Then he bent down and taking hold of the hem of her dress with both hands, he gently drew it over her head. She helped him by straightening up away from the wall and raising her arms.

Siglinde was naked. Again she stood immobile against the wall.

He put his hand on her hip, which was dry and warm and friendly. Then he bent forward, drew with the tip of his tongue from her collar bone down over her right breast and caught up her nipple between his lips. It was large and hard and tasted salty from the sea. After a second or two he took it further into his mouth and bit it, lightly and very carefully.

Siglinde did not move, but she had begun to breathe more quickly.

He straightened up and looked at her, drawing his hands across the curve of her stomach. Then he pushed his fingers through the thick hair, stiff and obstinate, and she moved her legs a little to open the way, to be able to feel his hand better.

With his other hand he stroked her head and throat roughly and took hold of her slim neck.

She liked his hands.

For perhaps the five hundredth time, he felt a vague and simple surprise that her loins seemed so large and broad and generous in relation to her body in general.

He caressed her with his open hand between her legs, first swiftly and lightly, then more slowly and more purposefully, with a growing sense of possession.

Siglinde trembled and moved her legs again. A little further

63

apart so that she opened herself completely and let him feel the whole of her flooding soft expectancy and hidden passive strength.

She raised her right hand and drew her splayed fingers down his face, increasing the pressure along his chin and throat, and then scratched him swiftly and hard down his chest. Then her hand changed, grew soft and spread across his stomach, and again strong and demanding as it slid round his loins and stayed there. She caressed him, hard and roughly, often changing her grip.

They spoke to each other.

'Am I doing it too hard?'

'No, no.'

'You must take me now.'

'You haven't your pessary on you.'

'It doesn't matter.'

Dan Pedersen bent down, laid his right arm round her thighs just above the back of her knees and lifted her over his shoulder, easily and swiftly.

He carried his wife across the room and carefully put her down on the outspread blankets.

He tried to kiss her body, but she flung her legs apart and pulled him down over her, wildly and violently. She pressed her pelvis up against him desperately and took him inside her at once, long and hard and releasing.

She was panting for breath and flung herself about wildly beneath him, as if pinned down. When it came for her, she put the soles of her feet on the warm stone floor outside the edge of the blanket and lifted him up in an arch whilst with a locked embrace round his hips, she tried to press him even deeper into her body.

Then the cramps came and released her from her impotence and lassitude. They began deep inside and then ran along her vagina and spread in concentric waves through her body. Her convulsions were transmitted through her thighs and calves and reached the soles of her feet as a slight tremor.

Siglinde lay flat on her back with her arms down her sides and outspread legs, and she felt her husband emptying his longing into her body.

64

After a while she put her arms softly and tenderly round his back and waited. She knew it was not at an end yet.

They lay like this for twenty minutes or perhaps half an hour, while the candle on the bedpost burnt calmly on.

Then Siglinde felt how he grew inside her and how the contact increased between myriads of small nerve ends and she knew it was her turn.

She slowly drew up her legs and with her toes drew a line along his legs and hips, then lowered her legs again, just as slowly, and began from the beginning again.

She grew deep and soft and simply an expectant friendly cradle and he took her, for a long time, and she placed her round heels in the small of his back and lay with her knees drawn high up and her arms round his back. He was hers and she clung to him with her arms and legs and thought she would never wish to let him go. But a little later she let go and brought her legs up round his arms so that she lay doubled up and completely smothered by him, and when it was necessary she bit her own hand to stop herself crying out.

Then she lay still.

Dan Pedersen knew he could take her again in an hour or two, if he wanted to, but he also knew that it would be quite unnecessary.

He thought that he had not been really concentrated on her all the time and that annoyed him.

He carried her to the bed and arranged the sheets, blew out the candle and got into bed.

Siglinde Pedersen was happy. She had drawn up her left leg across Dan and was sleeping with her head against his shoulder and her open loins against his thigh.

Just as she had felt herself falling asleep, she had thought: Soon we'll go home and live in a proper place with our own furniture. We'll work and earn money and buy nice clothes and if we feel like it then we'll come here and bathe now and again. We'll soon be going home. Now I know it for certain.

5

Willi Mohr was sleeping too. He had sensed rather than understood why no one had called goodnight to him from above.

He had forced himself to go to sleep. It was one of his great feats. But after a while he woke again and did something which he usually tried his hardest to avoid doing. In itself it was quite natural, but as he did it so seldom, it irritated him a little.

When he woke the next time it was light and the cat was lying asleep on his legs like a small heavy round lump of warmth. He sat up cautiously so as not to wake it.

The door opened and Siglinde came in from outside. She had just washed and was clear-eyed and bare-footed, wearing a clean green cotton dress. She had gone out so silently that he had not noticed.

'Morning, Willi,' she said brightly and went on out into the kitchen.

Willi looked listlessly at his pictures, yawned and scratched himself inside his pyjama jacket.

Half an hour later, Dan Pedersen came down the stairs, his hair untidy and tangled. He sighed, pulled the chair with the typewriter on it towards him, read through the last page of typescript and said gloomily: 'O.K. Let's go on for a while before it gets too warm.'

The keys clattered for a moment, but he stopped after only half a line, drank a little water and lit an Ideales.

'We'll go down to the puerto this afternoon,' he said. 'I feel like drinking a little today.'

Willi Mohr did not reply. He was already sitting painting.

A moment later Siglinde went out. She was going to do the shopping.

As she passed Dan on the stairs, she rumpled his hair.

She walked down towards the alley, briskly and energetically, playfully swinging her empty raffia basket.

66

6

Even before she got to the square, Siglinde noticed that something had happened.

Down the road she met two trucks packed with marine infantrymen. She had seen military vehicles before and was used to soldiers whistling and calling and throwing kisses at her, but this time they were sitting in silence, crouching on the wooden seats, their packs on their backs and their rifles across their knees. The vehicles were old and rasped noisily up round the corners in bottom gear.

On Avenida Generalissimo Franco she was passed by a rattling army ambulance with red crosses on the back doors. It was travelling fast, swerving about on the knobbly cobblestones, and then it swung round up a side-street towards the barracks.

The square was full of people, men and women, either sitting in front of one of the cafés or standing about in groups round the pump. Some of them were talking and gesticulating, but most were silent.

Siglinde bought some fish, taking her time over choosing, to get the best and the cheapest. Then she went to the bakery and on to the tienda to fetch wine and vegetables.

It all took quite a long time, as there were a lot of people in the shops, although there was very little business being done.

When Siglinde had finished she felt thirsty and went into the Central to have a café con leche. There were people in there too, at many of the tables, and she decided to have her coffee at the counter. A civil guard on a motor-cycle stopped outside, his face sweaty and his boots white with dust. He came up beside Siglinde, tapped on the counter with a coin and ordered a glass of wine.

Must be some kind of holiday or fiesta again, thought Siglinde.

Then she remembered the ambulance on Avenida Generalissimo Franco.

'Why are there so many people about everywhere?' she said to the proprietor, who was just blowing hot air from his expresso-machine into her milk.

67

He placed the glass in front of her, frowned and said: 'There's said to have been an accident up at the mine.'

'Has someone been killed?'

'Yes . . . it seems so . . .'

'Many?'

'They say so, yes. Quite a lot.'

'Only Asturians,' said the civil guard, turning to her with a smile. 'Only Asturian labourers. No one from round about here.'

'Why are there so many people about here then?'

'They're upset because the road construction work has been stopped,' said the civil guard.

After a brief pause, he added: 'Only for the time being . . . as an emergency measure, that is . . . in case help is needed . . .'

'They lose their wages,' said the proprietor.

The civil guard shrugged his shoulders.

'Have you been up there, at the mine?' said the proprietor.

'No,' said the civil guard curtly.

He emptied his glass and left.

'There's going to be an extra mass, they say,' said the proprietor.

'What happened? The accident, I mean?' said Siglinde.

'Don't know,' said the proprietor, throwing out his hands.

He stared absently in another direction, as if he would prefer to put an end to the conversation.

When Siglinde went back across the square, people had begun to move in towards the side-streets. In the distance she heard the church bells ringing.

Only Asturians, she thought.

It was not the first time she had heard the mine mentioned. It lay about twenty kilometres out of the town, west of the main road and in the direction of Santa Margarita. On one occasion they had driven up there and she had seen it in the distance, a huddle of stone buildings, tall constructions and a chimney. She had also seen some of the Asturians, small, soot-covered men who had appeared dragging a water-cart. Up towards the mine wound a narrow road covered with yellow stone flints.

So there had been an accident up there.

'Only Asturians,' said Siglinde Pedersen to herself. 'What a country!'

In fact the following had happened:

At seven the evening before, the workers in the mine had started a strike, which during the course of the evening had taken on the character of armed rebellion. The strike was a desperate measure caused by despair and hideous need, but no less well-planned for that. Something, however, had gone wrong. The works, which consisted of a zinc mine and an old-fashioned smelting works, employed two hundred workers. Practically all of them had been forcibly moved from Asturia, and most of them had criminal records, which meant that they had belonged to illegal unions or were suspected Communists. Only a few of them had been in the workers' militia during the Civil War. The rest were too young. Some had previously been condemned for political offences and had served long sentences in concentration camps or in the salt mines in Formentera. After being released, they had been moved to the mine to adapt themselves to society. The sanitary arrangements at the works were not without failings. The workers lived in two stone barrack buildings which had been built on one floor without inner walls and lacking drains, water-pipes and fireplaces. In each barrack lived approximately a hundred men; those who had the advantage of bringing their wives and children with them had sought to better their position by nailing up partitions of wood for themselves and their kin.

Wages were very low. For those with families, the money only just sufficed to cover their daily minimal needs for bread and dried fish. The workers' freedom of movement was officially limited to the district; through poverty and lack of transport, it was in fact limited to the mine and the surrounding mountains. Water supplies were erratic, as there was no drinking-water on the spot, and the water that was transported there in donkey-carts was polluted and contained a high percentage of iron, so had to be boiled before it could be used. There was no doctor at the mine, but a guard-post consisting of twenty-five men.

The riot had begun modestly: three elected delegates put forward a number of demands to the management. The demands concerned certain financial and sanitary improvements. The organizers had not, however, reckoned on much progress through talks. They knew that all signs of a strike were illegal and they had been smuggling arms into the mine for a long time. Should

69

it prove necessary, almost a third of the workers could be armed with pistols and carbines. Supplies of ammunition however, were small and the result of the enterprise depended on a supply which should have come that same evening. At a previously stipulated place near the main road, a truck from the transport department of the mine was to have taken over a load of ammunition boxes from an arms-smuggler and then take them on to the strikers. There was a guard on the truck, but he had been bribed, and the operation looked watertight, largely because it was to be carried out in broad daylight. The main outline of the plan was as follows: If the delegation was turned away, the workers would stay in the barracks, arm themselves and be divided up into operational groups. Then they would neutralize the guard-post and take over the dynamite store. Among those who had taken part in the Civil War were several who could handle dynamite and who knew their job. The strike leaders reckoned that with dynamite and fuses, they would be able to add a certain emphasis to what were in themselves very modest demands. The threat to blow the whole works up was a very strong argument.

Everything went wrong from the start. The employers immediately had the delegates captured and locked up in the guard-post, which was so situated that it controlled the only possible route to the explosives store. The ammunition had still not yet come. The strike leaders could not stop a spontaneous demonstration for the release of the prisoners. An engineer who tried to stop the demonstrators had stones hurled at him, and to set an example, the head of the gendarmerie had the prisoners shot and their bodies thrown on to the road. All three had wives and children and this event aroused great bitterness. Arms were dealt out among the workers and three officials who had not had time to get themselves to safety were shot down.

In the small hours, the workers made several attempts to force the guard-post and get at the dynamite, but the shortage of ammunition made their arms useless. Hour after hour, they waited in vain for the truck with the cartridge boxes and hand-grenades, and at dawn they were forced to retire to the barracks and smelting works, where they barricaded themselves in, prepared to hold out as long as they could.

Despite all this, they nevertheless in some ways had some luck. Immediately before the telephone wires had been torn down, the head of the gendarmerie had been in contact with another guard-post and had had time to leave a brief message about the disturbances. The report was sent on to the civil guard regional headquarters in the town, but was totally misinterpreted and remitted to Santa Margarita.

A cabo on duty at the civil guard-post later tried to 'phone through to the mine, but could not get through. As it was not uncommon that telephone communications were unreliable, he did not take much notice. Shortly after midnight, a road patrol came into the guard-post and reported sporadic shooting from the mine. The head of the guard-post again checked with regional headquarters, who again referred the matter to Santa Margarita. At three o'clock, three men finally received orders to cycle up to the mine.

The patrol took their time and did not arrive until half-past four, just as it was beginning to turn light. Twenty minutes later, both regional headquarters and the local division in Santa Margarita were informed that the Asturian mine-workers were in a state of total rebellion. The reports implied that the guards at the mine had been killed, that the approach road had been barricaded and that red flags had been hauled up on the smelting works and the barracks.

A state of emergency was proclaimed immediately over the whole district. It was feared that the revolt might spread and orders were given that workers at places where there were more than ten employees should be sent home. At the same time there were strict orders that the matter should be kept secret. All telephone and telegraphic communications were reserved for official purposes, and a number of unreliable people were woken and arrested.

The military commander of the district, a colonel by the name of Ruiz, was put in command of the cleaning-up operations.

The regional headquarters directed all available security forces and one-hundred-and-fifty men from the marine infantry to the mine. The soldiers brought with them machine-guns and grenade-throwers and in addition requisitioned two tanks from a tank regiment some miles inland.

71

It was only a quarter to six when the first security forces reached the barricade of iron girders, stones and upturned carts blocking the approach road. The small group of strikers behind the barricade retreated after a brief exchange of shots. The civil guard began to pull down the barricade, while they waited for reinforcements. It was still not quite light.

During the night the strikers made yet another desperate attempt to get through to the explosive store, but they were forced to give up because of lack of ammunition. Ten men or so were killed or wounded by the gendarmes' fire. When it was quite clear that the ammunition was not coming, or at any rate would be too late, the workers divided themselves up into three groups. The children and most of the women were taken away to a store-house, then the others shut themselves into the smelting works and the two barracks. Doors and windows were barricaded with stones. They had plenty of arms but only a few hundred cartridges.

By half-past six, so many police and regular troops had arrived at the place that Colonel Ruiz considered himself in a position to attack. He urged the rebels *pro forma* to capitulate by shouting an ultimatum through a megaphone. The reply was a few scattered shots.

The barracks were taken in turn. After fifteen minutes' firing with grenade-throwers and automatic weapons, holes were breached in the walls and the first building attacked. The workers who had used up their ammunition defended themselves with pick-axes and iron spits and many of them were shot down.

The screams and the knowledge that the women and children were in the hands of the attackers demoralized the men in the other barrack, and they surrendered with little resistance.

In the smelting works were forty men and about twenty women, most of them young. This group held out the longest and were also in possession of most of the ammunition. The strike leaders were in charge and the red flag had been raised on the roof.

It took almost two hours to take the smelting works, although it was continuously showered with grenades and automatic fire. A tank arrived finally and shot away the great iron doors and the walls round them. The assault was undertaken by a company of the civil guard, as the regular troops had begun to demonstrate

72

a marked lack of the will to fight. Many of the soldiers were Basques and Catalonians, and the firing had not always been exceptionally accurate. The civil guards showed good judgement and used mostly hand-grenades and tear-gas bombs. It took them only ten minutes to make the conditions in the smelting works unendurable and the strikers capitulated. Thirty-three men and fourteen young women came out of the building with their hands clasped behind their necks. Some were wounded and all were dirty, drenched with sweat, and exhausted. They had had no drinking-water for twelve hours. The women were wearing soot-covered overalls and most of them had tied red rags round their arms or waists. The rebellion had been crushed.

Of the strikers, thirty-four men and seven women had been shot or blown to pieces. A further six men, who were accused of murder and mutiny, were executed immediately. Many were injured, three so seriously that they died within a few hours.

A civil guard and five soldiers were killed, the latter in the hand-to-hand fighting in the first barrack. A few more were injured. In the guard-post, one gendarme had been shot dead and another injured.

The regular troops were put to work burying the dead Asturians in a mass-grave, and then they were withdrawn.

All roads were blocked within an area of ten kilometres.

Reprisals were left to the gendarmes, who had experience of the circumstances in the place and a good eye for the younger Asturian women, some of whom possessed a kind of wild, abandoned beauty. Of the fourteen women who had taken part in the fighting, one was raped and smuggled away and one simply died. The rest were driven into the machine-room where the gendarmes tore off their overalls and burnt them between their legs with blow-lamps.

Their screams were so prolonged and irritating that the windows of the mine office, which Colonel Ruiz and his staff were using as their headquarters, had to be closed.

During the course of the day the strikers were transported in small groups to different prisons and transit camps. The workers who were to have fetched the ammunition waited in vain at the meeting place, all night and most of the day. Not until the afternoon were they discovered by a patrol and arrested.

73

The rebellion at the zinc mine had widespread repercussions.

Ten workers were condemned to death for murder and mutiny. Five of them were garrotted six months later, the other five being reprieved and given life sentences of hard labour. All the rest received prison sentences of between five and twenty-five years.

The head of the civil guard-post was promoted and all his subordinates were decorated.

Colonel Ruiz was made a general.

Within the course of three weeks, all officers in the civil guard headquarters and at the local branch in Santa Margarita were changed and replaced with well-qualified personnel from other parts of the country.

The arms, of Spanish and Czech manufacture, could not be traced despite intensive interrogations. The strike leaders who might have known anything had, with ignorant industry, been executed immediately after the rebellion.

No official information about the event was publicized until long afterwards and then only in very vague terms.

In the surrounding communities during the morning hours of the day the rebellion was crushed, the state of emergency and increased military activity caused a certain unrest.

7

They drove down to the puerto at about four and although it was siesta time, they passed three road-blocks. The first two were manned by civil guards, who contented themselves with smiling in recognition and waving them on. The third consisted of a patrol of Policia Armada. Both policemen were sitting in a grey jeep parked in the shadow of a tree on the roadside. When they saw the camioneta had a Spanish number plate, they walked out on to the road and made a sign that they should stop. Then they walked round the truck and looked at it from every angle. Their faces were very serious. When they had convinced themselves that the passengers were foreigners they let them go on.

'I think everyone's mad today,' said Dan Pedersen. 'If I see one more cop I'll scream.'

74

The puerto seemed almost completely deserted, only two trawlers at the quay and all the shutters firmly closed. Everything had been done to keep the heat out.

They sat down under the awning outside one of the bars and Dan Pedersen clapped his hands. The proprietor came out and they ordered vermouth and soda-syphons. There was one other guest in the bar, a middle-aged foreigner in grey trousers, a shirt which hung outside them, sun-glasses and a white cap. He was sitting a few tables away, drinking brandy. A camera in an elegant leather case lay beside his glass.

Siglinde and Dan bickered between themselves over all kinds of things. Now and again they said something in German to Willi Mohr, so that he should not feel left out of things.

After a while the man in the white cap rose and came towards them, stopped two strides away from them and said: 'I happened to overhear that you were Scandinavians. I hope you won't think I'm intruding if I ask whether I might join you. It's a little lonely among all these . . .'

He made a gesture, but could not find any Spaniards to point at.

'No, do, by all means,' said Dan Pedersen.

The man fetched his camera and glass of brandy. Then he shook hands with all three of them and each time repeated his name: 'Berg.'

'Swedish, from Malmö,' he added, and sat down.

Siglinde and Dan had forgotten to say their names and Willi Mohr had not understood anything. After another pause, the man said:

'Excuse me . . . but I did not really catch . . .'

They all gave their names and there was another silence. The man cleared his throat and said: 'Perhaps I can get you a drink or something?'

He looked vaguely round for someone to serve him.

Dan Pedersen clapped his hands. The proprietor came out at once.

'You couldn't exactly do that at home, could you?' said the man. 'I mean, clap for the waiter.'

'Why not?' said Siglinde.

She had a feeling she was not going to like this man very much.

75

The proprietor came out with a bottle and poured out the drinks.

'Leave the bottle here,' said the man.

The proprietor shrugged his shoulders and put the bottle down on the table. It was still almost full.

The man raised his glass and said: 'As we're so far from home, we Scandinavians needn't be quite so formal, need we? My name's Ivar.'

They drank.

'Do you live here?' said the man, after a while.

'Up there.'

Dan gestured up towards the misty grey spot in the mountains.

'It looks wonderful,' said the man. 'This is a wonderful country.'

They considered this for a moment and the man filled the glasses again.

'As I was saying, wonderful. They don't cheat you and everyone's so nice and friendly and helpful.'

'Yes, they're good people,' said Dan Pedersen, for something to say.

After their third glass, the man said: 'I was here four years ago for a brief business trip—this is a business trip too, in fact. I've just taken a few extra days as a holiday before I fly home.'

'Oh yes,' said Dan Pedersen, who easily became quite unnecessarily rude when he drank spirits.

'Everything's much better since then,' said the man. 'Not at all the same bother at the borders and much more democratic.'

'This is no democracy,' said Dan Pedersen. 'It's a corrupt dictatorship which the fascists call democracy to kid foolish foreigners. One shouldn't really come here at all.'

'Why do you live here then?'

'Because we don't give a goddam what kind of régime they have as long as it's warm and as long as we're left in peace. It's fine living here, especially for foreigners and in many cases for Spaniards too. Most people do exactly the same things whether they live in a democratic community or under tyranny. The difference in daily life is very small. People work, eat, have sex, go to bed tired at night and wake up even more tired in the

76

mornings. On Saturdays they drink or sit at home listening to the radio or go out for a walk. We don't bother with politics and so we can live here. But that doesn't stop us thinking it's all wrong.'

Siglinde looked at her husband with amusement. She liked the way he said 'we'. She loved him. She thought about the night before.

'And it's all wrong here, is it then, as you put it?'

'Yes, definitely.'

The man filled his glass again, though only he and Dan were drinking now. Then he said: 'You're wrong. Franco has done a lot for this country. Before his time everything was chaotic and disorderly, the economy was even worse than it is now and people shot each other dead in the streets. He cut the Gordian knot and freed both the country and the people from their worst problems. He brought order. Aren't I right?'

'Yes, if the right way to free someone from his problems is to kill him.'

'Skoal,' said the man.

'Skoal,' said Dan Pedersen.

The bottle was empty now.

Santiago was approaching their table, still looking drowsy after the siesta.

Siglinde took the opportunity.

'Here's the friend we were waiting for,' she said.

They got up and said goodbye to the man from Malmö.

'Hell,' said Dan Pedersen to his wife. 'Lots of people reason like that. It almost made me angry.'

He thumped Santiago on the back.

'Now let's go on up to Jacinto and bust a bottle of champagne,' he said.

Willi Mohr walked a few yards behind the others up the slope towards the church. Although he had drunk very much less than Dan, his head felt fluffy and he felt abnormally light. The brandy had quite an effect in the heat. He definitely did not like being drunk and thought it would be best if he took things carefully for the next few hours. And yet he felt in a good mood and was expecting good of the evening. He had begun to feel a sense of solidarity with Dan and Siglinde, which he could not explain but

77

which gave a certain content to the days. He often found himself being curious to know what was going to happen next.

Dan Pedersen walked in the middle with his arms round the other two. Santiago was wearing his faded cotton shirt and blue trousers rolled halfway up his calves. He held himself very straight with his hands in his trouser pockets. Siglinde had pulled in very close to Dan, with her arm round his waist.

At the top of the hill, she freed herself and turned round with her hand stretched out.

'Come on Willi,' she said. 'You shouldn't be walking there all alone.'

She laughed and her grey-brown eyes shone clearly despite their indefinite colour.

The bar was dark and there were no customers sitting inside. Along the far wall was a bar counter with an old espresso-machine on it, and the shelves behind it were filled with bottles and a radio-set. In the middle of the floor stood a tall iron stove with a crooked chimney pipe leading up to a hole in the chimney breast, and in one corner there was a well with a single rope for the bucket. The ceiling was blackened with grease and soot, but the walls were covered with colourful posters for films and bull-fights. The abuela was sitting in an old rattan chair by the stove, knitting, with the cat sleeping on her knee, and behind the counter Jacinto was dozing on a stool, a sporting paper spread over his knees. He had been a civil guard from Santa Margarita and had resigned when he had succeeded in marrying into this bar. He ran it well with no concessions to elegance or modernity, and he did well out of it too, especially from the resident foreigners to whom he gave relatively generous credit. If he was ever cheated, then he retrieved more than just his losses through the juggled bills he presented after special parties. He needed the money, as he had to support both his own and his wife's parents, and his wife never for a moment forgot that the place was really hers.

When the customers came in, he rose sleepily from his stool and automatically wiped the counter in front of him with a dirty cloth.

'Champagne,' said Dan Pedersen, 'and bring a glass and come and join us.'

78

Jacinto got up on the stool and took down two bottles of the cheapest champagne from the rows hanging above the shelves. Then he went and sat down with the others at the table.

'Five glasses,' he said in passing to the abuela.

The old woman put down her knitting and shooed off the cat.

Jacinto opened the bottle skilfully and let the cork pop. They raised their glasses and drank.

Drinking began at six in Jacinto's bar and would go on more or less continuously for the next nine hours.

There was talk, noise and drinking. More people came and joined in. Some came and sat for a while and then vanished again. One man brought a guitar with him and started playing. He was one of those who stayed to the end, as were a young Englishman and his red-haired wife. Now and again a couple of patrolling civil guards came in and leant their carbines against the bar. They allowed themselves to be offered brandy, smiled with white teeth and went out again into the night. The talk was like crossfire, in several languages, and at intervals Jacinto went behind the bar to scribble on the bills. The little Finnish painter who had drawn attention to himself in the fight a few months before came in for a while and tossed back a row of conciliatory drinks. He drank too quickly, was soon drunk and staggered away.

At about ten, Santiago made an attempt to get Siglinde to go bathing, but she shook her head and patted him indulgently on the arm.

Willi Mohr, who was sitting between them, was probably the only person who saw this.

Dan Pedersen was deep in an endless argument about women with the Englishman and on the whole noticed nothing at all.

The drinking went on. Everyone seemed very happy.

Shortly before midnight Santiago got up and said indifferently to Siglinde: 'The boats'll be coming in now. Are you coming down to meet Ramon?'

'Shall we?' said Siglinde to Willi.

Dan Pedersen was still arguing with the Englishman.

Willi Mohr went with them.

When they came out of the steaming smoky bar, it was as if the night had fallen on them with an indescribable purity and

79

soft blackness. It had become considerably cooler and the stars in the sky arched with grandeur between the mountains. A bit further down the hill, the noise from the bar faded away and they heard the distant chug from the boats' engines out in the approaches.

At the quay, all the lights were out except a few melancholy flickering street lights.

They sat down on the edge of the quay and waited. The water lay black and smooth and far out they saw the mast-lights of the first trawler.

Siglinde, who was sitting in the middle, took off her shoes and lay down on her back on the warm concrete. She drew up one leg and placed her heel on the edge of the quay. The other leg she let hang out over the water.

'God, it's good to be alive, anyhow,' she said.

'Isn't it?' she said, when no one replied.

'Yes,' said Willi Mohr.

Santiago said nothing. He was smoking and looking absently at her legs.

Willi Mohr was not very sober, but it struck him that this was in no way an unpleasant feeling.

The first boat rounded the pier. The reflections from its lights lay like a long trembling strip over the water.

'Here they come,' said Santiago.

They had been fishing for sardines and behind the trawler were two small boats with large lamps in the stern. About fifty yards from the quay someone had lit an oil lamp on board the fishing boat and hung it up on the mast. A cold white light fell on to the silvery heap of fish on deck.

'They've had a good night,' said Santiago.

A few minutes later the trawler's bow touched the stone wall, Santiago caught the rope and fastened the boat. The whole boat seemed to be full of glittering sardines. Ramon jumped lightly up on to the railing and crouched there, barefooted and wearing an old black woollen jersey and torn blue trousers. His tangled hair stood on end and both his hair and his jersey glistened with small shining fish-scales. He laughed, swung up on to the quay, embraced his brother and shook hands with Siglinde and Willi.

'Here's Dad, so I'd better fetch the cart,' said Ramon.

80

Pedro Alemany climbed over the railing. He was a broad, short-statured fisherman with a thin mouth and cold eyes. He was wearing a beret, a black shirt and black trousers. He stopped in front of Santiago and said: 'Why didn't you drive into town with the fish last night?'

'I was thinking of going early tomorrow instead.'

'You should go when I tell you to go and not at any other time.'

'The van wasn't fit yesterday.'

'You're lying, as usual,' said Pedro Alemany coldly. 'See that this lot's shifted now.'

He made a gesture towards the heap of sardines on deck. Then he threw a scornful look at Siglinde, turned round and walked away up towards the village.

Santiago bit his lip but said nothing. He avoided the others' eyes.

Ramon came back with a cart full of empty boxes. Santiago gave the remaining three members of the crew some instructions and then they walked back up to Jacinto's bar. Ramon chattered all the time in Catalonian, his arm round his brother. Santiago interrupted him.

'How's your head?'

'All right now,' said Ramon.

'Poor Santiago,' whispered Siglinde to Willi Mohr, 'his pride's hurt.'

In the bar, the tobacco smoke was so thick that the miserable electric light bulb looked like a pale winter sun in the mist. They sat down at the table again and there was nothing to show that anyone had noticed their absence.

Jacinto, who was himself growing slightly unsteady, pulled the jalousies aside and closed the door to show that the party could now be considered over. The abuela had gone to bed.

The drinking went on. The champagne had come to an end and they continued on white wine. Ramon drank heavily. Evidently he was tired and was trying to liven himself up. Willi Mohr took one more glass and noticed he was becoming muddled. I won't drink any more now, he thought.

The girls were in high spirits. The English girl danced first with the guitar-player, then solo. Siglinde insisted on dancing

81

with someone and gradually it became Santiago. They danced very well and rhythmically together. Dan Pedersen, Jacinto and the Englishman were discussing something, loudly and with great energy.

The atmosphere grew even more gay and confused. Everyone was drunk and everyone seemed to feel the need to move in different ways. Siglinde and the red-haired English girl found it difficult to keep their legs still and performed a private can-can show on the bar counter. The guitarist was playing like a madman.

Suddenly Willi Mohr's mind sharpened and he turned quite sober. It was a minor victory for his strength of mind, he thought. At once he saw the people round him quite clearly and wholly objectively.

The man with the guitar, small, sweat-soaked, his shirt flapping, playing like a madman, stamping his feet.

The Englishman, his face beginning to stiffen as his voice grew slow and uncertain.

Dan Pedersen, just knocking a glass over but still talking away.

Jacinto, who had had a long working day and had drunk more than he usually did, looking tired but quite pleased.

The girls, laughing and screaming and trying to kick in time on the bar counter. The English girl was in an ecstasy from the rhythm and the champagne, her untidy red hair sticking to her forehead. They were not sober, but there was nothing distasteful in their behaviour. They just seemed happy.

Santiago sitting straight up in his chair staring at the bar, every now and again licking his lips.

Ramon leaning forward with his mouth open, staring at the girls, so naively and covetously that it was almost moving.

Although the English girl was probably the most accessible to them, and anyhow had the nicest legs, Willi Mohr had the impression that both of them were looking at Siglinde. But that might well have been wrong.

The scene was broken up almost at once. Siglinde grew tired and jumped down. She walked round the table and sat down, wiping the sweat from her forehead. Soon afterwards the Englishman rose unsteadily, lifted his wife down from the bar counter, took her with him and left.

82

'Where's my friend Santiago?' said Dan Pedersen suddenly, as if he had by chance just come back from a long trip.

He got up and drank to Santiago.

'You've known each other a long time now,' said Jacinto, yawning.

'Santiago,' declaimed Dan Pedersen, 'is one of the best friends I've ever had. Santiago and I have done quite a few things together. And there's nothing I wouldn't trust him with. Cheers!'

They stood opposite each other and raised their glasses. It looked like a parody of a declaration of fidelity.

'Long live their friendship,' shouted Ramon.

Dan Pedersen took a step forward and embraced Santiago, who stood without moving, his arms down his sides.

For perhaps a second Willi Mohr caught his look over Dan's shoulder, troubled, painfully moved, and the next moment he gently but firmly freed himself from Dan's embrace.

'The calamary fishing comes to an end on Wednesday,' he said, as a diversion. 'We'll go out fishing then.'

'Yes, by Christ, we must,' said Dan Pedersen.

Twenty minutes later the party broke up. Dan was very drunk and leant against Siglinde as they walked down the hill.

'You and your friendship,' said Siglinde, holding him more firmly with her arm. 'You're more Spanish than the most Spanish of Spaniards.'

As soon as he got into the camioneta, Dan fell fast asleep.

Siglinde took an uncertain step as she was getting into the truck, and Willi Mohr had to help her up.

'What a night,' she said. 'Willy, did I behave very badly?'

'Of course not.'

'I only get like that sometimes,' she said, and she yawned.

Willi Mohr drove home. He was feeling rather drunk and kept having to shake his head to be able to see the road clearly in the beams of the headlights. He saw no civil guards, but already knew the country so well that he was certain that they were there.

8

When Siglinde Pedersen woke, the daylight was flooding into the room through the open windows, but although it was very warm, the sun looked pale and veiled.

She was lying behind her husband's back, on one side, with one hand under her cheek and the other between her thighs, just above her knees, as she always lay when she slept. But now she was awake and had opened her eyes and was listening to her husband's even breathing and to the small noises outside. She could hear the chickens scratching round in the dry grass between the cobblestones and the rattle of a motor-cycle on the road and a donkey braying far away. For the moment she was feeling secure and happy about having woken to a new day.

Siglinde turned over on to her back and stretched her warm naked body. She ran her hands over her hips and waist and breasts and burrowed her head into the pillow, yawning widely, for a long time. Then she raised herself on to her elbow and reached over her husband for his watch lying on the stool by the bed.

It was half-past seven and the date-indicator showed it was the fifteenth of December.

She untangled herself from the sheet and cautiously climbed over Dan, who was sleeping so calmly and heavily that she took the risk of giving him a light kiss on the ear and she swung her body back and forth a couple of times so that her bare breasts brushed his shoulder. She found it difficult to leave him alone, but wanted to be up first as she needed longer time to get dressed.

Then she remembered something and stayed standing by the bed as she thoughtfully pinched her breasts to see whether they were beginning to feel tender. She could feel nothing and she rummaged round in the bag lying on the chair. Then she found her pocket diary, wet her thumb and leafed through it, looking at the dates and pouting as she counted in her head. She should be having her period on the sixteenth if her calculations were right and there was no sign as yet. That did not necessarily mean anything but things were not quite right anyhow.

Siglinde Pedersen looked down at her husband and smiled.

She took the dressing-gown off the bedpost and swept it round her as she walked over to the window. The sunlight was drab and dusty and a veil of greyish mist covered the sky. The town lay spread out below the window, flat, yellowish and lifeless, and visibility to the east was so poor that she could not see the sea.

She padded bare-footed down the stairs and crept out through the outer door. Willi Mohr was lying asleep on his back with his mouth open and his hands behind his head.

When Siglinde came back from the lavatory, he had turned over on his side, but still appeared to be asleep.

She went out into the kitchen, shut the door and quickly washed herself all over with cold water. As she was doing this, the rest of the household woke up. The dog came rushing up to her and wriggled round her legs, and she heard Dan and Willi calling to each other.

When she came out again, Willi was sitting curled up on the mattress, smoking. He grinned slightly when he saw her, as she was wearing Dan's dressing-gown and looked rather funny.

'Today's the day we're going fishing,' she said. 'Have you changed your mind?'

'No, but I'll come with you down to the puerto. I thought I'd wander round and do some sketching while you're out.'

'Perhaps you're right. I don't think it'll be up to much today.'

In the room above, Dan Pedersen was still lying in bed. He watched Siglinde as she took off the dressing-gown and moved round the room.

'What are you staring at. Haven't you ever seen me before?'

'It must feel silly to have a damn great mass of hair like that between your legs. All black, too!'

'I can think of something that must feel ten times sillier.'

Siglinde pulled on her pants and fastened her bra, then stood still for a moment deciding what to put on.

'Wrap up well,' said Dan. 'It won't be all that warm out there.

'It's hot and peculiar.'

She thought for a moment again. Then she got out her shorts and a clean white blouse, which ought to go well with her sun-

85

burn. When she had dressed and tied on her espadrilles, she was annoyed they had no proper mirror.

'I'll take my jeans and polo-necked sweater in reserve. Do you think that'll be all right?' she said.

'Sure to be,' said Dan, indifferently.

Siglinde put on her straw hat with green edges and fetched a bag from the kitchen. Before she went to the tienda she got another hundred peseta note from Willi Mohr and carefully noted the sum down on the wall alongside the kitchen door, where she kept her household accounts.

The tienda was dark, cool and very dirty. Along the one wall stood sacks of beans, sugar and dried green peppers, along the other the barrels of wine with their taps and galvanized metal measures. From the roof hung sausages, earthenware jugs, shoulders of mutton and pieces of harness. The proprietrix absently chased away a dog which was standing on its back legs slobbering in a sack of sugar. Then she took ten small oblong rolls out of a brown paper bag.

'Are you going out on a trip today?

'We're going out fishing.'

'It's not a good day to be out at sea,' the woman said gloomily. 'Better to stay at home.'

Apart from the ten rolls, Siglinde bought two litres of the cheapest red wine, a piece of cheese and a few slices of smoked sausage. She needed only the things they were to take out with them, for they were to have fish for their evening meal, and she had olive oil to fry it in at home.

As Siglinde walked up the hill back to Barrio Son Jofre, she peered several times up at the sky. She had a feeling of anxiety, but could not think of any plausible reason for it.

Dan and Willi were up and had made the beds and swept out the house in her absence. Siglinde sat down on the stairs, sliced through the rolls and put cheese and sausage into them. Then she packed the food into a bag and added her jeans and her polo-necked sweater.

Willi Mohr had gathered up sketching-block, pencil box, his box of water-colours and had fastened them all together in a bundle with a strap so that he could sling the lot over his shoulder.

86

Just as they were about to leave, Siglinde discovered that they were almost out of paraffin. She put the can down just inside the door and said: 'Don't forget to remind me about that, if I forget.'

Willi Mohr locked the door and pushed the key into the crack in the wall.

When they were in the truck, Siglinde found they had locked the dog out and she was sniffing round outside the house.

'We'll take Perrita with us, shall we?' she said.

'Out to sea?' said Dan.

He sounded slightly disturbed.

'She can go with Willi while he's sketching, and then he won't be lonely.'

Willi Mohr grinned. He seldom felt really lonely nowadays. He jumped down and lifted the dog up into the camioneta. Then he climbed up again and sat down behind Siglinde.

They left the house in Barrio Son Jofre.

The truck rolled down the hill at a moderate and reliable speed. Siglinde pushed her hat back and looked up at the sky with its smooth veil of shining white mist. The light hurt her eyes and although the cloud-veils appeared quite harmless, they frightened her. She had a vision of the sky suddenly opening and unloading on them some devastating, unimagined disaster. Siglinde lowered her gaze to the roadside and saw a small green lizard creeping under a stone in terror as the shadow of the truck fell across it.

She thought: Why is one afraid and why just today? And no one notices, only Dan, and even he doesn't usually. But he knows I imagine things and think up all kinds of nonsense and anyhow I'm no more afraid today than I've been hundreds of times before and nothing happened then.

She put her arm along Dan's back and tried to find security there, saying quietly to herself: 'It's really a great personal tragedy to be so stupid.'

They met the sheep at almost exactly the same place as the last time. But this time it was on a straight stretch of road so Dan saw them in good time and had time to brake.

They sat in silence and watched while the old shepherd ran about trying to shoo the flock off the road. He rushed hither and thither with his rags flying round him like an actor in an old slapstick comedy, and not once did he dare even glance at the people in the truck.

'The children of Israel leaving Egypt, directed by Mack Sennet,' said Dan Pedersen, spitting on to the dusty road.

At last the sheep-dog managed to arrange the sheep along the roadside. The old man stood with his hat in his hand and bowed his head as the truck rolled by. He was trembling all over.

Siglinde felt oppressed. She would have liked to get down and pat him, or give him some money, or anything.

When they came down to the quay, Santiago and Ramon were already in the boat. They had got bait and lines and were filling up the tank with petrol. Both were bare-footed and wearing blue trousers and black jerseys. Ramon raised his head and laughed, showing his white teeth. He was unshaven and his dark hair stood out in a cloud round his head. Santiago said nothing but glanced at his watch before raising a hand in greeting.

Dan Pedersen jumped down into the boat and Siglinde handed down the baskets with clothes, wine-jars and food. Santiago and Dan stowed the luggage in the space in the bows. Then Siglinde jumped down before anyone got around to helping her.

Santiago went astern and cast off. He held on for a moment, to give Willi a chance to go on board.

'He's not coming with us,' said Dan Pedersen.

Willi Mohr had understood and shook his head.

Santiago threw him a complicated look.

'Oh, aren't you?' he said, and pushed off.

Ramon began to turn the balance-wheel and the engine coughed.

'What about the weather?' said Siglinde.

'It's O.K.,' said Santiago, without looking at her.

The engine started up. Dan Pedersen gripped the tiller.

Willi Mohr was standing on the quay with his sketching things in a strap over his shoulder. He raised his right forefinger in farewell.

The people in the boat waved to him.

The boat swung out towards the lighthouse in the approaches and tore up a long wide bow of surf. Siglinde was kneeling in the stern watching the houses in the puerto getting smaller and smaller and becoming more and more indistinct and shapeless in the peculiar light. The misty sunlight seemed to fill out and fall over the valley and farther inland the first dragging clouds were going through the pass in the mountains. It was still hot and oppressive and she hoped there would at least be some breeze out at sea.

The engine chugged evenly and reassuringly, and the dinghy bobbed up and down in the swirling waters of their wash. The dinghy was part of the calamary fishing and there was no real reason why they should take it with them. But they had occasionally amused themselves with it out among the skerries. They rounded the lighthouse and steered close by the place where they had bathed a week or so earlier. Siglinde remembered the luminescence of the sea, the dark silence, and then the moment she had stood wet and naked and utterly defenceless in the pale light. She shivered, but did not know why.

Dan Pedersen pulled on the rudder and the boat set course for the mouth of the bay. The cliffs on each side were high and steep with a few pines and low bushes growing on them.

Ramon was sitting crouched in the bow peering at the sun. She could see his hairy muscular calves and the soles of his feet, which were leathery and grey with dust. Under his right heel he had a large dark brown patch of oil. Sometimes he turned round and laughed towards the others, his tongue playing between his white teeth.

Santiago was sitting cross-legged on the bottom of the boat as he systematically and carefully cut up small square pieces of white half-transparent calamary flesh. Each line had eight hooks on it and it took a long time to bait them. He did not once look up from his work. The knife in his hand was long and sharp and flashed in the sunlight.

They rounded the nearest point and met the breakers rolling in from the east, long and smooth and regular, and each time the bows rose on a wave a thin spray of salty water flew over the boat. Although it was still warm, Siglinde began to feel goose-flesh on her forearms and thighs. She felt like stretching out on the bottom of the boat but for some reason she wanted to be as near to her husband as possible, so she stayed where she was. When she turned round and looked towards the land, she saw a civil guard high up on the cliff farthest out. He had his carbine

89

across his back and was leaning on his bicycle. She watched him for a long time until he was nothing but a small dark protuberance on the skyline, and she wondered whether he really could have cycled all the way up there.

When they were farther out to sea, the waves grew larger, but they were still kindly and not at all unpleasant. The sea was moving towards them in long soft ridges and now the skerries ahead could be seen quite clearly, an irregular group of small black silhouettes against the shimmering horizon. It was about an hour's journey there.

Santiago was sitting as before, cross-legged on the bottom of the boat. He was still busy with the hooks and did not look up. Occasionally he hummed to himself quietly, but he said nothing.

Ramon had left his place in the bows and was crouching down beside the engine. He poked at the fuel regulator, then turned his head towards Siglinde and stared at her knees and thighs.

She felt naked under his look and wished she had put on her jeans and sweater. For a moment she considered changing, but then thought it would look silly. Her jeans were tight and she could not very well put them on on top of her shorts. Change clothes in this open boat, she did *not* want to do.

After a while Ramon raised his eyes, looked at her and smiled. He shouted something to Dan who shouted back, but she did not understand what they had said.

A shoal of porpoises went by on both sides of the boat. They tumbled joyfully and playfully in the dark blue-green water, and one of them came so near that she was able to stretch out her hand and pat it on the back, shiny and as grey as lead. She looked out at the islands again. They were much nearer now and she thought they looked ominous in their wet rugged blackness. She had seen them many times before but never like this.

Siglinde leant over the side and let her right hand drag in the bubbling luke-warm water.

Pull yourself together, my girl, she thought. This won't do.

And then: We'll be fishing for a couple of hours and in three, or at the most, four hours' time I'll be home again. Every minute that goes by is a minute nearer home.

And: If you look round you'll see that everything is just the same as usual, and it's quite fine weather, and you're sitting in

90

the same old boat together with the same old Dan ... and same old Santiago ... and same old Ramon ...

She straightened up hurriedly. The nearest island was very close now, a high black chunk of rock which rose straight out of the sea, girded by a narrow border of foaming surf. Ramon had sat down in the bows again. He was singing and smiling up at the sun.

Santiago had finished baiting the lines. He had turned his head and was looking at her legs, as he moistened his lips with his tongue.

They passed the first island by a few yards and steered into the archipelago. The swell was hardly noticeable now and Ramon adjusted the regulator so that the engine chugged more slowly. The pale blue exhaust gas floated astern in light clouds which dissolved over the water. The islands were volcanic and severely eroded.

Many of them were small and hardly rose above the surface of the water, but others were large and high, with steep towering cliffs. Once in amongst them, they resembled ruins of a long since devastated desert city. Here and there were lagoons and sheltered bays with small beaches of fine gravel and pulverized sea-shells.

'The usual place, I suppose?' said Dan Pedersen.

Santiago looked round and nodded.

'The wind'll probably get up this afternoon,' he said. 'Perhaps we'd better not stay too long.'

Not stay too long ... Siglinde became aware of an instant sense of relief, but she at once felt frightened again. Perhaps of the storm that was coming.

She found it difficult to sit still and twisted her fingers round and round each other. Once she noticed that Santiago was looking at her hands, she straightened her fingers and pressed the palms of her hands down on the thwart of the boat. She could feel the grain of the dry sun-warmed wood, but it gave her no comfort.

Dan had been here many times and knew the archipelago as well as the Alemany brothers did. He steered skilfully and purposefully through narrow passages and set course for the largest of the islands, a high narrow ridge of cliff lying almost farthest out towards the sea. A few minutes later he rounded the northern point and the boat glided forward along the outer side, close under the cliff wall. Ramon switched off the regulator and Dan Pedersen fastened the tiller. When the sound of the engine died away Siglinde could hear the cries of the sea-birds and the sound of the waves breaking and washing over the shoals farther out at sea.

The boat had stopped moving forward. It rocked slowly in the water only five yards from the cliff. The others started moving and handling the fishing gear. Siglinde sat still.

The island was a quarter of a kilometre long and perhaps a hundred-and-twenty feet high. On the outer side it plunged almost perpendicularly down into the sea, offering no foothold. Up on its highest point was a ruined stone lighthouse, built there with great labour a long time ago. It had later been discovered that the lighthouse was useless in bad weather, as the clouds sank so low, it became swallowed up in them. A number of lighthouse-keepers had been slowly driven mad in the place. Then the stone tower had been replaced by two automatic metal lights, one on each point. Nowadays the island was only visited by fishermen and police-boats hunting for enemies of the state.

When Siglinde turned her eyes upwards, she saw that the cliff wall was leaning in the wrong direction and the upper edge of the cliff was almost directly above her head. A long way up, large white birds were shooting over the edge as if they were being slung from a catapult. They flew in wide circles and disappeared again where the cliff cut off her field of vision. All the time, she heard them screaming. Even farther up the sky was covered with a silvery shimmering mist.

Dan slapped her good-naturedly on the shoulder and held out the line with the lead weights and eight baited hooks on it. She took it mechanically with her left hand. Dan lifted up the box-like wooden frame with the line on it and gave it to her.

'You seem to be in a hell of a daze,' he said, slightly irritably. 'Aren't you feeling well?'

Siglinde forced herself to smile slightly.

'I'm fine, darling, thank you.'

He left her and went forward to the bows. The boat rocked slowly as he moved.

Siglinde sat quite still and looked at the others. Ramon and Santiago had placed themselves roughly midships, one on each side. They had already got their hooks in the water. Ramon was squatting with his elbows on the side and the line over his coarse forefinger. He was staring at her with large glistening eyes, his mouth half-open, and she could see the tip of his tongue between his red lips. Santiago was half-lying against the side. He seemed to be looking straight into the cliff wall. Siglinde shook herself and let go the weights and hooks. They fell into the water with a small plop.

When she began to let out the line, Santiago turned his head and looked at her for the first time since they had left the puerto.

'Let out all the line,' he said.

His light brown eyes were cold and factual. He looked into her face and smiled a little.

The line was very long and she held it over her forefinger, feeling the vibrations as the water took it away. She looked at the cliff wall, wet and black and shiny, and at the small industrious waves which were slowly hollowing it out. She remembered that on all the occasions she had been here before she had enjoyed herself. But today everything was different and she could not stop thinking: In three hours' time I'll be home again.

And a moment later: A quarter of an hour must have gone by now. In two hours forty-five minutes I'll be home again.

She had no watch and she tried to reckon the time. She sat and counted the seconds for a long spell. One, two, three, four, five, six, seven, eight, nine, ten, eleven, twelve, thirteen, fourteen, fifteen, sixteen, seventeen, eighteen, nineteen, twenty, twenty-one, twenty-two, twenty-three, twenty-four, twenty-five, twenty-six, twenty-seven, twenty-eight, twenty-nine, thirty, thirty-one, thirty-two, thirty-three, thirty-four, thirty-five, thirty-six, thirty-seven, thirty-eight, thirty-nine, forty, forty-one, forty-two, forty-three, forty-four, forty-five, forty-six, forty-seven, forty-eight, forty-nine, fifty, fifty-one, fifty-two, fifty-three, fifty-four, fifty-five, fifty-six, fifty-seven, fifty-eight, fifty-nine, sixty.

There is nothing so long as a minute. Thought Siglinde Pedersen.

No one in the boat said anything, but they did not usually talk while they were fishing.

Now and again someone hauled in the line. There were always two or three small pink fish on the hooks. The fish were unhooked and flung down on to the bottom of the boat, where they thrashed about once or twice before dying. Then the empty hooks were re-baited.

Siglinde sat for a long while and registered the weak distress signals in her line before she began to draw it in. It went slowly and her arms felt feeble and without strength. She had got four of the red sharp-finned fish and when she jerked them off, she saw how the hooks tore their small red mouths. When she let out the line again she thought that if she waited for a long time between hauls, she would not have to take the line in more than three or four times more.

After a while she got another bite, but she remained sitting quite still, looking down into the dark greenish water. High above she heard the cry of the birds. They must have been here for half an hour already, perhaps three-quarters of an hour.

Siglinde was senselessly frightened and she did not know why. Now she used all kinds of small tricks to quell her disquiet. She thought about different things.

At intervals the others drew in their lines and unhooked small red fish. A couple of dozen already lay in the bottom of the boat.

Siglinde thought: Today I'll fry the fish. They are salmonetes and they're good. And expensive if you have to buy them. But I'll keep some and tomorrow I'll make bouillabaisse. First I clean the fish and boil the heads and insides and perhaps a couple of the poor ones if we get any of those. I'll use the big pan and put in two litres of water. They have to boil for a long time and be well salted and then I'll sieve it all through a cloth so that I have nothing but the stock left. The heads and guts the cat can have, when they're all boiled, but he can't have raw fish as he only gets worms from it. Then I'll buy saffron and dried pimentos and ordinary onions and cut them all up and put them all in the stock together with garlic and a little rice that I've already got at home. There should really be a few bay-leaves in it too, but perhaps they're hard to get hold of. I could ask of course, if I remember. And dried tomatoes too, and red pepper and a little oil, as Willi likes blobs of fat on his soup. Then I'll

94

let the lot simmer under the lid for half an hour at least and put
in some cleaned salmonetes, at least two each. Then we'll sit on
the stones in the kitchen and eat the soup and I'll really make it
good this time, as now I've learnt how to make it. It must be
strong and . . .

Suddenly she could not go on. She felt how the small jerks had
increased in strength, but it did not occur to her to pull in the
line.

Instead she forced herself to look in another direction. She
turned her head quickly and saw the open sea spreading beyond
the small rocky skerries. On the horizon was the superstructure
of a large passenger liner, slowly ploughing its way from north
to south. A minute or so later she let her eyes wander towards
the men in the boat. Dan was just hauling in his line. Ramon
was staring straight at her. Santiago was also looking in her
direction but as if he were observing something just behind her.

Siglinde shuddered and again looked at the rugged black cliff
wall.

She sought for another diversion. In desperation she fumbled
for one she used only seldom and then only when in direst need.

She thought about the man she had lived with before she met
Dan.

At the time she had been working in a drawing office and was
well, but life was dull. He was working in an advertising agency
and was a very well-dressed and well-brushed young man, well
brought-up and everyone said he had a way with him. She had
met him before at college and he had been much the same then.
They had quite a lot in common, and she quite liked him, at least
at times. He lived in two rooms, which were very neat and
clean and practical and decorated with a kind of modernistic
bogus-artistry, geometry on the walls and chilly impersonal
mobiles hanging from the ceiling. Gradually she moved in with
him, but it was some time before she did. Once or twice a week,
he became completely transformed and tore off her clothes and
threw her down anywhere, on the carpet, or the bed, or sometimes even the kitchen floor. This usually happened on Saturdays
and sometimes on Wednesday evenings. When she was naked,
he forced her legs apart and she remembered that his hips were
quite broad and that he had black hair on his chest and

95

stomach. He bit her on the breasts and shoulders and under her chin and on Mondays she had large red marks on her body which turned blue in the middle of the week and hardly had time to disappear before the next Saturday. He did everything very quickly and roughly and was sometimes impotent and bit her throat in desperation, and she was not frightened but very embarrassed, for she was inexperienced and had not learnt what she ought to do. At first she had thought that all this was rather good, but she had fairly soon lost interest. Long afterwards she discovered that she had learnt to loathe people who became transformed. But there were still situations from the kitchen floor or the carpet which she could not bring back to mind without feeling a certain excitement.

Siglinde saw the dripping black cliff wall in front of her again. She had goose-flesh all over her now and her fear had grown wild and unreasonable. Dimly she saw that her thoughts had chosen the wrong channel.

At that moment a large fish bit. Its heavy strong jerks made the line run through her fingers, but she contented herself with winding the line once round her hand and holding on. She sat like this for a long time, until Dan said: 'Siglinde, you've got a bite.'

Then she began to haul in the line slowly and all the time she kept her eyes on the line down in the water. Soon something shone down there, as the large fish threw itself about to free itself. It came nearer and nearer and it was not so large but quite big all the same, perhaps eighteen inches long. She had also got three small red fish and the other four hooks were empty. She swung her catch into the boat and at that moment the big fish flung itself loose and shot between her feet. It was fat and shimmering green and purple, and she saw a large cold circular eye. She took it in both hands and tried to break its neck against the big stones lying in the bottom of the boat, but although she hit several times she only succeeded in gashing it more and more. Finally she could not bring herself to hold it any longer. It slid away from her and down the length of the boat.

Without looking at her, Santiago put his bare foot on the fish and drew his knife out of its sheath and cut its throat. The fish died at once.

96

Siglinde sat still and looked at the knife. Her hands were sticky and cold and there was a little thin blood on her fingers.

'That's what I call luck,' said Dan. 'And you hardly able to hold the line today.'

Siglinde shuddered. She was sweating all over and her heart was beating violently.

Ramon was staring at her, greedily and openly.

She thought one single clear thought, over and over again: As long as I get home, as long as I get home, I'll do anything as long as I get home, as long as . . .

Santiago had pulled in his line and wound it up on the wooden frame. He half-rose and looked out over the sea.

'It's beginning to blow a bit now,' he said. 'Perhaps we'd better go back.'

Along the horizon the mist had grown greyer and more compact. The water was slapping a little more heavily against the cliff wall. High up above the birds were screaming.

Siglinde returned to reality. She blinked and looked round as if she had just woken up from a nightmare. Her heart was still thumping and she could still feel the fear in her diaphragm, but nevertheless everything seemed different. They were to leave now and nothing would happen and in an hour's time they would be home. She wiped the sweat from her forehead with the back of her hand and smiled confusedly, sitting down on the stern seat.

Santiago gathered up the fish and slung them into a flat basket. Dan and Ramon wound up their lines.

It grew slowly darker on the horizon and a cool breeze wafted along the cliff wall.

Dan rose, stepped over Ramon, walked to the stern seat and sat down. He freed the rudder and pressed the tiller.

'How are you feeling, darling?' he said, stroking her cheek.

'I'm all right. Yes, I'm all right.'

He looked at her in surprise.

'Are you frightened?'

'Yes, a little,' said Siglinde.

'Funny darling,' said Dan, laughing. 'There's nothing to be afraid of.'

Santiago had sat down cross-legged and begun to put the lines in order.

Ramon was kneeling on the floor of the boat turning the engine. The engine started on the second turn and the boat increased speed along the cliff wall.

Dan Pedersen steered slightly away from the land and held course southwards to go round the island. They came out of the shade and into the sun and he laid his hand on Siglinde's thigh, calmly and comfortably, and so high up that a couple of fingers crept in under her shorts and brushed a few hairs that had made their way out under the elastic of her pants. They had the tiller between them and were holding it from each side.

Siglinde felt her confidence returning. She looked at the Alemany brothers and they looked the same as usual. Santiago was standing bent over the hooks, humming slowly as he worked. Ramon was squatting by the engine, poking at the fuel regulator.

Dan moved the tiller over and rounded the south tip of the island. The swell here was already quite strong and the dinghy on the tow-line danced lightly on the waves.

Siglinde fumbled for cigarettes under the seat. In an hour they would be home.

At that moment the engine began to cough. It did not stop, but it was labouring heavily and unevenly.

'What is it?' said Dan Pedersen.

Ramon peered into the engine, fiddled with the fuel regulator and shook his head.

'We'd better fix it before we go on,' said Dan. 'We'll go in here into the bay and then we won't drift.'

He drew the tiller towards him and the boat swung back towards the island in a tight slow curve. The engine was misfiring badly now.

The west side of the island was different from the sea side. The mountain sloped more gently and the coast was cut up into a long row of separate stony bays, with calm water and small beaches of shell-sand. Just here, near the southern point, was a sheltered bay where they had bathed several times.

As they passed through the narrow approach, the engine stopped. The boat slid slowly through the water until the bows softly burrowed their way into the tawny yellow sand on the shore.

'Don't worry, I'll soon have it fixed up,' said Dan Pedersen.

'I know what it is,' said Santiago. 'Oil on the plugs.'

·He began to get up.

'Oh, let Dan do it,' said Ramon laughing. 'He wants to so badly.'

Dan knelt down by the engine. Ramon stood diagonally behind him with his hands on his knees. Santiago had got up.

'Give me the spanner,' said Dan Pedersen.

Siglinde was still sitting on the seat in the stern.

Time stood still. Every detail was visible with corrosive clarity, as if in a permanent flash of lightning.

Siglinde did not know why she had been afraid and she had been right and it was too late.

Dan Pedersen was dead and lay prostrate over the engine.

Ramon Alemany had bent down and lifted one of the diving-stones from the bottom of the boat and smashed in his head.

What remained was steely terror and reflections of horror in their eyes.

Siglinde lay on her back on the shore, while Santiago held her arms and Ramon tore off her shorts and pants. She smelt the smell of fish and sweat on their trousers. High up above her, she saw the white birds shoot over the ridge of the cliff, as if slung by a catapult.

She wanted to live and so she resisted.

Half-an-hour later, they killed her.

Part Four

1

Willi Mohr had a good friend called Hugo Spohler.

They had met at the end of 1951 in a repatriation camp outside Cologne, where they were living in a wooden hut and had top bunks in the same partition. In the daytime they were occupied with clearing rubble and in the evenings and at night they talked to each other. The winter was cold and grey and muddy and it rained nearly every day.

Willi Mohr had crossed the zone border in Berlin a few weeks earlier, received new identity papers from the Commandant of the British Sector and then he had been sent west. He was missing his mother and had already regretted having changed sides.

Hugo Spohler was from Dresden in Saxony and the whole of his family had vanished either in the great raids towards the end of the war, or in the confusion that followed. He was four years older than Willi Mohr and had already been chosen for the Life Guards when he was still at school. He was blue-eyed and broad-shouldered and nearly six feet tall, so more than fulfilled the physical requirements, although he was in fact not particularly strong.

Now he was troubled by stomach ulcers and occasionally by an old wound, and he had long since managed to get a doctor to remove the SS tattooed on his left upper arm.

So far as he was concerned, the war had ended in 1944 when he personally had capitulated to the Americans in Normandy after his unit had been surrounded and wiped out in small groups. It was a clear morning and very early as he had crouched down and run along a narrow path between high hedges. As he ran he held his pistol loose in his hand so that in a flash he could either use it or throw it away, whichever the

101

situation demanded. Round a sharp bend, he had run into an American soldier, so he had stretched out his pistol on the flat of his hand and said: 'Souvenir.'

The astonished American took the gun and with that Hugo Spohler managed to achieve his sole aim at that particular moment, to become a prisoner-of-war.

As he had been a member of the SS, he was sent to the United States and not sent back from there until the authorities were quite convinced that he was a reasonably insignificant figure.

Before that bright clear morning between the high hedges, Hugo had managed to experience the war fairly thoroughly. He went to France after the great offensive in 1940 and was posted to Bayonne. It was a pleasant posting and he had enjoyed it very much, but a year later he had overslept with a seventeen-year-old French shop girl and missed a parade. The following week he was sent to the Russian front. He spent fourteen months on one of the southern sectors of the front, in thirty degrees below zero in the winter and the same above zero in the summer. In the autumn of 1942 he got a grenade splinter in his right upper arm and was transported back to an Italian field hospital. The wound was a serious one, was badly treated, the Italian surgeon's eyes were red and sore, and he had had blood on his white jacket from operating for ten hours at a stretch.

He felt Hugo Spohler's arm for a while and shook his head. Then he took a piece of blue chalk out of his pocket and drew a line round the arm, just below the shoulder. Hugo tried to argue with him, but they had no common language and the Italian also appeared to be very tired.

When the doctor had gone, Hugo Spohler managed to get off the stretcher and walk out of the tent. Out on the road, he stopped a Service Corps vehicle, which took him to a German first-aid post farther away from the front. Two weeks later he was taken on a hospital train going west. He still had his arm but it hurt him so badly that he screamed with pain when the morphine he had been given lost its effect.

After three months he was more or less recovered but not yet fit for service. He was put on special service and sent to France again, to the north coast, where the sun was not quite so

102

seductive as in Bayonne. In addition to this, the spiritual climate had grown considerably harsher, but that he did not bother about.

Hugo Spohler knew the art of forgetting what he considered not worth remembering.

During the war he had not been able to avoid killing a number of people, perhaps six or seven, but he never talked about it and neither did he think about it.

He remembered the French shop girl's navel and eyelashes very well, but he did not remember that one morning, with the warmth from their bed still with him, he had executed three workmen who—probably mistakenly—had been suspected of sabotage.

He could describe a young Ukrainian woman partisan in detail, the one he and two others had raped in a stable (she had preposterously large nipples and black hair on her legs, and strangely enough had been a virgin) but he had no memory of the scenes of horror at the first-aid post or the Italian surgeon with his bit of blue chalk.

From his happy years he could remember the tunes and parades and the Fuehrer, whom he had seen several times at quite close quarters, but he had long forgotten a red-haired sergeant who had forced him to throw himself down in a deep muddy pool on the barrack square forty times, one after another.

When Hugo Spohler talked about the war it might have all been a fantastic escapade, full of absurd complications.

He conquered the past with forgetfulness and the present with optimism, romancing away from sorrows and difficulties. People liked him. He was warm and positive and he was always looking straight ahead.

His attitude to Willi Mohr was not very complicated.

He refused to believe that a person who had never experienced anything could be marked by his experiences.

As he had no understanding whatsoever for any form of depression or dispiritedness, he confused Willi Mohr's sullen coldness with the true integrity and perfectionism he had always admired.

Hugo Spohler filled the empty space round Willi Mohr with

103

talk. He had never forgotten Bayonne, and in the middle of the camp's grey muddy sordidness, he gave himself up to vague sun-drenched visions of the South. The South had become his Shangri-La, the happy land of naive escapism.

Hour after hour Willi Mohr lay with his chin propped in his hand, listening. Gradually he realized that even his own passive resistance lacked strength, that he was on the way to being convinced.

Hugo Spohler was the first to get away from the camp. A week later he met a girl from Berlin and made her pregnant. Then he borrowed two hundred marks from her, got himself a passport and hitched south. He landed up in the puerto by chance and managed to stay there for a while.

After four weeks he came home again, broke but happy. He was intoxicated by the experience and had painted four very bad paintings with borrowed paints. A little later he got himself a place and married the girl from Berlin. She was the only survivor of a well-to-do official's family and had no assets apart from a good physique, a respectable upbringing and a job in a betting-office.

Hugo Spohler had thus organized his own life and could again devote himself to Willi Mohr. He got him out of the repatriation camp, much as one fetches a forgotten trunk, and placed him in an attic room in a tumbledown, bomb-damaged old block in Zugasse, on the west bank of the Rhine.

Next to Willi Mohr's room was a large, open attic with a hole in the roof, the floor covered with broken tiles and charred bits of wood. They cleared away the rubbish and covered the ceiling with hardboard and corrugated iron. Then they had a studio and Hugo Spohler painted several pictures in it. He was totally lacking in talent, but not afraid of using bright colours, and he himself considered that his paintings were pretty good. He also succeeded in selling some of them for fifteen marks each and was greatly encouraged.

Willi Mohr had a view over the river from his window. It was autumn and wet and foggy, with tugboats, with their tall sloping chimneys, going by like ships in the mist, towing long barges behind them. One day he borrowed Hugo's paints and sat down at the window and painted a picture. He took a long time over it, dabbing carefully with the brush, now and again sticking out his lip and peering out into the pouring grey rain.

The result filled Hugo Spohler with astonishment and enthusiasm, but Willi Mohr was more dispassionate. He knew of old that he ought to be able to make fog look like fog and a tugboat like a tugboat.

Hugo got seventy-five marks for the picture, but he could not persuade Willi to paint any more like it. Neither of them had a definite job, but now and again they took temporary employment in the docks or on some building site. Willi Mohr mostly lay on his rickety old camp bed, smoking cigarette ends in a pipe as he stared at the ceiling. Sometimes he wondered vaguely what on earth he was doing there.

When Hugo's wife was eight months pregnant, she had to stop working and so he was faced with a wholly new problem. For the first time in his thirty-year-old life he was forced to take financial responsibility for both himself and someone else. He was in no way a soldier any longer. The war was definitely over. He felt that it had been going on for a very long time, beginning some time in the thirties when he was only a small boy and to a certain extent continuing through the years, even after that morning between the hedges in Normandy.

Soon after the New Year, Willi Mohr and Hugo Spohler applied for work as decorators at an English department store, which was there largely to serve the forces of occupation. Although Willi was undoubtedly the one with the qualifications, it was Hugo who got the job. He managed to get a week's wages in advance and they celebrated by drinking beer and a couple of schnapps at a beer-hall by the cathedral. Afterwards they went to a brothel. Willi Mohr liked the brothel because it was pleasant and clean and functional and wholly impersonal. It was in a new yellow-brick two-storey block, and the prostitutes lived in identical rooms along a long corridor, with numbers on the doors, exactly like a real hospital. The rooms were practical and kept clean, with coverlets and curtains in pastel shades, and the employees were dressed in garments which more or less matched the décor. The women who worked there had been chosen with some care so that the enterprise would be in a position to cater for different tastes in such matters as corpulence, stature and colour of hair. Willi Mohr had no particular bents, but he used to avoid those who were blue-eyed, though he did not know why.

Hugo Spohler said that the brothel was colour-conditioned and he expressed some disapproval of it, but Willi Mohr thought it was a considerable improvement on those he had been to in Gotenhafen.

After their visit to the brothel, they bought a litre of wine and sat on the bed in Willi Mohr's room and drank it. Outside it was raining steadily and dismally, and the tugboats hooted in the poor visibility. The German miracle growled and rattled along the streets by the river.

As in the repatriation camp the year before, Hugo did his best to talk away the cold and rawness from the air. After his expedition to the south he had not only his imagination to call on, but he also had access to certain facts. So his arguments became even more convincing.

Willi Mohr sat leaning against the wall and listened. He had drawn one foot up on to the edge of the bed and was balancing his wine glass on his knee.

'You have to express yourself and that's the most important thing,' said Hugo. 'Express yourself in colour or words or tunes. Why is it so difficult to express yourself here? Well, because there's nothing here one wants to express. And not only that, but also because here there's such a hell of a lot that stops us and ties us down. You'd be a great painter, if only you could work in the right surroundings and the right atmosphere. Perhaps I would too. Willi, listen to me for once . . .'

'I always listen to you, said Willi Mohr seriously.

'Wouldn't you like to try then?'

Willi Mohr sipped his wine, which was cheap and sour. Then he looked towards the window and nodded.

'O.K.,' he said. 'We'll try.'

They made the decision that evening, a decision which was of determining significance to Willi Mohr, but in fact made not the slightest difference to Hugo Spohler.

They were to work hard for eighteen months and save every pfennig. Then they would go to Spain and live there for a year and paint. Eventually, and if the money lasted, Hugo would take his family there too.

106

'But,' he said, 'on the other hand I don't think Maria would get very much out of it. Next year she can go out to work again and perhaps it's better if she supports herself and the kid.'

When Hugo had gone, Willi Mohr undressed and crept down into his bed. He was slightly drunk and the sheets felt damp and cold. But deep down in his mind, a minute speck of expectancy had come to life, and he wondered whether he would ever be able to experience even a small fraction of the exhilaration which Hugo seemed to be able to produce from his imagination.

Three days later he got himself a job and left the attic in Zugasse for ever.

During the following year, they did not meet once. Willi sent one or two postcards with laconic messages on them, but he never received one in return, perhaps owing to the fact that he never had a permanent address.

When the summer came Hugo Spohler had saved three hundred marks. He hitched to Spain and bathed for three weeks. When he came home again, he had made a lot of new acquaintances and had the Caudillo's portrait on one single Spanish duro, which no one would change for him.

Next summer Willi Mohr went back to Cologne. He was much the same as ever, if possible even thinner, more sullen and more blue-eyed. He had saved three-thousand-five-hundred marks and was going to go to Spain to paint.

Hugo Spohler had changed a good deal. Although he still had no money, he seemed plump and well. He had moved to another house and had a son of fourteen months and his wife was pregnant again. He moved in circles which enthused about Buddhism and Zen-Buddhism and he was convinced that he could cure his ulcers by will power. He spent his evenings working out involved betting systems, which were going to bring him in a fortune. He had stopped painting, but was still convinced that he ought to move to a warmer country. Sometime.

Willi Mohr felt slightly cheated, but smiled a sardonic smile and persuaded himself that this was in reality exactly what he had expected.

Hugo Spohler was, as usual, master of the situation. He took two weeks' holiday and borrowed two hundred marks of Willi's capital.

'We'll hitch down and then I'll show you the best place of all,' he said. 'I'll introduce you to people, good people, and then I'll come down and fetch you in a year or so.'

He laughed and slapped Willi Mohr on the back.

'You'll have to experience this year for us both,' he said.

They had good luck with lifts, but had to walk the last bit over the border in the Pyrenees.

About a hundred yards directly above the last tunnel on the French side, an iron chain was stretched across the road and a civil guard in green uniform and black shiny cap came out of a little tin shack in the mountainside. He had a carbine over his shoulder and glanced at their visas before he let them through.

'The real passport control is a couple of kilometres down the road,' he said, as he raised the chain.

They came to the puerto in the middle of the summer and Hugo Spohler could only stay a week. The day he left, he bought a thick notebook with a blue mercerized cover and gave it to Willi Mohr.

'I told you you'd have to experience this year for us both,' he said. 'I want you to note down your impressions day by day in this book, as if you were writing letters to me. Then when we meet again, we can go through what you've written. Don't forget you must express yourself, in every way.'

Half an hour later he left the puerto. The first bit he did in Santiago's fish-van.

He had just introduced Willi Mohr to Dan Pedersen and his wife. All three of them were standing outside Jacinto's bar, watching the van.

Hugo Spohler did not hear from Willi Mohr during the whole of the following year and neither did he think about him very often. Hugo got himself a better job shortly after Christmas and the following summer he did not have an opportunity to travel south.

2

When Willi Mohr woke in the morning of the sixteenth of December, he was alone in the house in Barrio Son Jofre. Although he had slept for only four hours, he was wide awake the moment he opened his eyes. The cat had evidently felt cold, as it had crept in under the blanket and lay curled up with its head in his armpit. It was quite quiet in the house, and neither were there any special sounds from outside, only the wind rushing over the mountain ridge far above. The wind had begun to get up after the siesta the day before and no boats had left the puerto, not even the old trawlers.

He pushed the cat away and looked at his watch lying in its usual place on the floor to the left of his mattress, together with his cigarettes and a box of matches. It was half-past seven.

Willi Mohr got up, took off his pyjama jacket and went out into the kitchen. He cleaned his teeth and washed his face and torso with cold water. Then he went back into the room and dressed. He shooed the cat away from the warm bedclothes where it had again curled up, opened the door and shook out the blankets and sheets thoroughly. Meanwhile the cat sat on the stone floor blinking sleepily, waiting for his bed-making to be completed so that it could go back to bed again.

Willi Mohr lit his first cigarette of the day and went upstairs. The sky was covered with an even grey blanket of clouds and although it was not raining the air was heavy and humid. Despite the mist and the low clouds, he could see that the wind was howling through the pines up on the mountain.

He fetched the gas can and the funnel from the kitchen and poured the remains of the gas into the camioneta's tank. When he put the things back, he took his straw hat down from the nail in the doorpost and was just about to leave when he stopped in the doorway, went back into the room and got the notebook out of his rucksack. Then he sat down on the bottom stair and leafed through it.

The last note was more than three months old and very brief.

4th September, 22.30. Today I fetched wood, bathed and played ping-pong with S. and D. I think I'm beginning to like . . .

He had never completed the sentence.

On the next pages were three or four small sketches of houses and streets and one of a donkey working a pump. There were also some calculations and some figures, but he had forgotten what they were about.

He leafed on until he came to an empty page, undid the top of his fountain pen, looked at his watch and wrote:

16th December, 8 a.m. Yesterday I waited all afternoon and evening in the puerto but they did not come back. It was past two in the morning when I got home.

He put the notebook in his hip pocket and went out to start up the camioneta. It took a while to get it going. The dog had been locked out again and he had not thought of taking her with him, but when she ran so far after the truck, he took pity on her and stopped. As he lifted the animal up on to the seat he could feel her trembling with the strain, her heart thumping violently.

In the puerto all was silent and calm, as if the inhabitants had not yet woken. The quay shone from the rain and the water was pale and smooth, reflecting the sky in shades of grey. There were a lot of boats lying in harbour, but he at once saw that the calamary boat was still not there.

Willi Mohr parked the camioneta on the quay and lifted down the dog. He listened absently to the sea roaring beyond the mountains and walked slowly across the broad open concrete surface. He had already waited for twelve hours the day before, from two in the afternoon until two in the morning. He had not sat in the camioneta all the time, but had moved from café to café, and no one had spoken to him or even noticed his presence.

He bought a roll and some red jam in the tienda, sat down outside the nearest bar and ordered café con leche. Although the basket chair was under the awning, its arms were sticky and slightly furry with the damp.

He gave the bitch half the roll and forced himself to eat the rest, although he did not feel at all hungry.

An hour went by. Willi Mohr remained sitting in the basket

110

chair, staring out across the bay. His eyes were blue and expressionless. There was no sign of life in the harbour.

Pedro Alemany came down from one of the steep side-streets and walked out on to the quay. He had a dead yellowish cigarette in the corner of his mouth and was wearing espadrilles, a black shirt, black trousers and a beret. He stood for a long while with his hands in his pockets, looking out towards the approaches, small and fat, his feet apart. Then he looked round, caught sight of Willi Mohr outside the café and slowly walked across the concrete space.

He leisuredly raised a thick, short forefinger to his temple and said something which the other man did not understand. Willi Mohr had no sense of language and knew only a few of the most ordinary words.

When the fisherman saw that he had not succeeded in making himself understood, he first pointed at Willi, then out towards the sea and then made a questioning gesture.

Willi Mohr shook his head and Pedro Alemany stood silent for a moment.

Then he threw out his arms and said with exaggerated diction: 'Probablemente Villanueva.'

Villanueva was a little fishing settlement several miles farther south, considerably nearer for those coming from the islands. Fishermen who were caught in bad weather often sought shelter there.

'Telephone,' said Willi Mohr.

'Telefono cascado,' said Pedro Alemany.

He realized that the last word had not sunk in and made a movement with his hands as if he were tearing something apart.

The fisherman pointed out to sea and put up a finger as if he were listening.

Willi thought at first he really was listening to something special, but then realized that the man just wanted to emphasize how bad the weather was out there.

'Malo, malo,' said Pedro Alemany, shaking his head.

The word needed no further explanation.

The fisherman thrust his hand into his trouser pocket and pulled out a turnip watch. He opened the front and held out the watch, putting his thumbnail on the large Roman two. With his

111

other hand he pointed first at the boats by the quay and then towards the sea, while making violent wave movements with his arm.

'A las dos,' he said.

Willi Mohr nodded. At two o'clock they were evidently thinking of going out to search, if nothing happened between now and then.

The father of the Alemany brothers turned round and walked away.

Willi Mohr watched him until he disappeared into one of the alleyways. Then he crossed his legs and lit another cigarette.

A dirty little girl was standing a short distance from the table, staring at the roll and jam the dog had not eaten.

A civil guard cycled diagonally across the quay. He was wearing a dark green rubber raincape over his uniform and his carbine was fastened with straps along the frame and carrier. As he cycled past, the barrel of the carbine was for a moment pointing straight at the man at the table.

Willi Mohr went on sitting in the damp basket chair for more than five hours, watching the meagre life in the puerto. He drank two cups of coffee and left the table once, to go into the estanco and buy another packet of cigarettes. The dog lay at his feet and occasionally he bent down and patted her. She then rolled over on her side and begged for more affection, which at once made him withdraw his hand.

He did not feel nervous or anxious, but he was incapable of doing anything else but just this, sitting and waiting. At half-past eleven, the green mail bus rolled down on to the quay towards the small group of black-clad old women waiting there. They gathered up their bundles and baskets, climbed on and remained sitting in the bus until the driver came back and started up again, three-quarters-of-an-hour later. Before the bus left, the driver repeatedly blew the horn, which moaned a shrill lament. A number of ragged small girls sauntered by with great bundles of brushwood on their backs. Then it was silent and empty again on the quay.

About half an hour later the bus returned laden, as far as could be seen, with the same old women and the same bundles.

Shortly before three o'clock, Pedro Alemany came down to

112

the quay together with three civil guards, all wearing dark green oilskins. The guards went across to the grey police barque, jumped down into it and indolently began to undo the cover over the well of the boat. After a while the cabo came cycling up.

The puerto had acquired another police-chief since Dan Pedersen and Siglinde and Willi Mohr had been expelled four months before. The new one was small and squat and older than his predecessor. He stood with one foot on a bollard, talking to Pedro Alemany. Now and again, he interrupted the conversation and mumbled some instructions to the men in the boat.

Willi Mohr rose and walked over to the group on the quay. He had been sitting still for so long that his back was aching and his joints stiff. At first the others took no notice of him, but then the father of the Alemany brothers looked in his direction and shook his head, saying: 'Villanueva . . . no.'

He turned back to the cabo at once, and the conversation continued, while the men in the barque slowly got ready to depart.

When the civil guards tried to start the engine they found that they had run out of gas. One of them hunted out a tin can and jumped up on to the quay. He walked slowly away towards the houses and it was twenty minutes before he came back.

What a sea-rescue operation, thought Willi Mohr scornfully.

The guards filled the tank with gas and manipulated the engine for a while. Then all three climbed out of the boat and walked up to the bar, where they drank a small cup of coffee each. Pedro Alemany was still talking to the cabo. Willi Mohr noticed that the fisherman's tone of voice had grown more and more irritable and that the cabo was frowning and making lively gestures, sometimes towards the boat, sometimes towards his subordinates and sometimes out to sea.

The three civil guards came back, received yet another stream of instructions from their superior and climbed on board. Then they started the engine and cast off.

The barque was broad and steady and made of riveted metal sheets. It had rope fenders along its side and in the bows there was a machine-gun covered with a tarpaulin. The boat steered in a wide curve across the harbour basin and in the strange light looked as if it were swirling through the mist. The men on the quay watched it until it disappeared behind the breakwater.

113

Willi Mohr stood a short distance from the others, quite still, his hands in his pockets.

The cabo seemed to notice him for the first time. He stared for a moment and then flung a question at Pedro Alemany.

When the fisherman answered, he spoke so clearly that Willi Mohr understood what he said.

'A friend of the Scandinavians.'

'Aha,' said the cabo. 'Poor man, his friends . . .'

'They're my sons,' said Pedro Alemany.

Willi Mohr went back to the bar and sat down in the same basket chair as before.

He drank yet another cup of coffee and looked indifferently at the proprietor's daughter who was serving him. She was perhaps sixteen years old and quite fresh, with small round breasts, clear skin and lively eyes. She still had a couple of years before child-bearing would begin, and then would come the fat, the dirt and the frustration.

A nun walked by and vanished behind the jalousies. When Willi Mohr went in a few minutes later to fetch some more sugar, she was standing by the bar testing the point of a hypodermic syringe on the tip of her forefinger. A small child, its backside bare, was sitting on the counter, staring at the syringe with large, dark eyes. The nun went and stood under the oil lamp and pushed back her coif to be able to see better, and he saw that she was young and had straight features. Her neck was dirty and she had a large pimple on her forehead, just above the nose. She glanced at him swiftly and timidly.

When Willi Mohr sat down in the chair again outside, he heard the child cry out shrilly from inside the bar.

Half an hour later a boat-engine could be heard chugging in the mist and the barque appeared from behind the lighthouse. Even from a long way away he could see the silhouette of the three civil guards, one sitting bent low over something, and to his surprise, Willi Mohr felt a contraction in his diaphragm as he got up and walked down towards the water. The boat was approaching very fast.

The gendarmes were alone in it. Their oilskins shone from the wet and one of the men had lifted the bilge-boards and was bailing out the boat with a scoop. The sound of the boat's engine

114

died away and the bows gently touched the quay. The civil guard flung out his arms in gesture of hopelessness and pointed out to sea. They had taken off their sou'westers and the face of the one sitting in the stern was pale and sweaty. They all talked at once and Pedro Alemany listened. Then he spat out the chewed yellowish cigarette-end, turned round and quickly walked away. The civil guards shrugged their shoulders and climbed up on to the quay. One of them looked at Willi Mohr and shook his head.

'Terrible,' he said, making violent wave signs with his arms.

Willi Mohr went back to the bar.

He sat in the basket chair and watched as Pedro Alemany and his men got the trawler ready to leave. They hauled down the nets and took a number of boxes ashore. The engine was warmed up and started. The cabo was there, as was another official in a blue uniform and a white cap, the harbour-master. Two other civil guards went on board.

The preparations did not seem to be either hysterical or panic-stricken, but were carried out with a professional calm which inspired a certain amount of confidence. Pedro Alemany stood up in the bows and supervised the work, only once losing his temper, when a middle-aged woman with grey hair and a shawl round her shoulders cautiously approached the boat. Then he shouted shrilly and uncontrollably and the woman at once hurried back up to the houses. Willi Mohr guessed that she was his wife.

It took less than an hour to get the trawler ready for departure and then it was already a quarter to five. Once or twice Willi Mohr considered going down to help, but he had a feeling that he could not do anything and no one bothered about him. And neither did he understand what they were saying.

So he remained sitting where he was and the trawler backed away from the quay, watched by the cabo and the harbour-master and several other people who had gathered there. He leant his chin on his hand and watched the fishing-boat until it had vanished round the lighthouse. It had begun to rain and the drops broke up the polished surface of the water with small, sharp pinpricks.

Willi Mohr listened to the sound of the engine and after a

while discovered that he could not hear it any longer, but only the light sound of the rain falling and the pulsating in his own body. He got up and went over to start up the camioneta. When he climbed up on to the seat he noticed that the dog had disappeared, but he had hardly driven more than a hundred yards or so along the quay when she caught him up and ran alongside the truck. He did not bother to stop.

At the end of the quay, a winding road ran on along the rocky shore. At first it was smooth and relatively wide, but then it quickly narrowed and became rougher. Willi Mohr drove past a row of square villas, built by summer visitors, now standing empty and closed up, then the houses came to an end and the road ran up the mountainside. He could just see the grey water of the bay between the pine trees on his right. The higher he got the more primitive the road became. The camioneta bounced and rocked, but it was constructed for just this kind of country and the wheels were so high that it could clear even quite large boulders without difficulty. The rain was beating down on to his face and once he nearly drove straight into a couple of civil guard who were cycling towards him.

A couple of minutes later, he passed a woman with her shawl over her head, who had stepped to one side and was standing quite still with her face turned away. He recognized Pedro Alemany's wife and stopped. He jumped down and pointed at the truck, saying: 'Please get in.'

But she stared stubbornly in the other direction and when he approached her, she took a step back among the stones. For a few seconds Willi Mohr stood irresolutely with his hand stretched out. Then he shrugged his shoulders and went back to the truck.

By this time, the dog had caught up and was panting exhaustedly, wagging her tail. He picked her up and drove on.

Up on the mountain he met the wind coming whistling straight at him, wild and capricious. He pulled down his hat and peered carefully out from under the brim, but although he slowed down, it was difficult to keep the camioneta on the road. Here he had to drive mostly over smooth rock slabs, where the road was marked with scraped white stones and one or two rusty iron pipes. In the dips they had built up primitive banks of macadam and cement during the summer, but in a number of places these had already collapsed into shapeless heaps of rubble. The road ended at a deeply eroded ravine, across which lay a few planks of wood and on the other side, the mountain rose in a gentle, smooth slope.

Willi Mohr stopped and got out. He wedged the wheels of the camioneta with stones so that it would not blow away and walked across the primitive wooden bridge, which creaked and shook. Then he struggled on upwards and although the slope gave some lee, the rain whipped into his face. The dog followed him for the first bit, but soon turned back and lay down under the truck.

He was right at the top of the highest point and could feel the merciless force of the storm. It was impossible to stand upright, so he was forced to crouch down and hold on to a rock. Below him the cliff fell almost perpendicularly and far down below he could see the sea heaving in long dark green waves. But the distance made the waves appear astonishingly small and still. The trawler was already quite a way out, heading south-east. It was rolling violently, at intervals the green colour showing below the dirty yellow boarding, and after a while its contours blurred in the rain and swirling foam.

Willi Mohr stayed there, not looking at his watch, so he had no idea how long for. It stopped raining, but the heavy salt wind still seemed full of small, swirling particles of water. His clothes were wet and he began to find it hard to see. He tried lighting a cigarette, but the waxed-paper matches refused to burn. When the box was empty, he threw it away and sat with the unlit cigarette in his mouth until it soaked through and disintegrated.

He turned round once and saw the woman standing about fifty yards away, leaning against the wind, her shawl tightly wound round her body.

About an hour or an hour-and-a-half had gone by when the trawler again appeared in the mist, at first an indistinct blur and then with sharper contours. It had the wind behind it and was not rolling so badly as before. Willi Mohr focused sharply and although his eyes were aching, he could see that the fishing-boat was towing something. A moment later the calamary boat was quite distinguishable, and he got to his feet and had stretched out his neck quite instinctively.

The trawler came nearer and nearer and rounded the point. He

117

could practically see straight down into it and there were a number of people on deck, but the distance was too great to recognize anyone. The boat vanished under the point and all he could hear was the sound of the engine, weak and uneven, through the storm.

When Willi Mohr turned round, the woman had vanished and he was nearly halfway to the puerto before he passed her. She was walking swiftly, with long strides and her head bowed. This time he did not bother to stop.

Willi Mohr got down to the quay before the trawler. He parked about fifteen yards from the boat's mooring-place and stayed seated in the truck, his forearms resting on the steering-wheel and his hat on the back of his head. His clothes were wet and his eyes smarted after the long wait on the top of the mountain. Then he heard the engine, weak and halting, through the suppressed roar from the sea, and then the top of the mast grew visible, a slim perpendicular line above the parapet.

The cabo and the harbour-master came out from one of the bars and crossed the concrete. They stood by the edge of the quay and waited. The cabo was searching for something in his jacket and there was a glimpse of an automatic pistol he was carrying under his rain cape.

The trawler rounded the lighthouse and was approaching swiftly, towing the calamary boat, and Pedro Alemany was already visible standing in the bows. At his side stood Santiago, his foot up on the side and one hand on the stay of the bowsprit.

So I've made a fool of myself, thought Willi Mohr.

The engine stopped and the trawler slid silently through the water. Before it touched the quayside, Santiago Alemany jumped up on to the bowsprit and then ashore. He fended off the boat from the quay as he fastened the rope round a bollard. Although he must have seen Willi Mohr in the camioneta, he did not once look in his direction.

On board the boat Pedro Alemany, the two civil guards and some of the crew were clearly visible. The others must be below decks. One guard jumped ashore, heavily and clumsily in his big boots, and began to report to the cabo. One of the crew dropped the anchor from the stern. The cabo listened and stroked his

118

small moustache with the tip of his forefinger. Santiago was talking somewhat subduedly to the harbour-master.

The doors to the cabin steps opened and Ramon's head and shoulders appeared. He came up on deck, small and bandy-legged, and looked for a moment past Willi Mohr. His face was quite expressionless, but down his left cheek he had a long coagulated scratch, running from the corner of his eye right down to his neck.

Some other people had come down to the quay, among them the bearded Finn who had fought in the bar.

The door down to the cabin steps was not opened again.

Someone hauled the calamary boat alongside. Some water was splashing about in the bottom of it, but not much.

The civil guard was still talking to his superior officer. Willi Mohr heard the word *desastre* over and over again. He knew it meant accident.

The cabo looked reluctantly towards the truck, then appeared to summon up his courage and walked over to Willi Mohr. He was poking thoughtfully at his moustache, as if hunting for suitable words.

'Catastrofe,' he said. 'Vuestros amigos . . .'

He stopped and pointed down into the water with a finger stained yellow with nicotine. Then he made a quick sign of the cross.

He saw that he had succeeded in making himself understood and went on talking, but Willi Mohr no longer understood what he was saying, and indeed was not even listening.

He was looking over the cabo's shoulder and he saw Ramon Alemany jump down on to the quay. Someone on board handed over a flat basket and when Ramon put it down on the ground, Willi Mohr could see a lot of small red fish and one which was large and greenish. Ramon lit a cigarette and picked up the basket again. The Alemany brothers walked across the quay and their father followed just behind them. Farther up, by the houses, stood the woman with the shawl, crossing herself continuously. When the men reached the house, she embraced them one after another and then all four vanished into an alleyway. Neither Santiago nor Ramon had even glanced at the man in the truck.

Willi looked at the cabo again. He had fallen silent and

119

seemed irresolute and unhappy. He looked round for help and waved to the Finn, who hesitantly came up to the camioneta The Finn spoke a little German.

'Your friends have been drowned,' he said.

Willi Mohr nodded.

'I don't understand all that well either,' said the Finn apologetically, 'but I think he's saying that both he and a family called something like Ale . . .'

'Alemany,' said the cabo.

'Yes, that's right, that they're sorry about the accident, that is.'

Willi Mohr nodded.

He was still sitting leaning over the wheel, his straw hat on the back of his head.

'What happened?' said Willi Mohr.

The cabo talked for a while, trying to explain something with a great deal of gesturing.

'He says the dinghy—bote is a dinghy, isn't it?—well, that the dinghy capsized in the storm. Out by some islands somewhere.'

The cabo saluted and went back to the group by the trawler. The Finn stood there hesitantly.

'What a hellish business,' he said. 'Would you like to come back with me for a while? I've got some brandy at home. I mean . . .'

'No, thank you,' said Willi Mohr.

He straightened up and jumped down from the truck. Before turning the handle, he said:

'What time did the wind begin to get up yesterday?'

'About six, I think . . .'

The camioneta started first turn. Willi Mohr climbed up and pushed the dog away from the pedals. He nodded to the Finn and drove away.

Dusk fell swiftly and when Willi Mohr arrived at the house in Barrio Son Jofre, it was already dark. He unlocked the door, went in and hunted out the lamp, but when he tried to light it he saw that the paraffin had run out, so he fetched a stub of candle from the kitchen, lit it and slowly walked upstairs, where there was a whole packet of candles. Before he went down again, he

120

raised the bottle with the candle in it and looked round the room. On the chair by the bed lay Dan's manuscript and a book he had evidently been reading two nights ago. Siglinde's green dress and a bra were hanging on a nail in the wall, and below them stood a pair of shoes which looked as if she had just stepped out of them. One or two of Willi's and Dan's shirts were hanging over a string by one window, shirts she had washed the day before. They ought to be dry by now. A packet of cotton-wool, Siglinde's blue bathing-costume, Dan's swimming trunks, a comb and a hairbrush lay on the window-sill.

Willi Mohr went down again to the ground floor. He lit two candles and put one on the stairs and the other on the floor by the mattress. Then he went out into the kitchen, poured water into the dog bowl and took out the packet of butcher's offal Siglinde had bought the day before. He chose a few good bits for the dog and patted her absently on the back as she ate. He blew out the candle and put it on the stone bench and then went back into the room.

He stood quite still and looked round.

His latest picture was on the floor by the chair where he usually sat and painted, beside it a bottle of turpentine and the jar of brushes. Just inside the door stood the paraffin can Siglinde had put there before she had left.

The cat came through the hole in the outer door and wove itself round his legs. Then it went out into the dark again.

Willi Mohr went over to the door and kicked the paraffin can as hard as he could. It flew up the stairs and knocked over the candle, then bounced noisily back down into the room again. He picked up the turpentine bottle and flung it with all his strength against the wall. The bottle broke and pieces of glass flew through the air. He rushed across the room and tore one of his canvases off the wall and with a great effort ripped it in two and crumpled up the pieces. He tripped over the metal can, and lifting it up with both hands, he crashed it time and time again against the stone floor. When it was completely buckled and crushed, he threw it away and went over to the little mirror on the wall by the door. Indistinctly, he made out his own sullen, closed face and his swollen, bloodshot eyes. He raised his hand and smashed the mirror with his fist. The candle on the floor

121

was still burning. He stamped on it and then flung himself down on the mattress.

Willi Mohr lay on his face in the dark, his chest heaving and great jerks convulsing his body.

3

The calamary boat lay drawn up at the far end of the harbour and several people were standing round looking at it. The village blacksmith and one of his apprentices had unscrewed the engine from its bed and were just lifting it on to a hand-cart. Ramon Alemany was squatting on the starboard side and was strengthening the props. He did not notice Willi approaching the boat and did not see him until Willi bent down on the other side, and their eyes met. Ramon turned his eyes away and hammered with renewed energy at a wedge between the props.

'Guten Tag,' said Willi Mohr, stretching out his hand beneath the keel.

Ramon responded hesitantly and weakly to the handshake, his face half-turned away, but he could not hide the long scratch down his left cheek. The edges of the wound were inflamed and red and his whole cheek was discoloured with some kind of greenish-yellow antiseptic.

Neither of them said anything more and Ramon went on listlessly fiddling about among the props. Suddenly he got up and disappeared from sight.

Willi Mohr stayed where he was and scanned the planking, which was not noticeably damaged. Then he heaved himself up on to the side and continued the inspection. There was nothing in particular to be seen there either. The inside of the boat seemed exactly as it had been when it had lain by the quay that morning two days before.

He jumped down and walked slowly away. The people standing about stepped to one side, almost respectfully, and he did not look at them.

The smithy was the village workshop and lay on the western edge by the road to the town, a large shed of corrugated iron,

122

originally built by the army but now turned over to civilian use.

The blacksmith was a Catalonian, a large man with reddish hair, strong arms and a bull neck. He had mounted the engine on to a work-bench and was already on his way towards the door to shoe an emaciated donkey waiting outside, its head hanging. On the cart beside the work-bench lay the parts of the engine-cover, which the smith had unscrewed and brought with him.

Willi Mohr went up and looked at the engine. He had a mechanical mind and had also been able to pick up quite a bit about small boats during his years at Gotenhafen. This engine was a Spanish one, rather old, but not very different from types used in other countries. It was immediately very easy to see why it had ceased to function.

The fuel pipe had broken off just by the nut, which was deformed and crushed in the thread, and the piston rod was bent and almost broken.

This was undeniably irreparable damage for anyone at sea with no access to spare parts and proper tools.

He picked up the parts of the wooden cover and fitted them over the engine. The box was more or less whole and had no noticeable scratches or marks on it. So the lid had not been on when the engine was damaged.

Willi Mohr pushed out his lower lip a fraction and took the wooden pieces off again. He ran his forefinger lightly over the piston rod and felt that the metal was lumpy and scratched round the break. The fuel pipe was cleanly broken off and the surfaces of the break were fresh.

He took a spanner from the bench and unscrewed the plugs. There was some oil on them, presumably sufficient to make the spark uneven. He put the plugs back again and straightened his back.

The smith had finished shoeing the donkey and came back to his bench. He shook his head.

'Terrible,' he said.

Willi Mohr nodded.

'Mucha agua,' said the smith, gesturing towards the engine, 'muy malo.'

This was right too. The engine had recently been in contact

123

with water. It seemed almost unnaturally clean. But presumably the man had meant something quite different.

It doesn't fit, thought Willi Mohr, as he left the shed. It doesn't fit at all. The time doesn't fit either. Nothing fits.

On his way back to the truck he caught sight of Santiago Alemany and he quickened his steps. But they had seen each other from a long way away and before they could meet, the Spaniard had turned into an alleyway and disappeared.

An hour later Willi Mohr was sitting on the steps outside the house in Barrio San Jofre looking in his notebook. At the top of the page he had written:

17th December, 8.30 p.m. They have been drowned. Found out about it at seven yesterday. Behaved strangely and spoilt a painting and a paraffin can. The time doesn't fit.

He unscrewed the cap of his fountain pen and added a few more sentences.

Should have been back at two o'clock. Wind got up at six. Fuel pipe broken. Engine cover whole. Scratch on Ramon's face. They seemed frightened.

He thought for a few minutes and then added three words:

Perhaps they're ashamed.

He stayed there for a while looking down at what he had written, and then he closed the notebook and put it into his hip pocket.

'It still doesn't fit,' he said to himself.

The next day Willi Mohr drove to Santa Margarita and sought out the builder who was the real owner of the camioneta. The man had hired the truck to Dan Pedersen for a lump sum a year ago and evidently had not reckoned on seeing it again. He shook his head doubtfully, but after the customary protests, thrust the money Willi Mohr gave him into his pocket. Then he offered Willi a cognac in the square and laughed and said:

'Y los amigos? Otra vez en Noruega?'

He apparently thought that Dan and Siglinde had gone home and no one sought to disillusion him.

It rained all the way back and Willi Mohr was soon soaked. He had paid five times as much as Dan Pedersen had for the old truck, but he had got used to having the camioneta always at hand and did not want to be without it.

And he was convinced that he would be needing it.

He used the truck every day during that time. So long as the bars were open, he was to be found in the puerto, and at nights he lay on the mattress in the house in Barrio Son Jofre, his head propped against his hand and the notebook open in front of him. Now and again he wrote something in it. The door was always locked and the paraffin lamp spread its trembling yellow light round the bare room.

Bit by bit, he drew out small fragments from his memories of the past months and fitted them into his terrible puzzle.

4

Early in the morning, one day between Christmas and the New Year, two consular officials from the provincial capital came to deal with Dan's and Siglinde's possessions. They brought a civil guard with them from the local guard-post to show them the way, and drove a large jeep with foreign number plates.

Willi Mohr had just got up and was standing in the kitchen washing himself. He pulled on his faded brown shirt, which had been with him since the days of the Hitler Jugend, and went out to the strangers, who had been discreet enough to stay out on the steps, although the door was open.

The consular officials shook hands and handed round American cigarettes. Then they went upstairs and Willi Mohr helped them tie up numbered cardboard boxes full of all the loose articles, and put them all into sacks. When they had carried down the sacks and trunks and loaded them into the jeep, the room upstairs was empty except for the bedstead.

One of the officials looked round downstairs and said: 'Is there anything left now, or have we got the lot?'

He spoke excellent German.

'The lamp,' said Willi Mohr.

'It looks as if it's needed here more than anywhere else,' said the man dryly. 'Nothing else?'

'The dog and the cat.'

'Their relatives in Norway would certainly be overjoyed if we

125

sent the menagerie to them as well. If you don't want to keep them, we can arrange for them to be shot.'

'I'll keep them,' said Willi Mohr.

The official took out a notebook with black cover, licked his thumb and leafed through it.

'Have you any claims against their estate?' he said.

'I beg your pardon?'

'Did they owe you any money?'

Willi Mohr glanced at the wall by the kitchen door, where Siglinde had kept her accounts. Above the long columns of figures and involved divisions she had written in her clear backward-sloping handwriting: We now owe Willi 1,125 marks.

He shook his head.

'No?' said the man. 'Otherwise they seemed to have had debts all over the place. Not exactly an orderly lot.'

He scribbled something in his notebook.

'These things will be impounded,' he added, pointing with his pen towards the heap outside the door. 'Not that they're worth anything . . .'

He put his notebook back into his pocket and held out his hand to say goodbye.

'Is the inquiry still going on?' said Willi Mohr.

'The inquiry? That was over a long time ago. The case is quite clear, don't you think?'

Willi Mohr nodded absently.

'An ordinary accident; nothing much to make a fuss about,' said the official. 'But the police down there have made a report. Haven't you read it?'

'I don't understand the language very well.'

'We've had it done in English too, for simplicity's sake. I think I've a copy out there, if you'd like to borrow it.'

'Thank you.'

The man went out to the jeep and fetched a black document case. He took out two typed sheets of paper clipped together.

'This is the official report,' he said. 'You can keep it if you like, as I've had several copies made.'

He shook hands and went out to his colleague, who had just finished loading.

Then they drove away, and Willi Mohr could hear the sound

126

of their engine for a long while as the jeep laboured up the long, twisting bends.

When it was quiet again, he put the paper down on the sacking in the corner, where he kept his clothes and rucksack and some other things. Then he went out into the kitchen, took off his shirt and went on with his morning toilet. He washed himself with soft soap and cold water and cleaned his teeth with coarse salt. The largest of the pieces of mirror he had kept and wedged up against a joist in the kitchen wall, and as he shaved, once or twice he met his own indifferent gaze and thought that he looked much as usual.

Before he left the house, he took out his wallet and counted his money. It would last for at the most four more months and he would have to be very economical.

Willi Mohr thrust out his lower lip, folded up the typed report and put it in his wallet.

In the puerto, he left the camioneta on the quay and went from bar to bar until he found Santiago and Ramon. They were sitting in Jacinto's, playing cards with a couple of fishermen. When Willi Mohr came in, Santiago looked up and nodded to him, but returned at once to the card-game. His brother peered up at him through his fringe of hair but could not manage a greeting. The air in the place was raw and chilly and Jacinto had put a large brazier of glowing coal in the middle of the floor.

Willi Mohr sat down by the door so that he would be able to see the faces of the Alemany brothers and be sure that they did not leave the bar without having to walk close by him. He ordered café con leche with his breakfast roll, but was in no hurry to eat, simply sitting still with his legs crossed, watching the card-players. On two occasions Santiago raised his head and looked fleetingly across at him, once with a weak, joyless smile. Ramon stared stubbornly down at his cards.

Willi Mohr ate the roll. Then he pushed away the mug, took the carbon copy of the report out of his wallet and spread it out in front of him on the table. He propped his head in his hand and began to read. As he was not particularly good at English, it took him some time to spell his way through the document.

Report on accident at sea. At a bathing accident which

127

occurred here on the 15th of this month, two foreign citizens lost their lives, Daniel Olaf Pedersen, born 1925 in Avendal (?) and his wife Birgit Siglinde Wolf (?)—Pedersen, born 1929 in (information not available), both Norwegian citizens of Protestant faith, entered Spain via Irun border-post on 12th August 1952 with entry visas numbers 63 428 and 63 429, issued by the Spanish Consulate in Paris, France, later extended by General Commissioner for Security, reference numbers 738/52, 739/52, 926/52, 927/52, 181/53, 182/53, 539/53, 540/53, 897/53, 898/53, 1012/53 and 1013/53. Since 4th September this year Dan Olaf Pedersen and Birgit Siglinde Wolf (?)—Pedersen have not been resident in this police district.

Other circumstances: On 16th December this year at 2.00 p.m. a smaller fishing-boat with four persons on board, which had on the previous day gone out on a fishing trip, was reported missing to the senior officer of this civil guard-post. The previous day the boat had been observed by a patrol between 8.30 a.m. and 9.00 a.m. moving in the general direction of the group of islands Islotes Redondos, for which reason it can be with certainty assumed that it was heading for these aforementioned islands. A motor-barque belonging to the harbour authorities and manned by personnel from the civil guard was sent out to search the area, but was forced to return to harbour on account of very bad weather conditions, where it arrived at 3.00 p.m. At 5 p.m. fishing-boat number 13–1698 *La Virgen Dolores* was sent out, manned by volunteers and personnel from the civil guard, to Islotes Redondos, where at 6.30 p.m. two survivors were rescued and taken on board, at which it was learnt that Dan Olaf Pedersen and Birgit Siglinde Wolf (?)—Pedersen had lost their lives through an accident some time during the afternoon of the previous day. The deceased's bodies could not be traced.

Testimony of Driver Santiago Alemany Ventosa:

Together with his brother and Daniel Olaf Pedersen and Birgit Siglinde Wolf (?)—Pedersen, he had during the morning gone to Islotes Redondos to fish. When the weather worsened during the day, he had several times suggested that they should return, but for various reasons the return journey was postponed until the afternoon. Both the foreigners insisted that they should bathe off one of the islands, although the witness several times advised them not to. During the bathe Daniel Olaf Pedersen and his wife took the dinghy which was being towed and despite repeated warnings rowed it out of the bay and close to a point which lay open to the sea. There the dinghy was hit by an unusually strong wave and capsized, at which Senor and Senora Pedersen were thrown in the water. Witness, who together with his brother was in the fishing-boat, at once tried to start the engine, but the engine, which had been giving trouble earlier, refused to function, and when they finally reached the place, the two persons had gone under and could not be found. Witness and his brother stayed at the place for more than an hour, during which time the weather worsened even more and then a wave hit the boat and the engine again stopped. Witness presumes that the dinghy was smashed by the waves and sank or drifted out to sea. On the island where witness and his brother took refuge there was good lee and access to water and provisions. During the day they tried to get the engine going, but did not succeed. Witness maintains that the conditions at the place of the accident were so bad that there would have been little possibility of saving the two bathers, even if the engine had functioned normally.

Witness could not give exact time of accident as neither he nor his brother had a watch, but he estimates it as between 3 p.m. and 5 p.m.

This testimony is confirmed in all essentials by fisherman Ramon Alemany Ventosa, who was at the time constantly in the company of the witness and similarly witnessed the accident.

17th December 1954
Puesto de Policia no. 413
Zona Oriental S.F.P.D.
(Signature)

'Not a word of truth in it,' said Willi Mohr slowly to himself. He did not feel especially surprised or angry, but more as if he had been faced with an already known fact. Possibly he was surprised that the story had been so clumsily put together and was so obviously untrue.

He raised his head quickly and looked at the men at the other table and he caught Ramon Alemany's gaze for perhaps a tenth of a second before it turned away. It was wild and frightened and then the moment passed and Ramon was again staring at his cards. Although he was leaning forward, and despite the bad light, Willi Mohr could see the thin white scar from the scratch down his cheek.

Santiago nudged his brother jokingly and said something. Then he put his cards together and laid them down. Both the other players began to argue loudly and aggressively, but Santiago flung a few small coins down on to the table and got up. He and Ramon walked towards the exit and just as they passed the table by the door, he looked straight into Willi's eyes, coldly and calmly.

Willi Mohr stayed there three or four minutes more and drank his cold coffee. Then he rose and began to go the round. He found them in a seedy little bar at the end of the quay, a place where there were very rarely any visitors. It was run by an old man who watered the wine and sold it cheaply to strange fishermen.

Santiago and Ramon were standing by the dirty little bar counter, drinking red wine. They were talking quietly to each other, but fell silent when Willi Mohr came into the room.

They daren't even rely on the fact that I can't understand what they're saying, he thought.

He nodded and went to stand beside them. Santiago called for another glass and Willi Mohr let the old man bring it and put it down, but he did not touch it. After a minute or so, Santiago said something to him, and he shrugged his shoulders to show that he had not understood. Ramon stared stubbornly down into his glass. Suddenly he emptied it in one draught, turned towards the door and walked out. Santiago stayed for a while, then he too left, without saying anything more and without looking at the man at his side.

Willi Mohr took his glass and went and stood in the doorway to watch the Alemany brothers, who had joined each other again some way up the quay. He knew that he had driven them indoors and that he need not follow them any longer.

130

They would probably go home now.

'We're getting into a routine with this now,' he said to the dog.

Willi Mohr stayed in the puerto the whole afternoon, but Ramon and Santiago did not show themselves again that day.

He read through the report again, and was again struck by the fact that it was so obviously false and easy to refute.

It surprised and confused him, and he felt disappointed and exhausted, as if he had used all his strength to burst open a door.

To go from bar to bar looking for the Alemany brothers had been an uncomplicated, almost mechanical occupation, and now he missed it. At the same time, it irritated him that he could not say definitely why he had done it.

He had a feeling that many small thoughts were slowly being drawn together into something liberatingly simple, but he doubted whether it would ever find the strength to burst free from his mind. Presumably it would stay there behind the wall and wither away. Perhaps it would drive him mad.

He drove home at about ten o'clock. The camioneta engine was running badly and he decided to begin overhauling it the next day, while he still had enough money for spare parts.

When Willi Mohr went into the house in Barrio Son Jofre, the silence and loneliness fell round him. It was then that the thought occurred to him that he was the only person who could refute Santiago Alemany's story. If there had not been a translation of the report, he would never have been able to read it and it must seem quite plausible to anyone else.

No one had reckoned with him. Neither with his memory nor his almost abnormal memory for detail, details which to a great extent he was the only one to know about.

Willi Mohr stood in the darkness, talking to himself. He asked: 'How did it happen? What did they do? And why?'

He held his breath for ten seconds, as if awaiting a reply, but nothing happened.

He undressed and crept down between the damp sheets. His head thumped and it was a long time before he fell asleep.

131

5

He jerked awake and sat up, violently, as if a cry or a shout had torn apart the silence and was ringing round the room.

It was all quite clear.

The Alemany brothers had killed Siglinde and Dan.

Naturally he knew why they had done it. Who would know better than he?

Now they were frightened and their fear was not without cause.

He would force them to confess, no matter how or when.

Then he would kill them.

Everything was quite simple.

Never before had he thought such clear and simple thoughts.

Willi Mohr lay down on the mattress. He felt completely calm and fell asleep almost at once, as if he had just been freed from some great uncertainty or recovered from a long illness.

It was in the middle of the night and the room was quite dark.

6

Willi Mohr underwent the change very quickly, but there was no one who knew him well enough to notice it. He was seen daily in the puerto, where he sat in bars or wandered about in the alleyways, a thin, lonely foreigner, who never did anything which aroused attention.

He did not seek the company of the Alemany brothers and was never together with either of them, but he was very often to be found somewhere in the vicinity of them. When they visited one of the bars, he was usually sitting in the same place, and seldom left before them. If they went to another place, it would not be long before he appeared there too. He was never seen drinking spirits, but he could sit for hours over a cup of coffee or a mineral water. Sometimes he appeared to be studying his surroundings, but he mostly stared straight ahead, his blue eyes quite expressionless.

132

He had a black and white mongrel with him and drove an old re-built Fiat truck, which he used to park on the quay where everyone could see it. In the shops where he bought things, it was noticed that he was learning more and more of the language.

At the beginning of April, he left the country as a temporary member of the crew of a private yacht. Barely two months later, at the end of May, he came back and again took up residence in the house in Barrio Son Jofre.

After that he never again visited the puerto.

Part Five

1

Willi Mohr was tired after the police interrogation and slept nearly all day. He woke at about eight in the evening feeling hungry, and as soon as he had washed and dressed, he went up into the town to eat. The eating-place he usually frequented was small and seedy, in a narrow side-street off the Avenue, up by the church. It was run by a couple of old maids and was mostly frequented by junior non-commissioned officers feeling the need for a change from army fare. The food was uninviting but cheap. Only two courses were served, either a kind of soup with green leaves floating in it, or black pudding with rice. The soup was thin and not very nourishing but the rice oozed with mutton-fat and refined olive-oil, so anyone eating both courses did not need to leave the table hungry. For three months, June, July and August, Willi Mohr had gone there every evening, but then his money had come to an end and he had been forced to live on bread and salted sardines bought on credit at the tienda. This did not matter all that much, as he was more or less indifferent to what he ate, but he was not domestic and did not like messing about with food.

Although he had paid his bill at the tienda, he still had some money left from Santiago Alemany's visit four days before, so he ate both courses. There were no other customers in the dirty little café and both the old women served him at table; he had not been there for a long time and their attentions were both ridiculous and moving.

Willi Mohr took his time. He wiped the grease and oil carefully off the plate with small pieces of bread and picked his teeth thoroughly and lengthily before getting up to say goodnight. The old women had already been paid and had withdrawn into a

corner where they were sitting like black shadows, silently waiting.

As soon as he had stepped out into the street, they locked the
door behind him.

It was already eleven o'clock. Willi Mohr went to the square
and drank coffee outside the Central, sitting there until everyone
else had gone and the proprietor had begun to yawn. Then he
went home to bed.

This was more or less his daily routine. True, now and again
he painted for a while on the picture of the house and cactuses,
but he doubted it would ever be more complete than it already
was and he had no desire to begin another one.

For four months he had done virtually nothing whatsoever.

He was waiting.

Before he had been waiting for Santiago Alemany to come to
the house in Barrio Son Jofre.

Now Santiago had been there and Willi Mohr was still
waiting.

For the visit to be repeated.

2

Today, thought Willi Mohr, I must do it.

He closed the notebook and put it in his back pocket and
went out into the kitchen.

He thrust his hand under the stone bench and one by one
lifted out the puppies, carried them into the room and put them
down on the floor in the patch of sun by the stairs. Then he sat
on the bottom stair and looked at them. There were three in all.
At first there had been four, but one had died almost at once and
the bitch had pushed it out on to the kitchen floor. Now she had
come in with him and was standing on one side wagging her tail.
She trusted him and had manifested this trust by licking his
hand every time he had thrust it in under the bench to take one
of her puppies.

The cat was sitting a little farther up the stairs watching the
scene with astonishment and disapproval.

The puppies whined and crawled slowly away in different directions. They were already old enough to begin showing some individual personality; their eyes were open and one of them whined more often and on quite a different note from the others. Two of them were black and white, the third brown and white.

The brown one would probably be an ugly dog. It was dirty brown on one side and white on the other, and in the white patches were a number of scattered small liver-brown spots.

One of the black and white ones looked very odd. It had a circular spot round its right eye, black legs and white feet. That was the one which was always whining. The other had a black head and back and was undoubtedly the least unfortunate in its markings.

It had taken Willi Mohr no more than thirty seconds to decide which of the puppies had the best markings, but nevertheless he still sat watching them.

He was no longer sure whether he accepted that markings were the best way of judging them.

After a while he got up, went out into the kitchen and fetched a basket. Then he sat down again and looked at the pups as they strayed uncertainly round in the patch of sunlight.

He lifted up the brown one and held it in his hand before putting it into the basket. It felt warm and small and softly alive.

The bitch sat there, quite unmoved.

After pondering for a few more minutes, he lifted up both the other puppies and sat there with one in each hand. Finally he put the black one into the basket and put the other one down by his feet. It immediately fell over and yelped shrilly as it scrabbled round the floor. It was the one with the spot over one eye.

Willi Mohr watched the chosen puppy, but now and again looked down into the basket, where the other two had crept close to one another and fallen asleep.

Suddenly he made an exchange. He put the pup with the spot round its eye into the basket and took out the brown one instead. It woke at once and began to crawl round, whining.

The bitch came up and licked it.

'No, this simply can't go on,' he mumbled.

He changed the dog again and put the brown one in the basket and the one with the spot round its eye on the floor, but this

137

manoeuvre confused him even more. He scratched his head and put the third pup into the basket too. The bitch wagged her tail and stared at him with her stupid brown eyes.

'Oh, shit,' he said.

He pulled the basket towards him and placed it between his legs, closed his eyes and thrust his hand into the basket, taking one pup out at random. It was the brown one.

He went out into the kitchen and put it under the stone bench. The bitch came with him and busily scratched away round it.

Before he left the kitchen, he sought out the few bits of rope he usually used for tying up brushwood, then placed them on top of the puppies, swung the basket over his shoulder and went out.

Behind the house was a rubbish heap and a few low, dusty cactus bushes and a little farther on was a stone wall which bordered a terraced field containing ten or so withered almond trees. One the other side of the field rose the mountain, steep and stony, thinly overgrown with spindly pines.

Willi Mohr walked across the terraced field, crunching old almond cases and dry lumps of yellow clay under his feet. Then he began to climb upwards through the stones. Now and again he heard the puppies whining in the basket.

He had to go quite far up the mountain to find any pieces of wood worth tying up and taking home, and the higher he went the more open grew his view over the countryside. When he turned round he could see the town lying below him, flat and dismal and yellowish-grey in the dip between the mountains, and also the road down to the sea, a winding white strip between the ridges, the glittering water far away and even the houses in the puerto, where he had not been for so long.

He climbed on until he came to a group of thickish pine trees which grew out from the stones below a perpendicular, rough cliff wall. There he put down the basket and stopped to get his breath back. The puppy with the spot over its eye was whining all the time, quietly, abandonedly.

There was quite a lot of brushwood here, so he took out the bits of rope and put them down on a flat stone. Then he took the basket to a point about three yards from the cliff. He took out the almost black puppy, looked absently at it and then swung it

138

swiftly against the rock wall. It smacked as if he had thrown a split rubber ball, and the animal fell and died immediately.

The other puppy was still whining, but fell silent the moment he picked it up. He avoided looking at it, but weighed it in his hand and it felt the same as the other one, small and softly alive. It lay on its back and fitted exactly into his half-open hand. He raised his arm to shoulder height and drew back his hand, but either he unconsciously held back or the animal slipped, for the throw was crooked and feeble and the puppy spun round in the air and bounced a bit away from the cliff wall.

He stood still without moving for a long time before he could bring himself to go forward and see where it had fallen.

It had slipped down into a deep wedge-shaped crack between two relatively large chunks of rock, and when Willi Mohr leant forward and peered down, he saw that it was still alive. The pup with the black spot round its eye was lying quite far down with its paws in the air. It moved its legs a little and he could see small pale trickles of blood running from its mouth and nose, which was pink and small and slightly wrinkled.

He put his arm down the crack but however hard he tried, he could not reach the puppy, not even with the tips of his fingers. It was moving more now and a feeble little whine could be heard from below.

Willi Mohr found a broken branch and stuck it down the crack. He could poke the animal but it had evidently got wedged between the stones and he could not move it. He threw away the branch and heaved at the outer rock to see if he could widen the crack, but the rock would not move outwards. But he could move it inwards so that the crack grew narrower.

He took a step back and put his right foot against the jagged stone and pressed on it with all his strength. Slowly it tipped over and he thought he heard the puppy yelp once and then it was crushed. He thrust his foot against the stone, keeping it there for a long time, then let it go and it swung back again.

It was a long time before he had collected himself sufficiently to return to the flat stone where he had put the bits of rope.

Then he slowly and systematically gathered up a large heap of dead branches. He tied them together, slung the bundle on to his back and began to climb down.

He was in no hurry, and about half-way down stopped to smoke a cigarette. As he sat there, he saw a civil guard pushing his bike up the alleyway towards Barrio Son Jofre. Despite the distance, he could see quite clearly that the man had his carbine over his back and that he stopped in the middle of the hill to fan his face with his cap. When the civil guard reached the house, he leant his bicycle against the outhouse and vanished from sight, presumably to bang on the door.

Willi Mohr finished his cigarette, then lifted his bundle of brushwood on to his back again and went on down. He kept his eye on the spot where the civil guard should appear, but the man did not show himself. The bicycle was still there, but after a few minutes he had got so far down that the outhouse was hidden by the almond trees and cactus bushes.

He crossed the crackling field and rounded the house. There was no one in the yard and the bicycle had vanished.

Willi Mohr shrugged his shoulders and went into the house.

On the floor inside the doorway lay a letter, apparently pushed in through the cat-hole by the civil guard. There was nothing written on it, only a blurred stamp in the top right-hand corner. Willi Mohr opened the envelope and took out his passport.

He turned over the pages but there were no new stamps or remarks. Then he shrugged again and put his passport into his back pocket, alongside the notebook.

3

It was the first of November. Twenty-four days had gone by since the police interrogation and nothing had happened to Willi Mohr.

The days had grown shorter, the nights colder, and it had rained twice during the last weeks, but otherwise everything was as before.

His money had long since come to an end and he had made no effort to acquire any more, although he could well have written to Hugo Spohler, who still owed him quite a sum. The tienda still gave him credit, as did the Café Central. His bills slowly mounted, although he had reduced his purchases to an absolute minimum and lived exclusively on bread, salted sardines and figs. Now and again he bought a box of Ideales, and by smoking very seldom and saving the ends for his pipe, he could make a packet last several days. He regularly increased his bill at the bar in the square by having a small cup of coffee every evening.

With the exception of the civil guard who had pushed the envelope containing his passport through the cat-hole, no one had come to the house in Barrio Son Jofre. The brown puppy had died three days after he had killed the other two, and he had thrown it on to the rubbish-heap behind the house. The dog came with him on his daily walks through the town again, and although he occasionally got bones and mouldering bits of meat for her at the tienda, she had grown much thinner, as he had himself.

Only the cat remained unchanged. It saw to its keep itself and came and went with a self-sufficiency which made it appear to be the only legitimate tenant in the house.

Willi Mohr did not do any painting, and he had also begun to be careless about some things. He was no longer so particular about washing and shaving and he seldom bothered about making his bed properly. And yet he managed to fill his days with trivial matters, fetching water, lighting the fire or collecting fuel. Unconsciously he did everything at a slower tempo than before and he had no definite impression of being unoccupied or having plenty of time.

He was waiting for Santiago Alemany, but he was not impatient and neither was he feeling nervous about the meeting.

He was convinced that Santiago would come back some time and he had already decided how he would behave when he did.

He would shoot him immediately. Then the matter would be over and his part of the problem out of the way.

He had no further plans for the future and nothing which tied him to this place, so to postpone the execution would simply be pointless.

On the first of November, Willi Mohr got up at nine o'clock. He lit the fire, boiled some water and drank it with two spoons of

141

sugar and half a roll left over from the previous day. Then he went out and relieved himself behind the camioneta, which was standing in the outhouse, filthy and dusty and unusable.

The tyres were flat and the engine would not start. When he had come back from his trip in May and driven up from the puerto to the town, he had forgotten to put any water in the radiator. The engine had got overheated without his noticing and the steam had blown the gasket. He had only just managed to get back and since then the truck had stood there, not because he could not afford to repair it, but because he considered he no longer had any need for it. Now the chickens lived in it and both the engine and the seats were white with their droppings.

Willi Mohr buttoned his fly and went into tackle his day's work, the cleaning of his pistol, something he had thought about doing for a long time.

He locked the door and got out the gun from its place under the mattress. There was not much light in the room but what came through the cat-hole and the cracks round the door was quite sufficient.

He spread a piece of cloth out on the floor, sat down on the bottom stair and appraisingly weighed the pistol in his hand. It felt cold and reassuring.

First he pressed the restraining catch and took out the magazine. There were seven rounds in it. He ejected the cartridges and put them in a row in front of him. Another cartridge remained in the breech, so he drew back the action and caught it in his hand. He put it down beside the others, poked out the spring from the magazine and tested the tension in it before putting it down. Then he picked up the cartridges one by one and looked them over carefully.

Willi Mohr had a reserve magazine too. It lay tucked away in the bottom of the rucksack, but as he had no intention of using it, he let it lie there.

When he had looked at the cases without finding any scratches or other visible defects, he set about the pistol itself. He removed the barrel and held it up to the square of light from the door. The bore was oiled. Then he examined the breech face, tried out the striker against his thumb, pressing the spring together, which was hard and tense, and laid the things down on the cloth, together with the screws and pins and cartridges and the parts of the magazine.

The cat, which had been lying asleep among the bedclothes, woke when two of the metal parts clinked together. At once it was inquisitive, and after stretching itself a couple of times, it went over to the stairs and sat on a corner of the cloth, its head on one side, eyeing the dismantled weapon. Then it raised its right fore-paw, dabbed cautiously at the spring, and then sat still again, staring with interest at the spiral wobbling back and forth. Suddenly the cat whipped out its paw again and hit the spring, which rolled across the floor with a metallic rattle. The cat crouched, took two long leaps, landing on it with its claws distended, stood on its back legs with the spring between its forepaws and then threw it backwards over its head.

Willi Mohr sat still, his hands hanging between his legs, and watched the animal playing with the spring. Suddenly the cat lost interest, yawned and went back to the mattress. The spring rolled away into a corner of the room and lay still. Willi got up and went and fetched it.

He got out the oil can and some soft rags from his rucksack and carefully cleaned all the parts before greasing them again. Then he dried the barrel and once again held it up to the light.

Willi Mohr looked for so long down the bore that all sense of proportion vanished. He saw a cold, polished steel tunnel, a reflecting corridor of terror, endlessly extended by the bore's twisting spiral.

When he finally took the barrel away from his eye, he was almost surprised to find it was so short and light and ordinary, an unassuming little object which could be carried in a breast pocket if necessary.

He put the lid on the oil-can again and began to re-assemble the pistol. Finally he slid the magazine into the butt of the gun, releasing the action to slip the first cartridge into the chamber.

He got up, put on the safety catch and then put the weapon back under the edge of the mattress, on the right and quite far down.

The pistol was a nine millimetre 1936 Walther. Willi Mohr had exchanged it for two tins of meat in Flensburg in the summer of 1945 and since then he had succeeded in smuggling it over all borders. He had never fired it, but knew both its construction and how it worked very well.

4

On the twenty-sixth of November, fifty days after the police-interrogation, Willi Mohr spent nearly all day lying on the mattress, waiting. He was weak with hunger, but did not want to go to the tienda, as the old woman had begun to look pityingly at him. When it grew dark, he went to the Café Central where he had pawned his watch. The proprietor was kind and gave him a glass of white wine and two thick slices of bread, soaked in olive oil. He ate them greedily and hurried back to the house in Barrio Son Jofre. He was afraid that Santiago might come while he was out, and dared not be away from home for any length of time.

5

During the first few days of December, the weather turned very warm, just as it had at the same time the previous year. The man in the house in Barrio Son Jofre had no calendar and did not know the date, having lost count about a week before and not bothered to ask anyone. It might have been twelve o'clock or half-past twelve, to judge by the sun.

Willi Mohr was listening to the sound of a motor-engine which had just swung up into the alleyway, and he knew that it was Santiago Alemany coming. He had already taken out his pistol and clicked off the safety catch with his thumb.

He felt calm and relaxed as he squatted down by the mattress and waited. The gun was aimed at the door and he had his finger on the trigger, but he had lowered the pistol so that the barrel was resting against the mattress. He had also pulled a piece of the blanket over the gun so that it was not visible from outside and would not give his visitor a chance either to flee or throw himself down behind the vehicle.

He would shoot immediately, but not until he was absolutely certain of hitting.

The sound rose slowly, for the alleyway was steep and careful driving was necessary round the sharp corners. The cat had already slunk into the room and taken up its listening-post by the door. Willi Mohr could see the tip of its tail slowly thrashing back and forth behind the edge of the door.

The fish-van drove up into the yard and stopped exactly opposite the open door. Santiago Alemany was sitting in the driver's seat in blue trousers and a faded striped cotton shirt. When he switched off the engine, it coughed once or twice and he listened thoughtfully to the bubbling sound from the over-heated water in the radiator. The back was loaded with fish-boxes, carefully tied-down. They were quite dry, so Willi Mohr knew that Santiago was driving with an empty load and was on his return journey from the provincial capital to the puerto.

The dog woke and rushed barking through the room, wagging her tail and running round the van.

The cat recognized the visitor and relaxed, indolently strolling out into the sun. On the step outside, it suddenly stopped and started biting itself energetically on its right foreleg.

Santiago threw his half-smoked cigarette away and climbed out of the van.

He bent down and patted the dog and when she turned over on to her back, he scratched her dutifully on the stomach.

Then he slowly walked up the two low steps and went into the room.

He stopped inside by the door and nodded at Willi Mohr. His gaze rested for a moment on the tangle of bedclothes before wandering on round the walls of the large untidy room.

His gaze rested for a long time on the picture of the house and cactuses, still standing on the easel, quite unchanged since he had last been there. When he walked over to the kitchen door, Willi Mohr saw that he had dried fish-scales on his trousers and on his right hip was a large sheathknife in his belt.

Santiago Alemany turned round and walked out of the house. He felt the top of the radiator carefully and then held on to it with his left hand while he turned the starting-handle with his right. At the third turn the engine started. He nodded to Willi

145

Mohr, climbed into the van and after fiddling with the pedals, backed out of view. Half-way down the hill, he switched the engine off and let the van free-wheel.

As he swung into the main road, the brakes squealed and the sound could be heard for a long time in the great empty silence.

Santiago Alemany had left Barrio Son Jofre.

Willi Mohr had not moved once the whole time. He was still squatting by the mattress with his right forefinger on the trigger and his hand closed round the butt, a piece of blanket covering the gun. He did not know how long the visit had lasted; whether Santiago had been there half-an-hour or perhaps only two minutes.

His calves prickled and he could feel the strain on his knees. Small white dots were dancing about in front of his eyes. He dropped the pistol and let it lie on the blanket. The palm of his hand was wet with perspiration and he wiped it on his trouser-leg.

Willi Mohr rose, stiffly and unsteadily, and went and sat on the doorstep, his elbows on his thighs and his head in his hands.

In front of the steps was a large dark patch of oil slowly spreading out over the cobblestones.

He thought: It didn't come off.

This was his first conscious reflection since he had heard the fish-van coming up the alley. The intervening time did not exist. And yet he had had all his senses under control and assembled in an orderly way. What he remembered most clearly now was the dog lying on her back on the ground, abandoning herself to the man who was scratching her stomach.

Willi Mohr picked up the cigarette-end Santiago had thrown down and took his pipe out of his pocket. Then he carefully tore off the cigarette-paper and let the dry tobacco run into the bowl of the pipe. Not a single flake was lost. He struck a waxed-paper match that was so poor that he had to hold it with his nails close to the top. He burnt himself a little and even more so when he pressed down the tobacco with his thumb. When he had smoked it, he knocked his pipe out on the step, rose and went back into the house.

He fetched the piassava broom from the kitchen and swept the floor. Then he put the safety catch of the gun on, placed the gun

146

on the cane chair, shook his bedclothes out in the yard and made his bed properly. He carried the water-jar to the well by the road and filled it. When he had washed and shaved and changed his shirt, he put the safety catch of the gun off again and placed the weapon under the pillow. He checked whether it were easily accessible, before sitting down on the doorstep again to wait for Santiago Alemany to return.

The heat was dry and thick and suffocating, but the sun was no longer in the zenith and the shadow of the house fell over the doorstep.

Willi Mohr sat still and listened as he watched a small green lizard on the outhouse wall. It seemed hardly real in its total immobility. If one did not know its behaviour-patterns one would have thought that the animal was paralysed with terror or simply stuffed. But the lizard was waiting, and its vigilance was exemplary, just as was its action when its victim came within reach.

Thought Willi Mohr.

There was nothing at fault with his own vigilance either. Twice motor-cycles came along the road from the puerto and once the mail bus. After three hours, perhaps four, he heard the fish-van. He was quite certain about everything as it approached the cross-roads and long before it swung up into the alley towards Barrio Son Jofre.

He looked at the lizard and sat still, waiting.

Santiago Alemany had not changed his clothes or unloaded the empty boxes, but on the floor of the cabin were two large baskets which had not been there last time.

He switched off the engine and listened to it boiling. Then he got out, repeated the procedure with the dog, and chased away a few small naked children who had come running after the van from the houses down the hill.

'Good-day,' he said to the man on the steps.

Willi Mohr nodded.

Santiago knelt down and looked under the van. The oil from the engine had already made a small patch, a few yards farther on from the first one.

'This van's finished,' he said. 'I can't use it much longer.'

Willi Mohr opened his mouth, but said nothing.

'The oil's running straight through,' said Santiago.

'Get a new engine,' said Willi Mohr.

'Not good enough. It's completely finished. I hardly dare brake any more. Anyhow, you can't get hold of engines like this that are any use any longer. They're all just as bad.'

'You can get a re-bore,' said Willi Mohr.

He spoke slowly, hunting for the words.

'You've learnt to speak Spanish since last I saw you,' said Santiago.

'A little.'

'Quite a lot, I think.'

Santiago turned round and took the baskets out of the van.

'Fish,' he said, 'Salmonetes and a calamary and a few langostinos. If you'd like them?'

He sounded slightly uncertain and kept moistening his lips with his tongue.

Willi Mohr looked indifferently at the fish and thought: He's waiting for me to say no and then he knows what he's got to cope with. He doesn't really want to come here but he must, because he's got to know. If I say no or just shake my head, then he'll just put the baskets down on the ground and after a while he'll drive away and then he'll know a little more than he knew before. If I don't kill him first, of course. Now I'll let him go out into the kitchen and then I'll fetch the pistol and kill him.

His thought processes were quite clear.

'Why not?' said Willi Mohr.

Santiago picked up the baskets and went into the house.

Willi Mohr waited a short while before following him in. Santiago was kneeling in front of the fireplace, heaping wood in the ashes on the hearth. He had emptied his baskets and set the contents up in a row on the stone bench. Two loaves, oil, a twist of salt, wine, one bottle of red, one bottle of white. Five packets of Ideales. Matches. Bones for the dog. Paraffin. A large green melon.

Although Willi Mohr had not eaten anything at all for several days, he did not feel hungry.

Santiago got up and gave some bones to the dog, and she at once began to chew them. Then he poured water into the large earthenware bowl and sat with it between his legs. He drew out

148

his sheath-knife and began to clean the fish. Bit by bit he put the guts and heads and tails down on to a piece of grey paper beside him. The cat was already there, purring as it ate and twisting its head to one side to enable it to chew with its back teeth.

Willi Mohr stood leaning against the doorpost, watching. Santiago's face was calm and purposeful. He looked totally absorbed in his occupation, but now and again the tip of his tongue ran along his lips. After a while Willi Mohr shifted his gaze to the man's hands, which nimbly and skilfully manipulated the broad-bladed knife and the small red fish.

They were not the hands of a labourer, although they were sunburnt and quite large. The fingers were long and well-kept with broad, short nails. Black hairs grew on his wrists as well as on the backs of his hands. His fingers moved, swift and supple, and between them ran small streams of pale, watery blood.

His hands seemed to settle the matter.

Willi Mohr went back into the room, bent down and thrust his hand under the pillow. The butt was scored and roughened to give a better grip and when he touched it he thought about the cold shiny steel tunnel and the bullet which would rotate through it, driven forwards with relentless force.

He stopped and listened to the sounds from the kitchen. Then he withdrew his hand and looked at it. It did not look like the hand of a labourer any longer, although it was sunburnt and quite large. The fingers were long and the nails broad and cut straight across. Sparse fair hairs grew on his wrists.

He shrugged his shoulders and returned to the kitchen door.

Santiago had cleaned the fish and was just wiping out the large frying pan, which had been thrown to one side for almost a year now and had got very dirty.

Santiago muttered to himself and rubbed at the iron with a bit of grey wrapping paper. Now and again he studied the results, finally pouring in the oil and putting the fish in after dipping them in salt. Then he poured paraffin over the wood and struck a match. The fire flared up at once and burnt with a clear orange flame.

As the fish were cooked he put them into the earthenware bowl, now rinsed out and thoroughly cleaned.

All this time Willi Mohr was standing in the doorway, watching. He still did not feel hungry.

Santiago finished cooking. He put the bowl down on the beaten earth floor between the two stone seats and cleaned his knife against his trouser-leg. Then he held one of the loaves to his chest and cut it up into thick slices.

He had also taken out two of the old tin mugs and poured out the wine.

'Let's eat,' he said.

They sat opposite each other, the bowl between them.

Santiago looked at Willi Mohr once or twice, questioningly and uncertainly.

Then he raised his tin mug and nodded.

When Willi did not react, Santiago took a gulp and put the mug down again without saying anything.

After a minute or two, he took a fish and began to eat. He ate with his fingers, occasionally glancing at the man opposite him.

His eyes are not like they were before, thought Willi Mohr. Not cold and bold.

When Santiago had eaten his third fish, Willi Mohr stretched out his hand and took a salmonete from the dish.

He looked at it for a long time, as if hesitating still.

'Good fish,' he said.

'Yes, very good. The fish are best at this time of the year, but it's difficult to catch them. The weather's usually impossible. It's just been good for a few days. The boats have had big catches. Last night's were the best for a whole year. Good business.'

Willi Mohr bit the salmonete in the back. As soon as he had taken the first bite, he was overwhelmed with hunger and had to stop himself gobbling the fish and at once stuffing his mouth full with another one.

'Lot of money,' said Santiago, rubbing his thumb and forefinger together. 'A great deal of money.'

Willi took a piece of bread and washed it down with a mouthful of wine.

'A lot of money,' repeated Santiago.

'Needed, too,' he added.

Another fish. Eating, slowly and carefully.

'If they'd gone out again tonight, we'd have earned a lot more money,' said Santiago.

'Aren't they going out then?' said Willi Mohr.

Santiago shrugged his shoulders.

'I don't think so,' he said. 'If they have a good night then they seldom bother to go out again the following night. Even if they could have earned a whole month's income on just that one night. They forget they haven't been able to fish for a month, and that the fine weather might well come to an end the next day. Then there'll perhaps be stormy weather for a month again. Perhaps two months.'

'Strange,' said Willi Mohr.

'They're like that. All of them. My father too. They're hopeless. But if things are bad, really bad, then they lie out there night after night and day after day, just to get a little, perhaps not even enough to pay for the fuel. It's what the priests call humility in the face of the inevitable. That's what's called work.'

Willi Mohr was eating.

He had not understood the last remark and looked up, shaking his head.

Santiago raised his right forefinger and made an effort to explain.

'Before I got hold of the van,' he said, 'they used to just sit down there, waiting for a buyer from the town, who came when he felt like it and paid whatever price he cared to offer. Sometimes he didn't come at all and they had to give away their catches or throw them back in the sea, if the fish were the kind you couldn't salt down. That's what they call work. What I do, that's not work. D'you see what I mean?'

Willi Mohr nodded. He felt very peculiar. Perhaps it was because his stomach was rebelling against the rich food after such a long fast.

He went on eating. It annoyed him that he could not stop.

Santiago had finished. He drank up his wine and wiped his mouth with the back of his hand. Then he picked up a dry piece of wood, shaved a piece off with his knife, and picked his teeth lengthily and thoroughly.

When Willi Mohr had eaten up the last bit of fish, Santiago threw away the toothpick and said:

151

'Which country do you come from?'

'Germany.'

'Hamburg?'

'No. I come from the south-east really, The German Democratic Republic . . . but I left several years ago.'

'Was it a bad country?'

Willi Mohr found the question difficult to answer. After a while he said: 'Yes, I suppose I thought so . . . then. From certain points of view, anyhow.'

'Do they let people starve there too? And do they shoot people who want better pay?'

'No, not that. No, no one starves.'

'What was bad about it then?'

'They were short of things, for instance.'

'What sort of things?'

'All kinds. Coffee, tobacco, certain sorts of clothes, cars, motor-cycles. There weren't any foreign things to buy.'

'And no work?'

'Yes, almost too much.'

'No industry?'

'It was being built up. The whole country was wrecked by the war.'

'But the factories must have made things?'

'Of course.'

'And you could buy those things if you had money, I suppose?'

'Only necessities, simple things. Everything else was called a luxury and was for export only.'

'Why?'

'To improve the economy. Our money wasn't worth anything in other countries.'

'But there was food?'

'Yes, everyone had food and clothes and somewhere to live. And work.'

'Why did you leave it then?'

The question was direct and caught him off his guard. Willi Mohr sought for words for a moment. For some reason he wanted to answer as explicitly as possible.

'Such huge sacrifices were demanded and so little given in return. Everything, your whole life, was built on a concept of a system. If you lived there, you had to be convinced that the system was really worth the sacrifices, you had to believe in the justification of the ideas, so to speak. If you didn't, then it was all pointless, and you couldn't stand outside it.'

'It was Communism there, wasn't it?'

'Yes.'

'Did you have to be a Communist?'

'Yes.'

'And otherwise? Prison? Or . . .'

He made an international gesture, raising his chin and drawing his forefinger across his throat.

'No, not like that. You didn't have to be a Communist like that. No one demanded it and you couldn't even be a member of the party just like that either, even if you wanted to. But you have to be one from conviction, to be really able to work in that way and on those conditions.'

Santiago sat in silence for a while and looked absently in the direction of the door.

'When I was a boy, during the war, there were Communists here too. I remember them arranging meetings. Andres Nin came here and spoke, on the quay in the puerto. I was about ten then. Or eleven. Then the war came. I had two brothers, older than me, and they were both killed.'

Willi Mohr nodded.

'Communism is forbidden here now,' said Santiago, after a minute or two.

'So are all socialist movements, aren't they?'

'Yes,' said Santiago.

He looked searchingly at Willi Mohr. Then he said: 'I've never bothered with politics. But last winter something happened which . . .'

Willi Mohr started and his eyed widened.

Santiago stopped abruptly and got up.

He pushed the dish away with his foot, picked up a packet of cigarettes from the stone bench and went out of the kitchen.

Willi Mohr gathered up the dishes into a heap and put them in the corner by the water-jar. Then he opened a packet of Ideales and smoked with deep long draws. He had not had any cigarettes for a week.

When he went out on to the steps, he saw that the evening was already drawing in. The sun was low and throwing long, violet shadows along the ground. The air was dry and hot and in the east the sky flaring in colours varying from indigo blue to purple above a thick black band of the rising dusk.

Santiago Alemany was standing by the camioneta, absently kicking one of the flat front tyres.

'Punctured?' he said.

'Yes.'

'It shouldn't stand like this. Wrecks the tyres.'

Willi Mohr shrugged his shoulders.

'What's wrong with it?'

'Gasket.'

'A gasket's not the whole world.'

'Perhaps the cylinder-head too.'

Santiago bent down over the engine and ran over it with his fingers.

'Don't think so,' he said.

Willi Mohr did not reply.

'It'll be difficult to get it going again.'

'Yes.'

Santiago walked round the truck and extracted the spare tyre lying on a rack above the back axle. He rolled it round a couple of times and pushed his fingers in it to test it.

'This is a good tyre,' he said.

He was right. There had been no spare tyre when Dan Pedersen had taken over the camioneta, and as that had been at a time when he and Siglinde had had money, they had bought one to be on the safe side, but they had never had a puncture and the spare had never been used.

'I could use it,' said Santiago. 'I've been thinking of buying one for some time, but haven't done anything about it.'

'It's not mine.'

'No, I suppose not, really.'

Santiago smiled joylessly. He took a roll of notes out of his pocket and extracted three hundred pesetas. Willi Mohr made no effort to take the money. He was looking suspiciously at the fish-van.

'They're exactly the same size,' said Santiago.

154

He put the notes down on the running-board of the camioneta, found a small stone and placed it on top of them.

'Not that anything gets blown away in this weather,' he said.

'It's too much,' said Willi Mohr.

'On the contrary, a tyre like that costs at least a hundred duros.'

Santiago rolled the tyre across to the Ford.

'Your Spanish is really good now,' he said.

He turned his back to the steps, bent down and jerked the starting-handle. The engine started immediately. Dusk was falling quickly and it was almost dark.

Santiago climbed into the driver's seat and switched on the lights.

He said something, but his words were drowned by the sound of the engine.

As he backed away, the beam from the headlights fell on the man on the steps, standing quite still, his hands in his trouser pockets.

When the sound of the engine had died away, Willi Mohr went back into the house and fumbled for the pistol under the pillow. He stood with the gun in his hand, talking to himself.

'It won't come off,' he said.

He had a sense of helpless unreasonable despair, as if the very foundations of his existence had suddenly collapsed.

He pushed over the safety catch and tucked the gun under the mattress. Then he went out into the kitchen and struck a match to look at the things lined up on the stone bench.

'Hell,' he said.

He went out to the camioneta and found the notes, rolled them up and pushed them into his pocket.

As he shut the door from the outside and turned the key, he had collected himself sufficiently to think: This won't do. I must wait him out as I did the other one. There's plenty of time.

Willi Mohr went to the Café Central to drink his evening coffee.

155

6

Although there were only fourteen days left until Christmas, the hot weather continued and the stone floor felt warm under his bare feet. It was half-past eight and Willi Mohr had just woken up. He was wearing creased pyjama trousers, his hair was untidy and he was yawning as he unlocked the outer door. The heat stood like a wall outside the house, white and blinding.

On the running-board of the camioneta sat Santiago Alemany, elbows on his knees, hat pulled down over his eyes, whittling boredly on a stick. At his feet stood a metal tool-box and beside it lay a gasket, a brand-new one, of shining copper.

'Good-day,' he said, pushing back his hat off his forehead.

Willi Mohr nodded. Then he cleared his throat and spat indifferently on the ground.

He was dumbfounded and painfully moved. This, to be caught in bed, was something he had not reckoned with and he looked round incredulously.

'I was forced to leave the van down there,' said Santiago. 'They were killing a pig in the middle of the road.'

He dropped the piece of wood, but still went on fiddling with his knife.

'It'll soon be Christmas,' he said. 'Then they'll eat themselves full.'

Willi Mohr glanced down at the knife and went back into the house. He did not like the situation and had no desire to stand naked in the kitchen with his back to the door. On the other hand, he could hardly take the gun with him and put it down beside the basin. He scratched his chest and thought. Then he shrugged, took off his trousers and began to wash.

When he came out again Santiago had taken out the tools and was already bending over the engine.

'This'll take several hours,' he said.

Willi nodded. They would probably have to carry on all day and perhaps the next day too, if they wanted to get the truck going. And then he would not use it, anyhow. The whole operation seemed pointless to him, unless something lay behind it all.

156

Perhaps Santiago was thinking of using the camioneta instead of his worn-out Ford.

'Let's start then, shall we?' said Santiago.

'We must drain it first,' said Willi Mohr.

Santiago handed him the spanner.

Willi hesitated a moment before getting down on his back to get at the stopper. He was painfully aware that he was lying with his head and arms under the camioneta and the rest of his body utterly defenceless outside. The stopper was jammed and it took quite a while for him to loosen it; the mixture of oil and rusty water ran out of the engine and was sucked up into the dry soil between the cobblestones.

They worked in silence and without haste. When they had taken off the cylinder head and exposed the broken gasket, they took a rest and ate some bread with slices of sausage, then sat in the meagre shade of the outhouse wall for a smoke. Santiago said: 'I've a friend who's a seaman. He's been to Hamburg several times. He says there are whole streets there full of bars and night-clubs, where the women dance with no clothes on and the girls parade naked in front of you in the brothels. And that the kiosks and ordinary tobacconists have books and papers full of naked women.'

'That's more or less true,' said Willi Mohr.

'Last time he told me he'd been to a place where a woman made love with a goat if you paid her twenty-five duros.'

Willi Mohr stuck out his lip and thought about Hugo Spohler, who had once told him that the whores in Egypt lay naked in the shop windows and smoked cigars from their cunts to demonstrate their professional skills. The world was full of exaggerations and anyhow Hugo had probably never been to Egypt.

'It's possible,' he said.

'Is it like that in your part of Germany?'

'No, things like that are arranged better in the Federal Republic.'

'Where?'

'In West Germany, I mean.'

'What are the women like in your country?'

'Well, they don't make love with goats,' said Willi Mohr.

He was not particularly amused by the conversation and would

157

have preferred to put an end to it, but when he looked at Santiago he realized that even the last question had been quite serious.

'They have quite different conditions from here,' he said. 'They work, at different things, in all kinds of occupations. As bus-drivers and building workers and engine-drivers, for instance. In factories and in the Customs. Well, everywhere. They have the same education as men and have quite a different place in society. So they also have the right to take the same liberties if they want to.'

They had gone back to the truck and were standing leaning over each side of the engine.

'Liberties?'

'Yes, to sleep with whoever they want to, for example, as often as they like and with as many as they like. They don't all do that, but some do.'

'And no one criticizes them?'

'Of course, but no one they need bother about or take any notice of.'

'And the brothels?'

'Aren't any.'

'How do things work then?'

'Quite well, I imagine. It's not a problem. The problems are of quite a different kind.'

There was a short silence as they levered off the gasket and trimmed the edges. Willi Mohr tried out the pistons and found that the play was pretty large. As he did so, he thought about a couple of questions he was considering asking. Silently he formulated them but waited until the other man was leaning over the engine, trying out the new gasket, before he said: 'It's different here in Spain, isn't it? It isn't easy for you to make contact with other women, except those in the brothels, is it?'

'No, it's not easy,' said Santiago.

He did not look up when he replied. He had taken off his hat, as it was in his way, and Willi Mohr stared at the back of his head with its smooth brown whorl of hair.

'But what about the tourists?' he said, grasping the spanner hard. 'Don't you try making love with them now and again?'

Santiago Alemany raised his head and looked at him, first straight in the eyes, then at the hand holding the spanner.

158

'It happens,' he said coldly.

He bent down and went on with the job. Willi Mohr had an impression that he had stiffened for a moment, as if expecting something, but he was not certain.

They said nothing else to each other for the rest of the afternoon.

The repairs were not complete and soon after six Santiago looked at his watch, picked up his tool-box and left. He did not say whether he was thinking of coming back the next day.

Willi Mohr did not allow himself to be surprised the next morning. When the little fish-van braked in front of the house, he was already sitting on the steps, waiting.

The engine was ready at midday but it took another hour before they could start it. Finally they pumped up the tyres, a tiring job as the foot-pump was old and inefficient, and they took turns at it. When Willi Mohr was doing the last wheel, Santiago stood just behind him and said: 'We've a very strong sense of family here.'

'I've heard that.'

'If anything happens to a member of the family, we look upon it as a very serious matter.'

'Oh yes,' said Willi Mohr.

He did not bother to look up.

A moment later Santiago left. Willi Mohr had a feeling that it would be some time before he came back.

7

The events of the last two weeks had had a confusing effect on Willi Mohr. His relations with Santiago Alemany had developed into a series of situations which were not simple and he had not anticipated their origins.

He was still certain that sooner or later he would kill Santiago, but he no longer knew when or how.

For the first time in a year he grew quite conscious of his loneliness and isolation; he no longer had anything to wait for and so his life suddenly seemed artificial and meaningless.

He realized that he would probably live on for a number of days, but because that future could not be foreseen and also was not limited by any particular aim, it seemed to him only vague and repugnant.

When Santiago had gone, Willi Mohr had been seized with a genuine desire for companionship which he had not felt for a very long time. By tiring himself out physically, he found a reason for postponing thinking about it, at least until the following day.

He found to his satisfaction that his fuel had again come to an end, so he hunted up his pieces of rope and went out to collect brushwood. The climb was a strain in the dry, still heat, but he made two trips and both times went higher up the mountain than he had ever been before. When he came back, it was already growing dark and he was able to fall in with his usual evening routine. Although he was tired and sweaty, he went up to the eating-place behind the church and after the meal spent his usual couple of hours outside the Café Central. At the next table sat some labourers from the road construction projects. They were not drinking but had expended a peseta on the loan of a couple of packs of greasy cards. They played in silence and their thin, sunburnt faces reflected nothing but poverty and spiritlessness.

Willi Mohr went back to the house in Barrio Son Jofre soon after midnight. He opened the door and went on into the darkness without locking it behind him. As he was very tired, he did not bother with the paraffin lamp, but struck a match and lit the stump of candle beside his pillow. He yawned and thought that he ought to go out into the yard to clean his teeth and relieve himself before he went to bed. He fetched his toothbrush and a mug of water from the kitchen and just as he was going towards the door, he heard someone moving outside.

He stopped and stood still, about two steps from the doorway.

He was certain no one had come up the alleyway behind him, and yet there was someone out there in the darkness.

Someone who had been there all the time and who was now already standing on the steps, just outside the closed door. The key was still in the door on the outside.

He was holding his toothbrush in one hand and the mug in the other, incapable of deciding what to do.

160

Then he heard the slight sound of cloth brushing against wood and he saw the handle begin to move.

Willi Mohr stood quite still and stared at the door, which silently and very slowly, was opening.

Out on the steps stood a small civil guard with a round face and a thin black moustache. He had his carbine in his hand and he looked indifferently into the room.

'Come,' he said. 'Let's go.'

8

Nothing in the room had changed.

It contained only four pieces of furniture, a small desk, a brown filing-cabinet, a black armchair and a rickety bench for two people—and yet it seemed overcrowded. There were no windows, but on the wall behind the desk hung a large photograph of the Caudillo in a heavy black frame. Beneath the portrait sat a man, writing in the circle of light cast by a ceiling light with a green glass shade.

When Willi Mohr came into the room, Sergeant Tornilla at once put down his pen and rose out of the armchair.

He saluted meticulously, held out his hand and said with a smile: 'So we meet again. A pleasure. I'm sorry to have to ask you to come here at this time.'

Willi Mohr stared at him with clear, blue eyes and mechanically returned the handshake.

The butt of a carbine rattled against the concrete floor outside. Someone was standing on guard out there, presumably the little black-moustachioed civil guard with a round face, the man who had brought him here and who had walked three steps behind him all the way. Willi Mohr had not seen him since they had left the house in Barrio Son Jofre, only heard the gravel crunching under the soles of his boots.

Sergeant Tornilla walked round the table and pulled the wooden bench nearer.

'The accused's bench,' he said, and he smiled as if they had exchanged a private joke, intended only for the initiated.

161

They sat down opposite each other and Sergeant Tornilla went on smiling. He had his elbows on the desk and slowly he pressed the tips of his fingers together, then the palms of his hands. As if he had just thought of something important, he suddenly parted them, fumbled for a packet of cigarettes from behind the telephone and held them out.

Willi Mohr felt that he must in some way or other break this farcical act and he tried to get out his own matches, but the man in the armchair was there first, leaning across the desk with a light.

Before putting his lighter away, Sergeant Tornilla weighed it in his hand for a moment and said with a smile: 'Still the same lighter. Excellent quality. Never goes wrong. Officially, I shouldn't use it. Impounded goods . . .'

Again he pressed his fingertips together and went on smiling.

Sergeant Tornilla was exactly as he had been before, that night two and a half months ago. The same friendly, apologetic smile and the same kind of cigarettes. The same smooth cheeks and the same well-pressed uniform, the same angle of his cap and the same gloss on his strap. On the table lay a pair of light-brown gloves, which had not been there the last time, but otherwise everything was the same. Even the papers and the documents were the same.

Willi Mohr crossed his legs and stared sullenly across the desk. He was not nervous, but irritated by the man's silence and steady eyes. He was sleepy too and had to suppress a yawn.

'Why have you had me brought here?'

No reply.

Willi Mohr finished his cigarette and carefully extinguished it in the ash-tray. Four cigarette-ends lay there already.

'Where are you living now?' said Sergeant Tornilla.

'In Barrio Son Jofre.'

'How long have you lived there?'

'Since August last year.'

'Exactly. Your Spanish is much better now. You'll soon be talking like a native.'

'Thank you.'

'Well, that's an exaggeration of course. A way of speaking, you know. But you really do speak much better now. I heard it at once. You've made great progress.'

162

He offered a Bisonte and again had a light ready before the other man could get out his matches.

Next time I'll get there first, thought Willi Mohr.

'There are only a couple of weeks to go before Christmas,' said Sergeant Tornilla. 'But I'm afraid you'll be disappointed in our Christmas celebrations here. They're not at all as they are in your country. I remember the German Christmas very well. Even in Russia, at the front, we had small trees in the posts and bunkers, and hung red and green paper garlands on the branches. And we sang melancholy songs. I knew many of your country-men and they complained that it wasn't a proper Christmas. That was about the only time I ever heard them complain. They described how it used to be too, before the war. How you put on beards and gave each other presents. How you impersonated a certain figure, like a carnival figure. He had a special name, didn't he?'

'Santa Claus.'

'Ah yes, Santa Claus. It's not like that here. That's not a Spanish custom at all. In the big towns the business men have taken it up but it hasn't caught on out in the country. The only thing that happens here is that people go home to their families and eat a little more than usual, perhaps a paella with meat. Then they drank an anis at some bar. You won't notice very much. Or have you already experienced a Spanish Christmas?'

'I was here last year.'

'Of course. I was forgetting. You've already been with us a long time. But you didn't see very much of it, did you?'

'No.'

'Easter is quite different. That's the great festival here. It lasts for several days, great processions and events, religious and secular. But perhaps you've experienced a Spanish Easter too?'

'No.'

'That's right. You weren't here over Easter.'

It began to darken in front of Willi Mohr's eyes and he thought: I'll fall asleep soon. But then he noticed that it was the electric light which was going out. The light flickered and faded until the coil looked like a small red zig-zag ribbon behind the dirty glass. The room was almost dark.

163

Sergeant Tornilla held out the cigarettes and clicked on his lighter.

'The electricity works here are not good,' he said. 'The equipment is old and very poor. It often fails in the winter and will soon be worse when the storms come. It should be modernized, but people seem satisfied with it as it is. They're proud to have electricity at all. As I said before, they're simple, good people.'

The light went out altogether, but after a minute or two it went on again, flickered once or twice and then remained stable.

'There we are. Now we can see each other again,' said Sergeant Tornilla cheerfully.

After a short pause he added apologetically: 'We are soon going to get an emergency generator here at the guard-post. Then this sort of thing won't happen.'

Willi Mohr yawned, making no attempt to hide it. The conversation was uninteresting and was exhausting him.

The man in uniform looked searchingly at him.

'My wife gets very irritated with the electricity works,' he said. 'She's got an electric sewing-machine which my parents-in-law gave her two years ago. As I said before, they live in Huelva. Her father has a shop there, quite a large one, but he's handed it over to my brother-in-law now. Have you been to Huelva? Pity, it's a lovely town. The sewing-machine often annoys her. When I was posted to Badajoz and we lived there, it worked admirably, but here it doesn't work so well. Sometimes the current is too weak to drive the motor and sometimes there's no electricity at all. They say it's something to do with the boilers. They're very old and on the whole it's surprising that they function at all.'

Willi Mohr blinked and looked at the portrait. The likeness between the Caudillo and the man in the chair was more marked than ever, but now it seemed more ridiculous.

He's dragged me down here under escort in the middle of the night to talk about his wife's sewing-machine. He's mad.

Thought Willi Mohr.

Sergeant Tornilla had fallen silent. Without moving his eyes, he picked up a piece of paper from the desk and said: 'There's been a complaint about you.'

He smiled in a troubled way.

164

'A person called Amadeo Prunera complains that you are stealing wood from his land.'

'Not wood. Brushwood.'

'I see. But that's not allowed either.'

'I didn't know it was forbidden.'

'Naturally not. But as I told you before, a lot of things are different here. A number of things which might well appear valueless have a certain significance to their owners. This is a poor part of the country and the people who live here are poor people. They want their rights.'

Willi Mohr did not know what to say. He was tired and this astonishing accusation had in some way robbed him of his certainty.

'Naturally this is not a serious crime, but it is still an offence. The man had complained and he has right on his side. The simplest thing to do is to offer him some compensation. It can't be more than an insignificant sum, and you have some money, haven't you?'

'Yes, a little.'

'Where did you get the money from?'

Willi Mohr did not reply.

'You got the money from Santiago Alemany, didn't you?'

Tornilla waited only a second or two for the reply and then he said: 'I mentioned your shirt when we last had a talk. You've got it on again today. How long have you had it?'

'Since 1941.'

'What kind of shirt is it?'

'A Hitler Jugend shirt.'

'So you belonged to that youth organization during the war then?'

'Before the war too. Everyone did.'

'That's right. Did you belong to any other organization?'

'No.'

'But during your time in East Germany?'

'No, not there either.'

'Did you ever see the Fuehrer personally?'

'Only once.'

'When?'

'1940, I think.'

'You don't know?'

'I'm not certain I saw him.'

'Can you explain yourself a little more?'

'It's very simple. They said he was coming past in a train and we were lined up along the track with flags and flowers in our hands. First came a train full of soldiers and police and soon after that a train with only two carriages. I think he was standing by one of the windows, at least they told us it was him. Everything went so quickly. Now I'm not certain whether I really saw him, but then I believed it.'

'You see, you speak quiet fluently. But let's go on to something else. You said you weren't here at Easter. But earlier on in the winter you were here?'

'Yes.'

'You were living here in the town?'

'Yes.'

'In the house in Barrio Son Jofre?'

'Yes.'

'When did you leave?'

'At the end of March or the beginning of April.'

'Why did you leave?'

Willi Mohr did not answer.

'When did you last see Santiago Alemany?'

'Today.'

'And before that?'

'Yesterday.'

'Had you asked him to visit you?'

'No.'

'Why did he come then?'

'Don't know.'

'What were you doing when he was with you?'

'Repairing a truck.'

'All the time?'

'Most of it.'

'Did he give you some money?'

'Yes.'

'Has he ever given you money before?'

'Once.'

'For what reason did he give you money?'

166

'Don't know.'

'Did he buy anything off you?'

'In a way, yes.'

'What did he buy from you? A painting?'

'No. A tyre.'

'And on the previous occasion? Did he buy anything then?'

'No.'

'He just gave you the money, just like that?'

'Yes.'

'Are you a friend of Santiago Alemany's?'

He did not want to reply but had to make a great effort to refrain from doing so. His resistance was wearing thin.

'Do you find it easy to remember events which happened, shall we say, six months or a year ago?'

'Yes, generally.'

'Let's go back a bit in time, then. You were living here in the town during the months of January, February and March this year, weren't you?'

'Yes.'

'You said, on the other hand, that you were not here during Easter week, in April. Is that correct?'

'Yes.'

'When did you leave Spain?'

'At the end of March or the beginning of April.'

'And when did you return?'

'At the end of May.'

'Quite right. You left on the second of April and came back on the fifteenth of May. What did you do during that time?'

'Worked on board a boat.'

'What boat?'

'A pleasure yacht.'

'Who owned this boat?'

'An Englishman.'

'Do you remember his name?'

'Thorpe.'

'Quite right. Colonel Thorpe. When did you meet this Colonel Thorpe for the first time?'

'Just before.'

'Just before what?'

'Just before we sailed.'

'Can you remember which day you met him?'

'The twenty-ninth or thirtieth of March.'

'Did he come to you or ask you to work for him?'

'No.'

'So it was you who went to him?'

'Yes.'

'To look for work on his yacht?'

'Yes.'

'You knew he was sailing to Corsica?'

'No.'

'You're not a seaman, are you?'

'No.'

'Why did you try for this work?'

Willi Mohr had anticipated this question and had an answer ready. After a short pause, he said:

'I had already lived here for seven months. I wanted to leave the country.'

'But you didn't know where Colonel Thorpe was going?'

'No.'

'In other words you were willing to go with him anywhere?'

'Yes.'

'If you'd never met Colonel Thorpe before, how did you know he was looking for people?'

'I happened to hear it.'

'Where did you happen to hear it?'

'In a bar.'

'Someone told you, then?'

'Yes, in a way.'

'Who was this someone?'

'Someone I didn't know. I just happened to hear it.'

'And then you went to Colonel Thorpe?'

'Yes.'

'Did he employ you just like that?'

'No.'

'Why not?'

'My papers weren't in order.'

'No, they weren't in order. You had no exit-visa.'

168

'No, but it was all right.'

'In what way?'

'The Englishman arranged it.'

'When?'

'The next day.'

'And the following day you sailed?'

'Yes.'

'Did you have any money with you when you left?'

'No.'

'None at all?'

'Practically none.'

'How much?'

'About a hundred pesetas, perhaps.'

'Were you the only crew aboard?'

'No.'

'So there was one other person employed on the boat?'

'Yes.'

'Who was that?'

'Ramon Alemany.'

'Quite right. It was Ramon Alemany. Do you know where this Ramon Alemany is now?'

'No.'

'Is he in Spain?'

'No.'

'Was he the one who asked you to go on the trip?'

'No.'

'So it was his brother, Santiago Alemany, who persuaded you to look for work with Colonel Thorpe?'

Willi Mohr was very surprised by the question. Without thinking, he said: 'Of course not.'

Sergeant Tornilla sat in silence for a few minutes. His eyes had remained on the man opposite him since the series of questions had begun and his expression was serious.

Willi Mohr looked down at the floor, trying to avoid those immobile eyes so that he could collect his thoughts. Under the desk he saw Sergeant Tornilla's legs. There was not a speck of dust on his shiny black boots.

'Are you tired?'

'Yes.'

169

'Pity. I'd very much like to continue our conversation a little longer. Have you any objections?'

'Yes.'

'Pity, a great pity,' said Sergeant Tornilla. 'Perhaps you'd like something to drink?'

'Yes, please.'

'I'll arrange for it in a moment. Well, how far had we got?'

'Then we sailed for Corsica,' said Willi Mohr.

Sergeant Tornilla put out his hand and took a file out of the filing-cabinet. He did it with a sleep-walker's certainty, without turning his eyes.

'No,' he said, 'of course it wasn't Santiago Alemany who gave you orders to go too.'

Willi Mohr stared questioningly at him.

'So it was Antonio Millan?'

'I've never heard of the name.'

'You're not telling the truth,' said the man in the armchair sadly. 'I myself have told you it.'

'I don't remember that.'

'You've a good memory usually.'

Sergeant Tornilla had opened the file and taken out a couple of pieces of paper clipped together. Without looking at them, he pushed them across the desk and said:

'Read that. It'll be a good exercise for you and the contents may also interest you.'

The pages were typed and seemed to be part of a police-report. Willi Mohr picked them up and shook his head to clear it.

'Read it aloud,' said Sergeant Tornilla.

Willi Mohr read:

'Report on interrogation of Colonel Thorpe, held on his yacht *Monsoon* in Puerto de Soller, Majorca, in the province of Baleares, on 10th September. Colonel Thorpe himself gave the information that he was born in 1893 in England and had retired nine years ago. During the last four years he had stayed for longer and shorter periods in Spanish Mediterranean ports. He is in the process of writing his memoirs. When asked about his relations with the German citizen, Wilhem Mohr, he said as follows: On the evening of the same day I had been told

170

that one of the hands I had employed could not be relied on, I was visited by a German (Mohr) who said he had been in the Navy during the war and was willing to sign on. He seemed very keen to come on the trip, in fact so keen that at first I was afraid that he was trying to get out of the country in a not very honest manner. However this proved to be wrong, for the following day he was given an exit-visa without any fuss from the authorities. I decided to employ him, although he had no references, as both my wife and I wanted to leave the place as soon as possible, especially while the weather was good, as due to certain circumstances we had already stayed there far longer than we had meant to. The man (Mohr) was in my service from the second of April until the twenty-ninth of the same month, when at his own request he signed off in Ajaccio. During that time he fulfilled his duties well and I think to the best of his abilities, but his experience of navigation and daily life on board appeared to be extremely limited, and he had obviously exaggerated his qualifications in his first conversation with me. He was a poor seaman and I shall not in future employ Germans on my boat. When my other man (a Spaniard by the name of Ramon Alemany) deserted in Ajaccio, the German asked to leave the boat. I saw no reason why I should refuse him, especially as I should anyhow have been forced to ask him to leave. On the other hand I was sorry to lose my other hand (Alemany) as he was a good and industrious seaman. On the question of his opinion of the relationship between the two men, Colonel Thorpe says that he is not in the habit of noticing the behaviour of his employees in their free time and that he had not talked to the man (Mohr) or even addressed him on any subject apart from his duties on board. However he considered that both men knew each other well when they first came on board. Of Mohr's character, the Colonel says that he seemed to be typically German. The Colonel's wife, Senora Clementine Thorpe, who was present during the conversation, says: The two of them (Mohr and Alemany) were always together and on the occasions when they went ashore, once in port on the French mainland, where the boat was tied up for two days, and twice in Ajaccio, they went together. She adds that Mohr and

171

Alemany kept the cabin they shared reasonably tidy and clean. Asked if he knew where Mohr was thinking of going when he asked to leave the boat, the Colonel says that as far as he remembers Mohr did not mention any place. On the question of wages received by Mohr for his work, Colonel Thorpe says he offered to work for his keep and the trip, and so did not receive any wages.'

Willi fell silent. His throat was dry and his head felt empty.

Sergeant Tornilla had sat quite still all the time and it was impossible to make out whether he had been listening or not. Now he smiled benevolently and said: 'You really do read very well indeed. Admirable that you've been able to learn so much of the language in such a short time. But your J's are not quite right yet. Much too hard. Say after me: Barrio Son Jofre, J-o-f-r-e ... J-o ... J-o ... J-o-f-r-e ...'

'Jofre,' said Willi Mohr.

'See, that's better.'

He stretched out his hand and took the paper, placing it in the cardboard file. Then he pushed the file into its place in the filing-cabinet without even glancing in that direction.

'How are you liking it in your house, by the way? I understand it's not in a very good state of repair. That's not so good at this time of year. The nights can be both damp and cold, and even at your age you can get rheumatism. My wife is often troubled with rheumatism. And yet our house isn't bad.'

He smiled and added thoughtfully: 'On the contrary, it's surprisingly good, when you think of the standard here. It's on the Avenue, by the church. Only a block away from the place where you usually eat when you've got any money.'

'May I have a little water?'

'Soon. Apropos money, you didn't have any with you when you left and you didn't get any from Colonel Thorpe. Then you came back here and then you had enough to pay the rent for six months and live quite well for three months. You didn't change any, so you must have had Spanish money.'

Sergeant Tornilla's stomach rumbled. The sound was very weak, but Willi Mohr heard it quite distinctly. It felt as if at last he had made some progress.

172

'You see, it's small things like that which puzzle a man when he's sitting and thinking. But experience tells you that everything has a natural explanation. Where did you get the money from?'

Willi Mohr said nothing. His face was sullen and closed and did not reflect his physical exhaustion.

The man in the armchair picked up a piece of paper from the desk, glanced fleetingly at it and said, as if in passing: 'On the twentieth of February this year, Colonel Thorpe appled for exit-visas for Ramon Alemany and Santiago Alemany. He said he was thinking of employing them on his yacht *Monsoon*. Fourteen days later a visa was issued for Ramon Alemany, but his brother's was refused. Thorpe appealed against the decision, and on the thirty-first of March both he and Santiago Alemany were informed that the decision was upheld. That same evening you went on board the yacht and offered to do the work for nothing, although you were obviously not capable of doing it in any way satisfactorily. The following day you go together with Colonel Thorpe in a taxi to the provincial capital, where the Colonel manages to arrange an exit-visa for you. As you are a foreigner and Colonel Thorpe knows the Governor personally, there were no difficulties. In France, Ramon Alemany disappears from the boat and immediately afterwards you sign off. Four weeks later you come back here and then you have some money. Earlier you have been seen together with or in the proximity of Santiago Alemany practically every day, but now you don't meet for three and half months. Then Santiago Alemany suddenly appears and gives you money. It is puzzling in some way. Don't you agree?'

The words bored into Willi Mohr's mind and stopped him from falling asleep and off the chair. He blinked several times, but had difficulty in seeing clearly, and the face in front of him seemed strangely unreal in the unsteady light from the little ceiling light.

'Give me some water, please,' he said.

'You're tired and thirsty?'

'Yes.'

'Not very. It can be much worse.'

Sergeant Tornilla had had his hands clasped in front of him, and now he leant on his elbows and pressed his fingertips together.

His smile died away and he said, swiftly and sharply: 'Have you ever been to Santa Margarita?'

'Yes.'

'When?'

'A year ago, just before Christmas.'

'And before that?'

'Once.'

'When?'

'In October or November, I think. Anyhow, in the autumn.'

'Try to remember the date.'

'Of the first time or the second?'

'Both.'

'I don't know, once just before Christmas and once earlier, during the autumn.'

'Let's try to reconstruct the events. Your Norwegian friends left the country at that time, didn't they?'

'Yes.'

'When?'

'On the 15th December.'

'Did you visit Santa Margarita before that or after?'

'The second time was after, just before Christmas, as I said.'

He counted on his fingers.

'It must have been the eighteenth of December.'

'What did you do in Santa Margarita?'

'Hired a truck.'

'Right. You talked to a builder there about taking over an old truck your Norwegian friends had had before. But the first time? Was that in December too?'

'Earlier, I think.'

'Might it have been the first or the second of December perhaps?'

'No, it must have been earlier. In November or perhaps October. It was raining.'

'Did you go to Santa Margarita alone?'

'No.'

'Who was with you?'

'My ... Norwegian friends.'

174

'What are their names?'

Willi Mohr did not reply.

'They are called Pedersen, aren't they?'

'Yes.'

'Let me see, what are their first names? Yes, Daniel and Sig . . . something like that. You know their names, don't you?'

'Yes.'

'Would you be good enough to tell me them?'

Sergeant Tornilla sat quietly, waiting for a reply. His attitude grew thoughtful, as if he had gone on to think about something else.

'Do you know my name?' he said finally.

'Yes.'

'My first name too?'

'No.'

'I've told you it.'

Willi thought.

'Yes,' he said, 'now I remember it.'

'Would you please say it.'

'José Tornilla.'

'Exactly, José Tornilla. But your j's are still too hard, J-o-s-é.'

'José.'

'And what are your Norwegian friends called?'

Silence.

Willi Mohr looked at the man beneath the portrait, sullenly but not defiantly.

'You think your Norwegian friends are dead, don't you?'

'Yes.'

'You're probably right. Well, you went with them to Santa Margarita. Will you tell me what happened?'

'We drove there and looked and then we drove back again.'

'There's a mine up there. Did you look at that too?'

'We weren't there, but I remember seeing it, in the distance.'

'Was Santiago Alemany also with you?'

'No.'

'You don't remember the date, but you think it was November and anyhow before the third of December?'

'Yes.'

'We shall look at those days for a few minutes, the second and the third of December. What did you do then?'

'No idea.'

'I'll help you. On the second of December in the evening you were in the puerto. A police patrol saw you out by the pier at half-past one in the morning with your Norwegian friends and the Alemany brothers. What were you doing out there?'

'Nothing.'

'What were you doing out by the pier?'

'Bathing.'

'At half-past one in the morning? And by the pier? Why not at one of the ordinary bathing-places near the village?'

'We didn't have our bathing-costumes.'

'Not the woman either?'

'No.'

'It's not permitted to behave like that. There's even a special law which forbids it. Do you know that?'

'It's a silly law.'

'That's possible. Did you have sexual relationships with the woman too?'

'No.'

'But you practically lived with her for four months. She's said to have been physically attractive and not especally ... particular. She could hardly have failed to make an impression on you. Were you in love with her?'

Willi Mohr did not answer. He felt less tired now, but very uneasy and he wanted at any price to get the other man away from this subject.

'What do you really want to know?' he said.

'For instance, what happened on the following day, the third of December?'

'I think we went to the puerto then too. Let me see, one moment, it was very hot then too. We didn't bathe but went to a bar and stayed there until late into the night. It was a kind of party. We sang and drank quite a bit ... and ... well, there was nothing else.'

'Were the Alemany brothers there too?'

'Yes. Santiago Alemany was with us all the time. His brother came later, after being out in the fishing-boat. Yes, I remember

176

now. We were down on the quay when the boat came in. The Alemany brothers' father spoke sharply to Santiago because he had not been to town with the fish the day before. Then we all went back to the bar again.'

'What did Santiago Alemany answer to that?'

'I don't remember. Not definitely. Yes, that the van was out of action, I think. Then we started drinking again and then we went home. I drove the camioneta, I remember.'

'Did you drive although you were drunk?'

'Yes.'

'That's not really allowed.'

Sergeant Tornilla smiled. His expression was again friendly and good-humoured.

'Tonight you've admitted three offences already. Wherever will this end?'

He put his hand down behind his chair and lifted up the water-jug. Then he got up and walked round the desk, just as elegant an unmoved as before. Willi Mohr drank and was given a cigarette and a light. The other man returned to his place.

'The electricity really is poor,' he said, looking at the bulb, which had again begun to flicker.

Then he sat in silence for a while, looking at the man on the bench.

'You should have a family,' he said, pointing with his middle finger at the three photographs in the leather frame. 'It's very important for a man to have a family. It gives him a wholly different anchorage in life. I well remember after all those years as a soldier, what a change it meant. Perhaps you don't really appreciate it to the full until you have children of your own. You ought to get married. Then you have two essential things to live for, your work and your family. The family makes your work more worth while, even if as in my case, you sometimes don't see all that much of them. You get a more definite understanding of what you're working for, evidence that your aims really correspond to the work you do to achieve them.'

Willi Mohr was not listening. His cigarette had gone out and he was holding it between his fingers, staring at the portrait. It seemed to him that the Caudillo's lips were moving, like the last time, and he did not like it.

177

'Have you a fiancée in Germany perhaps?' said Sergeant Tornilla.

'No.'

'Not even before either?'

'Yes, perhaps, in a way. Once.'

'A long time ago?'

'During the war.'

'You were in Poland in the war, weren't you?'

'Yes, in Gotenhafen.'

'Was it a nice town?'

'No, not especially. Rather small, wide streets and small, square houses. A very large harbour. Full of army people.'

'I was in Poland once or twice too. My impression of the Poles was not particularly favourable. They seemed very hostile, almost irreconcilably. Like the Russians.'

'They had good reason to be. It was an unjust war.'

'That's right. But why? Well, because it was lost. Even here that's thought to be a historical truth now, although it's admitted that the opposite result would have been better. The war became unjust the moment it was lost. And the result might well have been different.'

'Don't talk about the war,' said Willi Mohr, crushing his cigarette-end out in the ash-tray.

Sergeant Tornilla pushed the packet of cigarettes across the desk and followed up with his lighter. Then he sat in silence and waited.

'Gotenhafen was a dreadful town,' said Willi Mohr. 'I was there for a year, from February forty-four to January forty-five. Second Submarine Cadet Division. More than two thousand men, jammed into an ex-luxury liner which had been painted grey. Everything was grey, except the snow, and that turned grey too, as soon as it reached the ground. It was always windy and the whole of your damned war went through the town like an endless grey snake. Stores and tractors and hospital ships and grey boats which came and went and grey voices bawling out lies from a grey loudspeaker. And every night one lay in terror that they'd bomb the place and the ship would heel over and drown you. It did in the end, and drowned five thousand people, mostly women and children. And almost half of the Second Submarine Cadet Division.'

178

He fell silent.

'What happened?'

'The Russians torpedoed it, a Russian submarine.'

'I've read about that. During the evacuation, wasn't it?'

'Yes.'

'Ruthless.'

'Not at all. That's your war, just as it should be. Anyhow, what d'you think one can see in a bloody great storm in the middle of the night? Woman and children? Huh.'

'And what happened to you yourself?'

'Nothing. Nothing happened to me. I never saw the enemy, not until the war was over, and then there weren't any enemies any longer, were there? That's the rules. I just saw thousands of grey people with grey faces. They came from somewhere or other and stood on the quays and waited in their tens of thousands. In snowstorms. Some died, I suppose. There were air-raids sometimes, so they say. But no bombs ever fell where I was, and I saw nothing. And the boat I was on got through. That was a liner painted grey too, but an older one. And it didn't drown me.'

Unfortunately, thought Willi Mohr. And the next second he thought about himself talking like this with great surprise. He must pull himself together.

'But you had a fiancée there?'

'Yes, if you can call her that.'

'What was her name?'

'Barbara.'

'German?'

'Yes.'

'Born in Gotenhafen?'

'Posted there. Women's Naval Corps.'

'What happened to her?'

'Don't know.'

'Did she disappear after the torpedoing?'

'I don't know which boat she was on. Most got through. We were soldiers. Never knew anything about anything.'

'You never met her again?'

'No.'

'Did you look for her?'

'Everybody was looking for someone. But there was no one looking for everyone.'

'And you loved each other?'

'We made love.'

'Do you mind talking about it?'

'Not at all. But it's not worth it.'

'No, perhaps not,' said Sergeant Tornilla.

He picked up a photograph and handed it over.

'Do you recognize this man?'

A thin, ordinary Spanish face. Like a road-labourer's, perhaps a little more lively.

'No,' said Willi Mohr.

'Well then, so you sailed with Ramon Alemany for almost three weeks, nineteen days to be exact?'

'Yes.'

'Do you know where he is now?'

'No.'

Answer in monosyllables, thought Willi Mohr. Don't let him get you talking again.

'Let's talk a little about the trip to Corsica. Was the weather good?'

'I'm tired,' said Willi Mohr. 'I need some sleep.'

'Naturally. I should have thought of that before. You can sleep here. Or would you rather go home?'

'Yes.'

'You want to go home?'

'Yes.'

Sergeant Tornilla got up, smiled and held out his hand.

Willi Mohr swayed as he got up. He was drenched with sweat and everything blurred in front of his eyes. The other man looked exactly as he had done when he had got up from the arm-chair the first time, an eternity ago.

'I'm sorry I've had to wear you out,' he said. 'And now, until the next time.'

He threw his hands out apologetically. Smiling.

Then he walked to the door and opened it politely.

Reprieve, thought Willi Mohr as he stood out in the porch. The dawn light hurt his eyes.

The sun had just risen behind the ridges on the sea side and

180

the mountainside was bathed in its clear white light. A little of the cool of the night remained and although it was already hot, the heat had not yet become oppressive. The long, low, yellow stone building of the guard-post appeared empty and dead, and the silence lay like a hood over the countryside. Willi Mohr stood quite still in the great dusty stillness and looked at the buildings which rose in a jumble beyond the olive-trees. This was the town up in the mountains. Here lived a number of priests and a doctor and some officers and policemen and naturally someone who owned the sheep and most of the land. and three thousand people too, simple and poor and happy over the miracle that they were allowed to create new families for this community. Most of them had fought for three years in the war to avoid experiencing this miracle.

He had lived here for more than a year, sufficiently long to get to know the milieu without breaking through or carrying out systematic studies. Now he was standing there, waiting for the town to wake, rise and cry out, not in revolt, but in an agony of death and despair.

He was beyond fatigue now, and could not control his thoughts, which had broken through the barriers and become impulsive and irrational.

Willi Mohr shrugged and began to walk along the road between the olive-groves. It was still straight and smooth but the rains of the last few months had crumbled the edges and washed away most of the gravel.

He looked straight ahead and walked through the town with long strides, calmly and mechanically. The only people he saw were two civil guards standing in the middle of a cross-roads staring out to the east. They were smoking and had leant their carbines against the low wall along the edge of the road.

He went into the house in Barrio Son Jofre and shut the door behind him without locking it. Dimly, he was aware that such details would no longer change or even influence his situation. He poured water into the bowl for the dog and gulped down what was left in the jar. Before he left the kitchen, he glanced at his watch. Nearly six o'clock. The interrogation had not been especially long, at the most three or four hours.

He did not bother to wash, but went back into the room and

181

lay down on his back on the mattress, his straw hat over his face, without undressing or taking off his sandals.

Thirty seconds later it struck him that they were going to kill him, presumably without telling him why and without giving him another opportunity to kill Santiago Alemany. But that did not matter any longer. He just wanted to sleep.

Just as he was about to fall asleep he thought once again about Barbara Heinemann.

9

In December 1944, Barbara Heinemann was just twenty-one and two years older than Willi Mohr. She was five-foot-eight, weighed ten stone and had fairish hair drawn into a small knot at the back of her neck. Dressed, she seemed plump, but that was largely due to her thick stockings and ill-fitting uniform. She did not have any special physical advantages, apart from her youth, but together with Willi Mohr she was undeniably beautiful. Once, when he had pointed this out to her, she looked in the spotted mirror on the wardrobe door and said: 'Why, you're quite right. I can even see it myself.'

The room was small and shabby and they had scrounged together three rolls of adhesive tape and an unwarrantable number of emergency rations to be able to rent it.

He slept with her sixteen times and before that he had had only a few misleading experiences from field-brothels, where the exhausted whores were shaved for hygienic reasons and usually refused to take off much more than their woollen bloomers.

Barbara was the first woman he had seen naked, and with astonishingly photographic clarity he could remember what she looked like, especially from behind.

It was snowing outside and the room was full of a greyish soft light. She was standing on the bare floorboards some way away from the bed, calm and relaxed, her head bowed and her arms hanging loosely at her sides. Her feet were slightly apart and she had lifted her right heel a few inches off the floor so that her knee was slightly bent and her weight was resting on her toes

182

and the front part of her foot. Her legs were not slim and nor were they exactly shapely, but they were quite long, with well-rounded calves and the muscles ran in soft ridges at the back of her knees. Although the distance between her heels was no more than an inch or so, her legs touched each other in one place only, a few inches below her crotch where two slight bulges caused the insides of her thighs to meet. Above this point he could see the daylight between her thighs and a few curly hairs outlined against the light background. Although her hips looked firm and reassuring, her backside was small and her buttocks firm and well-shaped, a horizontal crease below the left one making them look uneven in size and shape. The narrow cleft between them opened out into a diffuse cavity, soft and kindly, and farther up, on each side of the small of her back, were two dimples, irrationally placed with the left one higher and a little farther away from her spine. Her hips had no even curve, but ran in an irregular line which was both beautiful and inviolable and beyond all geometrical definition. Her shoulders were a little broader than her hips and the contour from armpit to waist was soft and pure and simple. Her shoulder-blades were like resting wings under the soft skin, and a little farther down, shadows gathered in a shallow hollow down her spine. Her arms looked loose and relaxed, and he could not see her hands as they were resting against the front of her thighs, just below her loins. Neither could he see her breasts, but he knew they were small with pale brown, quite circular nipples. She was standing quite still with her head bent forward and her eyes directed at some point on the floor, just in front of her and a little to the left.

He could never decide whether he had seen her stand in this way just once or whether it had been repeated every time they were together.

Anyhow that was their starting-point. Then she turned round, swiftly and softly, and came over to the bed with her blue eyes shining with confidence and expectation.

Later on, he had on numerous occasions found that she was a steady and well-made girl, but that she would probably have grown fat on a diet containing high-quality nourishment. And that her eyes were shining because she wanted him, which she undoubtedly did. But that made no difference.

She was by no means a virgin when they met, but he persuaded himself that she changed with him and showed the same tendencies to awakening and liberation as he did himself. Naturally he was quite right, even if he did not know whether he wanted it.

They made love quite uninhibitedly, in every way they could think of and with a persistence and systematic eagerness that even they themselves found surprising, at least at first.

He remembered this part of their life very well and found he usually remembered her from behind.

Lying on her stomach with her cheeks against the coarse grey pillow-case, her thighs apart as she thrust away with her elbows and knees to try to get in a better position. She whimpered and whined, her tongue running over her lower lip and beneath him her body thrashing about with wild uninhibited frenzy. During her orgasm, she kicked out desperately with her legs and threw her head from side to side, biting the dirty pillow.

He had a whole gallery of memories of her, mostly in various attitudes of abandonment.

She was sitting astride him, panting wildly, her mouth open and her eyes glazed, riding him until her shoulders and breasts grew shiny with sweat, and as it came for her, she bit her lower lip and beat him on the chest with her fists.

Or she was lying on her side along the wall with her head towards the end of the bed, her knees wide apart and the soles of her feet together so that her loins were wide open to him. He caressed her, lightly but methodically and inexorably over one single spot, tenderly extending her until she broke and collapsed, sobbing and helpless in total surrender.

That happened one of the last times, when they had already discovered most of each other's nerve-points, late one January evening, with refugees seething round the quays and the thunder from the front a dimly distant sound beyond the banks of fog and driving snow.

There were other memories too, less photographically and coldly registered, but he had managed to make a chrysalis of those a long time ago, and they appeared only seldom, mostly when he was ill or totally exhausted.

Her hands on his body, for instance, and the times he had
184

woken with his head on her shoulder, enveloped in her soft, safe warmth.

Barbara reminded him of Hugo Spohler in one way. She possessed a capacity for reacting normally under abnormal circumstances, and for finding simple positive ways out of apparently hopeless situations. And she was a great fixer. She found it easy to tackle things and considered a problem something to be solved. It was she who arranged for the attic room, and if she had not taken the initiative it was doubtful that they would ever have found a mutual bed to lie in. It was she who got fuel for the cracked tiled stove in the corner behind the wardrobe, and it was she who began to undress the moment she had slammed the door shut and put on the hook. It was she, too, who got hold of contraceptives the first time, though they did not bother to use them later.

It was she who had stood naked a little way away from him, her head bowed and one heel raised off the floor, staring at something, before turning round and looking at him with eyes shining with happy expectation.

She was not a nymphomaniac, which otherwise would have been a cheap explanation and later could have been an evasion. On the contrary, she was, as far as he could make out, a perfectly normal young woman with normal sexual reactions. After their meeting she was happy and content, but pale with exhaustion, occasionally finding difficulty in walking.

The very first time, she had known more than he had done, but only a little of what they both knew when they parted. He was quite certain of that.

But she wanted to use her hands and her lips, her mouth and her tongue, her tenderness and her body for something which all those were meant to be used for. Before it was too late. As he did. And they did not have much time.

This in itself was banal. Many other people behaved in just the same way at that time and naturally there too, even if most of them had to make do with tin shacks and empty goods-wagons. But that did not make any difference either.

At first he often thought about how they had met and made love to each other on sixteen different occasions, mostly with two or three days in between, because of the difficulties of

185

arranging leave at the same time. The first time was a Sunday and they did not use contraceptives. It was in the middle of the day and quite light in the attic room and they were naked and he lay over her on the bed. When it began to fire in his loins and the paralysis began to spread, he was seized with his old uncertainty and thought of stopping. But she noticed it at once and drew her legs high up and grasped his testicles and forced him to spurt his hot fluid seed deep into her. She did not let go until his convulsions had stopped and his organ had begun to soften. Then he lay in her arms and she held him as if he had been a toy teddy-bear or a doll. After that neither of them had hesitated, not on any occasion, and this gave him cause for thought. Even ten years later.

They spoke very little to each other and then only of the present, never of the past or any possible future.

She was happy and lively and was never irritable. Neither did she ever raise her voice, but once she had wept, quite without cause.

She came from Königsberg.

This was more or less what he knew of Barbara Heinemann.

Otherwise he knew very little.

The most ridiculous thing of all was that he did not know whether she was dead or alive.

The evacuation came more quickly than had been expected. It was carried out in haste and confusion, after a stream of orders and counter-orders. Much was hurriedly planned and did not go well. The grey liner which had been the quarters of the Submarine School was torpedoed at the height of Stolpmünde, keeled over and sank with more than five thousand people on board. Exactly how many, no one knew. There were nearly four hundred Women's Naval Auxiliaries on board, their quarters in the bowels of the ship. One of the torpedoes landed there and all of the girls but two were killed, the others trapped when the watertight doors were closed, drowned like mice in a sealed tin. The name Barbara Heinemann was not on the passenger list, but that was nothing to go by. On the other hand, she had been on special duties on some staff and might well have been put on another ship. Most of these got through, as did the old liner Willi Mohr ended up on. But two others were sunk.

Though most got through.

And tens of thousands of people were left ashore.

It was an insoluble equation.

And he had not done very much to solve it. At first he had had no opportunity, then he had not devoted sufficient energy to the task, and as time went by it grew too late.

When he ever thought about the matter, he preferred to think of her trapped behind the hydraulic steel doors, deep down in the great passenger liner, which had turned over and sunk into the ice-cold water. Even if this alternative was not really the most believable. Or was it after all the most logical?

He did not know, and in time, forgot. Most of it, but not all.

Nothing more ever happened to him, he met no one else, and when he made casual acquaintances, nothing much ever came of most of them. He had long ago got used to this being the case. If there were a brothel in the vicinity, he perhaps went there, but he usually did not bother.

And yet he had had Barbara Heinemann with him for ten years. It was her hands and shoulders which haunted him when he was tired and defenceless and could not stop dreaming. But most of all, it was his memories of her physical attitudes which he turned to when he occasionally thought of sex. She was also the one who was his free-pass when it came to that kind of sense of inferiority. No one could possibly possess another person so fundamentally as he had possessed her.

At least, not physically.

For a short time, perhaps six months, she had been thrust aside for someone else, a woman who used to come padding bare-footed through his room very early in the morning, when she thought he was asleep. She used to be wearing a dressing-gown, but once he had seen her naked, her body covered with small pearls of glass in the trailing pale beam of a lighthouse. He had resisted her as long as she had been there, but gave way after she had gone.

A short while ago. Barbara Heinemann had returned, with her bowed head and loosely hanging arms, and now it already seemed that she had never been away.

Barbara was also the only person who had been able to touch

187

him while he was asleep without the usual consequences. Several times when she had woken first or he had fallen asleep from exhaustion before her, she had woken him. She never said anything on these occasions, but just caressed him awake with her hands.

Ever since he was very young, he had always disliked people surprising him in his sleep, and he detested anyone touching him. During the early days in the house in Barrio Son Jofre, he had even found it difficult to get used to the cat, which used to creep in under his blanket when it was cold.

10

Willi Mohr felt a hand on his shoulder and opened his eyes. He had been dreaming about something, deeply and vaguely, and when he felt the hand, he knew whom he had been dreaming about. It was a large, sunburnt hand, with broad curved nails and a signet ring with a reddish stone in it. A man in a green uniform was leaning over him, shaking him slowly, the middle-aged civil guard with a heavy, sleepy face and a stubby grey moustache. He was holding his carbine in his left hand with the butt on the floor. Willi Mohr violently threw off his hand and sat up.

'You didn't hear when I knocked,' the man said apologetically.

Willi Mohr shook his head and looked at his watch. It was a quarter-past eight. The morning sun was shining outside the open door. Two hours had gone by since he had come home from the previous interrogation.

'Come,' said the civil guard, slinging on his carbine, 'let's go.'

11

They walked down the steep crooked alleyway and turned right on to the main road. Then they passed the fork in the road, continued along the Avenida Generalissimo Franco and crossed the square with its pump and three cafés. Willi Mohr, as usual, strode along, light and energetic; it was he who decided the tempo, and the civil guard with a stubby moustache walked on his left, half a stride behind him. Although his rest had been short and uneasy, he did not feel sleepy or thick-headed, and in the clear white sunlight he noticed details along the road with an almost unnatural clarity. He had stopped reflecting, and his movements and actions were mechanical, exactly as if he were following a well-rehearsed schedule. At the Café Central, he stopped and asked the same question as before, the guard shrugged his shoulders and leant his carbine against the edge of the table. They drank their vermouth and walked on, and in some way everything was as it should be. He was on his way to Sergeant Tornilla and they would sit opposite each other in the little windowless room with its portrait and filing-cabinet and green lampshade, and he would be very tired and thirsty and suddenly would be given water and everything would come to an end, so that he could go home and sleep. It was also part of the scene that it was the man with the grey moustache who had come to fetch him, not any other of the civil guards, the small one with the round face, for instance. Just before they got to the straight gravelled road between the olive trees, a fat, shabby woman appeared in a doorway and tugged at the civil guard's sleeve, his wife presumably, and she embarrassed and worried him. Then he made a sign to the arrested man and followed the woman into the house. This was not part of the schedule, and as a result was a cause of irritation. Willi Mohr felt badly treated and shifted his feet as he stood out on the street listening to the excited voices inside. A small child with a dirty face in a short yellowish garment was standing in the doorway staring at him. After a while, the civil guard came back, lifted up the child, patted its bare backside and gave it a smacking kiss on the cheek. This seemed to cheer him up, for as they walked on, he smiled and said apologetically: 'Women . . .'

The guard-post seemed quiet and peaceful and the striped flag hung immobile in the still air. Willi Mohr looked at his watch and noted that fifty-five minutes had gone by since they had left the house in Barrio Son Jofre. The guard tapped lightly with his knuckles on the door of the interrogation room. Then he opened

189

it slightly, peered in and at once shut it again. He pointed at a narrow wooden bench in the porch and said: 'Wait.'

Then he went farther in, opened a side-door and was gone. Willi Mohr sat with his elbows on his knees and waited. He had nothing against waiting and also found a certain pleasure in the fact that he seemed to be the first at the meeting-place. It strengthened his self-confidence and in some way gave him a better starting-point. His brain was functioning a little better now, but he could not draw any lines of direction for the coming conversation or even concentrate on the present or the near future. If he was thinking at all, it was only of an irregular and capricious series of pictures and tableaux. He sat leaning forward, staring down at the smooth concrete, thinking about the stone floor in the house in Barrio Son Jofre, and then of the spanner he had clutched in his hand two days ago as Santiago Alemany had stood leaning over the engine of the lorry, his head bare, only a foot or so away from him. When he had got that far, he tried to begin from the beginning again and reconstruct the chain of associations. He could not remember all the links, but anyhow most of them. He had thought about floors in general and then about the metal plates in his quarters in Gotenhafen and the varnished boards in the attic room and about Barbara Heinemann's feet and pink heels and what they felt like in his hands, and then about another woman and her left breast which had lain in his hand like a small frightened animal, and about a kitten which he had once held when he was small, and the puppy with the black spot over its eye, and the sound when the other puppy, the near-black one, hit the rock wall, and about a man in blue trousers and a black jersey on all fours in front of him, whining and whimpering, trying to creep under a narrow screwed-down table, and about a system of concentric circles in the water, and—the smooth brown curl in Santiago Alemany's hair, and then he was there. The last part of the chain made him feel so ill that he felt sick and his forehead grew hot. He shook his head roughly, and turned to look at what was going on round him. Which was practically nothing. A telephone had rung twice inside the building and someone must have answered it at once, because each time there was only one signal. A thin pig, evidently belonging to the guard-post, walked past outside the entrance, sniffing with its long black snout along the ground. From the military camp on the other side of the town a few scattered shots could be heard, then a donkey braying and far away there was the rumble of an explosion, presumably from the road works.

Exactly half an hour had gone by when the civil guard with the grey moustache came out into the porch, bareheaded and with his jacket unbuttoned. He grasped Willi Mohr's arm, lightly and in a friendly way, and led him the few steps across the porch, opened the door without knocking and pushed him into the interrogation-room.

Willi stood inside the doorway.

The door was closed at once and the guard's footsteps faded away.

The ceiling light was on and under the green glass shade a coil of grey cigarette smoke was just spreading out and dissolving.

In the circle of light below sat Sergeant Tornilla writing.

He had been there all the time.

He put down his pen, rose and held out his hand. Willi Mohr took it apathetically and thought: You can tell him everything except one thing. One single thing. One single thing.

Sergeant Tornilla pointed to the bench, but did not repeat all the old phrases, making something of this, as if wishing to emphasize that even a very small joke is spoilt if you use it once too often.

His uniform looked more perfect and newly-pressed than ever. His white shirt-collar was fresh and he must have shaved at the most an hour ago. He politely continued to stand until the other man had sat down, and then he drew the armchair up, sat down behind the desk, pressed his fingertips together and slowly shook his head.

'You should have taken my advice,' he said with a sorrowful smile. 'You should have stayed here at the post. It would have saved a lot of valuable time.'

Willi Mohr said nothing.

'Excuse me saying so, but you really ought to have washed and changed. And shaved. You've eaten, I hope?'

'You're much too thoughtful.'

'Not at all. On the contrary, it is my fault that you are in this

191

state. I should have made the position clear earlier, and been more definite about you staying here. I can't think what I was thinking about.'

He sighed reproachfully and frowned.

'But you've slept, haven't you?'

'Yes.'

'Well, that's something.'

Willi Mohr sat waiting for a cigarette, but he was not given one.

He could see a corner of the green packet of Bisontes lying in its place behind the telephone. He was so used to being offered cigarettes that quite a long time went by before he thought about using his own. He had a box of Ideales in his pocket but as usual no matches. When he thought about it, he remembered putting them down beside the candle a few hours earlier, as he always used to do before going to bed.

'Could I have a light?'

'Soon,' said Sergeant Tornilla.

He smiled, but made no move towards getting out his lighter.

Instead he went on looking at Willi Mohr, who was waiting with the unlit cigarette between his lips. The only sound in the room was that of flies buzzing round the light and the small dry blows of them hitting the green glass shade.

A minute went by, perhaps two. The smile slowly died away from Sergeant Tornilla's mouth and the next time he spoke, his voice was clear and business-like.

'So you left Spain on the second of April on board the yacht *Monsoon* together with Colonel and Mrs Thorpe and Ramon Alemany?'

'Yes.'

'To sail to Corsica?'

'Yes.'

'Did you go straight there?'

'No.'

'You went into another port on the way?'

'Yes.'

'What was it called?'

'Port Vendres.'

'Quite right. Port Vendres in France, just north of the border. Why did Colonel Thorpe go into this port?'

192

'He wanted some spare parts, which he couldn't get here.'

'You didn't know you were going to visit this port before you sailed from here, did you?'

'No.'

'So it was a surprise for you when Colonel Thorpe did not sail directly to Corsica?'

'Yes.'

'Did you go ashore in Port Vendres?'

'Yes.'

'Together with Ramon Alemany?'

'Yes.'

'What did you go ashore for?'

'Nothing special.'

'What did you do?'

'Nothing. Went into a bar, looked around.'

'Did you go on board any other boat in the harbour?'

'No.'

'Who did you go to see?'

'No one at all.'

'Were you together the whole time?'

'Yes, more or less all the time.'

'What do you mean by more or less?'

'Ramon Alemany went away for a while, while I was sitting at a bar.'

'How long for?'

'A hour perhaps.'

'What was he doing?'

'He went to see a woman, he said afterwards.'

'What did he say before he went?'

'Nothing. He just vanished and was away for a while.'

'Have you any reason to believe that he was not telling the truth?'

'No, none at all.'

'Was Ramon Alemany interested in women?'

Willi Mohr took the unlit cigarette out of his mouth and rolled it between his fingers.

'Did you hear my question? Was Ramon Alemany interested in women?'

'Yes.'

193

'Very?'

'Yes.'

'How do you know?'

'He often talked about women.'

'And you then? Weren't you interested?'

'Not in the same way.'

'How could you sit for hours at a bar without any money?'

'I only drank a glass of mineral water.'

'Was that all you did? In Port Vendres? Drank mineral water?'

'Yes.'

'Well, and then you went to Corsica?'

'Yes.'

'Did you have good weather for the trip?'

'Almost too good. We were becalmed and we had to use the auxiliary engine all the way. The Englishman was very dissatisfied.'

'As he was with you?'

'Yes, but this was meanness.'

'And then you got to Ajaccio. How many days were you there?'

'Six or seven, while I was on board.'

'And during that time, Ramon Alemany disappeared.'

'Yes.'

'Which day?'

'Twenty-first of May.'

'How do you know it was that day exactly?'

'I simply remember what the date was, that's all.'

'I meant this: it was discovered that he was not on board on the morning of the twenty-second. How did you know that he left the day before and not on the morning of the same day that he was missed?'

Willi Mohr squeezed his cigarette out between his fingers. He said nothing and stared sullenly and defiantly across the desk.

'You knew his plans of course, didn't you?'

'No.'

He had been preparing himself for so long for this part of the interrogation that Tornilla's next question was an anti-climax

'Do you think you were badly treated on board?'

194

'No, it was all right.'

'Did you get good food?'

'Relatively.'

'Where were your quarters on board?'

'In the fo'c'sle.'

'Together with Ramon Alemany?'

'Yes.'

'What was it like in this fo'c'sle?'

'It was a small triangular space below deck with room for a table and two bunks.'

'So it was very cramped there?'

'Yes.'

'Were the bunks opposite one another?'

Willi Mohr hesitated for a moment.

'Yes,' he said.

'Are you certain?'

'Yes.'

'Strange,' said Sergeant Tornilla.

He stretched out his hand, took a file from the filing-cabinet, opened it and pushed a paper across the desk.

'Here you are,' he said. 'Read it out aloud.'

It was another typed page with a reference number in the top right hand corner. The text was quite short. Willi Mohr cleared his throat and read:

'As requested I have today inspected certain parts on board the pleasure yacht *Monsoon*, the property of British citizen Colonel Archibald Thorpe, which has been here since 15th August this year. The space where the crew (two in number) had their quarters lies below deck in the front part of the boat. The floor is triangular and measures nine square feet and is partly taken up with a fixed table, three feet long and two feet wide, and two moveable stools. The bunks (two in number) are contained in alcoves, round at both ends, and placed one above the other along the side of the room on the boat's left side. The exit consists of a hatch in the ceiling up to which there is a ladder which is screwed to the floor about a foot away from the bunks' head-end (the space narrows towards the foot-end). To get out you have to climb past the upper bunk at the head-end. On the question of which of the two members of the crew had used which bunk, Colonel Thorpe says that he has no idea and that he never visited the space in question except possibly to shout down the hatch. Colonel Thorpe's wife, Senora Clementine Thorpe, says however that she knows that the man Mohr (German) used the top bunk and the man Alemany (Spanish) used the lower one, and she is certain as she inspected the place several times in the men's absence. She adds that it was always kept clean while Mohr and Alemany were on board. Police Post. Puerto de Soller, Majorca, Baleares, 15th September. Signed Juan ... I can't make out the signature.'

'That doesn't matter,' said Sergeant Tornilla.

He put out his hand, took the paper and placed it back in its file.

'The person who wrote that is probably an even worse seaman than you are,' he said jokingly.

He smiled in a friendly way and let his fingertips play against each other for a while.

'But it doesn't matter all that much, as you can understand what he's saying, can't you?'

Willi Mohr did not bother to reply, and anyhow the question could be regarded as a rhetorical one. Instead he silently contemplated the result of his first direct lie.

The man in uniform went on smiling.

'Who was it who did the cleaning? Was it you?'

'Yes.'

'Did you clean up after Ramon Alemany too, when he had left?'

'Yes.'

His fatigue began to come back. Naturally he should not have answered. Thought Willi Mohr.

Sergeant Tornilla picked up the packet of Bisontes, tapped it against the edge of the desk so that a cigarette shot half way out and politely handed them across. Then he took his lighter out of his pocket and lit it.

'Smoking before the siesta is a bad habit,' he said. 'I fall into it myself sometimes, especially when I've got some hard work to

196

do. But when I'm at home, my wife usually keeps me in order. As I said before, from many points of view one should marry. You should have a family.'

He played with the lighter and smiled at Willi Mohr, who was drawing long, deep drags on his cigarette.

'So,' he said, summing up, 'you don't know where Ramon Alemany went to, or in what way he left the boat. You didn't notice when he left the fo'c'sle and took all his possessions with him, but you're sure he went on the evening of the twenty-first and not on the morning of the twenty-second. The dinghy, which he obviously used, was not found until two days later, drifting outside the harbour. Naturally you don't know how it got there.'

Willi Mohr smoked.

'On the other hand, you're certain that Ramon Alemany has not returned to Spain and is not here now, as you've said several times before.'

He opened the file and took out another paper, and this time did not hand it over, but simply absently eyed through the typed text.

'This is your own account which you gave to the French gendarmerie in Ajaccio on the twenty-fourth of April,' he said. 'I presume you remember it so well that you don't need to read it? Briefly, it says that when you woke up on the morning of twenty-second, Ramon Alemany and all his possessions had gone. As you had no rowing-boat left on board, no one knew about this until Colonel Thorpe and his wife came back that evening. Where had they been, by the way?'

'At a friend's somewhere out of the town. Maretti, or something like that.'

'Quite right. Mazetti was the name of the friend, Lieutenant-Colonel, to be precise. You've a good memory. Otherwise then, you didn't know anything either about why Ramon Alemany had run away or where he had gone to. Well, it's of no great interest.'

He slipped his lighter into his pocket with a swift movement, as if preparing to go on to something else. When he spoke again, his bantering tone had gone.

'There are two dates that interest me considerably more than this twenty-second of April. Namely, one the day before, and

197

two, a day two weeks later, the fifth of May, to be exact. Let's try to reconstruct both those two days. First the twenty-first of April, the day before you discovered that Ramon Alemany had gone. What did you do that day?'

Willi Mohr drew the back of his hand across his face, as if to wipe away his fatigue and confusion. He was at a decisive point and knew he would have to be very careful.

'We had been there three days, I think,' he said hesitantly.

'Quite right. You came into Ajaccio on the eighteenth of April. When did you go ashore for the first time?'

'The day after we got there.'

'With Ramon Alemany?'

'Yes.'

'And on the twenty-first, what happened then?'

'In the morning, I rowed the Englishman and his wife ashore. They were going to visit those Mazettis.'

'Did you know that they were staying there overnight?'

'Yes.'

'Were they usually away from the boat so long?'

'No, that was the first time.'

'Shouldn't someone have stayed on board when neither the Colonel nor his wife was there?'

'Yes, someone had to be there to be able to fetch them when they wanted to come on board again. We were lying out at a buoy just inside the breakwater. The Englishman used to blow a whistle from the pier when he wanted fetching.'

'So it had been decided that either you or Ramon Alemany was to stay on board?'

'Yes.'

'And yet you both went ashore as soon as it was certain Colonel Thorpe had left the town?'

'Yes.'

'And left the yacht unguarded?'

'Yes.'

'It doesn't sound very conscientious, does it?'

'No.'

'Did you perhaps have an important errand that demanded that both of you were present?'

'No.'

198

'Was it your idea to go ashore?'

'No.'

'So it was Ramon Alemany's?'

'Yes.'

'Why did you go with him then? You could have stayed on the boat?'

Willi Mohr did not reply at once, but looked at the portrait of the Caudillo. Finally he said: 'I didn't want to let him go alone.'

The answer was a dangerous one but truthful.

Sergeant Tornilla's next question showed that he was either going to ignore the logical continuation or else save it for some later opportunity. He said: 'So you went ashore. What happened then?'

'We walked round just looking for a while.'

'For how long?'

'All the afternoon.'

'And nothing unusual happened?'

Willi Mohr looked at the portrait again. The photograph had been heavily touched up and there was a vague halo round the General's egg-shaped head. Screwed to the bottom edge of the frame was an engraved brass plate, and to gain time, he laboriously spelt his way through the inscription.

> *General Franco, al frente del movimiento*
> *bajo cuya espada, invencible se cubren*
> *de gloria los Ejércitos nacionales, el*
> *general Franco, al frente del movimiento*
> *salvador, vindica ante el mundo entero,*
> *con una emocion de admiración y respeto*
> *universales, el nombre sagrado de nuestra*
> *querida España, Caudillo de España por*
> *la gracia de Dios.'*

He understood the thread of this harangue only, but at once thought of the labourers up on the road works and the Asturians along the road to Santa Margarita and the nuns and their syringes and dirty black robes. Then he grew conscious of the silence in the room and lowered his gaze to Sergeant Tornilla, who was sitting absolutely still, waiting for an answer, his gaze steady and his fingertips together.

199

'Ramon Alemany drank,' said Willi Mohr.

'A lot?'

'Yes.'

'Did he get drunk?'

'Yes.'

'Did he usually get drunk?'

'This was the first time during the trip.'

'Was there any unpleasantness?'

'The police came.'

'Why?'

'He was very drunk and was accosting women outside a bar.'

'Was he arrested by the police?'

'No, but they took us down to the quay and let me take him on board.'

'Had you been drinking yourself?'

'No.'

'Why not?'

'I very seldom drink.'

'You told me yourself that you'd been drunk in the puerto, didn't you?'

'That was much earlier.'

'That's right. That was much earlier.'

Sergeant Tornilla looked at him long and thoughtfully, before picking up a piece of paper apparently at random from the desk.

'Good, that saves you the bother of reading aloud again.'

Sergeant Tornilla smiled gently and silently ran through the typed sheet. Then he looked at Willi Mohr and said, as if answering a question that had never been put: 'Senora Thorpe once more. Seems to enjoy telling what she knows, that lady. She went of her own accord to my colleague in Majorca and told him this some time ago. She happened to hear the story by chance in Ajaccio after you had gone, and she also says she was very upset, as she has always been very particular about the people working on board the *Monsoon* behaving properly. Was pleased to testify to your good character. According to my spokesman, the German behaved with presence of mind and irreproachably, she says, while the other man behaved worse than a pig.'

He placed the paper in the file and added: 'She doesn't say anything about the cleaning this time.'

As usual, the little joke was a prelude to a change of scene. Tornilla straightened his back a fraction and placed his hands on the desk, palms down on the blotter, as if just about to rise

'We'll go on to the next day,' he said, 'that is, the fifth of May. What were you doing on that day?'

Willi Mohr had felt danger coming and had held his breath. Now he felt a great liberating relief.

'Don't know,' he said.

'Try.'

'I don't even remember where I was.'

'You were in Ajaccio.'

'That's possible.'

'It was your last day in Corsica.'

'Oh yes.'

'How did you leave the island?'

'By boat.'

'Where did you go?'

'To Marseilles.'

'How did you get a ticket?'

'I bought it.'

'You had stayed in Ajaccio for ten days after signing off the yacht. Is that right?'

'Yes.'

'Where did you live?'

'In a boarding-house.'

'What did you do during those ten days?'

'Nothing.'

'Didn't you go out?'

'Seldom.'

'Who were you waiting for?'

'No one.'

'Did you pay your hotel bill?'

'Yes.'

'Did you pay for your boat ticket?'

'Yes.'

'Did you visit the Spanish Consulate in Marseilles?'

'Yes.'

'What for?'

'To get an entry-visa.'

'Did you pay the stamp fee?'

'Yes.'

'Then you came here?'

'Yes.'

'Did you pay for the trip yourself?'

'Yes.'

'You always pay for yourself?'

'Yes, when I have money.'

'Did you pay the fee at the Consulate in French currency?'

'No.'

'You had money with you when you entered the country, although you didn't declare it at the currency-customs at the border?'

'Yes.'

'From whom did you get all that money?'

Willi Mohr did not reply to the question. He looked stubbornly at the shiny black boots under the desk and waited for the question to be repeated, or followed by another one. The seconds went by, lining themselves up into a long, silent minute. And another and another. And yet another. And yet another. And yet another. But of course he was misjudging the time; a minute did not go by so quickly. He glanced at his watch. It was ten to twelve. He began to watch the second hand wandering round the face of his watch with small, short steps. One—two—three—four—five—six—seven—eight—nine—ten.

He shuddered and found he had lost count. Then he raised his head. Sergeant Tornilla was still sitting there with his hands on the desk, watching him, but his gaze was unclear and his face with its plump cheeks and strong dark eyebrows looked relaxed and expressionless.

He's had a stroke and lost his power of speech, said Willi Mohr silently to himself, and the next second he thought that if this were a joke and designed to distract him, then it had not worked. He tried to stare into those brown eyes, but was able to hold his gaze for only a few seconds.

He crossed his legs and looked at the portrait instead, again spelling his way through the inscription on the brass plate. Then he cleared his throat and said: 'What does that mean there beneath the portrait?'

Sergeant Tornilla neither moved nor spoke.

Willi Mohr realized that he was sitting uncomfortably and changed his position again. He tried to relax and think of something else, such as the cat or the dog, but it did not work and instead of relaxation he felt a rising desire to talk or listen or at least move.

He listened, but all there was to hear was the silence. Not a sound came from the man in uniform and even the buzzing of flies had stopped. When he looked up, he saw only two small flies circling round the light, always exactly opposite each other, the glass shade between them, engaged in a grotesque, silent roundabout dance.

He dug into his pocket for his Ideales, took out the packet and placed it on the edge of the desk, sat a moment with the unlit yellow cigarette an inch away from his lips until he said, calmly and politely: 'Please would you give me a light?'

Silence.

After a minute or so, Willi Mohr took the cigarette out of his mouth and carefully put it back into the packet. Then he sat still. He made no attempt to look into the other man's eyes, but looked intently at his hands instead. Somewhere or other he had read that no man could help being irritated if one demonstratively looked at his hands.

Sergeant Tornilla's hands were lying absolutely still. His fingers were short and a little fat, but only slightly sunburnt, very well-kept, with neatly polished nails.

Willi Mohr raised his right hand and scratched the back of his neck, a purely reflex action which annoyed him intensely. When he began to itch again, he controlled himself and kept his hands still.

A little later he had to change position again because his right leg had begun to go to sleep. As he was moving anyhow, he took the opportunity to scratch his head and between his shoulder blades. That was a big mistake; he saw he was behaving like a caged monkey in a menagerie and the measures he was taking were also quite pointless, as the itch immediately grew worse and spread to other parts of his body.

He began to think about the silence. Despite its elasticity it had from the beginning been very small and enclosed and compact, but as it continued it began to vibrate. The more it was

203

extended, the more brittle it became, and the higher grew the number of oscillations. It undoubtedly had a breaking-point but he did not know this point's place in time and was convinced that Tornilla did not either. But he knew that sooner or later he would open his mouth and begin talking. He would answer and the answer would be a very full one. Then it would be over. But first the silence must reach breaking-point. Perhaps that was not so far away. He felt the pressure within him mount and grow explosive and importunate. Many months ago he had become aware that this pressure existed, but it had never been anywhere near as strong as it was now.

Strangely enough he was not sleepy. But that was not strange at all. The crucial moment was all too close.

Nevertheless he went on trying to find ways out, inventing possibilities.

There were only three. That the man on the other side of the desk would collapse, that someone would come into the room, and that the telephone would ring.

The light might possibly go out, but that would not make any essential difference.

The thought of Tornilla collapsing was unrealistic, and in all probability no one would come into the room. So there was the telephone left. He had never heard the telephone ring of course, but on the other hand he had never before been here in the day-time. He delved even further into the world of clichés and thought: There's always got to be a first time.

For nearly an hour his whole mind was concentrated on the telephone. Then he decided to count to a thousand, slowly and silently to himself, without moving his lips, and if the telephone had not rung by the time he had finished—

The thought broke there.

One—two—three—four—five—six—seven . . .

. . . five hundred and ninety-eight—five hundred and ninety-nine—six hundred—six hundred and one . . .

Willi Mohr fainted and fell off the bench. He lay on the stone floor with his eyes closed, half on one side with his head thrown back and his knees bent.

Sergeant Tornilla leant forward in his chair and placed his wrists against the edge of the desk. He moved his shoulders and legs and exercised his fingers. Then he yawned, took a cigarette out of the green packet and lit it. As he smoked he sat hunched up slightly, his left elbow on the arm of the chair and his finger running over his cheek up towards his eyebrows, as if to check whether the growth had already begun to make itself felt. His gaze was directed straight out into the room, but it looked as if he were not really seeing anything.

When he had about an inch left of his cigarette, he extinguished it carefully in the ash-tray and folded the stub in the middle. Then he yawned again, pulled out a drawer in the desk and got out a tube of simpatinas. He shook two of the small white tablets into his hand and looked at them for a moment before grasping the earthenware jug behind his chair and swallowing them with a gulp of water.

Then he got up and walked round the table, the jug still in his hand.

Willi Mohr opened his eyes. His face was wet and he saw the shiny black of boot legs a few inches away from his nose.

Sergeant Tornilla had not bent down, but was standing upright with the water-jug in his hand, apparently looking down at him from a preposterous height.

As Willi Mohr began to get up and was leaning on his elbow, Tornilla put the water-jug down on the wooden bench and walked back to his seat on the other side of the desk.

'Get up and sit up,' he said.

Willi Mohr obeyed. He sat down on the bench, picked up the jug and brought it up to his mouth. He drank for a long time, with deep gurgling gulps.

Sergeant Tornilla sat at his desk, in exactly the same position as before, watching. After a while, he said: 'Well? From whom did you get all that money?'

Willi Mohr felt more confident now, despite his recent collapse and the fact that his head was still empty and whirling. The telephone had evidently remained dumb, but similarly nothing unexpected had happened and he had not been the one to break the silence. He glanced down at his watch and saw that it was already a quarter-past two. The previous silence had lasted more than two hours then. The present one lasted only a minute or so.

'From Ramon Alemany.'

'So he gave you at least twenty thousand pesetas then? I must say, that's a considerable sum.'

'No. I stole it.'

His reply seemed to overwhelm or surprise the man in the armchair in some way. But he asked immediately: 'Didn't you find it strange that a poor fisherman like Ramon Alemany should have so much money on him, to steal?'

There was a brief pause before the word steal, very brief, but quite noticeable.

'Yes,' said Willi Mohr.

Sergeant Tornilla smiled kindly and put his hand in his pocket.

'You asked me for a light,' he said. 'Here you are.'

Willi Mohr took out one of his yellow poor-man's cigarettes and began to smoke.

'My German isn't good enough for me to give you a perfect translation of the text on that portrait, but naturally I shall make an attempt. Let me see now, it would run roughly like this: General Franco, our undefeated Leader, beneath whose invincible sword the National Army is covered in glory, General Franco, who at the head of the Salvation Movement defends and vindicates before the whole world our beloved Spain and her sacred name, in a manner that arouses a universal wave of rapture, respect and admiration, the Leader of Spain, by the Grace of God. That's it, roughly.'

'Thank you.'

'Unfortunately I cannot give you a translation which gives the words their full meaning. Much of the beauty is lost. Your language is a powerful one, but it lacks poetry and greatness. I hope I have succeeded in making the content clear. Those words were true when they were written and are to a great extent still true. Here and for us. But you haven't been here long enough to realize that.'

Willi Mohr stared at him with tired astonishment.

'Every word is not taken literally, of course, like certain parts of the Bible,' said Sergeant Tornilla.

Willi Mohr's jaw-muscles twitched. For the first time for years, he almost burst out laughing.

Tornilla looked at him searchingly and then with a sleep-walker's certainty, he picked up one of his papers.

'There's one detail missing in your personal file,' he said.

'Oh yes.'

'Your faith isn't down here.'

'No.'

'I presume you're not a Catholic?'

'You're right.'

'Protestant then?'

'No.'

'What religion do you belong to then?'

'None at all.'

'What do you mean by at all?'

'Exactly what I say. I was baptized, purely routinely, into the Lutheran Church, but I left it seven years ago. I've even got a receipt to prove it.'

'When you lived in East Germany, was it? Obligatory?'

'Not at all. So far as I could make out, you could pray to whatever god you liked, Buddha or God or thunder or anything. I had a workmate who wore both the Communist Party badge and some Catholic emblem on his lapel.'

'Not even a bad Catholic can be a Communist.'

'Oh yes.'

'And you yourself? Don't you believe in God?'

'Don't know.'

'What do you mean, you don't know?'

'Again, just what I say. The question does not interest me. So far as I can see, it doesn't make any difference if there is one god or a thousand or none at all. Anyhow, not while one's alive.'

'And what if you should die suddenly?'

'I hope I do die suddenly.'

'Unprepared and without even being honourably buried?'

'My father died seven years ago, unfortunately not particularly suddenly. A friend of his, who knew him well, officiated at the funeral. He was a guard on the railways. I don't think any priest could have done it better.'

Sergeant Tornilla offered him a cigarette and lit it.

'Are you very unhappy?'

'No.'

207

Willi Mohr glanced at the portrait and shrugged his shoulders.

'Anyhow, not for that reason,' he said.

'And so you went from Gotenhafen to Flensburg?'

Tornilla plunged into the subject with no kind of transition whatsoever and at least thirty seconds went by before Willi Mohr was able to say:

'Yes, via Kiel.'

'And how long did you stay there?'

'Until the end of the war.'

'Went on with your training?'

'Yes, at the Torpedo School. We were even having a lecture on the morning the British came.'

'Wonderful.'

'You think so?'

'And then?'

'Went home.'

'To Thüringen?'

'Yes. The Americans had gone from there by then. They exchanged it for a bit of Berlin instead.'

'How did you get there?'

'By goods-train to a place somewhere south of Hanover. It was very slow and we were standing packed in open wagons. Then I walked the last bit.'

'Was your home-town very changed?'

'No. The Russians had nailed up a huge wooden construction in the middle of the square. When I saw it I thought it was some kind of apparatus to execute people in, but it turned out to be a gong they used when the soldiers were to eat.'

'And your home? Had it been destroyed?'

'No, not at all. The town wasn't in the battle-line and had hardly even had a raid.'

'And your parents were still alive?'

'Yes, but my father was ill and never really recovered.'

'Did you suffer much?'

'The first winter there was a shortage of food, but then things got a little better.'

'Did you join the Communist party?'

'No, I told you I wasn't interested in politics.'

'Yes, you said that before. Did you manage to get work?'

208

'Yes, with a firm of decorators in Jena. I painted signs and placards.'

'How long did you work there?'

'Five years.'

'Why did you leave?'

'I fell out with the owner.'

'Why?'

'He maintained that I sabotaged his work and behaved in a manner hostile to the state. He even reported me to the police.'

'Was he a Communist?'

'Quite the opposite, and he was afraid that someone might discover it.'

'How did you fall out with him?'

'It was a crazy business. The man was an idiot and a coward too. The President, Pieck was his name, was going to make a speech in Jena, and we had got the order for a large placard with his portrait on it. I made it in the usual way, stuck up a litho on a board, and the picture didn't cover the whole surface, so I drew a few lines with a brush from the portrait out towards the edges. I thought it'd look like a halo or rays of the sun or something like that and it'd look all right. My boss was away and didn't see the placard until it was put up. I had painted with a round brush and there was a circle at the end of each line. He decided that they looked like gun-barrels pointing out from the President and that we'd all be sent to Siberia. He'd got Siberia on the brain. So he hurried off to report me to the police.'

'And what did the police do?'

'Laughed.'

'And you?'

'I decided to go.'

'Why?'

'I didn't want to stay in a country where people, rightly or wrongly, were so riddled with fear that they made fools of themselves in public. Things weren't up to much there, and I thought I'd be able to earn much better money in the British Zone.'

'Didn't you then?'

'Yes, when I got work. The money was more usable too. Otherwise everything seemed even more meaningless.'

'Where did you work?'

'With a travelling ice-show, a sort of circus, which performed all the year round. In Germany and France and Luxembourg.'

'What did you do there?'

'Drove a truck, and helped put up and take down the tents and seating. It was nothing special, just heavy manual labour.'

'But you earned money?'

'Not all that much, but I had practically no expenses so I could save my wages.'

'Were you saving for any particular purpose?'

'To come here and paint.'

'Did you dream of becoming an artist?'

'No.'

'But you wanted to paint?'

'No, I didn't want anything.'

'Are you painting now?'

'No.'

'Why are you here then?'

Willi Mohr raised his head and his eyes met the friendly, steady gaze from the other side of the desk.

'I don't know any longer,' he said.

'One must believe in and want something,' said Sergeant Tornilla, shaking his head slightly.

'Possibly,' said Willi Mohr.

He sat in silence for a while, looking absently at Tornilla. He had stopped regarding him as his tormentor and had given up longing for the interrogation to end. On the contrary, he had begun to feel a strange sense of communion with this room and this terrible smiling man, who never perspired and never lost control. He was very tired and his thoughts were undisciplined and muddled. Suddenly he began to talk again.

'It's stupid to believe and want things, but sometimes one envies those who do. There, in Jena, I knew a girl who was in the Party. She was an editor of a paper which dealt with tractors and she ordered placards from us. I talked to her, and we met quite often. She was very enthusiastic and always talked about all sorts of things and had views on everything. It was laughable.'

'Was she your . . . er . . . girl?'

'No, she was shy about things like that and got confused when you touched her, talking twice as fast about everything, mostly

210

about collective agriculture and production increases. Nothing ever came of it. Once it looked as if it might, but she got no further than taking off her dress. Then she began to sweat all over and look as if she wanted to run away and hide. I didn't know what to do and then I laughed at her and she cried. But she really was enthusiastic. I remember she had newspapers from West Germany and looked at the advertisements for clothes, nylons and that sort of thing, and she was always talking about how much she'd like to have such things. That was when I'd already decided to go and I said it was quite simple for her to get all those blouses and stockings she wanted. All she had to do was to go to Berlin and then cross the border. But she said that we already had something much more important and in time we'd get everything else too. She said she had time to wait. Why are we talking German, by the way?'

'Because you're tired,' said Sergeant Tornilla.

Willi Mohr sat in silence for a moment and then said, as if to himself: 'I've been wondering these last few days whether I ought not to go back and find her again. But that's too late of course, that too. She's probably met someone who's less clumsy than I am. One should be able to find another like her, I suppose, though most of them are probably different. If I ever get away from here.'

'Exactly, if you ever get away from here,' said Sergeant Tornilla.

He shook his head seriously and offered yet another Bisonte.

'You really have gone astray,' he said.

After he had lit the cigarette, he sat for a moment with the lighter in his hand, looking at the flickering flame. Then he blew it out and said as if in passing: 'There are a number of things you haven't told me. I suggest you do that now.'

Willi Mohr shook his head stubbornly.

'No,' he said.

Tornilla smiled regretfully and opened up one of his files.

'People who are led astray are at least sometimes guiltless,' he said. 'And yet they do irreparable damage and they themselves are the ones to suffer most. The real criminal is the one who leads others astray and provokes people into actions against their common sense, their instinct for self-preservation and their inner-

211

most wishes. I'll give you a few concrete examples of what I mean. The disturbances at the zinc mine in Santa Margarita a year ago. You know about them, but perhaps you don't know so much about the practical consequences.'

He had taken out a thick report and was leafing absently through it.

'There should be some figures here,' he said. 'Yes, here they are. Ten people murdered, three engineers massacred by the mob, and one civil guard, one man from the Policia Armada and five soldiers all killed while trying to restore order. The civil' guard and three of the soldiers were from the town here. The guard left a widow and three fatherless children behind him, the soldiers were young recruits with their parents alive, and at least one of them was the only son in the family. A million pesetas worth of damage was done. Can you tell me what the point was of all this?'

He paused briefly and looked seriously at the man on the bench.

'None at all, of course. Who is to blame? Well, those who provoked these crimes and put weapons in the hands of simple, ignorant creatures who do not know how or at what moment arms should be used. Earlier I mentioned that there were still a few exceptions amongst us. There are not many, but they must be eliminated. In addition, there are foreign provocateurs, who abuse our hospitality. They are the ones who are to blame.'

Willi Mohr slowly stubbed out his cigarette-end in the ashtray and tried to concentrate on what the other man was saying. He had never heard about the disturbances in Santa Margarita before, but he was aware that he had at last got hold of the end of a thread which was leading somewhere, though where he did not know.

'Well now, all this happened before I came here,' said Sergeant Tornilla, 'but as you lived here already, I thought perhaps the matter might interest you. It happened on the night of the third of December, while you were amusing yourself bathing naked with that Norwegian woman, if I remember rightly.'

He put the report back in the file.

'How many of those . . . who were led astray lost their lives?' said Willi Mohr.

He did not want to let the subject go just yet.

'Oh, quite a number. I don't remember the figure exactly. They also died unnecessarily, of course. The whole thing was quite pointless. No one could have gained anything from the affair, not even the Communists, who started it. A few hundred workers striking for a couple of hours. Then the strike's over.'

'But if sufficiently many do it at the same time in sufficiently many places?'

'There won't be any more strikes,' said Sergeant Tornilla, 'anyhow not in this district. I suppose you know strikes are illegal.'

'Yes.'

'They are illegal because they're pointless, because they do nothing but harm. They're quite simply outbreaks of ignorance. Before, during the dark years before 1936, there were always strikes. The country was impoverished, it was impossible to keep order, everything was chaotic and confused, poisoned by foreign lies and criminal ideas.'

He put the file aside and added: 'Nothing like that will ever be repeated again.'

For the first time for some hours, a few scattered sounds from outside began to penetrate the door's dark-brown panels. Nailed boots and butts of carbines scraped against the concrete floor in the porch, and a few remarks could also be heard, sharp and brief, like words of command. Evidently some kind of parade.

In the interrogation room, a new and alien sound had also begun to make itself heard, rhythmical and creaking.

The man in the armchair was winding up his watch. He wore it on his left wrist with the wide gold band half hidden by his cuff, and Willi Mohr had never seen him look at it.

'Changing the guard,' said Sergeant Tornilla. 'That means the siesta is over. We haven't had much sleep during it today, have we? Oh well, we'll have to catch up on it another time.'

He pulled his cuff to rights without checking on the time. His watch was broad and strong and had extra buttons for a stop-watch and automatic timing. He listened to the guard stamping away in the porch and then said absently: 'During those weeks on the yacht, you must have got to know Ramon Alemany pretty well. Did you like him?'

213

'No.'

'What was he like?'

'Rather primitive.'

'Your opinion seems to fall in line with what I've been told. I myself have not had the pleasure of meeting him.'

'Oh yes.'

'No loss, perhaps. He was physically strong, wasn't he?'

'Relatively.'

'Well, perhaps my informant was exaggerating. But his brother is said to be quite different. Is that right?'

'Yes.'

'Yes, I've been told so. I've never met him either.'

It was not a question and so Willi Mohr did not have to answer, a fact he was grateful for, as if he had been granted a welcome and unexpected favour.

Willi Mohr stared absently at the man in uniform and slowly formulated a question which he had a reason for asking.

'You've killed people, haven't you?'

Sergeant Tornilla smiled sadly and threw out his hands.

'That's been unavoidable,' he said. 'In nine years' soldiering. Later too, it's happened. The Service has not always been as pleasant as it is now.'

'How do you feel?'

'Thanks, I feel fine. Not especially tired. Our conversation has stimulated me.'

'I mean how do you feel, to have killed and to know you're going to do it again?'

'So far as I'm concerned, it's always happened in wartime or in situations comparable to war. One doesn't analyse such situations afterwards, and beforehand the problems are largely of a technical nature.'

'Thank you. You don't mind my asking?'

'Not at all.'

'You don't mind that I ... so to speak ... took over the interrogation?'

'What interrogation?'

For the first time in their time together, Tornilla seemed genuinely surprised. He looked round his desk and seemed to be searching among his papers.

214

'Of course,' he said, 'that man and the wood. Amadeo Prunera. You won't forget him?'

'No,' said Willi Mohr.

Sergeant Tornilla rose and walked round the desk.

'This has been a very pleasant and fruitful conversation,' he said. 'I hope I haven't tired you out too much.'

He smiled and put out a hand to help Willi Mohr up on to his feet.

'I also hope you will excuse my curiosity and obstinacy if I once again mention those details you have not wanted to tell me. If you should change your mind in the near future, do come here. Well, naturally you're welcome under any circumstances, I need hardly tell you.'

After following Willi to the door, he suddenly stopped with his hand on the door-handle and said: 'Otherwise perhaps we won't be meeting again. It pains me that I've not had an opportunity to see your paintings.'

Sergeant Tornilla opened the door and held out his hand. His handshake was dry and firm and heartfelt.

Willi Mohr stepped out of the shadow of the porch straight into the heavy, muggy afternoon heat.

He was fifty yards from the entrance before he realized that he was carrying his hat in his hand, and he stopped to put it on. When he had pressed it down over the back of his neck, he turned round and looked back at the guard-post, lying there like a long yellow brick in the white dust.

Black and white lines were vibrating in front of his eyes, but all the same he could distinguish Sergeant Tornilla quite clearly.

The man in the elegant green uniform was standing with his feet apart beneath the flag. He had a cigarette in the corner of his mouth and was just wiping the palm of his right hand with a clean white handkerchief.

'He'll break me next time,' said Willi Mohr to himself.

As he wandered on between the silky grey olive trees he thought: Hope it's not too long before then.

Part Six

1

It began to rain on the night of the fourteenth of December, at first in large scattered drops, and then it poured down in the dawn light, like a wall outside windows and doorways. The people of the town up in the mountains woke and blessed the rain.

It was steady and inexorable, numbing in its grey monotony, and the cool of the first few hours was soon exchanged for a raw chill which ate its way through the stone walls and penetrated into the houses. There was no defence against it, for the rain thrust the smoke back down the chimneys and smothered the embers in the open fires. At first the dry ground greedily absorbed the water, but gradually that too became soaked.

On the third day, four buildings collapsed as their foundations gave way and the walls caved in. In one case it happened quite unexpectedly and several sleeping people were crushed by the rubble, beams and sharp yellow stones. After the accident, many tried to shore up their houses with planks and poles, but there was a shortage of wood and in the worst affected parts people dared not sleep under their roofs, spending the nights in small provisional shacks of sacking and corrugated iron.

Now it was raining for the fifth day running.

The house in Barrio Son Jofre stood on rock foundations and showed no greater tendency to collapse than usual, but the white-washed wall of the room downstairs was already spotted with grey mould and everything in it was covered with a misty layer of damp.

Willi Mohr was sitting on the stairs watching the cat cowering by the doorway. Its head was down between its shoulders, its tail stuck straight up in the air, stiff and thick and staring, and

217

although it was on heat, even this inducement could not persuade it out into the wet just like that. Now and again it miaowed, hoarsely and urgently, staring reproachfully at the man on the stairs.

Willi Mohr laughed to himself and shook his head.

Ten minutes earlier he had been behaving in exactly the same way, and for a reason which was even more peculiar. The pistol under the mattress had irritated him as he slept and when he transferred it to his rucksack he discovered two reddish corrosive spots on the clip. So the rust had probably already begun to spread into the dry barrel, and the thought of a little damp obliterating that mirror-corridor of terror had filled him with a cheerfulness which a moment later had seemed both misplaced and inexplicable.

He defended himself by saying that he would only be using the pistol once anyhow, and quite soon too, so a little rust in the barrel would not affect the effectiveness of the gun at such short range.

With that, the thought that he would very shortly be killing Santiago Alemany had brushed across his mind. It was the first time he had thought about the matter since he had parted from Sergeant Tornilla beneath the drooping red and yellow flag at the guard-post. He had been busy during the last few days with things that had already happened and had not had time to reflect on what might happen next.

The cat at last made up its mind, crouched down, took a long leap out through the doorway and vanished into the pouring grey rain outside.

Willi Mohr shivered. His trousers were crumpled and his shirt so damp that it was sticking to his back, and he longed for a dry change of clothes, knowing full well that that was a luxury he could not aspire to. Instead he took off his shirt and tried to wring it out, but managed to squeeze out only a few drops, which did not even leave a mark when they fell on the damp tile of the stair. He spread the shirt out over the wooden railing in a vain hope that it would at least get a little dryer. Then he rose and fetched a towel from his rucksack. Even if not dry, it was at least clean and he went out into the kitchen and took off his sandals, trousers and long pants. He stood naked on the stone

218

floor and rubbed himself systematically with the coarse towel, beginning with his legs and working upwards over his hips, stomach, chest, and back. When his body had warmed up, he put on his wet clothes again with a reluctant grimace, flung his thin, wrinkled, plastic raincoat over his shoulders, and went out into the rain.

The dog splashed faithfully at his side, after a few minutes her black coat as smooth and shiny as a seal's along her back.

'Why don't you stay at home?' said Willi Mohr, poking her with his foot.

A moment later he thought: And what on earth am I doing out at this time of day?

It was no later than midday and he did not usually go up to town so early. But he felt lonelier than ever shut in by the rain and was tormented by a mounting anxiety which he could only counteract by keeping moving.

Willi Mohr wanted to see people and hear them speak. He was aching, quite simply, for company.

He had felt like this since the day before the rain had started, and he was perfectly aware that this change had become noticeable after his eighteen hours together with Tornilla at the guard-post.

But he was not going to admit it, not even to himself.

In the middle of the cross-roads stood four civil guards and on Avenida Generalissimo Franco, he met two more. With their hoods and long dark-green oilskin coats, they looked strangely alien, but they blended into the surroundings in a way that made it seem quite natural that it was they who inhabited this world of rain and no one else. Although they did not appear to notice him and he could not see their faces, he was sure that they would not forget him in their reports.

His wet trousers flapped round his legs as he crossed the square, and his hat was already so wringing wet that the rain simply went straight through it. He felt the water making its way under his shirt-collar and trickling down his neck and shoulders.

Outside the Café Central stood a grey jeep with its canvas hood up, and beside it a small black Renault of the kind that had just begun to be manufactured on licence in Valladolid. These cars were not especially good, but extremely expensive, and most

219

of the first series had been reserved for the authorities. Private individuals who could afford a car of their own for pleasure only were usually able to afford to get themselves a foreign car in some way or other.

The car was empty, but in the front seat of the jeep sat two gendarmes from the Policia Armada. They were smoking cigarettes and gazing philosophically out at the rain.

Inside the café there were about a dozen people.

Near the door sat two civil guards filling in their football coupons. They had hung up their raincoats and leant their carbines against the wall behind the table. The crumpled sports page from *Vanguardia* lay spread out on the marble table-top and now and again one of them bent over the paper and frowningly studied the tables in it.

Two strangers were standing by the bar, drinking coffee. One was small and thin and bald, the other a little taller and much younger, almost handsome, with dark hair parted at the side, a dimple in his chin and gentle brown eyes. They were obviously strangers to the town, but their appearance was ordinary and they could have been anything from commercial travellers to fish-merchants or travelling showmen. Their relatively well-cared for clothing, shirts with starched cuffs and detached collars, sleazy suits of some striped purplish material, bore witness to the fact that they had come at least from Santa Margarita, though more likely the provincial capital. The bald one had hung his black plastic coat over the rail round the bar, and the other was wearing a thin pepper-and-salt overcoat of very poor quality which would not stand up long to heavy rain. Willi Mohr concluded that these were the owners of the black private car in the square.

The other people in the café were road-workers. They were squatting in the middle of the floor round a large brazier of glowing charcoal. Not one of them spoke and their expressions were serious and closed.

Willi Mohr hung up his hat and coat and went over to the bar. He ordered a cognac and café con leche. The proprietor shrugged his shoulders and began to carry out the order. He was Willi Mohr's landlord and the owner of the creaking bedstead which was still up on the first floor of the house in Barrio Son Jofre. He

220

had also saved his tenant from precarious situations on several occasions during the past six months. This had always happened in exchange for some kind of consideration or guarantee, but Willi Mohr reckoned the man would probably show the same goodwill without the guarantees. He knew the road-workers came here because it was the only place they could warm themselves and because it only cost a few reales to hire a pack of cards. There was always a crowd at the Central, but the bar was probably not very profitable, as all the road-workers together spent less in one year than the Scandinavians spent in an evening at Jacinto's down in the puerto.

The café owner had never shown himself to be intrusive and neither was he particularly talkative, due perhaps to some extent to the fact that he was a Catalonian and came from a place in the far north of Gerona Province. Lately Willi Mohr had also begun to like the man for his way of coping with the unavoidable pictures of the Caudillo and José Antonio Primo de Rivera. They hung squashed between posters for films and bull-fights and were so incredibly filthy that it was very difficult to make out what they represented at all.

Today the proprietor said nothing whatsoever. He put down the coffee and brandy with his eyes averted and returned to drying glasses.

Willi Mohr drank the coffee quickly and in long gulps to make the most of its warmth, before it had time to cool.

Outside, the jeep started up and roared away across the square, the sound of the engine soon disappearing in the monotonous drumming of the rain.

Another road-worker came in, wet and ragged, and in silence a place was made for him in the circle round the brazier.

The two men by the bar were talking quietly to each other. As far as Willi Mohr could make out, the conversation centred on the question of when and where they should eat their dinner. The bald one, who was drinking some colourless spirits with his coffee, emptied his glass and pushed it across the bar.

'Give me the same again,' he said.

The proprietor said nothing, but took a bottle down from the shelf and poured out the drink.

'This is a very good sort,' said the bald man.

221

'It's the usual,' said the proprietor.

'Do you sell cigarettes too?'

'Yes, Ideales.'

'Nothing else?'

'No.'

'They won't do. Give me a cigar instead.'

'I haven't any cigars.'

Willi Mohr listened absently to this exchange of words as he sipped his cognac. The remarks were quite ordinary and yet they reminded him of Sergeant Tornilla and the room with its four pieces of furniture and green glass lampshade.

'You should try some of this,' said the bald man to Willi Mohr, pointing to his glass. 'Just what you need in this weather. The peasants drink it in the mornings before they go out to work in the fields.'

Willi Mohr had gone out to find company and listen to human voices. Now when someone was actually talking to him, he did not like it.

'Cazalla,' said the man. 'A genuine Spanish drink. Very good for you.'

'Not for your liver,' said the handsome one in the overcoat, taking a gulp of his coffee.

'Everything should be enjoyed in moderation,' said the bald man philosophically.

Then he raised his glass to Willi Mohr and said with a laugh: 'Health and money and good luck with your virility.'

'Your health,' said Willi Mohr.

'You must be a foreigner from those spots of paint. English?'

'No, German.'

'Do you live here?'

'Yes.'

From the other side of the bar the proprietor caught his eye, for one brief second only and without saying a word or making any sign whatsoever.

'This is an unusually dull town,' said the bald man. 'Thank God I'm only passing through.'

He seemed to have given up the idea of getting a conversation going and stared ahead of him, emptying his glass.

The man's inquisitiveness and obvious garrulousness had

222

irritated Willi Mohr. The strangers were probably commercial travellers or at the most lowly government officials.

The bald man seemed quite unable to keep silent.

'It really is very raw and chilly out,' he said, pulling on his fingers so that the joints cracked. 'Must warm up a bit.'

He went over to the brazier but could not get near, as the circle round it was tight and not one of the men moved.

'Is the fire reserved for honoured guests?' said the handsome one sarcastically.

'Move up so the man can get in,' said the proprietor.

The road-workers moved up.

'Thanks boys,' said the bald man genially, and he knelt down with his hands outstretched over the glowing charcoal.

No one replied.

The tall man in the overcoat leant over the bar and asked: 'Are those men unemployed?'

'Their place of employment has been washed away,' said the proprietor. 'They've lost their wages.'

After a while the bald man came back, paid and picked up his raincoat.

'Fine,' he said, for no apparent reason. 'See you again some time, my friends.'

The strangers walked towards the exit, but did not go out, remaining standing just inside the door, again discussing the question of food.

Without being asked to, the proprietor took a bottle down from the shelf and filled Will Mohr's glass. Then he dried a glass and helped himself.

'That man's right,' he said. 'Cazalla is good in weather like this.'

'Bottoms up,' he added, raising his glass.

The dry anise-spirits burnt his throat and sank like a ball of fire into his stomach. Willi Mohr was shaken by an involuntary shudder as the cold from his wet clothes chilled his skin. The air coming in from outside was heavy and raw and damp.

'Warm yourself up a bit,' said the proprietor.

Willi Mohr went over to the brazier and the men round it at once made room for him. He sat like the others, squatting and spreading out his hands to the warmth. They all sat apathetically

223

in silence, sullenly staring down into the sinking embers. Only the man on Willi Mohr's right moved, nudging him slightly in the side, a small toothless man with a thin face and deep-set eyes. He looked much like the others, just as ragged and emaciated, though his eyes were perhaps a little sharper and livelier.

The men by the door seemed to have come to some agreement at last. The jalousies rattled behind them, then car doors slammed and a starter began to rattle. After the third try, the engine started up and the car drove away.

'The bastards have gone,' said the toothless man.

The others sat without moving. Willi Mohr was the only one to raise his head and glance questioningly at the man who had broken the silence.

'Policia Secreta, the secret police,' said the man contemptuously. 'I can recognize the swine anywhere and anytime, even if they dress up as nuns or priests.'

'Perhaps mostly then,' he added, spitting on the floor.

'Careful,' said one of the men sitting opposite him.

He made an almost imperceptible movement of his head towards the civil guards still doing their football coupons.

'Huh, we needn't bother about them,' said the toothless man. 'They're locals and they're deaf when they're not on duty. What's so special about them? Nothing, just ordinary peasants and workers like us—who've taken on a shitty job to be able to live. But those other snooping swine . . . just think, did you hear . . . do you sell cigarettes here too . . . oh, only Ideales . . . give me a cigar then . . .'

He looked round wildly and shouted to the proprietor: 'Juan, you've got cigarettes here, haven't you? Supposing they'd looked under . . .'

He stopped and nervously bit his thin lips.

The café-owner gave him a long look and put his hand on the tap of the vermouth keg. He poured out two generous drinks, put them on a tray and carried them over to the table by the door. Neither of the civil guards looked up from their task, but one took his glass immediately and emptied it.

The proprietor went back towards the bar, but on the way stopped behind Willi Mohr, gently striking his leg with the tray.

'It's true,' he said. 'They're looking for contraband, coffee and foreign cigarettes.'

The man on Willi Mohr's right chewed at his bottom lip with his toothless gums and said wildly: 'To hell with that. They're after one of us, or some other poor bastard. I know them, I know...'

'Calm down,' said the man sitting on Willi Mohr's left.

He was a black-haired man in a ragged faded overall, with large gnarled hands.

'Calm, careful,' said the toothless man in a hoarse whisper. 'I don't know anyone who's as calm and careful as we are and this is what we get in thanks. Fifteen pesetas a day and nothing when the weather's bad or when they stop the work to hold their damn manoeuvres up there. I've a woman and three kids who're starving to death and yet I've got to be calm and careful. And grateful for my three duros a day. I met someone who worked at some swanky spa hotel where there wasn't even a well and the water had to be carted there in a truck. Formentor, the hotel was called, and he said people staying their paid four duros for every glass of water they drank and most of them weren't foreigners, but Spaniards... d'you hear that... Spaniards...'

He fell silent and hunched up a little, perhaps because none of the others seemed to be listening to him.

They were sitting as before, silent and immobile.

They had presumably heard all this many times before and were satisfied that the conversation had become sufficiently low-toned that what was said could not be heard over by the door. A couple of them moved a little nearer to the brazier as the warmth from it began to decrease.

After a while the man in the overall turned his head towards Willi Mohr and said quietly: 'Have you any children?'

He spoke with a strange dialect, making an effort to speak clearly and understandably.

Willi Mohr shook his head.

'I've two,' said the man, 'a son of nine and a daughter of five.'

'Here?'

'No, far away, near Bilbao. I come from there; Basque, that's my home country.'

225

There was a moment's silence. Then he put two fingers up in the air and said:

'My son's already done two years in school and he's learnt to read and write. Look at this. My wife sent me his first writing book.'

He thrust his hand inside his overall and pulled out a folded much-thumbed exercise book with a dog-eared yellow cover.

'Would you like to look?'

Willi Mohr nodded and took it.

'I never learnt to read and write myself,' said the man seriously, 'but my son can already, although he's only nine. It's a pity I can't read what he's written and see if he writes well.'

Willi Mohr weighed the thin exercise book in his hand without opening it.

'Why do you do nothing?' he said suddenly and quite unpremeditatedly.

'I work,' said the man in surprise. 'Work and send home the money I earn.'

After a moment's silence he added: 'Though someone has to help me with the envelope.'

'I didn't mean that,' said Willi Mohr quietly.

'No, I understand what you mean. You mean the other, but that's over a long time ago. It was no good. When we were to fight against . . . them. We were at it a whole year and everyone said the whole world would help us but I didn't see anyone. We were going to be independent, we were, but we weren't all that many, although we had rifles and a few old guns and tanks. Then those . . . those . . . they had awful great aeroplanes and bombs and tanks; it was many years ago, in March 1937, and we had nothing but our rifles, and we fought up in the pass in the mountains and every day they rained their bombs down on us, and there was something in the bombs which set everything on fire, thermite, I think it was called, and everything burnt all round us. They went on all through May and June and we got orders to counter-attack and retake a mountain, and we did too, and then they came with more aeroplanes and more bombs and more guns. Urquiola Pass . . . that's the name of the place where I was. They took Bilbao from us later, when there weren't so many of us left, and then the end came. I don't want to talk about it.'

226

The man in the overall sat in silence for a while. Then he laughed roughly and said: 'It's not so strange that I've never learnt to read, because I never had a chance. But you see, we who were in on that then can't do it again, as that's the kind of thing you only do once. Someone else has got to try next time, the younger ones, who've learnt more. We went on for a whole year and we gave the bastards what for many times, although they came with their aeroplanes and bombs and tanks. And I was a prisoner-of-war later and when the war was over, I couldn't go home after all, and that didn't matter all that much because nearly all of them were dead, but I wanted to all the same. But then they put me in Formentera for six years and we dug salt there. You don't do that again, even if you are still starving and have to look at those bastards on the streets.'

Willi Mohr knew very little about the Basque tragedy, but it was not the first time he had heard about the concentration camps in Formentera.

He said: 'In the salt mines? Were you a Communist?'

The man in the overall started and although he had been whispering all the time, he looked round anxiously and licked his lips.

'No,' he said. 'No, not that . . . no, you mustn't think that . . .'

In this case the teacher had evidently succeeded in his task without the need to kill his pupil. Willi Mohr was ashamed that he had even begun the conversation and even more that he had been the one to continue it, forcing the other man to reveal himself and talk about things he did not want to remember. He lowered his gaze and looked at the yellow exercise book.

'My son wrote that,' said the Basque. 'You can read it if you like.'

Willi turned the pages of the book. It contained three compositions, printed in laborious childish handwriting. The first was about Francisco Franco Bahamonde, the second about José Antonio Primo de Rivera and the third about Jesus. With each composition was a coloured illustration which the children had been allowed to copy from some publication. The first was the best, and despite various irregularities, one could distinguish the General's egg-shaped head, high curved hairline and small triangular moustache. The picture had probably been copied

227

from the same original as the portrait in Sergeant Tornilla's office.

Willi Mohr shut his eyes for a few seconds and then he opened· the book at random and read:

'José Antonio Primo de Rivera was a youth with more courage than any mature man, who sacrificed his life for the sake of the fatherland, its greatness and perpetuation, in the great just struggle for liberation against the bestial red hordes. This noble young Falangist ...'

He shut the book again and handed it back.

'Very good,' he said. 'Very well written.'

'He's only nine,' said the man in the torn overall.

Before putting the book back, he looked at it tenderly and lovingly.

Willi Mohr straightened up and went across to the bar and paid. He still had a few duros in his trouser pocket and wondered for a moment whether to offer the Basque a couple of bottles of wine. Then he decided against. It would be a meaningless gesture, almost an insult. He put on his hat and thin plastic coat and walked away. The men round the rapidly cooling brazier had begun to sing melancholy and sentimental songs about their home country, the words indistinct and incomprehensible and all he could catch was the refrain:

No somos de aqui—somos de Bilbao ...

We are not from here—we are from Bilbao ...

The civil guards had left unobtrusively, but at the doorway he had to make way for two more just coming in from the square. As they folded back their pointed hoods, he recognized one of them, the middle-aged man with a grey moustache, who had already fetched him twice from the house in Barrio Son Jofre. He was now looking very tired, his eyes swollen and bloodshot, but he smiled in recognition and shook his head, saying as he jerked his thumb out towards the rain:

'Terrible.'

Nothing had changed outside. The rain was still falling straight down, just as heavily as before. The dog splashed round his feet. During his visit to the Central he had not noticed her, but she had almost certainly been there, lying flat under one of the tables.

228

He would be wetter than ever when he got back, but that did not matter.

On the way home he saw two people and a car. The people were two half-naked children yelling and shrieking as they played about in a deep puddle, yellow with stirred-up mud, and the car a covered gas-powered army truck which drove along the Avenida so close to him that the camouflaged side-flaps brushed his sleeve in a shower of spattering drops of water.

There were no civil guards at the cross-roads.

When he had covered three-quarters of the alleyway up to Barrio Son Jofre, the dog began to bark and run on ahead. He realized that someone was waiting for him up at the house.

The fish-van was parked beside the camioneta. Santiago was sitting in the driver's seat, staring out at the rain. He was wearing a sou'wester and a short oilskin jacket, and he needed both, as the Ford had no doors and the windscreen was shattered. It must have happened recently as there were still bits of glass between the wooden beading and the metal frame. Santiago had unbuttoned his jacket and was holding his large sheath-knife in his right hand. He seemed irritable and restless, and had evidently been sitting whittling away at a wet piece of wood, for the floor of the van was covered with long fresh shavings.

When he saw Willi Mohr, he got down from the van and said: 'I've been waiting for you for a whole hour.'

'I was at the Central. You could have gone there.'

'No, I didn't want to meet you there.'

Willi Mohr stood on the steps and looked irresolutely at his visitor, who was still holding his knife in his hand.

'Open the door. I don't want to have to wait any longer,' said Santiago impatiently.

Willi Mohr shrugged his shoulders and turned round to stick the key into the lock.

He thought: Now he'll lift the knife and plunge it into my back, but I don't care any longer.

2

The door swung open on its creaking hinges and nothing had happened.

Willi Mohr stepped to one side to let Santiago Alemany walk past. Santiago put his knife back into its leather sheath and buttoned it down as he stepped over the threshold.

Before following him into the room, Willi Mohr turned round once more and looked at the small Ford van, with its high load of fish-boxes. The boxes were securely tied down and covered with a worn tarpaulin.

'What happened to the windscreen?' he said.

'They shot at me,' said Santiago.

'The civil guards?'

'No. Policia Armada. Two idiots in a jeep. They could have turned the jeep and overtaken me instead.'

'Why did they shoot at you?'

'I didn't stop at their halt-signal. For that matter, I never even saw it.'

His voice was tense and impatient and it seemed as if he thought the episode incidental, hardly worth mentioning.

Willi Mohr did not say anything more, but kicked off his sandals and hung his hat and plastic coat on the nail inside the door. Then he sat down on the stairs and wrung out his soaking trouser legs before rolling them up.

Santiago was walking uneasily back and forth across the floor, hunting in his pockets for something, presumably tobacco, and he looked irresolutely at the man on the stairs several times.

'There are some cigarettes over there by the rucksack,' said Willi Mohr, without looking up.

Santiago took an Ideales and lit it. His hands were shaking and he stood staring for a long time out into the rain, as if trying to regain his composure.

Finally he said: 'Do you like things as they are in this town and this country?'

'Not much,' said Willi Mohr.

'I was thinking of asking you to do something.'

'Oh yes.'

Santiago turned violently and flung the half-smoked cigarette out into the rain.

'Do you see what I've got on the van out there?'

'Yes, fish.'

'Fish, yes. There are some funny fish there too, not much like the usual ones.'

Willi Mohr said nothing. He was still busy with his trouser legs.

'Would you like to see my fish?' said Santiago Alemany sarcastically.

'Why not?'

Santiago laughed, and it sounded subdued and peculiar. Then he went out to the van and loosened the straps and pulled up a corner of the tarpaulin. Although it was the middle of the day and the distance from the van not more than six feet, Willi Mohr found it difficult to see and was not really able to distinguish what the other man was doing out there. The heavy rain softened the outlines and the more he stared the more blurred things became.

Santiago had taken down one of the fish-boxes and dumped it on the floor inside the doorway. Without speaking, he went back to the van fetched another box and placed it beside the first one, at the bottom of the stairs.

Willi Mohr sat still and looked at the fish.

'Do you see what these are?' said Santiago, kicking the first box.

'Squids.'

'Exactly, pulpo, the worst kind. They don't look very edible, do they?'

'No.'

'They aren't either. If you boil them for ten hours they're still just as tough as old rubber tyres. And these then?'

He kicked the other box.

'Sardines.'

'Not even that. Alachas, the poorest fish of the lot. Hardly worth bringing them ashore. But people who're really badly off eat them all the same. They salt them down in jars.'

'Oh yes.'

Santiago took the key out of the lock and shut the door from the inside.

'Feel in the bottom of the box,' he said.

Willi Mohr leant forward and thrust his hand down the edge. The unappetizing-looking squids were cold and slimy and in amongst the flabby jumble of tentacles were lumps of sepia-coloured secretion.

'No, not there. Try in the middle.'

Willi Mohr was irritated by his feelings of distaste and did not want to show it too clearly. He shrugged and thrust his fingers into the cold, sticky slime. Then he raised his head and looked at Santiago standing over him in the dim light, black and shiny in his wet oilskins.

'I didn't ask you to stir around in that mess just for fun,' said Santiago. 'And that's the best box. The other one's even worse. Alachas have sharper fins than any other fish I know. And I've four boxes of butcher's leavings too, entrails and half-rotten pig's stomachs, and two boxes of sea-urchins. If you touch them without gloves they puncture your skin and if you use gloves they spoil them.'

He knelt down and thrust both hands like a scoop into the mess and began to shovel the squids over into the other box. Not until he had scraped the rest away against the edges did Willi Mohr see that the box was unusually deep and stable.

On the rough bottom boards, among the lumps of squid secretion and torn-off tentacles lay a dismantled machine-gun. Despite the bad light, he could see that it was covered with a thick layer of green small-grained grease.

Neither of them said anything for a long time. Santiago had suddenly grown as calm as Willi Mohr, his breathing no longer uneven and panting, and he sat crouching with his elbows on his thighs, his filthy hands hanging loosely between his knees.

'I've got four more like that and six automatic-pistols. Out there. And underneath are three hundred rounds of ammunition and two dozen hand-grenades.

'Where does all this come from?' said Willi Mohr.

'From the sea.'

Outside the rain poured down with undiminished force.

'Not in our boat. That used to happen, when there were two of

232

us. My father would be mad if he knew about it. He believes in adapting himself, like most people of that age. They're burnt out, and say they've given all they had once and for all.'

'Who brings it ashore then?'

'Someone else. Hardly anyone knows anything about it, only him and me. And you.'

After a short pause he added:

'Things are going wrong. I must have help. From you.'

It grew silent again. They sat quite still and listened to the rain. Then Willi Mohr wiped his fingers on the stair and said: 'And if I refuse?'

The cat had come in through the hole in the door, wet and miserable, with a long bleeding scratch from its nose up to one eye. Santiago Alemany pulled out his knife and stirred round in the box of alachas until he found a flat red one among the other nickel-coloured fish. He lifted it out by the tail and put it down in front of the cat.

'Then I'll kill you,' he said.

'If you can,' said Willi Mohr.

'Yes, if I can.'

The cat sniffed at the fish, put one forepaw on it, turned its head sideways and sank its teeth into the fish's back.

'What's gone wrong?' said Willi Mohr.

'Something's up today. Something big. I know the signs. There were two road-blocks on the road from the puerto, and those idiots in the jeep too.'

'What happened?'

'They stopped me at the first and searched the van, even took off the tarpaulin and looked in the top boxes. There's never anything in them. Then they saw all this shit and the butcher's stuff and they gave up. They were people from hereabouts and they're never very dangerous. They've stopped me so many times that nowadays it's just automatic. Once I made them search through the whole load and lay the fish out along the side of the road. I pro ... pro ... what's it called?'

'Provoked.'

'Yes, that's it. I provoked them. Since then they've not been so fussy. The next road-block let me straight through. They've got some signalling system between them. But then that Policia

233

Armada patrol came. They'd parked their jeep under some trees and I didn't see either it or any halt-sign until they shot after me and the bullet came sailing through from behind and smashed the windscreen. However, they didn't feel like messing themselves up with fish and they didn't want to be out in the rain either. The one who had shot at me was a bit ashamed too. He said it must have been a ricochet.'

Santiago Alemany got up and went and fetched the cigarettes.

'I daren't go on now,' he said. 'It's worse on the other side of the mountains, on the main road. There are real barricades there. And tonight or early tomorrow morning this scare will have blown over. That's what usually happens.'

He lit two Ideales with the same match and gave one to Willi Mohr. Then he kicked the boxes and said: 'These have got to be there tonight or at the latest tomorrow morning.'

He stood still smoking, for perhaps thirty seconds, before he finished the sentence: '. . . they say.'

'Who?'

'You ask too many questions.'

'Antonio Millan?'

Santiago started and said roughly: 'What do you know about him?'

'Nothing. Just heard his name.'

'Where?'

'At the police.'

'Have they had you down there? Then I shouldn't have come.'

He paused briefly and then said thoughtfully: 'But I had nowhere else to go. You and I . . .'

He fell silent again.

Willi Mohr experienced a vague astonishment over the fact that he was not surprised, and also over the fact that the conversation was running so naturally and logically. He asked another question.

'Why are you doing all this? For money?'

'I don't think so. Not now. Anyhow, they don't pay all that well. At first I did it for money, but then something happened about a year ago, last autumn. Did you hear about the revolt in Santa Margarita?'

'Yes, a little.'

234

'Forty or fifty people were butchered there. They hadn't got any ammunition or hand-grenades. Do you know why?'

'No.'

'Because I didn't take the stuff there, although they'd said it was important and although I'd promised to do it and had already been paid for it. And do you know what I did instead? Went bathing with you and . . .'

He stopped suddenly and crashed his right fist into his left palm.

'Those people fought all the same, though they had nothing to fight with. There must be something in that. This time they've said again that it's important and this time the stuff's got to get there. No one's going to stop me.'

Then he began to breathe heavily and his voice grew suddenly hostile.

'Not even you,' he said.

'You must realize that this has really nothing to do with me,' said Willi Mohr with chilling politeness.

He did not like the change of tone, and he was always made uneasy by uncontrolled outbursts of emotion. A moment later he said: 'What are you going to do?'

'Leave the stuff and fetch it tonight or tomorrow when the extra patrols have been withdrawn. I'll drive into town with the fish this afternoon as usual. There are four boxes that are to be sold there anyhow.'

'What were you going to do with the arms and ammunition?'

'Put them in the outhouse or in here upstairs.'

'There's a rubbish heap behind the house. That'd be better.'

'As they're already on to you, it's dangerous wherever they're put.'

'No one'll think of the rubbish heap. There are a whole lot of old scrap metal and other things to cover them up with. And there's straw in the outhouse.'

'Perhaps you're right,' said Santiago. 'I'll get going now. The siesta's practically over.'

Willi Mohr fingered the dismantled machine-gun.

'Good stuff,' he said. 'Who are they for?'

'Don't know. Someone who needs them.'

Santiago swiftly and methodically scooped the squids back into

235

the box. Then he opened the outer door. Outside the rain was like a thick living curtain.

'This weather's saved us,' he said. 'Visibility's no more than thirty feet. If anyone comes, then my van's broken down and I've had to borrow the camioneta and am loading it up.'

'Yes, perhaps that'll do.'

Santiago lifted the box of sharp-finned, sardine-like fish.

'Are you going to help?' he said.

Willi Mohr got up from the stairs, pulled on his plastic coat, and pried the box of squids up off the floor. Then he took it in his arms and walked bare-footed round the house, just behind Santiago.

It took them only a quarter of an hour to transfer eight boxes of fish and sealed metal boxes of cartridges and hand-grenades from the Ford to the rubbish heap, and no one appeared as they were doing it. When they had covered over the boxes with old abandoned reed fencing and rotted straw from the outhouse, Santiago roped down the rest of the load and without looking up from the job, said: 'I'll be back this evening or tonight.'

Then he put his shoulder to the little van, got it moving and clambered into the driver's seat. The vehicle vanished into the rain long before it reached the alleyway, and if the engine started, it was not possible to hear it.

Willi Mohr stood on the flat steps in front of the door and stretched out his naked feet for the rain to rinse the mud off them. Then he did the same with his hands, which stank of fish and tainted offal.

As he stood there, a large piece of masonry loosened from the wall and fell down on to the soaking ground. He thought he heard the crack of a shot through the noise of the rain, but he was not certain.

3

Willi Mohr did not once leave the house in Barrio Son Jofre during the afternoon or evening. Once or twice he considered getting himself something to eat, but he only had to think about

236

the squid tentacles and the offal for his appetite to disappear immediately. Although he was wet through and everything indoors was quite damp, he did not feel especially uneasy and was not cold.

Although he did not think the arms-smuggling story was of any great significance and was convinced no one would find the compromising goods on the rubbish-heap, he sensed a rising excitement in face of the events ahead. He knew that something was about to happen, but he did not know what.

Most of the afternoon he sat on the stairs and thought. For more than an hour he turned over the pages of his passport. He studied the different visas thoroughly and suddenly found himself wondering about when and where and for what reason his passport would be stamped next.

His thoughts were muddled and undisciplined for long spells at a time. The events of the day had indeed enriched his store of new facts and lead-threads, but he was incapable of sorting them out or following them up. Nothing fell in with the pattern he had already defined and held to for a long time. The equation was not working out, although it ought to be doing so, and as a result life refused to appear simple and free of problems.

And it seemed to him that if his will to live was about to return, then it was doing so at a particularly ill-chosen moment.

Even after darkness had fallen, Willi Mohr still went on sitting on the stairs, thinking that there were altogether too many pieces of the jig-saw puzzle. Then he started listening. The downpour continued with the same monotonous force, but when he listened carefully and grew familiar with the sounds, certain nuances began to come through, for instance that sometimes it decreased in order to work itself up again to new strength soon afterwards. As if the rain itself were alive and breathing.

It was nine o'clock. He closed the door, undid his belt, pulled his shirt out of trousers and went and lay down on the mattress, flat out under the blanket, now swollen and decomposing like a piece of grey paper in a plant-press.

He fell asleep twenty minutes later, but before that he experienced a moment of sexual obsession, coming suddenly and violently and its physical manifestation was so ungovernable that he realized that using his will-power to overcome it would be useless. There was only one way of freeing himself.

Willi Mohr lay on his back and looked at naked women. Barbara Heinemann, and the Norwegian woman who had lived upstairs, and oddly enough the girl on the tractor-paper too. He had in fact never seen her undressed and the only time he had let his fingers glide over her cheek and neck down under her vest, she had blushed and perspired and gone on talking. He remembered a collar-bone which was slender and brittle and a breast beneath her bra and her polo-necked sweater. It lay in his hand like a terrified animal, soft and warm and small, its hard little nose hidden in his palm. And all the time she had talked on and on, her head down, quickly and disjointedly and mostly about production. The course of events was violent and strictly mechanical, the cramps beginning in his testicles and spreading out all over his loins. Then his thigh and calf muscles knotted and all his sinews stretched, first in his feet, but soon after in his neck and arms too, and then the dam burst into a scarlet pulsating haze.

He was almost naked, as he had had enough presence of mind to take his pants and trousers off and unbutton his shirt. He lay in the dark dripping room, on a flock mattress which had begun to go mouldy, alone, his heart thumping.

A minute or two later he found his damp clothing and pulled them on again.

Eighteen months had past since he had slept with a whore in a brothel in Cologne. Since then he had had only one other opportunity, in Marseilles at the beginning of May, and then he had had other things to think about. So it was natural that he masturbated, but it irritated him all the same. More than anything else, it seemed ridiculous.

Willi Mohr fell asleep and was woken by the sound of the fish-van's engine. It was one o'clock, and raining as before. Santiago came in from the darkness in his shining wet oilskins. He took off his sou'wester and said: 'The whole district is crawling with police and soldiers. I was stopped twice on the way here. The last time I thought they were going to take the van apart.'

He took out a cigarette and lit it above the paraffin lamp.

238

'The stuff must be got there before the siesta tomorrow. The action will presumably be postponed, but the man I spoke to didn't think it'd be abandoned. But they must have got wind of something. There can't be that many people on the roads for a round-up or an ordinary routine check.'

'What action?' said Willi Mohr.

'The strike. Four hundred factory workers above Santa Margarita are going on strike tomorrow afternoon. They must have that load before then.'

'I wonder if violence is the right way,' said Willi Mohr.

'The strikes that can be achieved now, and which can in some way be organized beforehand, are not very big ones. As strikes are illegal and the ones that occur are small and local, then they're always broken with violence. And as that's what happens anyhow, there's no point in the workers letting themselves be butchered like a flock of sheep, without putting up any resistance. Instead it's important that they show that there are still people who dare fight and that we can get help from outside, with arms for instance. In that way it'll be possible to carry through bigger actions later on and those actions needn't be armed, but will be effective all the same.'

Willi Mohr looked questioningly at him. Santiago smiled joylessly and said: 'I didn't think all that up. Do you know who said that?'

'No.'

'A man you mentioned earlier today.'

'Antonio Millan?'

'Yes, I asked him about it one day.'

'Where is he now?'

'No idea.'

'Has he got a wart between his eyebrows?'

'How did you know that? Have you met him?'

His voice had turned suspicious again.

'No. They showed me a photograph at the guard-post.'

Santiago had been kneeling down by the lamp as he smoked. Now he crushed his cigarette-end against the stone floor and got up.

'The arms must be got away from here at once,' he said. 'This isn't a good hiding-place.'

239

'Are you going to try now? Tonight?'

'No, I'll get through in daylight in the morning. That'll be better. But I'll move the stuff now, to a safe place, not far down the road to the puerto. I couldn't take it there this morning because of that jeep.'

'But the patrols?'

'They'll withdraw them later on, or at dawn.'

'You might as well let the things stay here. The rubbish-heap's a good place.'

'When I came from town, it had stopped raining there. It'll stop here too, perhaps tonight, perhaps early tomorrow morning. Then you can see this house with its rubbish heap and everything from miles away, up in the mountains. There are always people up there. I know the ropes in this business. Been at it a long time. It was coffee and cigarettes before. There's always been something, ever since I was small. The priest, one of them that is, for there are lots of them, once said I was too intelligent to get caught. And my father says I'm a wastrel. Although it's thanks to me he earns more money than any other fisherman down there. Although he was all through the war on the *Libertad*, even at Cabo Palos where we won a great victory, he would still do nothing against *them*. Not now, and neither would he agree to me doing so. He argues that if you're once beaten, then you'll never rise again. Lots of them who were in on it seem to think that way.'

'Not all that strange, perhaps.'

'Perhaps not. And he's right about me. I am a wastrel.'

Santiago took out a plug of tobacco, drew out his knife and cut off a piece with a quick slash.

'Good knife,' said Willi Mohr.

'All my tools are perfect,' said Santiago and he laughed loudly. When Willi Mohr looked at him, he saw that his eyes were shining and exalted under the rim of his sou'wester. His sunburnt face was tense and glittering, not with raindrops, but with sweat.

'I must load up now,' said Santiago. 'Goodbye.'

'I'll help.'

'No need. This is nothing to do with you.'

'I'll help all the same.'

They went round the house, slipping and stumbling over the half-buried stones sticking out of the ground. The rain was heavier than ever, beating down with a roaring sound, as if wishing to do its very best before its predicted end.

The move was troublesome in the darkness and wet, and although they worked as quickly as they could, it took them forty minutes to get the boxes stowed on to the fish-van. On one occasion Santiago tripped and fell against the wall. The box slipped out of his hands and the parts of two automatic-pistols hurtled down into the mud, together with a foul mess of stinking pig's stomachs and rotten intestines. He hit his knee against a stone in the fall and found it difficult to move. While Willi Mohr shovelled up the horrible mixture, Santiago leant against the house and held the paraffin lamp, shaded with a flap of his oil-skin jacket.

When the boxes were on the back of the van, well roped and with the tarpaulin over them, they went into the house and locked the door behind them. They had been working hard and were breathing heavily. Both were soaked with sweat and rain, and in spite of the downpour, their arms and legs were covered with clay and filth under their clothes.

Santiago stood with his back to the wall beside the door. He drew in a deep breath and said, unevenly and jerkily: 'Hope there are no guards at the cross-roads. Then I can free-wheel the whole way with the lights out and the engine switched off.'

Willi Mohr nodded.

'You can go down first and check. I'll stop the van at the entrance to the alleyway and wait. If anyone's down there, then hurry back. Otherwise I'll count to a hundred before I take off the brakes. If there's a checkpoint, then I'll start the engine and drive in the other direction.'

Willi Mohr nodded again.

After a brief pause he said: 'O.K. Let's get going.'

'Yes,' said Santiago.

The house was silent. Outside the rain was crashing down with apocalyptic force. Santiago was still leaning against the white-washed wall, now grey with damp. Willi Mohr stood in the middle of the room, his feet apart and his arms hanging. Neither of them moved.

241

Time floated by, perhaps a minute, perhaps two, long and unreal.

'Where's my brother?' said Santiago Alemany.

'He's dead.'

'I know. Where is he?'

'On the sea-bed.'

'How did he die?'

'I killed him.'

The cat came in through the hole in the door, thin and soaking wet, with scratches round its eyes. It looked from one man to the other and miaowed.

'Who killed Dan Pedersen?' said Willi Mohr.

'My brother.'

'And Siglinde?'

'I did.'

'How?'

'With the knife. From behind.'

Neither of them moved. The cat sat between them and licked its behind.

'I don't ask you to believe me,' said Santiago Alemany, 'but we didn't mean to, not from the beginning. And when I did it I thought it the only solution. Ramon didn't want to do it. It was a . . . a necessary action.'

Willi Mohr noted those last words 'una cosa forzada'. It was a good expression.

'That's no excuse,' said Santiago. 'It wasn't planned, but I knew it might suddenly happen. I have never wanted anything so much as I wanted her. I betrayed two hundred people, who were relying on me, just for the chance of seeing her bathing. After that I didn't know what I was doing. And yet everything happened quite by chance. It wasn't a matter of chance that you killed Ramon.'

'No,' said Willi Mohr.

'It was planned. You lay in wait for him.'

'Yes. Especially towards the end. Every minute, for twenty days. It was a long time before he realized it.'

'He didn't think all that clearly. Especially the last six months.'

The conversation was being carried on quite calmly. They still hadn't moved.

242

'You took the money he had with him,' said Santiago absently, as if he were thinking of something else.

'Some of it.'

'It wasn't his. He was supposed to give it to a contact over there. In Corsica.'

'I didn't know that. And if I had, I shouldn't have bothered about it.'

'It was all wrong,' said Santiago Alemany. 'I haven't thought about anything else except those people for the last six months. I'm no good at killing people.'

'Neither am I.'

They looked at each other, silently and blankly.

'It's time we got going now,' said Santiago Alemany, pushing himself away from the wall.

He stopped with his hand on the handle and turned his head.

'What are you going to do now?' he said.

'Go home.'

'To your country?'

'Yes.'

Santiago opened the door and went out, and Willi Mohr followed him. When the other man had climbed into the driver's seat, Willi Mohr put his shoulder against the back and got the van moving. It ran easily on the gentle slope and he felt it rolling away from him. As he made his way down the narrow crooked alley, he felt surprised that Santiago had been able to get there without lights. Suddenly he bumped into a corner of the back of the van and realized that he had reached the main road. As he walked past he rapped on the mudguard with his knuckles to show he had passed. There was no patrol at the crossroads. He walked ten yards in each direction but saw nothing. Then he stood on the roadside with one foot on the stone wall and waited. A few seconds later the fish-van rolled past. He heard the bearings squeaking and the splashing round the wheels, but all he saw was a vague movement in the darkness.

When he walked back towards Barrio Son Jofre, it was as if he had lost all sense of hearing and sight in the dark. He stumbled round in the rain, and up in the alleyway, he collided several times with walls of houses and protruding corners. The intuitive ability to react he had become used to having at his disposal had suddenly deserted him, like cutting the whiskers off a cat. But he was thinking, and again and again he put a hypothetical question to himself: What would have happened if he had broken off the conversation, gone over to his rucksack and fetched the pistol, or if Santiago Alemany had drawn his sheath-knife?

4

The paraffin lamp was still burning when Willi stepped into the room. He noticed that the floor was wet and muddy and that the half-drowned cat had curled up in his bedclothes and spread a large wet patch round itself.

When he took off his raincoat he saw that his legs and feet were muddy and his arms filthy with the offal from the fish-boxes. The smell was foul. He felt an intense repugnance and looked irresolutely round the room. Then he went over to the corner where his rucksack and dirty clothes and his painting things were standing, moved them all aside and picked up the ripped-up sack that had been lying spread out on the floor.

After shaking it out several times, he put it down on the mattress, took off his clothes and with his sandals in his hand, went out on to the steps. He stood for a long time letting the rain wash over his body before he put on his wet sandals and returned to the mattress. He dried himself with the sacking, which was so coarse it scraped great red marks on his skin. Then he locked the door, pushed aside the wet cat and lay down under the blanket. Before putting the lamp out, he smoked a cigarette and looked at his watch. It was half-past three.

He was nervous and restless and not at all sleepy. He knew that the last thing he had said to Santiago Alemany was true. If he could only get away from here, he would go home. To Dornburg or Jena or perhaps Berlin, it did not really matter which. But preferably Dornburg, as his mother was not all that old and was probably still alive. His motive was not yet really clear to himself, but he was quite certain it was not for his mother's sake that he wanted to go home. He also knew that he would not shoot Santiago Alemany, and that there was no reason for him to stay any longer than was absolutely necessary.

And why should it be necessary at all? What had Tornilla said when they had parted at the door?

Otherwise perhaps we shall not meet again.

This was undoubtedly otherwise.

Willi Mohr went on thinking. He would probably not be able to sleep, and as soon as it grew light it would be time to get to work. He would destroy his notebook and throw away the pistol, which could cause unpleasantness if it were found in his luggage. It would be easy to let it disappear into the rubbish heap behind the house. Then he would load his things on to the camioneta and drive to the provincial capital. He could be there by midday and the first thing he would do would be to hand in his passport for an exit-visa. That he had no money was a minor problem. At worst the Federal Republic would be forced to help him. All that seemed futile, as long as he got away from this house and these mountains, these stone streets and these faces. For the first time he had seen the town up in the mountains as a death-trap, and the year he had been there as a long, paralysing illness.

For the first time too, he was free of the memories of that day he had sat and waited on the quay in the puerto, and the last minutes with Ramon Alemany in the fo'c'sle of the Englishman's boat.

He did not want to kill anyone. He wanted to live.

There's a chance, he thought. This has gone, is past, is nothing to do with me any longer.

It was nothing to do with him any longer. He repeated the words silently to himself, then formulated them with his lips.

Willi Mohr lay there in the darkness and whispered: 'It's nothing to do with me any longer.'

He thought: I want to sleep now and get a couple of hours in, then wake when it's light.

And: Perhaps it'll stop raining.

Someone knocked on the door, not very hard, but urgently and persistently.

'Coming,' he called.

The knocking went on. Whoever was standing out there in the

245

pouring rain obviously could not hear sounds from within the house.

Willi Mohr fumbled for the matches. They were damp and he used about ten before he managed to get one alight and light the lamp. He wrapped the blanket round him, thrust his feet into his sandals and went over to the door.

He opened it in the certainty of seeing Santiago Alemany, but the figure on the steps was wearing a dark-green oilskin coat with a pointed hood and was so protected from the rain that neither hands nor face were visible.

The civil guard stepped over the threshold without saying a word. Willi Mohr nearly burst out laughing. The man stood in the room as if he had grown out of the stone floor. He looked like a Martian from some foolish newspaper strip, but he could equally well have been a half-erected tent or a successful carnival figure.

A green arm came out of the cape and tugged at the hood to draw it off from the shiny cap, while at the same time the mouth of an automatic-pistol protruded through a crack in his oilskins.

Willi Mohr had never seen the man before. He was quite young, with plump cheeks and reddish hair, but when he spoke his voice was sharp and cold.

'You're Willi Mohr, aren't you?'

'Yes.'

'I must ask you to come with me to the guard-post.'

Willi Mohr nodded.

'Please get dressed. It's urgent.'

Willi Mohr shook his head and pulled on his damp clothes. Meanwhile the man in the oilskins stood on the same spot and looked round the room.

When they were out on the steps and Willi Mohr had locked the door, the man put out his hand and took the key.

'Please may I have that. Walk to the left. I'll be just behind you.'

It was in fact raining slightly less heavily than before, but it was still quite dark. Although they walked right through the town, Willi Mohr saw not a single light, and the only thing to be heard apart from the rain were the occasional brief instructions

246

from the man behind his back. Go on straight ahead. Turn left here. Look out, there are some steps here. Walk a little faster.

The street lights were still out. The electricity works had evidently given up.

What a town, thought Willi Mohr.

He was not nervous about the meeting with Tornilla. At this stage he thought he knew the man and his habits, and the thought of exchanging the dripping house in Barrio Son Jofre for the relative comfort of the interrogation room was not entirely repugnant to him. He might have to spend a few hours in a cell, of course, as he had the first time, but that did not matter either. And so far as their conversation was concerned, he knew exactly what he had said before and what he ought to say now. Perhaps there would even be a brazier in the room. The thought cheered him and he lengthened his stride. The civil guard had hustled him several times, which implied that Sergeant Tornilla was already sitting waiting in his place under the circle of light from the green shade. As he had nothing special against meeting him, there was no reason to keep him waiting any longer than was necessary. He himself had several matters to settle when it grew light, and so the interrogation ought not to take too long.

Willi Mohr knew that this was his last day in the town up in the mountains. It was also the first day for a very long time that he looked forward to with some expectations.

They were already walking along the straight road between the olive trees.

'A little more to the right,' said the civil guard, poking him in the back. 'We're there now.'

There was not a single light to be seen in the building.

They were inside the hall. Behind Willi Mohr a pair of nailed boots clanged on the concrete floor. Five seconds later, the civil guard jerked open a door and pushed him over the threshold.

5

The room was large and bare, with whitewashed walls, a concrete floor, and filled with the blinding glare of an oil lamp hanging from a hook in the ceiling. There were four people inside and not one of them was Sergeant Tornilla.

Willi Mohr looked round and blinked in bewilderment in the cold, clear light. The interior was spartan. In the middle of the floor was a long, sturdy, wooden table, on which were a number of scattered papers and an old American typewriter. Round this table were half a dozen plain wooden chairs and there was a window with a blind drawn down over it in the far wall. An iron stove stood in one corner, the smell of soot and smoke emanating from it. That was all.

At one end of the table sat a tall officer with his jacket unbuttoned and gold braid on his sleeves. His shiny cap with its broad gold band lay in front of him and beside it was his belt and shoulder-strap holding his pistol holster. Willi Mohr had seen him before and even remembered his name: Lieutenant Pujol.

Beside him, nonchalantly leaning against the table, stood the small bald man who had been drinking anis at the Café Central the day before. He had hung his jacket over the back of the chair and was wearing a blue striped shirt with sleeve-bands and yellow cuff-links. A little farther away sat the handsome youngster with smooth hair and a dimple in his chin. He was not in his shirtsleeves, but had unbuttoned his collar and turned round so that he could rest his forearms on the back of the chair. His soft brown eyes looked indifferent and bored as he rocked slowly back and forth on his chair.

The fourth person in the room was a civil guard in green linen uniform and brown shoes. He was kneeling in front of the table busy adjusting the mantle of an oil lamp with a cone-shaped black metal shade.

The bald man glanced without interest at the newcomer and said: 'Have you searched him?'

'No,' said the civil guard in a rain-cape, who had come into the room immediately behind Willi Mohr and was still standing just behind him.

'Do it then, for God's sake.'

The civil guard took off Willi Mohr's hat and plastic coat and fumbled through his pockets and down his trouser legs. Finally he said: 'Nothing.'

248

'Good,' said the bald man. 'Then you can go.'

Then he turned to the officer at the end of the table and continued the conversation that had evidently been interrupted when the door had opened.

'So you sent a man to the electricity works. What did they say?'

'They're repairing the line. And a steam-pipe's burst.'

'And the telephone?'

'Don't know. They didn't tell us,' said Lieutenant Pujol.

His forehead was glistening with sweat and he seemed tired and irritable.

'Are things always like this?' asked the man in shirtsleeves in a complaining voice. 'There's been no light now for eight hours or telephone for five. And the stove smokes. It's just as well the actual building is still standing.'

Lieutenant Pujol did not reply.

'So this is the man you've been interrogating for three months?'

'This is Willi Mohr,' said Lieutenant Pujol.

'Yes, you and your experts. The civil guard is all right, I suppose, for scaring peasants, but not much use for this. Anyhow it's not your department, so there's no cause for offence. Where is this expert of yours, anyhow?'

'Don't know.'

'You're his superior officer, aren't you?'

'Yes, officially.'

The bald man sighed and leant over the table.

'How are you getting on? Have you finished?'

The guard in linen uniform had stopped fiddling with the lamp and seemed to be fully occupied listening.

'Oh yes,' he said hastily. 'It's O.K. now.'

'Perhaps you'd try lighting it then,' said the handsome young man in a friendly way.

The civil guard hunted through his pockets for a while, apparently for matches. When he found them, he fumbled for a long time with the box before succeeding in lighting one. He pumped up more oil, and the lamp spread a harsh light over the floor.

'No more?' said the man on the chair.

249

The guard gave the lamp a few extra pumps and the white light intensified.

'I daren't any more. It might explode.'

'We brought that with us, so it's good stuff,' said the bald man. 'But that's all right now. Put the shade on and hang it up.'

The man in the linen uniform fiddled with the screws and managed to let down three sections of the black shade. Then he got up on to a chair and laboriously hooked the lamp on to two hooks in the ceiling.

'Not in that direction, you idiot,' said the man in the striped shirt.

The lamp was finally placed as it ought to be. The harsh light fell on to a sharply limited section in front of the table.

'Bring the wretch here and we can get it over and done with.'

The guard went over to the door, grasped Willi Mohr's arm and led him up to the table. The light was so bright that he could not see any of the other men, only hear their voices. He fumbled for the chair and sat down.

'No one asked you to sit down, as far as I know. Get up!'

That was the younger of the two civilians.

Willi Mohr got up.

'Are we taking a statement now?'

That was the guard in the linen uniform.

'No, we'll write out the whole confession later.'

That was the bald man.

Willi Mohr felt himself seized with rage, cold sullen rage, which rose slowly and inexorably, making him think quite calmly and with crystal clarity. He said: 'What are you playing at? American gangster-films?'

'Keep quiet when you're not being spoken to.'

'Take me straight back to my house and then leave me alone. I'm a foreign citizen and whatever happens I'll report you to the authorities. If you want to ask me something, then you must first get in touch with the nearest German Consul. Anyhow, I don't even know who you are.'

'These gentlemen belong to the Security Forces,' said Lieutenant Pujol.

Willi Mohr had been looking down to avoid at least some of the blinding white light. He heard someone laugh, presumably

250

the younger of the two civilians, but the one to speak first was his colleague, the man in the striped shirt.

'That's the situation. We'll do you the service of telling you from the start that the game is up. Your friends have confessed everything and denounced you. All that remains is for you to do the same.

'I haven't any friends.'

Willi Mohr's eyes could not get used to the light and he was unable to distinguish anything. But the voices from the other side of the table penetrated through to him, hard and metallic, in a shower of questions and statements. Both the men from the Policia Secreta spoke swiftly but never simultaneously. All through, it was the younger man who used the most caustic phrases and threatening tones.

'You're a Communist provocateur, sent here from East Germany.'

'Oh yes.'

'Where have you hidden the arms?'

'Don't know.'

'If you try being awkward, it'll be very unpleasant for you.'

'Oh yes.'

'How long have you been in Spain?'

'Don't know.'

'Where is Antonio Millan?'

'Don't know.'

'We seriously advise you to stop prevaricating and answer our questions.'

'Oh yes.'

'Were you trained in Moscow?'

'Don't know.'

'When was the consignment sent to Santa Ponsa?'

'Don't know.'

'Who's in charge of the transport?'

'Don't know.'

'Don't you realize that we have the whole situation in hand and you're simply worsening your own position by crossing us.'

'No.'

'Both Antonio Millan and Baltazar Rodriguez have been arrested. The headquarters in Santa Margarita has been found and dispersed. The whole of your organization is shattered. Do you want to know any more?'

'Of course.'

Willi Mohr smiled faintly. He felt quite calm and although he could not see his tormentors, he had seen through them all. They knew nothing, least of all about him, and most of what they were saying was either bluff or half-truths.

They went on showering him with questions and accusations, names he had never heard before, dates and figures which meant nothing whatsoever to him, and he varied his replies each time; no, oh yes, don't know, of course.

How long this had already gone on for he did not know and neither did he care.

Gradually their statements and questions grew more and more far-fetched.

'Do you know your mother's been taken by the Russians and sent to Siberia?'

'Of course.'

'Don't you realize that your martyrdom is pointless and we'll continue until you confess.'

'No.'

'We know you received a consignment of arms last night.'

'Oh yes.'

'Where did you hide it?'

'Don't know.'

'We also know that both you and your foreign friends, who've fled from the country, belong to the Communist party.'

'Oh yes.'

'Don't you think we've lit a nice reading lamp for you?'

'No.'

'Do you think it's fun standing like that in the light?'

'Of course.'

'Are you getting thirsty?'

'Don't know.'

'We won't give you a drop of water and you may not move from the spot until you see reason.'

'Oh yes.'

'We'll appeal to your instinct for self-preservation for a while and make you a generous offer.'

252

'Oh yes.'

'If you tell us everything you know, you won't be punished in any other way except deportment. That's a very generous offer.'

'Of course.'

'You can trust us. We're not barbarians and the Lieutenant here will confirm that we keep our promises. Do you agree to that?'

'Don't know.'

'If you haven't confessed within ten minutes, I myself will personally ask some questions, which will be very unpleasant for you.'

'Oh yes.'

'Where are the arms?'

'Don't know.'

'Your fellow-criminals in Villanueva have been arrested and have confessed.'

'Oh yes.'

'You needn't protect anyone, because no one's protecting you. The smugglers put ashore the goods in Villanueva, we know that. So you can admit that.'

'Don't know.'

'You've eight minutes left. You remember what I said two minutes ago?'

'No.'

The lamp hanging from the ceiling exploded with a bang and the mantle hissed angrily as it was burnt by the oxygen streaming in with the air. Red-hot pieces of lamp-glass hit Willi Mohr in the face, but he scarcely noticed them.

There was still too much pressure in the holder and the flames rushed out into the room with a roar that soon faded. The lamp had gone out and Willi Mohr looked at it with a smile.

'Good stuff,' he said.

'Shut up,' said the youth with the pomaded hair angrily.

He had also taken off his jacket now and was sitting sideways on the edge of the table. The bald man had unbuttoned his collar and was leaning back in his chair, chewing a yellow pencil and staring at the lamp in astonishment.

Lieutenant Pujol was sitting as before, his legs crossed and his jacket unbuttoned. The clerk in linen uniform was standing over

253

by the wall, a cigarette hanging out of his mouth and a non-plussed expression on his face.

Willi Mohr felt calm and clear and in astonishing good condition. Shining white points of light danced about in front of his eyes, but now he could distinguish the objects round him again, he felt sure of himself. They knew nothing and were simply barking up the wrong tree. Presumably they wouldn't dare go on very much longer.

It was Lieutenant Pujol who broke the silence.

'I appeal to your common sense,' he said, 'and I'm talking as one man to another now. I'm an officer and chief-of-police in this district and I beg you to tell us what you know. I'm doing so not only as a representative of the law and the government, but also as a man of honour. Stop denigrating yourself by playing the fool. If you know anything, then tell us. I give you my word as a Spanish officer that you will be correctly and humanely treated. If these gentlemen say that your eventual punishment will be deportation, then you can rely on me as a witness and guarantee that their promise will be fulfilled.'

The bald man belched. He seemed to have recovered from his surprise and had turned round to get a cigar out of his jacket.

Willi Mohr looked calmly at Lieutenant Pujol and carefully thought out what he had to say.

He found that his Spanish was inadequate and asked: 'Do you speak German or English?'

'Yes, English, passably anyhow.'

'Good. I'll tell you everything I know. Namely, nothing at all. All this is a mistake and I'm innocent of all that you suspect me of and are accusing me of. I assure you that I am not in any party, and I've never been a Communist, and no one sent me here. I came here as a tourist and I have not smuggled in arms or been involved in any kind of propaganda. That's all I have to say on the matter. I shall not play the fool, as you put it, but neither will I answer any more questions until I am allowed to contact my Consul. Now I demand to be released.'

Lieutenant Pujol turned to the others and translated, slowly and thoroughly. It did not seem to make any special impression.

Willi Mohr felt cold rage bursting behind his forehead, making his mind clear and increasing his self-confidence. He said:

254

'Before I am silent for good, I'd like to say one or two more things, and they are to you personally. You shouldn't talk about your honour and your word as an officer, as long as you let yourself be treated in this way by these ... cretins. Isn't that what you say in Spanish? So far as I can see, you're no more than an underling and a representative of a corrupt and miserable régime. You are a coward too. Now I refuse to say another word.'

Lieutenant Pujol turned scarlet in the face and the skin stretched tightly over his cheek-bones. He found it difficult to keep his fingers still and he fingered his belt and shoulder-strap, biting his lower lip as he pulled the broad leather belt out of the slits for the holster. Then he folded it in three and rose.

'I demand an immediate apology,' he said.

Willi Mohr said nothing.

'Did you hear what I said? I demand an apology, here and now.' Both the men from the security forces were watching him with interest. He took another step forward and stood in front of Willi Mohr, less than an arm's length away from him.

'I demand an apology,' he repeated.

Willi Mohr looked sullenly at him. You daren't, he thought coldly. The man was still red in the face, but his eyes had taken on an almost childish expression, uncertain and appealing.

'Apologize,' he said.

It was not an order, but an appeal. Willi Mohr said nothing.

Lieutenant Pujol raised his arm and hit him as hard as he could across his face with the folded belt.

The leather belt hit him over the cheek-bone, just below his left eye, and the heavy brass buckle caught the bridge of his nose, stinging him below his eyes and making his head crackle all over as his nose broke. Willi Mohr took an involuntary step back. It had not hurt especially and he felt surprise more than anything else when the passage of air through his nostrils was suddenly blocked and blood began to pour down his mouth and chin. His head was whirling and everything blurred before his eyes, and yet he could see that the officer's round-cheeked face expressed nothing more than astonishment and confusion. He also noted in passing that the bald man was snipping the end off his cigar.

'You're coming on, Lieutenant,' said the young man with a

255

side-parting in his hair. He jumped down to the floor and took a pair of gloves out of his jacket.

'You should have done that three months ago,' he said, as he walked round the table.

He pulled on his gloves and straightened out the fingers as if to soften them up.

'Well,' he said, and struck.

It was a good blow, hard and swift and precise, and it struck just below the ribs between the navel and the upper edge of the hip-bone. Willi Mohr did not fall, but sucked in his breath and groaned with his mouth wide open.

'Well,' said the man with the side-parting, and struck again, with astounding precision in exactly the same spot.

Willi Mohr whimpered loudly and everything went grey before his eyes.

'You've got fifteen seconds. Then I'll do it again.'

'You don't know Vicente,' said the bald man genially. 'He can go on for ever.'

'Is this really necessary?' said Lieutenant Pujol.

'Who began it?' said Vicente. 'This at least doesn't mess up the floor.'

He hit out again, for the third time on the same spot. Willi Mohr fell over. He lay on his side, curled up with both arms across his diaphragm.

'Well,' said Vicente, bending over him. 'You've fifteen seconds this time too. But next time it'll be worse.'

He pulled off his gloves and walked round to the other side, gazed absently at his watch and then kicked the prostrate man from behind with the point of his shoe exactly between the legs.

The pain was excruciating and exact and penetrating. Willi Mohr yelped, shrilly and abruptly and rolled over on the other side with his knees drawn up high. This protective measure was a reflex action, and a second later only, he turned over on his back and lay flopped on his back with his eyes half-closed and his legs stretched out, his arms falling down by his sides.

'Hell,' said Vicente, kicking him experimentally below his left knee.

Willi Mohr did not react at all.

And yet he was not unconscious. It had stopped hurting and

256

in general he felt he had no organs left capable of causing him pain. But his hearing was still intact and he could hear the men in the room talking to each other.

'It's not worth going on,' said Vicente.

'Waste of time, all of it,' said the bald man. 'Where are the reports on this case?'

And then later on.

'What's all this? Some sort of thesis or other? Where's the person who put this together?'

'I don't know,' said Lieutenant Pujol.

'Who is Santiago Alemany? This has been incredibly mishandled. Isn't there any evidence against this cretin or have we been wasting our time on him quite unnecessarily?'

'Sergeant Tornilla has been in charge of the case.'

'We've gathered that. Best if he gets on with it himself too. Is the telegraph working?'

'It'll be open at seven o'clock.'

'Oh yes, excellent. At this stage perhaps half the province is in a state of rebellion and we're just sitting here. Nothing happens here. People who put up with your electricity works don't smuggle arms. Naturally everything's wrong.'

And a while later:

'It's stopped raining.'

'That's the only positive thing we've heard since we came here. We'll leave this to you and the Sergeant. That's no doubt best all round.'

'It's beginning to get lighter.'

'See to it that this wretch doesn't die on your hands, won't you? That might prove awkward. If I'm ordered here again I'll hand in my resignation.'

'My God, he's not dead, is he?'

Then there was silence.

Willi Mohr was not dead. He was asleep.

6

He was fully conscious and the only person left in the room was the clerk in linen uniform.

They talked to each other.

'I've only washed you and put a dressing on your face. I'm to take you to a doctor.'

'There's no need.'

'The Lieutenant said I was to. Orders.'

'Don't bother.'

'Wait, I'll help you. There we are now, you can stand on your own feet after all. And it's stopped bleeding.'

'What's the time?'

'Just past eight. Shouldn't I . . . ?'

'No, I said. There's no need.'

'I can ring him up. The lights aren't on again yet, but the telephone's working.'

'Don't bother about it. I'll go there myself if it's necessary.'

'You're finding it difficult to walk.'

'It'll be better soon. Where's Sergeant Tornilla?'

'Don't know. Perhaps in his room. Otherwise he'll be here soon.'

Willi Mohr left the room. As he slowly moved down the corridor, the electric light went on.

He came out into the entrance hall, about five yards farther in than usual.

Tornilla's door was locked and he got no reply to his knock. He crossed the hall and sat down on a narrow wooden bench opposite.

Willi Mohr cautiously fingered the clumsy amateurish dressing on his face. It seemed to consist entirely of cotton wool and pieces of adhesive tape. His nose was quite blocked but that injury was not aching much, only throbbing slightiy. On the other hand, his loins were burning like fire and the whole of the lower part of his body felt drained of strength. The pain in his midriff was more tolerable, although he noticed it each time he breathed.

He shifted his bruised body to rights on the bench. He was not thinking about anything at all. He was waiting.

Outside it had stopped raining, but the small wedge of sky he could see was grey and cloudy.

He had been sitting there for perhaps a half-an-hour, when Lieutenant Pujol came into the hall.

At first it looked as if he was going to walk past, pretending not to see the man on the bench, but then he hesitated and turned round.

'Have you been to the doctor?' he said.

'No.'

'Why are you sitting here?'

'Waiting for Sergeant Tornilla.'

'Why?'

'I want to speak to him.'

'I don't know when he's coming. You can talk to me instead.'

'I'd rather wait.'

'Just as you like.'

He was about to go, but stopped again and said vaguely: 'Do I need to point out ... well, that I'm sorry about what happened tonight ... it was largely your own fault, however, but ...'

He stopped and Willi Mohr said nothing. Lieutenant Pujol coughed with embarrassment and went away.

An hour later, Sergeant Tornilla got off his bicycle outside the porchway. He pushed it into a bicycle-stand at the end of the hall, took out a bunch of keys in a leather case and unlocked the door into his room.

'Good-day,' he said in a friendly way to the man on the bench. 'I must say you don't look too well. Most distressing.'

Before stepping over the threshold, he unhooked a brush from the inside of the doorpost and carefully eliminated a couple of small spots of mud from the leg of his boot. Otherwise he was just as usual, fresh, dapper and newly-shaven.

'Have you been waiting for me?' he said. 'Not for too long, I hope.'

'I want to speak to you.'

'Of course. Do please come in.'

He held the door open and Willi Mohr limped past him into the room.

'Just look, our mechanics have once again achieved a miracle,' said Tornilla, as he switched on the light.

Willi Mohr sat down unasked on the bench and the other man walked round the desk, straightened out the goatskin in the armchair and sat down. He looked behind the telephone and shook his head. Then he opened one of the drawers in the desk and brightened up a little. He took out an unopened packet of Bisontes, opened it with a paper knife, struck it against the edge of the desk and held them out.

Willi Mohr shook his head.

'I want to speak to you,' he said again.

'Of course. I have an unusual amount of work to do, but I can always find time for you. I'm sorry you've been kept waiting, but I have in fact had a very troublesome and busy night.

He looked at Willi Mohr anxiously and hurriedly added:

'Well, naturally nothing in comparison with you. You really do seem to have been in trouble. As I said, I hope that you've not been waiting too long. I was here for a while at about seven, but I didn't see you then.'

He fell silent.

Willi Mohr shook his head slightly and coughed to clear his throat. Tornilla raised his forefinger and interrupted him before he had had time to say anything.

'Take your time, by all means. There's no need to hurry just for my sake.'

He settled down, as if preparing to listen.

'You said that I was hiding something from you,' said Willi Mohr. 'You were right. Ramon Alemany did not run away from the boat in Ajaccio. I killed him. It was not an accident, but murder, carefully planned and thought out. Afterwards I discovered the money and stole it, almost thirty thousand pesetas.'

It grew quiet in the room. A minute or so later, Sergeant Tornilla said: 'Does it help if I say anything? I could, for instance, ask: Why did you do it?'

'I thought he'd killed Dan Pedersen, the Norwegian I lived with when I came here, and raped his wife, Siglinde Pedersen. I couldn't prove anything, but there were a number of small points which did not fit and which convinced me I was right. I wanted revenge, and I followed Ramon Alemany and his brother about

260

for months. That was why I signed on with the Englishman. Then I just waited for the right opportunity. I never let him out of my sight. I lay in wait for him and gradually he realized it and grew more and more frightened. He was physically courageous but a moral coward.'

There was another pause. Tornilla looked as if he were trying to think of some way of being helpful. Finally he said kindly: 'And when did this happen?'

'On the evening of the twenty-first of April, when the French police had taken us down to the quay. He had drunk a great deal because he was frightened. I knew that all the time. He was out of his mind with fear. When we had been down in the fo'c'sle for perhaps an hour, he sobered up a bit and that was also because he was afraid, I think. I accused him of what I thought he'd done. Then I deliberately turned my back on him. But I was on my guard all the time. I wanted him to begin it all, take the initiative for his own execution. I had seen that this was the only way I could kill him. As it turned out, I was right, but it was very difficult all the same. He drew a knife when I turned my back on him, but I disarmed him. Then he tried to kill me with his bare hands. He was crying with fear all the time. It was horrible. He was strong but I had the upper hand. Even physically I was in very good shape at the time. I knocked him down and he crept round the floor and whimpered and begged for his life and called on the saints and people and gods. He confessed and protested his innocence alternately. He tried to get away, but there was nowhere for him to hide. It lasted several minutes before I finally knocked him out. I banged his head on the floor several times, as hard as I could. Perhaps he didn't die then. I don't know. I collected up all his belongings and stuffed them down in his seaman's bag and put several large stones in it as weights. That was when I found the money and stole some of it. Then I rowed out to a boat which had been abandoned farther away, and took the anchor chain. I carried the body down into the dinghy and wound the anchor chain round it over and over again. Then I rowed round the pier out into the approaches where I knew the water was deep, and tipped the body and the bag into the water. When I got back, I let the painter drop and the dinghy drift. Then I cleaned up everything and went to bed. I couldn't sleep

261

and I've not been able to forget any of it since. That's what happened then, and if you want a statement before you lock me in down there, then I can sign it.'

Tornilla made a movement, but Willi Mohr went on at once: 'Wait a moment, if you can. There are one or two more things I want to say. I came back here, because I'd decided to kill Santiago Alemany too, before I was caught. I've always believed that I would do it, but it didn't work, although I've had several opportunities. I've still got a pistol which I smuggled in when I came to Spain.'

'Where is it now?' said Sergeant Tornilla.

'At home. In the house in Barrio Son Jofre. It's near the top of my rucksack.'

Someone knocked on the door and a civil guard he had never seen before came in with a telegram. Tornilla opened it and read it with a frown. Then he looked at Willi again and smiled.

'Duty,' he smiled, 'Full of complications. And the telephones have broken down now. Go on.'

'There's one more thing I want to say. I know what you suspected me of. At that time, I was as good as completely innocent. I have not been involved in any political activities whatsoever, and I have not been smuggling arms. I know practically nothing about all that. The events in Santa Margarita which you told me about, I had never heard about before. I promise you that is true. I have never transported arms from one place to another and neither have I done anything else illegal.'

Sergeant Tornilla grew very serious and made one of his old gestures. He pressed his fingertips together.

'I believe you,' he said.

'I've nearly always told you the truth. But I've refrained from telling you two things. That I murdered Ramon Alemany and that I was thinking of killing his brother. I don't know why I'm telling you this now. It's not because they mistreated me here at the guard-post tonight. At least, I don't think so.'

It was silent again.

Suddenly the telephone rang, shrilly and jarringly.

'Look at that now,' said Tornilla. 'It's been out of action almost continuously since yesterday evening. If you'll excuse me . . .'

He picked up the receiver and appeared to be listening to a message. He nodded several times, but said nothing more than a few words such as yes and no.

And once only: 'We'll see in an hour or two.'

He put the receiver down and made a few notes on a piece of paper. Then he said: 'Excuse me. I had not reckoned on your visit and must do one or two things at the same time.'

Willi Mohr sat in silence for a while. He was breathing unevenly and heavily, but that was because his nose was blocked.

'I don't think there's anything else,' he said.

After another few minute's pause, he added: 'I was really going to leave here today.'

Tornilla showed signs of surprise, raising his eyebrows and inclining his head.

'Oh yes? Were you thinking of leaving the country?'

'Yes.'

'Don't you like it here?'

'No. The more I see of it the less I like it. In as far as I've understood the situation, I think it's untenable. And loathsome.'

'Where were you thinking of going?'

'To the provincial capital first. And then home.'

'To West Germany?'

'No, to the German Democratic Republic.'

'What are you going to do there?'

'Work.'

'And become a Communist?'

'I don't know.'

'You really have been led astray,' said Tornilla sadly.

Another silence, long and guarded, as if they were both waiting for something. The man in the armchair stared at his visitor, steadily and thoughtfully. Then he said at last: 'What do you want me to do about it?'

Willi Mohr looked round in confusion.

'Arrest me of course,' he said, shrugging his shoulders.

'Why?'

'Well, I've murdered a man.'

Sergeant Tornilla slowly took a cigarette out of the packet and lit it. He blew a couple of smoke-rings and followed them with his eyes until they dissolved beneath the green lampshade.

263

'I can't really lock you up for a crime committed in another country. There's no body and no one has maintained that Ramon Alemany is dead. Except you. You've heard of corpus delecti, haven't you? In addition, if your statement is true, the case would be considered as killing in self-defence. Even in court with you as a witness, you would probably be acquitted.'

'But I did in fact kill him.'

'Even I have managed to grasp that fact, at last,' said Sergeant Tornilla.

'I had to. I couldn't go to the police. There wasn't any proof and I couldn't even speak the language.'

'I understand.'

'But what are you going to do?'

'Nothing. What can I do?'

'So I can leave here?'

'Of course.'

'And leave the town today if I want to?'

'I can't stop you. As long as you don't commit a crime before that, of course. Have you paid Amadeo Prunera, the man with the brushwood?'

'No.'

'Do that, then.'

'I've still got the pistol.'

Sergeant Tornilla smiled secretively. He pulled out a drawer and placed the Walther pistol on the desk. Willi Mohr recognized it by the spots of rust on the clip. Fastened to the butt was a stamped piece of cardboard.

'For certain reasons, your house was searched early this morning. My men found this, in a rucksack, as you said. They found no reason to bring anything else.'

He pointed at the pistol and said reproachfully: 'You haven't looked after it very well. Well, you can't have it back. The loss of impounded goods will in this case be the punishment. On the other hand, you'll be given a receipt. I'll have it sent over today.'

'So I can go?'

'Of course.'

'From here?'

'Of course.'

'I didn't come to Spain to smuggle arms.

264

'I believe you.'

'I'll leave as soon as I can, perhaps today even.'

Sergeant Tornilla rose.

'Of course, I doubt the wisdom of your decision, but that's nothing to do with me.'

He took Willi Mohr lightly by the arm and led him towards the door, opened it and put out his hand.

'Good luck,' he said.

Willi Mohr stopped in the doorway.

'I really am leaving,' he said. 'And I've no intention of ... well, of killing the other one any longer.

Tornilla looked past him out into the hall, at a pair of civil guards who were loading ammunition belts on to a bicycle-cart. Then he said absently: 'I believe you on that point too. Anyhow, you would be too late. Santiago Alemany was arrested in the puerto just before six o'clock this morning, suspected of several serious crimes. He resisted and was wounded before he could be overpowered. Quite badly, I believe. He has been taken to the military hospital some way away from here, and from what I heard, the doctor was not very hopeful about the case. That's some hours ago now, so he's probably already ... well, I don't know anything about all that ...'

The telephone rang. He smiled apologetically and closed the door behind Willi Mohr.

7

Slowly and stiffly, Willi Mohr walked along the straight road between the olive trees. He came to the narrow cobbled street where the civil guard with a grey moustache lived, crossed the square without even glancing at the Café Central, and continued along the Avenue with its grey façades and neat paving-stones. He was quite certain that he was walking this way for the last time.

The whole way he repeated several simple statements to himself: I won't bother with this any longer. It's all over. They are all dead, and I don't care. I want to live. Now I've got the chance.

Although Tornilla had not said anything of the kind, he was sure that Santiago had been shot in the stomach and had not died until three or four hours later.

He did not notice anyone or anything during his walk through the town. Not until he reached the alleyway which led up to Barrio Son Jofre did he stop and listen to something which he had not at once recognized. But a few seconds later he realized it was the sound of the streams from the mountain rushing and bubbling through their underground passages.

The door to the house was shut but the key was outside in the door. He went in, looked round and everything was just as before, apart from a large number of muddy footmarks on the floor.

Then he went back out on to the steps. The truck was still there and was standing where it had always stood. Seven months had gone by since someone had last driven it, but only a week since they had tried out the engine, so it ought to function still. And there was enough gas in the tank to get him to the provincial capital.

A plane flew low over the town and with a narrow margin rose up over the mountain ridge. A slow grey military plane; he did not know what type, but he could see that it was anything but modern. As he had never before seen a plane over the town, he gazed after it and the episode had the effect of at once making him more aware of his immediate surroundings.

He looked round and observed a number of things, the dog rolling about at his feet for instance, and a small, bare-legged boy standing in the shadow of the houses down in the alley, and the sun beginning to break up the clouds, first in the east, over the sea. What could he do with the dog? Take her with him? Let her loose? Try to find someone to look after her? In that case, who?

It was a problem, and he brooded over it as he went into the room and aimlessly began picking over his scattered possessions.

He was out in the kitchen when he saw a shadow fall over the patch of sun on the floor and someone knocked on the door, energetically and decisively.

The little civil guard with a round face was standing on the steps.

No, thought Willi Mohr, it's not possible. It can't be.

266

The man thrust his hand inside his uniform jacket and took out a brown envelope with an official stamp on it.

'From Sergeant Tornilla,' he said, saluting.

By the time Willi Mohr had opened the envelope and was standing with the receipt for the pistol in his hand, the civil guard had already gone.

In the upper left hand corner of the receipt, Tornilla had clipped a small piece of torn-off paper and written on it in his neat backward-sloping handwriting:

You won't forget about Amadeo Prunera, will you?

Willi Mohr felt the dressing pulling on his face. It must have been because he was smiling. He was smiling because he had been frightened for the first time for more than a year.

He began to gather up the articles in the room again, a little more systematically, but still slowly and indolently. He thought about the dog and said half-aloud: 'I'll have to take her with me after all.'

There was a rustle at the door and he turned round. The small ragged boy he had seen down in the alley was standing with one foot in the doorway, watchfully, as if prepared to run away immediately.

'Are you the German gentleman?'

Willi Mohr nodded.

'Are you quite sure?'

'Yes, absolutely.'

The boy took two steps forward, cautiously and suspiciously, like a cat in a strange house, then stretched out his clenched right fist and opened it. On the dirty palm lay a piece of paper, crumpled and folded firmly.

Willi Mohr did not understand and several seconds passed before he came to sufficiently to take the piece of paper and unfold it. It was the back of an old envelope and the pencilled writing was unsteady and feeble, as if written in the dark.

Fetch 600 yards from cross-roads side-road right
left first fork second farm. Abandoned. In big
house under stairs. Deliver to S. Margarita Fontane's
garage right of entrance brown Dodge with load of
wood. Inside garage Definitely before three

Under the last sentence the writer had drawn a wobbly line,

267

and slightly lower down there were six more words, very carelessly written:

Caught now am sending money gas.

Willi Mohr read through the text twice. His brain was working slowly and sluggishly. Then he looked for a long time at the boy, before saying: 'Who gave you this?'

'Santiago, mister.'

'Have you shown it to anyone?'

'No, mister.'

'Have you read it yourself?'

'Can't read, mister.'

'How did you get here?'

'Ran, but didn't dare come near at first.'

'Where's Santiago?'

'Don't know, mister. He ran into the fish-shed and there was a bang. There were civil guards there too.'

The boy was perhaps eleven years old. He was ragged and dirty and it was clear that he had recently been sweating profusely, for there were long light streaks down his brown face. He dug into his thin shirt and took out a roll of filthy tatty notes.

'That's all of it, mister.'

They were hundred-peseta notes. Willi Mohr thanked him, then gave him back two notes. The boy's mouth fell open in dumb astonishment.

'You can go,' said Willi Mohr, 'and you must promise not to tell anyone about this.'

'Yes, mister,' said the child, backing towards the door.

'No, wait a minute.'

Willi Mohr took out two more hundred-peseta notes, folded them into a piece of wrapping-paper and wrote on the outside with a red crayon that happened to be lying on the stairs: To Amadeo Prunera for the brushwood from the German.

'Take this and go and sit somewhere where no one can see you. Wait until you've seen me drive away in the truck. Then wait for two more hours and then go and find someone called Amadeo Prunera and give him this.

'I haven't got a watch, mister.'

'Listen to the church clock. When it strikes three times you can go. Understand?'

268

'Yes, mister.'

The child walked backwards to the door and vanished.

Willi Mohr sat down on the stairs and stared out through the open door. Clouds of flies were buzzing round in the sun that was just breaking through. He sat there for twenty minutes without moving.

Then he looked at his watch. It was already a quarter-past one.

He got up, fetched the piassava brush and went out to sweep out the truck. Then he began to carry his belongings out from the house. He did not possess much and in ten minutes everything was placed between or under the seats; clothes, painting gear and pictures. He had put only two things in his pockets, his pocket-book and his passport.

Willi Mohr returned to his place on the stairs, unfolded Santiago's note and read through it ten times. Then he went out to the kitchen, tore the paper up and put the pieces in the fireplace. He got out the notebook and systematically tore out page after page. When he had crumpled them up one at a time and placed them in a heap on the hearth, he struck a match and set light to them, watching until there was nothing left but a small pyramid of white ash on the blackened stones.

Willi Mohr went out of the house in Barrio Son Jofre, locked the door and left the key in the lock. He picked the dog up by the scruff of her neck and lifted her into the truck. Then he stood in front of the radiator, bent down and turned the handle. He had to keep turning for a long time before the engine finally got going.

He looked round once more and raised his hand to the cat which was just slipping round the corner of the house.

''Bye,' said Willi Mohr.

He climbed up into the camioneta and drove away.

Two civil guards were standing at the cross-roads. They were smoking, their carbines on their backs, and one of them raised his arm in a vague gesture which might have been either a greeting or a halt-signal.

Willi Mohr braked. One of the guards looked idly at his luggage, raised a corner of the blanket and drove his arm at random under the heap of clothes and canvases and other

269

rubbish. The other one came round to the driver's place and shouted: 'Are you moving?'

Willi Mohr leant out of the truck and bent forward to make himself heard over the sound of the engine.

'Yes, but I'm coming back soon. I'm just going down to the puerto to leave the dog.'

'Difficult with bitches,' shouted the civil guard. 'I'll shoot her for you if you like.'

He laughed and waved. Willi Mohr drove on.

The side-road was narrow and twisty and stony and the camioneta rocked violently. Just beyond the fork lay the first abandoned farm and six or seven hundred yards farther up the second. Willi Mohr drove into the stony yard and stopped.

The place had been well chosen, wedged between bushy, inaccessible mountain hills and hidden from sight by the ruined terraced fields. The house was built of rough yellow stones and was half in ruins. The pump pointed crookedly up towards the sky above the dried-up well, like a tombstone commemorating wasted toil.

The air in the house was oppressive and hot, the mud feet deep after the rain, and a heavy smell and the buzzing of myriads of flies indicated where the boxes were standing piled up beneath the remainder of the staircase.

Willi Mohr dragged them out one by one, turned them upside down and carried the arms out to the camioneta. The fish and butcher's offal lay there in heaps, the entrails and pig's stomachs already crawling with maggots.

He worked for half-an-hour before he was satisfied with the loading. The weapons, hand-grenades and boxes of ammunition lay well hidden under his own modest possessions. He had one automatic-pistol over and did not dare put it in. As he carried it over to the well, he absently tried to make out the Czechoslovakian inscription on the barrel. Then he dropped the weapon down the well and went back to the truck, lifted down the dog and starting-handle. When he had turned the first bend, the dog was already far behind him.

The civil guards at the cross-roads had not been relieved. They smiled and saluted carelessly as he drove by.

Willi Mohr was out on the main road. He jammed the accelerator down to the floorboards and drove into the first serpent-like coil. High above he could see the pass in the mountain range, its outlines shimmering beneath the clear blue sky.

The camioneta roared and shook, slowly making its way upwards.

He felt excitement tugging at his diaphragm, making him draw in his stomach and lean over the steering-wheel.

He considered it unlikely that there would be any more check-points in the district at this time of day and if there were one, then it would be on the other side of the pass. On the other side it was downhill, and then he would soon be out of the district and would again be able to benefit from the advantages of being a foreigner.

He grew calm again and remembered the civil guards at the cross-roads. They would laugh when the dog turned up and would think she had run all the way up from the puerto. He hoped they would not shoot her.

He was already half way up the series of bends. The pass seemed to lie directly above him. He felt as if he were one with the truck, functioning as an integral part of a rational and purposeful piece of machinery. The old engine rattled and roared, but he knew it well and was sure it would not let him down.

The sky had cleared and the sun blazed down on his back and shoulders. He drove round the next bend. And the next. And the next. It was slow going but he was nearly up now.

He knew that for every yard the chances of people from the guard-post taking the trouble to go that far on their bicycles lessened. At that, he immediately realized that he was in the process of committing a crime which they had attributed to him in advance.

Just before he got to the pass, he overtook a donkey-cart loaded with jumble and scrap-iron.

He drove round the last bend. He was up.

The pass was empty.

He switched off the engine, let the truck roll over the crown, put his foot on the brake and stopped just by the low stone wall.

On the other side of the crown, the road changed. It did not wind down in snake-like curves, but ran in a long uneven curve

271

along the side of the mountain. From up here he could see several kilometres of it, far into the next district. The whole of the bit that he could see was quiet and desolate, with no vehicles or people.

And yet he stayed there and listened to the hard metallic clicking from the cooling engine. He waited until the old man with the donkey-cart came past, his head down, moving at exactly the same jog-trot as the donkey.

'Good-day,' said the old man, without looking up.

'Good-day,' said Willi Mohr.

He gazed after the cart until it was nothing but a dark dot which vanished round a protruding rock far away.

It had been moving at the same even jog-trot all the way. No one had stopped it. The coast was clear.

Willi Mohr took his foot off the brake and let the truck roll, at first slowly, then swiftly and accelerating rapidly. He smiled and felt the adhesive tape pull at his face. For the first time in his life he was doing something positive, something he found meaningful and with a point to it. He enjoyed the situation and relished controlling the rushing truck. Half the road surface and sometimes even more was dotted with rocks and stones washed down from the mountain. But drive a truck he certainly could, and he avoided them without much difficulty.

His speed was now quite considerable and at the approaches to the first bend he began to brake. The braking system locked for a fraction of a second, then freed itself completely and the brake pedal sank unresisting to the floorboards.

He managed to think: It doesn't matter, I'll brake with the engine.

Then he was round the bend and he saw a civil guard rush out on to the road, making a halt-signal thirty yards ahead of him. Two others were standing at the roadside, their bicycles flung down against some low bushes.

The situation gave him no choice. He drove on. The guard on the road only just had time to leap aside, and then he was past. No shots came from behind.

He felt no fear. He saw with lightning speed that he was past and still had a chance to get through. First he could drive away from them, and then there were dozens of ways of tricking

272

them. He could turn off anywhere. He could stop at the first suitable hiding-place, unload the arms and turn back and then fetch them again later. He could . . .

Three hundred yards below the barrier a bicycle was leaning against the cliff-wall. A little farther up the mountain lay the middle-aged civil guard with a sleepy face and a stubby grey moustache. He aimed calmly and shot Willi Mohr at less than fifty yards range with an ordinary six millimetre grooved army carbine.

The bullet hit him head on, shattering his breast-bone and leaving his body about an inch to the left of his spine. Willi Mohr was already dead when he pulled the steering-wheel hard over to the left so that the truck swerved and hit the low stone wall.

The air was light and clean after the long spell of rain and so Sergeant Tornilla heard the shot. He was standing two kilometres farther away, at the cross-roads where the old coast road from the puerto joined the main road.

He looked at his wristwatch and unscrewed the top of his fountain pen. Then he wrote down the time on a small piece of paper, folded it up and thrust it into his breast pocket.

'Twenty-eight minutes to three,' he said to himself.

Soon after that he saw a thin pillar of swirling smoke rising in the still air.

Sergeant Tornilla turned round and went over to an ancient hired car that was parked under the tree.

'Uhuh,' he mumbled. 'That's that then. But it'll get worse. We're beginning to be alone.'

The civil guard standing nearest to him thought he had missed an order.

'I didn't catch that,' he said, standing to attention.

'What? No, it was nothing. Come now, let's get back.'

8

Several months later, Hugo Spohler and Sergeant Tornilla were sitting under the awning outside the Café Central, drinking an aperitif before dinner.

Hugo Spohler had come to the puerto on the fifteenth of April and on the following day had taken the mail-bus to the town to go through Willi Mohr's belongings. The police had put them all into a wooden box which was standing in an outhouse in the back yard at the guard-post, and Sergeant Tornilla himself had gone with him to unlock the door and break the seals. The day was hot and the heat in the tin shed appalling, but Tornilla did not seem to notice it, although he was wearing leather boots and a white shirt and a stiff collar with his well-pressed uniform.

'That should be the lot,' he said. 'He had a pistol too, and a dog and a cat. We were obliged to impound the pistol, the dog was shot by the police and they couldn't catch the cat. It's still around I suppose, if the Basques up there now haven't already eaten it.'

'In Russia in forty-four, cat was counted as a delicacy,' said Hugo Spohler.

'That's quite correct.'

'Oh, were you there too?'

'Blue Division, Third Brigade.'

'SS. Fifth Panzer Regiment.'

Hugo Spohler emptied the box of its contents and was sorting things into heaps on the floor.

'Most of this can just be chucked away,' he said. 'The pictures are the only things worth anything, really. But he hasn't painted very many, considering he's been here for a year and a half.'

'I got the impression that he had grown more and more depressed during the months before the accident.'

'You knew him?'

'Yes, we met several times.'

'He never had much zest for life.'

274

He spread the canvases out on the concrete floor and looked at them appraisingly.

'This interests me,' said Sergeant Tornilla. 'We talked several times about my coming over to look at his paintings, but nothing came of it.'

'Do keep one if you'd like to.'

'Do you mean that seriously.'

'Of course. Take which ever one you want.'

'I like that one there with the house and cactuses very much. It's most realistic. Very well done.'

'Yes, he was clever. Take that one, by all means.'

'On one condition only. That you do me the honour of dining with me and my wife.'

'Thank you very much. I'd like to.'

Later, at the Café Central, Sergeant Tornilla pointed at the rolled canvas and said: 'That'll really be the only souvenir I'll be taking with me from here. So I'm doubly pleased.'

'Are you moving?'

'Yes, in a few weeks time, to Asturia. I belong to a special department and you're often moved about. It's a bit difficult if you've got a family. I've got two sons, twelve and nine. You'll soon be meeting them.'

'I've got two children too, a boy of three and a girl of twelve months. There's nothing like family life.'

'You're absolutely right there.'

'Tell me, it's struck me, there was one thing I'd hoped to find in that box of his things. A kind of diary which he promised to write.'

'Unfortunately I can't help you there. It wasn't amongst his things. Perhaps he had it on him. You see, the truck turned over in the accident and whatever was on it was thrown off. Then it hurtled down a ravine and caught fire. The body was badly burnt.'

The dinner was excellent and afterwards they drank a glass or two of Jaime Primero in the shady patio behind the house. Sergeant Tornilla had taken off his uniform jacket and exchanged his boots for slippers. His wife and children had withdrawn, and the two men were sitting in comfortable basket-chairs, digesting their food.

'The Blue Division,' said Hugo Spohler, 'was an excellent unit. Fine fighting morale and good tactical leadership. If all sectors of the front had been held by such first-class soldiers the result would've been a very different story.'

'That's true. The reserves never came up to scratch. I was thinking especially about the Italians. Their discipline was poor and even the officers lacked any will to fight. They couldn't get their men to stay lying down under fire, and panic was a reaction which was always near to hand. We noticed that quite early on here, during the Civil War.'

'There were others who were just as bad. On our right flank we had a Rumanian regiment. Their tactical leadership was wretched and the standard of men almost worse. I assure you the officers strutted about in their shiny boots twenty or twenty-five miles behind the front. When the counter-offensive began, it was just as if there had been no one there at all. The Bolsheviks went straight through the front and made a gap of ten kilometres in less than an hour. That was the tragedy of it. To have failed because of useless allies.'

'You're right, the war needn't have been lost. If we'd been able to hold the front through the winter, we'd have broken the backs of them during the next summer offensive, and then things would have been very different. But to hold a line in which every third sector was being held by Italians and Hungarians and Rumanians wasn't easy.'

'Naturally there were some strategic mistakes too. If the Fuehrer's idea of one line of attack instead of three had not been tampered with by the General Staff, we'd have taken Moscow that first autumn.'

They continued discussing the subject for another hour or so.